Fabulous Machinery for the Curious

The publisher and the University of California Press
Foundation gratefully acknowledge the generous
support of the Joan Palevsky Endowment Fund in
Literature in Translation.

Fabulous Machinery for the Curious

The Garden of Urdu Classical Literature

Translated and edited by

Musharraf Ali Farooqi

UNIVERSITY OF CALIFORNIA PRESS

University of California Press
Oakland, California

Illustrations by Michelle Farooqi

Library of Congress Cataloging-in-Publication Data

Names: Farooqi, Musharraf, 1968- translator, editor.
Title: Fabulous machinery for the curious : the garden of Urdu classical literature / translated and edited by Musharraf Ali Farooqi.
Description: Oakland, California : University of California Press, [2023] | Includes bibliographical references. | Contents: Introduction — Qissa 1 : the Ingenious Farkhanda and the two conditions : translation of Char Gulshan by Rai Beni Narayan — Qissa 2 : the adventures of a soldier : translation of Qissa Sipahizada by Khushdil Kiratpuri — Qissa 3 : Chhabili the innkeeper : translation of Chhabili Bhattiyari by unknown author — Qissa 4 : Azar Shah and Saman Rukh Bano : translation of Nau Aaeen-e Hindi by Mehr Chand Khatri Mehr — Qissa 5 : the victim of malice: translation of Qissa-e Maqtool-e Jafa by Amiruddin Khan Maani — Qissa 6: a girl named King Agar : translation of Qissa Agar o Gul by Saadat Khan Nasir — About the authors and narrators.
Identifiers: LCCN 2022027168 (print) | LCCN 2022027169 (ebook) | ISBN 9780520388239 (paperback) | ISBN 9780520388246 (ebook)
Subjects: LCSH: Urdu literature—Translations into English.
Classification: LCC PK2211.E1 F33 2023 (print) | LCC PK2211.E1 (ebook) | DDC 891.4/3908—dc23/eng/20220824
LC record available at https://lccn.loc.gov/2022027168
LC ebook record available at https://lccn.loc.gov/2022027169

Manufactured in the United States of America

32 31 30 29 28 27 26 25 24 23
10 9 8 7 6 5 4 3 2 1

For
Robert B. Wyatt
Friend

CONTENTS

ACKNOWLEDGEMENTS

I am indebted to the past and present scholars of qissa literature whose work facilitated my translation. *The Ingenious Farkhanda and the Two Conditions* is based on Ibadat Barelvi's edited text of *Char Gulshan*. *Chhabili the Innkeeper* and *The Adventures of A Soldier* are based on Professor Abdur Rasheed's edited texts of *Qissa Chhabili Bhattiyari* and *Qissa Sipahizada*, respectively. *The Girl Named King Agar* is based on Khalil-ur-Rahman Daudi's edited text of *Qissa Agar o Gul* and earlier Naval Kishore Press editions. *Azar Shah and Saman Rukh Bano* is based on Syed Suleiman Husain's edited text of *Nau Aaeen-e Hindi* and the Khuda Bakhsh Oriental Public Library Patna manuscript. *The Victim of Malice* is based on Naval Kishore Press's published text of *Qissa-e Maqtool-e Jafa*.

My friend Rafaqat Ali Shahid provided important information about the qissa narrators, and helped find the different editions which allowed me to make a comparative study. Simar Puneet copyedited the first five qissas and her enthusiasm for them gave me hope that many other young readers will also connect with these delightful stories. Professor Abdur Rasheed prepared the Urdu glossary for these qissas which helped me immensely when making these translations. Professor Ahmad Mahfooz helped with the meaning of Persian verses in *Qissa Agar o Gul* from which I made the English translation. For Awadhi and Braj translations I was helped by my friend Aftab Ahmad of Columbia University.

It was a privilege to work with the wonderful Eric Schmidt at University of California Press who acquired these qissas for publication in the World Literature in Translation program, and LeKeisha Hughes who ably supervised the editorial and production stages. I am grateful to both of them for accommodating my various requests and bearing with my delays. I would also like to thank UC Press Production Editor Francisco Reinking for seeing the book through to publication.

Finally, I would like to thank Khalid Mahmood who generously sponsored the Library of Urdu Classics (urduclassics.com) where the original Urdu texts and these translations were first published.

Musharraf Ali Farooqi

Introduction

Musharraf Ali Farooqi

In the days before the written word, stories germinating in human imagination grew with each retelling, and flourished with each new generation of storytellers, until whole orchards of story trees had sprung up. Storytellers tended them well, with time adding the written word to their branches. The story trees grew and spread. Their canopies merged and the branches intertwined. In time, it became difficult to tell where one story tree ended and the other began.

Through our many story trees we are connected to a Story Tree that grew at the beginning of time, and which is our link to other civilizations. To lose this link is to lose our common human inheritance.

The story tree of Urdu language is the collection of tales composed in the qissa, dastan, and masnavi[1] genres. These stories were invented by storytellers, or retold from the oral and written literature of the Indo-Pak subcontinent. These absorbing, joyous, colorful tales are full of marvelous characters, the happy and tragic play of fate, and adventures in earthly and magical lands.

As the present volume offers six translations from the qissa genre, it is useful to understand the nature of the qissa genre; or rather, qissa's non-genre nature.

In Urdu, the word qissa is used for both short and long narrative literature. It encompasses works in both prose and verse. When looking at narratives that belong to qissa literature, one is struck by their

1. Masnavi: A genre of narrative poetry.

diversity. These narratives include everything from folk literature, to historical narratives, to adventure tales, picaresque narratives, comic and tragic stories, accounts of pilgrimage, and religious texts. Their structure varies from frame and interior stories, to linear narratives, to collections of disparate tales, joined loosely together. Each such narrative enriches the possibilities of the qissa, while at the same time making it more difficult to describe the genre neatly.

Stories must have played a paramount social role in a society for it to create such a profusion of narratives meant for narration and retelling. Did the qissa literature grow from an impulse to give a story-like structure to every narrative? The diversity of texts published as qissas certainly suggests that. This extraordinary engagement with stories at a social level becomes clearer when we take a closer look at the qissas and realize that a number of them have a function beyond idle entertainment. To their audience, they offered everything, from social guidance, physical well-being, and moral training. The qissas were meant to be life's finishing school.

The riches of this literature can be sampled in the six qissas presented here in their first English language translation.

QISSA 1: THE INGENIOUS FARKHANDA AND THE TWO CONDITIONS

Rai Beni Narayan's wonderful storytelling and linguistic achievements in *Char Gulshan* (1811) never came to light during his lifetime. The manuscript of the qissa remained unpublished until 1967.[2]

Narayan compiled the qissa but did not claim its authorship. He only mentions that he has *'narrated this qissa that he had carried in his heart since long'*. His statement is notable when considered with interior evidence from the qissa which suggests *The Ingenious Farkhanda and the Two Conditions* was authored by a woman. We know that women contributed to qissa literature in both the oral and written literary traditions, but except for a few rare instances their works remained unknown and unpublished, and may well have been forever lost. The unknown author of the present qissa was a brilliant storyteller

2. *Char Gulshan* by Beni Narayan Jahan, edited by Ibadat Barelvi, *Silsila-e Matbuaat-e Urdu Dunya*, no. 16 (Lahore, 1967).

and mythmaker whose radiant imagination has created an unforgettable character and story.

The qissa begins with a faqir arriving at Kevan Shah's court and offering to sell him three injunctions. Intrigued by the mysterious injunctions and the high price the faqir is demanding for them, the king purchases them against his better judgment. Acting upon the injunctions, the king is swept into a chain of events that reveals to him the secret love lives of his own and the vizier's daughter, and ultimately introduces him to Princess Farkhanda, who is forced to marry him.

In the beginning the qissa may read like a violent, misogynistic narrative where women's bodies are an extension of men's honour, and they pay the ultimate price for any transgressions. It may even appear as a tale where a higher order reinforces this worldview. But this view is called into question as soon as Princess Farkhanda enters the story, and we realise that the first part of this qissa is only staged to illustrate that a woman who allows her private life to be easily penetrated by men, is really a novice who deserves all the punishment the world has in store for her.

With her instinct for survival and the ploys she employs to achieve her purpose, Princess Farkhanda belongs in the pantheon of great trickster heroines. At the outset we know that she, like her sisters, does not put too great a value on marriage or becoming a queen, and is more interested in hunting and watching public spectacles. She and her sisters wear men's clothing, which signifies a certain independence from conventions and traditional roles. While Farkhanda tempts men with the promise of sex to achieve her ends, her actions never invite any dishonour. She makes her moves from a position of strength and integrity, neither acting treacherously nor vindictively. She honours her word and ensures that the conditions she sets are inviolable. She first makes the king fulfill the condition she had set him, before fulfilling with aplomb the impossible conditions he set her. Farkhanda demonstrates how a clever woman can do as she pleases by duping those who think they control her.

QISSA 2: THE ADVENTURES OF A SOLDIER

The translation presented here is from the *Qissa Sipahizada* (The Adventures of a Soldier) written in the masnavi genre by Muhammad Ibrahim Khushdil Kiratpuri (d. 1788 CE). Besides his authorship of six works, not much is known about Khushdil. He relates that he versified the qissa after hearing its narration by the storyteller Bhikari Das Bijnori. Versification of prose works and prosification of works in metric verse often took place within Urdu literature.

A later version by Zahoor Ali Zahoor, titled *Qissa Bel Wala* (The Man with the Bull), was also written in the masnavi genre.[3] The compiler of the qissa mentions that the story comes from the repertoire of the 'decent qissas', the allusion (and distinction) making it plain that the indecent qissa existed as a subgenre. It is not currently known if any of the indecent qissas were transcribed, or remained within the oral tradition until the tradition slowly died in the first half of the twentieth century.

The Adventures of a Soldier narrates a soldier's encounter with thugs. Khushdil Kiratpuri's era coincided with a time when thuggee had become widespread. Campaigns to exile or eradicate thugs were carried out sporadically across India from as early as the thirteenth century, but it was in the early nineteenth century that a concerted effort was made to rout them by the East India Company.

The protagonist of the qissa is an out-of-work soldier who is tricked by a band of thugs into selling the prize bull he had received in lieu of wages after much hardship. The family in the qissa—a father and two sons—are from a band of aseel thugs who operate as a family unit. When the soldier realizes their true identity and the imminent danger to his life, he readily agrees to their terms. Later, he returns to the thugs' house, and using daring and disguise, the very tools of thuggee, delivers their comeuppance.

Qissa Sipahizada is unique in Urdu qissa literature for the picaresque effect it creates by the soldier's trickery and use of disguise. There is much droll humor in the use of the versified sarapa (cap-a-pie) for the soldier, a narrative device typically used to describe the beauty and charms of the female body.

An adaptation of the qissa into English was made by M. L. Dube in 1892—interspersed with poetry from Shakespeare, Milton, and Pope—and titled, *The Adventures of a Sepoy*.[4] In his preface, Dube mentions certain alterations he made to the text in the process of translation. He writes:

3. *Makhtootat Anjuman Taraqqi-e Urdu* (vol. 1), compiled by Afsar Siddiqi Amrohvi, Syed Sarfaraz Ali Rizvi (Karachi: Anjuman Taraqqi-e Urdu, 1965), pp. 297–299.

4. *The Adventures of a Sepoy* by M. L. Dube (Agra: Rashid Press, 1892).

> *Its style—as is the case with almost all Urdu books—is flowery and figurative and consequently no translation can fairly reproduce its charms and beauties. Taking into consideration this last drawback the undersigned has made a free rather than a literal translation, adding at the same time a great deal of matter from his own imagination, to make the book still more interesting.*

In view of Dube's statement that he retold the qissa, the present text qualifies as the first translation of Qissa Sipahizada from its earliest known written version. In translating from verse, a few words were added in some places to round off the sentence in the interest of narrative flow.

QISSA 3: CHHABILI THE INNKEEPER

The first known printing of *Qissa Chhabili Bhattiyari* (Chhabili the Innkeeper) is from 1864. Shortly thereafter, in 1869, a versified version was compiled.[5] There were numerous printings of this qissa throughout the nineteenth and twentieth centuries. It was even published as 'sangit natak', a musical form particularly suited to shorter tales performed by travelling troupes.

One of the reasons for the popularity of this qissa could be the difficulty in assigning a protagonist to the story. There is a tradition of cautionary literature both in Indian and Persian literature to instruct men about the deceitfulness of women. The title of the qissa's versified version, *Qissa Fareb-un Nisa* (Tale of the Deceitfulness of Women), which contains some gruesome details of Chhabili's punishment, suggests this particular category for this qissa in public consciousness. Looking at the qissa's details we see that the versions of the narrative and the type of audience can also decide the protagonist.

Kumkum Sangari has explored the integrated role of caste and female rivalry in this qissa,[6] and how, through the cruel punishment meted out to Chhabili, 'husbandliness, kingliness, and wifeliness are built on the battered and burnt body of a low-caste woman'. We should consider that the details of torture were perhaps meant for the

5. *Qissa Fareb-un Nisa* by Khuda Bakhsh Gharib (Lucknow: Samar-e Hind Press, 1870).
6. 'The Prism of Caste: Chhabili Bhattiyari', *Politics of the Possible: Essays on Gender, History, Narrative, Colonial English* by Kumkum Sangari (New Delhi: Tulika Books, 1999), pp. 247–278.

edification of a female audience, serving as a warning to the lower-caste women, and conferring the protagonist's role on the prince's wife Bichhittar. It would change the qissa's nature from Chhabili's tragedy into a triumph for Bichhittar, who settles scores with Chhabili for her humiliation by the prince. It is important to note that in one of the versions of this qissa rendered in the sangit natak form, it is Bichhittar's name, not Chhabili's, that is used in the title.[7]

Urdu dastan scholar Muhammad Salim-ur-Rahman offers another interpretation by suggesting the qissa is an allegory. In a personal communication he mentioned that Chhabili represents the ephemeral world, which indulges our senses and puts blinders on our eyes so that we remain blind to reality. Bichhittar represents the truth, or the reality whose sight fulfills us and allows us to turn away our gaze from the false world.

It is likely that the qissa enjoyed such a huge appeal because beyond the boundaries of caste and time, and the gullibility and capriciousness of the prince, lies the story of a woman dispossessed of her love and life through palace intrigue, the fecklessness of her lover, and the vengefulness of a slighted, spiteful woman. Unlike characters in a novel, Chhabili and Bicchhittar are not internally complex; they are situationally complex, and the modern reader may also find their respective situations, and how they respond to them, difficult to judge.

QISSA 4: AZAR SHAH AND SAMAN RUKH BANO

The frame story of Mehr Chand Khatri Mehr's *Nau Aaeen-e Hindi* holds one of the most glorious tales of love and adventure, and also a little-known secret: Qissas were traditionally employed in the Indo-Pak subcontinent as healing devices, and a book of qissas is the best pharmacopoeia one could possess. When Azar Shah's new wife Saman Rukh Bano is poisoned by her rival, medications fail to restore her to health. But healers tell Azar Shah that a certain holy man called Sheikh Sanaan could possibly cure her through his ministrations. Sheikh Sanaan consents to do so, and by way of treatment, summons his disci-

7. *Bichhitra Kumari, Sangit* by Natharam Sharma (Hathras: N.S. Sharma Gaur Book Depot, 1924).

ples to narrate stories to Saman Rukh. The first disciple tells Saman Rukh the story of the adventurer Malik Muhammad and pari princess Giti Afroz, which unfolds in the human world and Paristan. Giti Afroz puts Malik Muhammad through many trials of loyalty, often transforming him into an animal, in punishment for transgressing the bounds set by her for their relationship. Despite these hardships, Malik Muhammad remains steadfast in his love. As Saman Rukh listens to Malik Muhammad's engrossing tale, she begins to recover, and her faculties, which had declined from poisoning, are slowly restored. Just as Saman Rukh becomes fully engaged with the qissa—and yearns to know how Malik Muhammad's story will end—Sheikh Sanaan orders a pause to its narration, and asks his second disciple to narrate other adventures instead. This disciple tells the tale of Zarivand, a down-on-his-luck young man, whose love and loyalty are tested through a great sacrifice asked of him. While Saman Rukh longs to hear the end of Malik Muhammad's tale, she listens with enough attention to Zarivand's tale to point out a weak link in the plot, which we realise was purposely planted, to check whether the person listening to the story has discernment enough to discover it. Like a symphony conductor, Sheikh Sanaan orchestrates the delivery of the stories in a way that engages Saman Rukh's mind and heart, and helps him diagnose the state of her faculties. Zarivand's tale soon ends and Sheikh Sanaan finally allows the narration of Malik Muhammad's adventures to resume. *Nau Aaeen-e Hindi* is not the only qissa to be structured and narrated for healing: According to legend, the stories in *Qissa Chahahr Dervish* (Tale of the Four Dervishes) were also begun by Amir Khusro as a way to cure his ailing master and Sufi saint Nizamuddin Auliya. Another qissa, *Qissa-e Pur-Asar, Dafa-e Dard-e Nim-Sar* (An Efficacious Qissa, the Dispeller of Migraines) is actually meant to cure migraines. *Nau Aaeen-e Hindi* is Mehr Chand Khatri Mehr's 1803 retelling of the *Qissa Azar Shah o Saman Rukh Bano* from the Persian into Urdu. The earliest known Persian manuscript is from the eighteenth century but it may well be a much older qissa. The retelling was commissioned as an educational aid for Baron Cowley to learn Hindi—as Urdu was then called—and was not published. Even though it remained unpublished, Mehr's stylistic feat in employing a simple, almost conversational idiom in telling the qissa became known. His work was considered important enough that in 1856, Urdu prose stylist Rajab Ali Beg Suroor did his own, shorter retelling of the qissa by making significant changes to the story and its structure. He criticised Mehr's style as old-fashioned, and retold it in his signature ornate style as *Shagufa-e Mohabbat* (The Bud of Love). Two copies of *Nau Aaeen-e Hindi*'s manuscript are extant. Mehr's important and delightful *Nau Aaeen-e Hindi* was finally edited and published in 1988 by Syed Suleiman Hussain.

QISSA 5: THE VICTIM OF MALICE

Unlike most qissas, we have in *Qissa Maqtool-e Jafa* (The Victim of Malice) a clear chain of transmission between the oral narrative to written text. It was transcribed by Muhammad Ameeruddin from the oral narration of his father, Hafiz Ghulam Nizamuddin, in the late nineteenth century.

The story revolves around Vizier Masud Ali Khan and his accomplished and pious wife who becomes the subject of discussion at the court one day, when the king asks his viziers if any of them has ever met or seen a woman who is beautiful, a master of musical arts, a scholar of religion, and so modest that none has ever glimpsed her shadow nor heard a word of her speech.

Forced to acknowledge that his wife has all aforementioned qualities, Vizier Masud Ali Khan invites the wrath of the first vizier whose answer to the king's interrogation had been in the negative. Later, finding an opportunity, he seeks the king's permission to verify the truth of Vizier Masud Ali Khan's claim by attempting to corrupt his wife.

The qissa has an older provenance. The seed of this qissa is found in an episode from 'The Legend of Raja Rasalu,'[8] a second-century CE legend from the Sialkot region. Raja Rasalu is tempted by his vizier Mehta Chopra's description of his wife Chandni, to put her chastity to the test. He secretly visits Chandni, but is unable to tempt her despite his many inducements. Later, Chopra confronts Raja Rasalu with proof of his visit, and the raja proves Chandni's chastity by putting himself and Chandni through a miraculous test. Raja Rasalu later chastises his vizier for publicly praising his wife which led to his temptation.

8. *The Legends of the Panjab* (vol. 1) by R.C. Temple (Bombay: Education Society's Press, 1884), pp. 35–39.

The incident from Raja Rasalu's legend is presented in a more detailed form—and a version closer to the present qissa—in 'The Legend of Sila Dai'.[9] In this version Chandni's role is assumed by Sila Dai or Sila Devi.

The qissa's connection to the legend of Raja Rasalu becomes more obvious as Sialkot is mentioned as the hometown of the vizier's wife. Another version of the story is *Fasana-e Ghaus* (1864)[10] by Sheikh Muhammad Karimullah, which more or less follows the story in the present qissa but ends on a happy note. We know from other examples in Urdu qissa literature that variant traditions of qissa could have variant endings.

A clue to the present qissa's tragic ending is revealed in an admonitory passage in the text written in the narrator's voice. It reads:

> *Dispel ego from your heart. Make yourself proof against vanity and arrogance. Avoid conceit, and do not be boastful. Lower your head before the True Lord in humility and meekness. Do not make tall claims before anyone, lest you, too, should be humiliated and degraded before the True King—like the fourth vizier—and find no refuge. Had he not boasted about his wife's chastity before the king, he would not have seen such humiliation and disgrace. The world is not a place where one should vaunt.*

The passage suggests that *The Victim of Malice* was structured in the Islamic tradition of advisory literature. While advisory literature does not necessitate a tragic end, it is effective in imprinting the story's intended message on the minds of the audience.

The qissa is also given the title *Fasana-e Gham Aamood,* derived from the chronogram in the letters of the title, which add up to 1289 AH (1872 CE), the year in which the text was published.

QISSA 6: A GIRL NAMED KING AGAR

With a dense plot and numerous characters, this qissa, according to its author Saadat Khan Nasir, is derived from an Indo-Persian version.

9. *Ibid.* pp. 243–366.

10. *Fasana-e Ghaus* by Sheikh Muhammad Karimullah known as Munshi Sheikh Ghaus Muhammad (Agra: Aftab-e Qudrat Press, 1864), p. 118.

Dastan scholar Gayan Chand Jain has identified two Persian texts containing the qissa.[11] It was also written in Deccani Urdu.[12] The present text was published a number of times in the nineteenth and twentieth centuries.[13] A version of the qissa was also composed as masnavi *Gulshan-e Mahwashan*[14] by the poet Lutf-un Nisa Begum Aseema.[15]

A Girl Named King Agar tells the story of a vizier's daughter, Agar, who is enthroned in the disguise of the heir apparent who is kidnapped by Lal Dev. Agar lives as a prince and receives occult powers from a jogi. The story unfolds in the human world, and a magical domain. Agar travels between these worlds through a tunnel. Her love of adventure brings her to the lands of Lal Dev, whose son King Gul learns her secret, and falls in love with her. Too busy with her adventures and accomplishing feats of daring and courage, Agar publicly spurns Gul's advances, but is mindful of his passion. Outwardly, one can draw a parallel between the protagonists' behaviour in *A Girl Named King Agar* and *The Adventures of Amir Hamza*: it is on the pretext of new adventures and military campaigns that both Agar and Amir Hamza hold love in abeyance. However, in *A Girl Named King Agar* there seems to be a deeper strategy at play.

Agar begins with conquests in the human world by defeating forty kings. She then earns the loyalty of all four of King Gul's viziers by accomplishing great feats of daring to unite them with their beloveds. The brave deeds Agar performs in service to King Gul's viziers are

11. *Qissat ul Jawahar,* MS (Persian) (1179 A.H./1765–66, Property: Rampur Raza Library) and *Shahanshah-e Adil,* MS (Persian) (?, Property: Anjuman-e Taraqqi-e Urdu).

12. *Urdu Ki Nasri Dastanen* by Gayan Chand Jain (Karachi: Anjuman Taraqqi-e Urdu Pakistan, 2014), pp. 172–73.

13. *Agar Gul* (Lucknow: n.p. 1846), Property India Office Library; *Agar Gul* (Lucknow: Naval Kishore Press, 1873), 62 pp.; *Agar wa Gul* (Lucknow: Naval Kishore Press, 1876), 62 pp.; *Agar wa Gul* (Lucknow: Naval Kishore Press, 1880), 62 pp.; *Agar Gul* (Lucknow: Matba Anwaar-e Muhammadi, 1881), 60 pp.; *Agar Gul* (Lucknow: Naval Kishore Press, 1929), 118 pp.; *Agar Gul* (Kanpur: Matba Majeedi, 1937), 96 pp.; *Agar Gul,* edited by Khalil-ur-Rehman Dawoodi (Lahore: Majlis Taraqqi-e Adab, 1967), 190 pp.

14. *Gulshan-e Mahwashan (Qissa Jahan Zarb)* by Lutf-un Nisa Begum Aseema (MS. 272 p., 5376 verses, dated: 1277 AH/1859–60 CE, Property: Asafia Kutubkhana).

15. "Aseema" by Maulvi Sakhavat Mirza, Quarterly *Nava-i Adab*, vol. 4, (Bombay: Anjuman-e Islam Urdu Research Institute, October 1952), pp. 4–40.

reminiscent of the adventures of the legendary hero Hatim Tai, who selflessly helps a stranger win the woman he loves. Finally, Agar comes to the aid of the jogi—the source of her occult powers—and vanquishes his enemies and restores him to his land.

This qissa is a complex commentary on gender. Agar pursues other women on the pretext of winning them for men. In one instance, one of these women also offers to lie with Agar if she would switch her gender with the help of magic. While Agar undertakes these adventures, she also removes the signs of manhood from King Gul who pursues her.

Agar sets out to prove herself as superior to men in the world of humans, to King Gul in his own magical realm, and to the jogi in the use of occult powers. *A Girl Named King Agar* is the only known qissa where a woman not only appears as the protagonist in a man's disguise, but outclasses most male heroes, if not all of them, in deeds of bravery, daring, and selflessness.

The translation follows the text in describing Agar's gender as masculine where Agar appears as a man, and feminine where the character is described as a woman.

. . .

Any notion or understanding of why the Urdu qissa literature was eclipsed in the twentieth century, must take into account the history of linguistic politics, social reform ideas, and literary movements in the Indo-Pak subcontinent, which played out in the background of the revolt of 1857 and British rule; the two world wars; sectarian political movements in the twentieth century; the uncertainty, panic, and large-scale violence ushered in by the Partition; and the necessities of the world that emerged thereafter.

But the importance of the qissa literature may be judged from one simple fact alone: It was composed by Urdu's finest prose writers and stylists, each one of whom selected one or more qissas from the hundreds that existed—in Braj Bhasha, Sanskrit, and Persian—to make their own version. Their collective work was a distillation of a vaster body of oral and written literature, and an informal canon of our classics.

To modern sensibilities the world of these qissas may appear unexpectedly brutal and discordant, but all worlds from a bygone time deliver a bit of a culture shock to those encountering them for the first time. The qissa literature addressed the world in which it grew. While it reflects the biases and prejudices of its time, it can also be stunningly subversive. And even the biases can be deceiving. If one finds that in these qissas a great importance is attached to the continuation of kingship and the need for an heir, one also finds this concern only being voiced by just and good kings for the preservation of order. If women's lives and fates are cruelly and arbitrarily apportioned by men in the qissas, the qissas also feature women who prove themselves to be men's equals or superiors in all matters.

Nor are the discordant, anachronistic worlds encountered in qissa literature too far removed from the world of our lived experience. There is no special barbarism which infuses these works that is unfamiliar to us. With greater resources in their hands humans have only become crueler. The despicable portrayal and cruel treatment of humans we sometimes encounter in the qissas is a window not into our past but the present—a dark reality that hides behind superficial conventions and fine words. Long before the novel, the qissas intimately knew the true nature of the world, and exposed its face.

• • •

The title of this collection is borrowed from Lewis Ferdinand Smith's 1813 Preface to *The Tale of the Four Durwesh*, the translation of *Bagh-o Bahar*, a qissa compiled by Mir Amman Dehlvi at Fort William College, Calcutta. Making a utilitarian translation of one of Urdu's greatest prose stylists, and the best-known qissa, as an aid to teach Urdu language to the officers of the East India Company, Smith disparaged the supernatural elements in the qissa and described the potential readers outside India.

> *The Tale itself is interesting, if we keep in our minds the previous idea, that no Asiatic Writer of Romance or History was ever consistent, or free from fabulous credulity; the cautious march of undeviating truth, and a careful regard to* vraisemblance *never enters into their plan; wildness of imagination, fabulous machinery, and unnatural scenes ever pervade through the composition of every Oriental Author: even their most serious works on History and Ethics are stained with these imperfections. . . . Some of the Notes will be superfluous to the Oriental Scholar who has*

been in India; but in this case I think it better to be redundant than risk the chance of being deficient. Moreover, as the book may be perused by the Curious in Europe, many of whom know nothing of India except having seen it in the map of the world, these notes were absolutely necessary to understand the work.

This translation, from a different tradition, aims to harness the fabulous machinery of Urdu storytelling to connect all curious about it, so that we can reach into humanity's common inheritance to discover and grow more stories.

M.A.F
Lahore, 5 May 2022

Qissa 1

The Ingenious Farkhanda and the Two Conditions

A first translation of *Char Gulshan* from the Urdu
as compiled by Rai Beni Narayan

NARRATOR'S PREFACE

Praise be to God! How to write, and what qualities to state, of the Progenitor whose luminance lit up the earth and the heavens; how from His perfect Nature one droplet materialized as Adam, and became the envy of earth's garden. The fork-tongued pen lacks all ability to narrate His praise; and the weak-natured man has no power to dare fathom His divine essence. The earth's garden grew lush and luxuriant from His tending. One who steps outside His command loses his honour and stature before long. The Maker forms a child's shape in his mother's womb and five months before the birth fills up the mother's breasts with milk from His providence. Thus, it behoves man to repeat His name night and day, to disassociate himself from all others, and present his devotion only to Him. May I become a sacrifice to the beneficence of the One, who, as the Giver, made the moon and the sun and the earth and the heavens a means of obtaining sustenance for the man made of clay. Pity the existence of the unenlightened one who never utters His name with fervency. The leaves on the trees appear as ledgers of divinity to the wise, and all the beasts from life's garden sing night and day the anthem of His virtues and purity in their speech. Flower petals become as many tongues in His praise. From its heart's ardency the narcissus is watchful and absorbed in wonders in the garden, desirous of the sight of the True Gardener's world-adorning beauty. Perhaps the tulip defied the True Gardener in some way and was thus marked upon its heart; and the heart of jasmine, which held back scattering its wealth in His praise, was pierced by the needle to reduce the flower to an ear-ornament. The cypress stands on one leg in the world's garden to offer its devotion and recite the name of the True Progenitor. There is no end to praising the oneness of His divine essence. Every flower is occupied with His praise in the language of rapture.

PRAISE OF PROPHET OF GOD AND THE FIVE HOLY ONES

Praise without end on the blessed existence, that is, Ahmad the most select one of God, and Muhammad the interceder on the Day of Reckoning. Benedictions on his progeny and companions.

I have found this rosary of the Five Holy Ones
Who are Muhammad, Ali, Fatima, Husain, and Hasan

AN ACCOUNT OF THE COMPILATION OF THIS BOOK AND THE NARRATOR'S LIFE

This insignificant mote, sinner, and reprobate being, Beni Narayan, son of Rai Sudarashan Narayan, and grandson of the late Maharaja Lakshmi Narayan, from the Khatri Mehta clan, resident of Lahore, the seat of empire, arrived in the select city of Calcutta in the middle of the year 1215 AH [1800 CE] during the reign of the Most Honourable Governor General Lord Marquess Wellesley, in the companionship of his stirrup-fellow and master Naimat Rai Khem Narayan, who had received an appointment as the representative of the Wazir-ul Mumalik Hindustan, Khan Bahadur Nawab Saadat Ali Khan II—may his glory be everlasting.

For ten years since that day this humble person found no employment. In the year 1225 AH [1810 CE], in the reign of the excellent lord, the powerful ruler, the sun of the noon of state and prosperity, the luminous moon of the skies of grandeur and power, protector of friends, destroyer of foes, scorcher of villainy, benefactor to the poor, the most select of the privy counselors to the lofty as Saturn King of England, the cream of the grandest monarchs, Governor General,

Ashraf-ul Umara,[1] Lord Minto, may his glory be everlasting, this reprobate being narrated this tale that he had carried in his heart for so long, before the kind Munshi[2] Imam Bakhsh, who is the very mine of benevolence and generosity, by way of presenting himself for any employment prospects.

Munshi Imam Bakhsh, my benefactor, was greatly pleased by hearing the tale's narration, and said to this lowly man: 'Do transfer this pleasant tale and rare story from the stylus of speech via the tongue of pen by inscribing it on paper in the Hindi language; and present it in the excellent service of the eminently learned Captain [John William] Taylor who, rightfully, nay, as a rule, may be called the soul of discourse. The narration of this qissa will amuse him and give him reason to remember your name.'

As per the command of the kindly Munshi Imam Bakhsh, this sinner transferred from the stylus of speech via the tongue of pen what his imperfect mind could put together. It is my hope from the bounty of the one who values men of letters, and is the benefactor of the universe, that he may look upon this poor offering with the eye of favour. I hope that the learned readers and the scholars of high stature will not hesitate in correcting, from their superior learning, any textual or scribal errors they come upon here. As they enjoy this colorful qissa, they may also remember this humble creature with favour.

1. Ashraf-ul Umara: Choice among nobles.

2. Munshi: Scholars of language responsible for teaching, correspondence, and some bureaucratic offices.

FIRST STORY: RELATING HOW KEVAN SHAH BOUGHT THREE INJUNCTIONS FROM A FAQIR, LEARNED OF HIS DAUGHTER'S MISDEMEANORS THROUGH THEM, AND PUNISHED HER AND HER PARAMOUR

The chroniclers of past times and the storytellers of yore have strung together the lustrous pearls of these rare tales and wondrous yarns in the skein of narrative thus, that in a land among the auspiciously founded, vastly populated lands of Hindustan, the image of heaven, there lived a king who was majestic as Jamshed, glorious, and of noble lineage. The praiseworthy God had conferred such grandeur, dignity, augustness, and exaltedness upon him that no other monarch of the time could claim equality with him. He was so formidable and daunting that even Rustam was unable to hold his ground before him.

He was Kevan Shah, majestic as the heavens
The sun and the moon were his two torchbearers

One day the king was looking out at the river from his fort window. Crowds of people were going about their businesses. Crowded boats were ferrying passengers across the riverbanks. The king was regarding their arrival and departure with interest when a crowded boat moored near his fort, and its passengers got off and set out for their destinations.

A faqir had arrived in that boat, and after everyone had disembarked, he too stepped off and headed for the king's fort, arriving under the window where the king was watching the riverside.

The guards and mace bearers of Kevan Shah, Shadow of God, said to him, 'O faqir, why do you stand here? This house is above the stature of the likes of you. Even angels dare not alight here, let alone a beggar like you. Tell us your purpose in coming here.'

The faqir answered, 'Good fellows, I have not come to beg. Go and tell your king that a faqir at His Radiant Majesty's palace door is desirous of an audience and speaking to him.'

The royal attendants went before the king and communicated what the faqir had said. The king said to them: 'Show him in.'

As per the king's instructions, the faqir was brought before Kevan Shah and said to him, 'O Refuge of the World, you possess all things that the praiseworthy God from his perfect nature has created in this world.

But I wish to sell you three injunctions. You may buy them if the proposal finds favour with you, and thank this faqir when they serve you.'

The king said, 'Speak! What are these three injunctions?'

The faqir answered, 'I will not share them with you just yet. I will do so once you have sent for three lakh[3] gold pieces and agreed to pay out one lakh gold pieces upon hearing each injunction.'

The king marvelled upon hearing this demand and told himself that surely it went against good sense to spend three lakh gold pieces for some injunctions. But the desire to hear them did not leave the king's heart; it merely grew. Kevan Shah considered the fact that while he could always acquire more riches, he would not get another chance to hear the rare wisdom the faqir might have to impart.

Becoming possessed with the thought, he ordered, 'Send for purses of three lakh gold pieces and put them before the throne.'

The royal servants brought the gold as instructed and put it before the throne.

Kevan Shah said to the faqir, 'Respected sir, three lakh goldpieces have been arranged as per your wishes. Now do share the injunctions.'

The faqir answered, 'O Refuge of the World, the first injunction is this: It is preferable to wake up rather than continue sleeping.'

The king was stupefied to hear this, and said to himself: 'It is known to the whole world that waking up is preferable to sleeping. This faqir has robbed me of one lakh gold pieces!'

When the faqir saw Kevan Shah looking apprehensive, he said, 'O Refuge of the World, it seems that the injunction I shared did not find favour with you. You must therefore restrict yourself to this injunction and not listen to the other two which remain.'

The king said to himself: 'I have already heard one injunction; perhaps the other two will be valuable.' Thus deciding, he said to the faqir, 'Respected sir, I have bought the injunction you shared with me, regardless of whether or not I found it to my liking. Pray take one lakh gold pieces from the pile.'

At the king's words, the faqir counted the gold pieces and put them aside.

The king now said, 'Pray share another one of the remaining injunctions.'

3. Lakh: One hundred thousand.

The faqir answered, 'O Refuge of the World, the second injunction is this: It is preferable to rise, rather than lie awake in bed.' Thus speaking, he took away another one lakh gold pieces from the pile before the king.

Kevan Shah was confounded by the injunction shared by the faqir, and said to himself: 'Why did I waste two lakh gold pieces over worthless commonplaces.' However, he did not let on. After brooding much over it, he decided that he had already lost two lakh gold pieces, and may as well hear the third injunction, which might be more useful than the other two. He said to the faqir, 'Respected sir, now tell us the third injunction.'

The faqir answered, 'O King, Conqueror of the World, the third injunction is this: It is preferable to walk around rather than sit in bed.'

The king was dismayed upon hearing this, and sent off the faqir after paying off the remaining one lakh gold pieces due him, and got up and left the fort for his palace.

. . .

However, the king kept thinking about the three injunctions and their import, all day long. In the evening, after he had had dinner and retired to his bed to rest, he again recalled what the faqir had told him. He opened his pen box and wrote out the three injunctions on a leaf of paper and ordered that it be put up on the wall facing his bed, so that he may see the inscription when he woke up. Then the king lay down to rest.

The first half of the night having passed, the king woke up and his eyes fell on the first injunction, and he said to himself that he should do as the faqir had instructed. Having made the resolve, he rubbed his eyes and woke up from his slumber. Then he read the second injunction and sat up in his bed. When he recalled the third injunction, he arose from his bed and stepped out to walk in the palace courtyard.

As Kevan Shah walked there, he saw someone gain the palace wall from without with the help of a snare rope. Greatly alarmed at the sight, he said to himself: 'All thanks to the faqir! Had I not woken up, this man would have surely murdered me in my bed.

These words by Abu Ali have been written in gold
The sleeping traveller places himself in danger

'Had this intruder been after gold and riches, he could have stolen them from the houses of the many rich men who live in the city. It would have been a far simpler matter to break into their homes. This person, who has bartered away his life and risked the royal guard and soldiers to climb the sky-high palace wall, is most certainly after my life. Surely one of my enemies has sent him here, with the promise of riches, to kill me. Or else, it could be someone whom I punished for some past misdemeanor, who nurses an injury and has now found the opportunity to settle the score by taking the trouble and undergoing the hardship of breaking into my palace.'

The king decided that this must be the case. He quickly picked up his short sword that lay on his bed, took out a black dushala[4] from its wrapping cloth and put it on, and with his sword stuck under his arm, hid himself behind a column, keeping an eye on the intruder.

Meanwhile, the intruder, an Abyssinian, climbed down from the wall onto the roof and went down from the stairwell into the palace courtyard, and stood there watchfully, looking around. The king resolved that when he headed towards his bedroom, he would surprise the intruder from behind, and cleave him in two with a blow from his sword.

That man did not go towards the king's bedroom, however, and headed instead towards the palace inhabited by the king's daughter. Kevan Shah realized that the intruder did not have designs on his life, and may, after all, be there to steal the gold which was why he seemed to be headed towards the princess's palace. He decided that it would be unwise to remain there, and he should follow him, and learn the truth of the man's intentions. Having settled on this course of action, the king stealthily followed him.

When the intruder lifted the curtain of the women's chambers, Kevan Shah was greatly surprised to see the entrance door lying open. He said to himself: 'What could be the reason that the door to the women's chamber is open in the middle of the night? It portends some mischief.' Kevan Shah steeled his heart and followed the Abyssinian into the women's quarters.

When Kevan Shah entered the palace he found the princess, his daughter, asleep in bed. As the intruder fearlessly approached the

4. Dushala: Shoulder mantle.

princess's bed, the king thought that he meant to steal her jewellery. He decided he would kill the thief when he headed out after removing the jewellery from the princess.

Approaching the princess's bed, the Abyssinian gave it a kick that made the princess sit up with a start. The wretch said to the princess, 'O whore, you were so languid that you could not wait even a little for me, and fell right away into slumber? From tomorrow you will not catch sight of me!'

The princess got up and gestured to take his troubles upon her head, and with her hands pressed together in plea, said, 'Do find it in your heart to forgive this slave girl's transgression; it shall never happen again. I shall keep awake until you arrive, and never fall asleep.'

When the wretch heard her answer, he climbed into the bed and, holding the princess's hand, seated her in his lap, and gave her a few kisses.

Beholding this scene, Kevan Shah's heart conflagrated with anger and he perspired from ecstasies of embarrassment and shame. He said to himself: 'I will not be able to overpower him; in fact, it would be a matter of shame even to confront him. It is preferable to hide somewhere and witness all that passes, and then serve the two of them their just deserts.'

The king stood behind a column to watch the spectacle. The wretch stepped down from the bed, holding the princess's hand, and the two of them lifted and moved the bed to one side. Upon their so doing the door of a subterraneous passage revealed itself, and the Abyssinian, holding the princess's hand, opened the door and stepped into it.

The king silently followed them. After going down a dozen or so steps he found himself in a paved passage. After travelling behind them in the passage for a quarter of a kos, he came upon another staircase and climbed out aboveground.

Upon emerging from the underground passage, the king saw a royal garden and luxurious apartments with doorways draped with curtains of figured silk brocade, worked with gold and silver. Every chamber was appointed with colourful velveteen carpets and decorously placed seats. Trays full of flowers and perfume boxes full of a profusion of perfumes lay before every seat. On the niches in the wall were aromatic unguents and burning wicks of ambergris. Salvers full of fresh and dried fruit lay in one corner of the courtyard. Jonquil bouquets and rosewater sprinklers were displayed in niches. Above the courtyard a large pankha was hung. In front of the apartment was a cross-shaped watercourse filled with clean water, as lustrous as a pearl, in which fountains and jets-d'eau ran. These extended in the form of channels in four directions, and one heard the sound of water falling in sheets from all sides.

The gardens were so wondrously decorated around the promenades that, seeing their marvelous trim, even the Gardener of Nature retired in chagrin and lay down His mattock. The bed of blooming lilies perfumed the lovers' minds. Branches of trees laden with fruit were hung over the gardens.

The rose bough dances with the breeze
For the breeze has engulfed and kissed her lips

From one end of the garden, the flowering bushes of white jasmine and Arabian jasmine intoxicated the souls of beloveds with their perfume. From the other, the tulips and purple poppies bloomed with such vigour that Shaddad's Garden of Iram seemed blighted in comparison. A carpet that rivalled Spring's bloom was laid out for the lovers to promenade in the garden. The narcissus stood solemnly watchful for the beloved.

The narcissus wiped slumber from her eye
For it had sought to nurse a wound
In one corner the plantain stood alone
Elsewhere the jasmine gathered with the Arabian jasmine

The twining Cyprus vine surrounding the promenades appeared as a chain of love around lovers' ankles. Beside the flower beds the cypresses reverentially stood like devotees immersed in thoughts of the True Creator. The henna hedge fenced the red poppy and eglantine flower beds like satin edging on silk turbans. The place rang with the chirping of crickets and the sound of water falling. The garden perfumed the world's senses, blooming with French marigold, double jasmine, medlar, Cupid's arrow, champak, screw-pine flower, juhi, tuberose, Arabian jasmine, the weeping nyctanthes, globe amaranth, gillyflower, marvel of Peru, rose-chestnut flower, iris, peacock flower, calendula, and Cape periwinkle. The rosebuds opened to blossom, and a perfumed miasma enveloped the garden.

In the courtyard there was an octagonal platform on which a canopy of silver cloth, which shone with gold and silk twine, was set up, supported on gold and silver inlaid steel poles. A bed with jewel-studded legs lay underneath it, covered with a sheet of fine muslin and redolent with a rare perfume. Flower trays and wine ewers were placed around it, along with salvers of fresh and dried fruit.

Fie! Fie! The debauched Abyssinian climbed into the bed holding the beauty's hand and began making merry with rounds of wine. Repressed rage wrenched the king's heart at the sight of them. He watched the scene from behind a tree but, unable to bear it, said to himself: 'O God, I had no inkling that my home would be consumed by the fire of ignominy. It was a fallacy to imagine that my adolescent daughter was unfamiliar with such matters, and that after she had grown up and come of age, I would betroth her to some majestic king of noble lineage. I wished to have a regal ceremony befitting my status, as God Almighty has not blessed me with another child besides her. Indeed, I wished to leave the crown of kingship and throne of the kingdom to her husband, and retire to a life of prayer and devotion. Little did I know that this depraved strumpet would find herself a husband while enclosed in her palace. Alas and alack that it was her destiny to fall into the hands of this vile Abyssinian, and smear herself with turpitude in this world and the next. There is nothing to be done now, except wait.'

It is impossible to wipe away the word of fate,
It is not her fault if she was destined to fall

Feeling dejected, the king stood under a tree watching the two of them. Meanwhile, the flame of prurience lit up in the Abyssinian's depraved mind and he began fondling and taking pleasure with the princess.

Engulfed by the flames of rage, the king could not bear to look at the scene. Unable to interrupt them, however, he put a lodestone on his heart and bided his time, waiting for an opportunity. After the Abyssinian had ravished the princess, lassitude overcame the lovers. As they fell into the embrace of sleep, the king found his chance and he rushed and dealt with both hands a powerful blow of the sword which severed the heads of both iniquitous creatures.

After beheading them, the king prostrated himself before God to offer thanks, and proclaimed: 'They reaped as they had sown!'

He decided that it would not do to return from the same subterraneous passage to his palace, and that he should go around the garden and find its entrance and the way to his palace. Thus decided, as he began surveying the garden, he was most surprised to behold its luxurious elegance and charm, and said to himself: 'I am the king of this land, and there is no place within my writ which I have not visited. It is a marvel that such wonderful garden was constructed so near my palace and I lived in ignorance of it. And let alone myself, none in my service knew of its existence. That harlot, despite the strict watch and guard over her, carried on so wantonly in her maidenhood that even married women would be left dumbstruck with shame upon hearing her exploits. In any event, I stand to earn nothing but disgrace by bringing the matter to light. There is nothing to be done but maintain silence. I must now find the garden's gateway and leave.'

SECOND STORY: RELATING HOW THE VIZIER'S DAUGHTER'S SECRET BECAME KNOWN, AND HOW HER PARAMOUR DIED AT THE KING'S HAND AND SHE WAS ALSO KILLED

Thus deciding, Kevan Shah searched the garden. In one place he came upon the entrance, at which he felt very pleased, and said to himself: 'I must now extricate myself from this situation and get back to the palace.' Arriving at the doorway, he found it barred from within, with a lock placed on the portal. With his sword hilt he struck and broke the lock, and opened the door and came out. He regarded that his palace lay at a distance of a quarter kos[5] from there. He told himself that he should quickly get to the door of the palace, and hide somewhere nearby and spend the night there, as some time yet remained until dawn. When it is morning and the palace door opened, people would come out to go about their business, and he would mingle with them, and secretly enter the palace and go and sleep in his bedchamber. Later in the day, he would take measures to attend to the matter at hand, without disclosing the secret to anyone who was not in his close confidence.

5. Kos: A distance approximately equal to two miles.

As he was headed towards his palace, immersed in these thoughts, Kevan Shah heard a dreadful shout behind him, saying, 'O murderer of my brother, do you think you can escape with your life after killing him? While I live, I will not allow you to escape retribution after you had inflicted on me the forever grief of mourning my brother. Indeed, your life's allowance was severed when you committed your heinous act. And much did I try to convince my brother to refrain from his deeds, but he would not take heed. He received just deserts for his actions and reaped as he had sown, meeting a terrible end that matched his miserable deeds. Be that as it may, may my life be cursed should I live and not avenge myself for my youthful brother's murder and seek recompense from my enemy.'

The king marvelled upon hearing these dreadful words, and exclaimed to himself: 'O God, who could that be?!' He looked around in apprehension and beheld another Abyssinian gaining upon him like a billowing dark cloud. Kevan Shah was petrified at the sight of him; fear gripped him, and his heart quivered like a fish out of water. He tried to get away but his legs failed him; with each step he took, he seemed to fall backwards, until the Abyssinian rushed forward and caught him. Kevan Shah's senses were in disarray. When he compared his size to his foe's, he found himself in no wise the Abyssinian's match. The man was so marvelously frightful that the sum total of ghastliness and loathsomness of all the hideous and repulsive creatures from the entire world would not add up to even one part of his ugliness. The Abyssinian had such strength that he could pick up an elephant and fling it away or crush it like a gnat should he so wish. Had Rustam[6] dreamt of his face in sleep, he would have woken up with a start like a withered old crone. Had Isfandiar[7] encountered and beheld him on the battlefield, he would have been terrified of being made into a morsel by him, and run to hide himself in the Seven Labours.[8]

The Abyssinian secured such powerful hold on Kevan Shah that he lost the use of his senses, but he nevertheless fought back to save his

6. Rustam: A legendary hero from Persian mythology, known for his great strength and bravery.

7. Isfandiar: Rustam's son. A brave warrior from Persian mythology.

8. Seven Labours: The *Haft Khvan* or Seven Labours refer to the series of challenging tasks undertaken by Rustam.

life. When that mountain of a man attacked Kevan Shah, he picked up the king like a twig and threw him down. Sometimes Kevan Shah mustering all his strength pushed him back a few steps. Then Kevan Shah received divine aid, and the foot of that Abyssinian landed in a hole and he fell down supine. Seeing his chance, the king secured him by his legs and lifted him up above his head, resolved to deliver him a terrible death blow. He saw a dead tree, one of whose branches was cracked and its sharp edge protruded out, and in no time he impaled the Abyssinian on it, bringing him to death's door as he writhed in ecstasies of pain.

Joyous, and pleased beyond measure, Kevan Shah prostrated himself in gratitude before God. He said to himself: 'To have escaped the clutches of this monster means that I still have some days of life left in this world.'

Thus conversing with himself, as he started for his palace, the wretch called out to him: 'O man! You killed my brother and also murdered me, but there is no helping the fate which ordained that we die at your hand; you are not blameworthy in this matter. Whatever had to happen, came to pass. If you could now do me a favour in God's name, He will grant you great recompense.'

Kevan Shah said to himself: 'I have put paid to him and there will be no harm if I approach him now, for who knows what injunctions he may part with in his last moments.'

Thus decided, he went back to the impaled man, and said to him, 'What you have to say?'

The Abyssinian said, 'O fellow! You killed my brother in a manner which quickly released him from all cares of this world, and returned him to his True Home; whereas you kill me in a manner that will keep me in the throes of death for four or five days; beasts will peck at my flesh while I am still alive, and my last breaths will leave me after great suffering. But whatever had to happen from fate came to pass. I have no companion or friend here to console me, and if you could do me a favour I will die easily, and with your aid be released from the world's cares.'

At these words the king took pity on him, and said, 'What is your wish? Speak so that I may fulfill it.'

That foul man joined his hands together in pleading, and said, 'O fellow, allow me to tell you that my brother and the king's daughter were intimate for five years and you have put them to death. The king's vizier Khiradmand also has a daughter. She is unmarried, and she and I have been intimate for a long time. In the same way that the princess had built a garden for pleasure-seeking, the vizier's daughter, too, constructed a garden near it, where we would rendezvous every day. Today, destiny had this fate in store for me, and she will be awaiting me in the garden and shedding tears over our separation. If you could find it in your heart to go to her and inform her of my terrible state, I will be forever indebted to you.'

The king was greatly surprised to hear this account about the vizier's daughter, and said to himself: 'Here's more mischief! I lamented the princess's fate and had no idea that the vizier's daughter would surpass her in wickedness. But never mind! Regardless, the princess reaped the reward of what she had sown, and the vizier's daughter, too, God willing, shall get her just deserts.'

Thus conversing with himself in his heart, the king addressed the Abyssinian, saying, 'O fellow, I am willing to carry out this errand, but my life is not such a burden to me that I would attempt breaking heedlessly into the vizier's house as a thief.'

That wretched Abyssinian said, 'If you have the determination to carry out the errand, I can convey you inside without trouble.' Thus speaking, he took a ring off his finger and threw it before Kevan Shah, saying, 'Wear this on your finger. It has the property that if you wear it and go into an assembly you will be able to see everyone, without anyone seeing you.'

The king was very pleased to have the ring, and as instructed by that wretch, put it on his finger, and headed for the vizier's house.

When he arrived there, he found the gate open and all the guards and watchmen at their posts, carrying out their duties. Four torchbearers were sitting in the courtyard with five-pronged torches set in the ground. Seeing this, the king feared lest one of them should recognize him, and all the pains he had taken to conceal himself come to naught. Weighing these considerations, he stood next to one of the torchbearers and slapped his head hard. The torchbearers started fighting amongst themselves and did not see Kevan Shah. The king felt greatly relieved and went into the vizier's house after lifting the curtain.

Upon entering it he looked in all directions to find the entrance into the women's quarters. As he searched for it, he saw a wall with a magnificent doorway. An embroidered curtain worked in gold and silver hung over the door, which was flanked by mace bearers standing on duty, wielding gold- and silver-inlaid maces. The king fearlessly lifted that curtain, and stealthily entered the women's quarters. He found female attendants and slave girls busy with their duties, and several female Calmuck, Abyssinian, and Turkic guards standing alert at their stations. In an apartment a beautiful maiden whose forehead was resplendent like the moon was sitting on a bed; looking dejected, her face betraying that she was expecting someone. Every now and then she would sorrowfully recite this couplet:

'Step out of home, O Beloved, it is the time for intimacy
Into the garden where the blooming eglantine is bathed in moonlight'

The king reckoned that she must be the vizier's daughter. Having arrived at this conclusion, he went close to her and whispered into her ear: 'O vizier's daughter, go and search for your beloved whom some enemy has put to death.'

The girl rose uneasily from her bed the moment she heard these words, maddened by transports of grief, imagining it was a voice from the Unseen World.

Verily, the Sea of Love is boundless and none has fathomed its depth. Whomsoever has stepped into its waters soon learns of its power to destroy households.

'Assets of faith and worldly riches both drowned in the waves of love
The bellicose waves drowned the habitation from end to end
The Moon of Canaan[9] has no need of a well
The pull of Zulaikha's[10] love drowned him in an instant
Why would the state of imprisonment kill the nightingale
Who has drowned from the weight of love's collar
Alone in the night of longing I cried
Until my flood of tears washed away my home
The heartless Sheikh and the prosecutor were punished by wine
Which blighted their robe and turban of office
The waves of love spared neither the pious nor debauched
Wherever its torrents turned they drowned alike the sober and intoxicated.'

9. Moon of Canaan: Allusion to Joseph.
10. Zulaikha: Potiphar's wife.

In short, that damsel could think of no recourse except to rush out and behold with her own eyes the state of her beloved, to learn what calamity had befallen him, and who was the wretch who deprived her of the pleasure of life. Having decided on this course of action, she got up and raised her bed, and opening the door underneath, stepped into a subterraneous passage. At that moment the king, too, stealthily and silently followed behind her.

The vizier's daughter, in her anguished state, rushed headlong towards the garden, conjuring in her imagination her beloved's face. She made much effort looking for him in all garden nooks but could not find him anywhere. Losing self-control, she broke into tears and recited the couplet:

'The moment the nightingale was caught in the net it said, "My fate!"
God shall unite me another day with the rose'

Then she said to herself: 'I am so unfortunate that I live and am unable to even behold my beloved's face while he undergoes terrible misery. That he should die and I live on! By God I shall not return home until I have set eyes on his face.'

Feeling helpless, she decided in the end that she must open the garden gate and step out, and either find her beloved's corpse, or relinquish her life in search of him.

That faithful lover disregarded all considerations
She headed out of her garden into the forest

Thus speaking to herself, she opened the garden gate and stepped out, looking for him in all directions. From afar she saw the tree on which her paramour was impaled. She said to herself: 'I must head for that tree and climb it and look around, perchance to discover where my lover's corpse lies.'

When she arrived under the tree she found him affixed to it. The sight of the body terrified her. The wretched man called out, 'O my mistress and confidante, it was fated that a savage should kill my brother and the princess in this garden, and bring me to this pass. I have just a few breaths of life remaining. It was my desire to somehow set my eyes upon your face, so that my soul may fly unencumbered from this ephemeral world to the Everlasting Domain.

'I have neither friend, nor a companion, nor a kind soul
To whom I could narrate my grief, my sorrow, my pain
I am full averse now to such an existence as mine, where
I have neither food nor drink and have a forest for my home'

The vizier's daughter implored him, crying, 'Tell me, where did the man go after wounding you?'

The wretched man said, 'I gave him my ring and begged him to go and narrate my condition to you. I do not know where he went after giving you the news.'

The vizier's daughter expressed much regret, and said, 'Had I known that he was my beloved's enemy, I would have found and caught him, and with my teeth ripped out and eaten his flesh. But no use crying over what is no longer in one's power. What has come to pass was fated. Now there is nothing to do except endure it.'

That condemned man said, 'O my consoler and solace of my restive soul, indeed, whatever was written in fate has happened, and no purpose will be served by crying and wailing. Come near me and press your breast against mine so that the fire in my heart may be quenched. But as it would be difficult for you to climb the tree to reach me, I wish that you would put your finger in my mouth so that I fulfill my desire and my soul leaves my body with ease.'

It so happened that the king had entrusted his signet ring to the vizier, and from affection for his daughter the vizier had given it to her to wear, and she was wearing it on her finger. In her anxiety, she put the same finger into her paramour's mouth. Upon receiving it that dissolute man breathed his last, with his jaw clamping shut in the throes of death, severing the vizier's daughter's finger along with the ring, leaving them in his mouth.

The vizier's daughter writhed in pain as her finger was severed, and from the shock of his passing. She shed many a bitter tear of helplessness and left after reciting these verses on his corpse:

The nightingale departs after her house was set afire on account of the rose
Alas no trace remained in the garden of the bird
The desire remained unfulfilled to bide life in pleasure
In a garden of one's own, and with one's own rose and gardener
The nightingale departed the garden with the words, 'How to argue with fate?
It was destined that I should leave the garden in the spring quarter'

When she returned to her garden, she shed many a tear, overwhelmed by the garden's lushness and bloom, and went away after reciting this couplet:

'O my bird companions, I now leave the garden
Alas the eve of exile, when I depart from my home'

She returned to her palace through the subterraneous passage and kept reciting this couplet until she lay down, and sleep overcame her.

'O tears, let not the string of your pearls be broken
They may fill up the robe skirts but keep continuously falling'

Kevan Shah witnessed all this and then returned to his palace and lay down to rest.

. . .

When the night was almost at an end, the vizier's daughter started screaming and crying in pretense, and wailed, 'Someone cut off my finger to steal the ring!'

Upon hearing her baleful cries, her attendants, handmaids, and slave girls rushed in a frenzy and surrounded their mistress's bed. One slave girl hurriedly woke up the vizier from a peaceful sleep and informed him that some thief had cut off his daughter's finger and stolen the king's signet ring which she had been wearing.

The panic-stricken vizier got up and rushed to his daughter's bedside, and beheld her writhing on the bed in pain and saw her finger missing. He marvelled at this and felt apprehensive, and considering the matter anxiously, said to himself: 'Should I mourn my daughter's injury, or the signet ring's theft? What will I say to the king when I go before him? Why would the king give credence to the story?'

Feeling helpless, the vizier spent the remainder of the night on tenterhooks. When it was time for morning prayers, and the moon, prison-keeper of the gaol of heavens, headed west after a head count of the stars, and the brilliant king, the world-illuminating sun, gave audience in the ninth heaven.

The night passed and the sun rose

Vizier Khiradmand got dressed and arrived in the king's illustrious presence. He made his salutations and said, 'Your Honour, the whole world is indebted to your scrupulousness and equitableness. The populace sleeps with doors open on account of Your Honour's excellent justice. The lion and the goat drink at the same water hole in your reign. Then what injustice that a thief should cut off my daughter's finger to steal a ring! Your Honour must deliver justice in the matter, or else I, your slave, will have no recourse but to kill myself.'

The king laughed at his words, and said, 'O Khiradmand, have no fear. We shall provide justice in the matter, and also recover the ring.' Thus speaking, the king held the vizier by his hand, and led him towards the princess's palace.

Upon arriving at the doorway to the female quarters, the vizier stopped in apprehension. The king said, 'Follow where I lead you, and witness the marvels of God.'

Then the vizier followed the king, who went with the vizier to his daughter's bedchamber, and said to him, 'Move the bed.' Upon the vizier moving the bed, the door of the subterraneous passage was revealed. The vizier's senses became disarrayed at the sight, and he said to the king, 'O Refuge of the World, in the name of God, do enlighten your slave about the particulars of this secret door.'

The king answered, 'There is nothing to tell. Once you have witnessed everything, you will know for yourself. For the present, quietly follow me.' Thus speaking, he descended into the subterraneous passage with the vizier and after crossing its length, emerged into the garden.

When they arrived in the garden the vizier became alarmed and agitated but did not utter a word for fear of the king. The king went and stood beside the corpses and said to the vizier, 'O vizier, do you recognize whose corpse this is?'

The vizier fell unconscious from ecstasies of trepidation. The king splashed some water from the stream onto the vizier's face. When he came to, he saw the king's daughter sleeping in the arms of a hideous looking Abyssinian, and that both had been beheaded.

The vizier fell at the king's feet from distress, and said to him, 'O my Lord and Master! Pray quickly tell what this mystery is, before my soul flutters out of my body from distress.'

The king answered, 'You have seen this much, and now you shall see the rest. Then I will share the particulars of this mystery with you.'

The king then led the vizier by the hand outside the garden and brought him to the tree on which the body of the vizier's daughter's paramour was impaled. Seeing the tree with the corpse affixed to it, the vizier marvelled to the limits of marvelling.

The king said to the vizier, 'Use something to open his mouth.'

As the vizier pried open the mouth of the corpse with a piece of wood, a severed finger with the ring fell out. Seeing these, the vizier turned pale and became dumbstruck like a beast.

The king said to him, 'O Khiradmand, identify the finger and tell me how the ring came to be in this man's mouth! You had stated that a thief cut off your daughter's finger. Who then put the finger with the signet ring in this man's mouth?'

The vizier found himself unable to answer the king's query, and tears issued from his eyes. Feeling helpless, he submitted before the king, 'O my Lord and Master, I have no knowledge of this mystery. I know not how I was caught in this mischief. My daughter has blighted my dignity and honour. All I wish now is to kill myself, and never show my face to the world.'

Kevan Shah consoled the vizier and returned with him to the princess's garden where they sat in an apartment, and the king gave him the whole account from beginning to end. Then he led the vizier by his hand to the other garden which had been constructed by the vizier's daughter.

Arriving in the garden, the vizier saw that it was in no wise less lavish than the one constructed by the princess. A gilded canopied bed lay in a corner of the courtyard. The king pushed the bed and a door was revealed in the floor. The king opened the door and, holding the vizier's hand, descended into the subterranean passage. After travelling for a quarter of a kos, they emerged into the vizier's daughter's palace. Now the vizier fully believed what the king had told him. The vizier's daughter fainted from fright when she beheld the two of them emerging from the underground passage.

The vizier asked the king, 'My master, what should be this depraved creature's punishment for her iniquitous deed?'

The king answered, 'You must kill her.'

As per the king's order, the vizier dealt a sword blow to his daughter that severed her head from her body. The king then said, 'O Khiradmand, bury the heads of these wretches, and have the corpses of the two Abyssinians interred. Then have the bodies of the girls displayed outside the magistrate's hall and depute two scribes and twenty messengers to faithfully transcribe whatever comments are made about them, and bring these for my perusal.'

After issuing these instructions, the king left the palace, went to the bath, and gave audience.

Royal scribes and messengers were placed at the magistrate's hall, and whenever anyone made a comment about the two headless corpses, they transcribed and dispatched it to the king.

THIRD STORY: RELATING TO RAJA BAIDAR BAKHT'S DAUGHTERS ARRIVING AND COMMENTING UPON THE CORPSES, OF KEVAN SHAH MARRYING THE RAJA'S FOUR DAUGHTERS, AND RETURNING TO HIS PALACE

There reigned a powerful raja in the environs of Kevan Shah's kingdom. God had conferred such dignity and grandeur upon him that thousands of men lived off his bounty, and travellers and journeyers from all over received sustenance from his charity and largesse. The raja's name was Baidar Bakht. God Almighty, from his bounty and favour had endowed him with four daughters. The raja had everything, including wealth, possessions, and grandeur, and his four daughters contributed to his fortune and felicity like the four elements that sustain life. All four of them had come of age, and were beautiful, amiable of disposition, and highly intelligent and sagacious.

Raja Baidar Bakht had named his eldest daughter Dil Aaram, his second girl Dilruba, the third Zaibunnisa, and the youngest, Farkhanda. While the other three sisters were older and taller than Farkhanda, they were no match for her in discernment and sagacity. Farkhanda was the youngest, but she was the craftiest of the four sisters.

The raja tried to have them married off into good houses, but his daughters always showed their displeasure at the prospect, and would say to their father, 'We do not wish to be betrothed. We will pass our lives in banter and recreation, as we do not need to get married.'

They would bathe, dress up in men's clothes, decorate themselves with arms and armour, and leave for the forest astride their horses. There they would spend the whole day in hunt and chase, and return home in the evening. Their father tried to stop them from following this pattern and beat his head in frustration, but none of them listened to his remonstrations.

One day, as the four sisters headed home after customarily spending the day in hunt and chase, Dil Aaram said to the others, 'I wish to watch the sights of the city on the way home.'

The other three sisters consented to her wishes, saying, 'We are willing. Let us go where you please.'

The four sisters turned their horses towards the city and, as they rode past the city square regarding its sights, they beheld a crowd of people gathered outside the magistrate's hall.

Dil Aaram said, 'Sisters, let us go and find out why people have crowded there and a throng is assembled.' Thus speaking, the four sisters arrived near the headless corpses.

When she saw the corpses, Dil Aaram, the eldest, said, 'These girls knew well how to tinge their teeth with missi.'[11]

All the men assembled there marvelled at the remark, as it was a strange comment to make about the headless corpses, and they wondered how the rider would know about that particular.

The second sister, Dilruba, said, 'While they were good at applying the missi, they also showed great finesse when lining their eyes with lampblack.'

Again, the comment surprised the crowd.

The third sister Zaibunnisa said, 'And they had such long hair!'

The people were yet again left shocked by the comment.

Then the fourth sister, Farkhanda, laughed and commented, 'These two idiots did it, but knew not how to do it.'

The crowd was astonished, but no one recognized that the four riders were women disguised as men. When the riders had made their comments and picked up their reins, the royal servants guarding the corpses surrounded them, and asked: 'Who are you and from where have you come? Give us your domicile and names.'

11. Missi: A powder (composed of yellow myrobalan, gall-nut, iron-filings, vitriol, etc.) used for tingeing the teeth (Platts).

Dil Aaram replied, 'What business do you have asking of our particulars?'

The royal servants answered, 'We have been ordered by the king to note down and send him the name and address of every person who makes any comments about the corpses. That is the reason we demand your names and particulars.'

Dil Aaram answered, 'My name is Dil Aaram, my second sister is Dilruba, my third sister is Zaibunnisa and my fourth sister is Farkhanda. We are Raja Baidar Bakht's daughters. We had gone hunting in the forest and decided to take the path through the city and visit the city square on our way home. Seeing a crowd gathered, we were drawn here, and are now headed home.' Thus speaking, they picked up their reins and galloped off. The royal servants wrote down their names and particulars and sent them to Kevan Shah.

The king marvelled upon learning of the incident, and said to himself: 'Indeed God Almighty from His power has created marvelous creatures, and given such power of perception to every woman, that although the corpses were headless, they deduced their tingeing of the teeth with missi, lining of eyes with lampblack, and the length of their hair. But the fourth one seems the most cunning of all. I would to God that they come into my possession, so that I learn how they arrived at their conclusions.'

Thus deciding, the king ordered the royal scribe to write out an order to Raja Baidar Bakht to convey his wishes.

Kevan Shah's order to Raja Baidar Bakht read: 'From the day God, Glory be to Him, has created mankind and inhabited the stretches of the world with His Perfect Nature, it is customary for rajas and badshahs to maintain links of love and affection. Now this abject being is desirous that you look upon him with the gaze of generosity and indulgence, and grant a favour like an elder to this well-meaning soul, accepting him into your family. I wish you to give to this well-wisher of yours, your four grown daughters in marriage, so that I do not forget my debt to you for as long as I am of this world and a single breath remains in my body. I shall carry out all my obligations of subordination and tending to the senior and venerable. It is incumbent upon you to grant my request by a favourable reply to this expression of my wishes, and take me as your son-in-law. I have now dispensed with the duty of presenting my suit, and it is up to you to decide the matter. You must not refuse it, as it will not augur well for you.'

The royal scribe wrote out the letter as ordered, and dispatched it after sealing it with the king's signet.

When the missive arrived, Raja Baidar Bakht felt very pleased to be the recipient of royal orders, and said, 'It is an auspicious day that the king has found me worthy of sending a royal injunction.' He stood up to honour the missive and received it with an obeisance. But upon opening and perusing its contents, Raja Baidar Bakht felt as if someone had broken his back, and tears issued from his eyes.

He summoned all his daughters, and said to them, 'O ill-starred wretches, it was for this that I forbade you your ways. I feared a day would come when your name would attract disgrace, and mine invite ignominy. You would not be checked in your conduct, and thus you lost yourselves your reputations, and me my honour. It would have been preferable by far had my wife given birth to a stone, because a stone would not have shaken the foundations of my house, whereas your birth has brought nothing but ruination upon my household. I cannot now show my face to the world, and shall neither eat or drink, and turn my back upon life. A pox upon a daughter's life who could not give up her dishonourable ways, and who robs her father of his dignity and honour. Now it would be better for me to murder all of you and then kill myself, as it would allow me to preserve my honour's essence.'

The four of them became dumbstruck upon hearing their father's speech and made no reply.

After some time had passed, Baidar Bakht threw Kevan Shah's missive before them and said, 'Read it, and then I will reply as you suggest.'

Dil Aaram picked up the royal edict in her hands, and read it to her sisters, but none dared make a reply before their father.

Then Farkhanda, who as we know was the craftiest of all the sisters stepped out and made an obeisance to her father, and said, 'Dear father, you are our Lord and Master in both letter and spirit. We came into this world because of you, and attained sense and intelligence. Far be it from us to suggest how you must answer this letter. If your dignity and honour would be preserved by killing us, we willingly submit our necks before you; it would be a fine bargain if our deaths should benefit you. May God preserve you and keep you in this world for a long while. Whether we live or die is of little consequence. Killing us, however, will not secure you any benefit, and we would have lost our lives.

It would be preferable that you give us to the king, for what is written in our fates must come to pass. You must then think of us as dead.'

Upon hearing her reply, Baidar Bakht felt grieved, and said to himself: 'If they themselves are amenable to the proposition, what use is my worrying over it? Nothing will be better than giving them to the king.'

Thus resolved in his heart, the raja sent a message to his liege. The reply sent by Raja Baidar Bakht to the king's order read: 'What power has a tiny particle to set himself up as an equal to the world illuminating sun, and how could a beggar dare to be a king's equal? This meritless being knows his true worth, but regarding the matter in which Your Excellency has expressed his preference, nothing could be more opportune for this inconsequential person than to be counted among the king's devotees, and considered among his well-wishers. Even though this worthless fellow has no wherewithal to organize a grand wedding ceremony, and his mind cannot grasp the enormity of the honour, he shall yet set a date in accordance with his means and resources, on which to give away his daughters as tribute to his king.'

The reply being written, he sent it to Kevan Shah.

The king was delighted upon reading the raja's reply. He was beside himself with ecstasies of joy, like a flower bud that tears open its clothes. He was unable to think of anything else but his impending union with those beauties, who were like thornless roses, and counted the days and hours to the wedding.

Raja Baidar Bakht summoned geometricians and astrologers to determine an auspicious moment and felicitous path of planets for the betrothal of his daughters, and said to them: 'Determine an auspicious moment for their nuptials.'

The astrologers and Brahmins reflected on their almanacs and inscribed leaves, as per his orders. They made calculations about the stars, and when they saw the moon, Mercury, and Venus gathered in felicity with Mars, Jupiter, and Saturn, and in auspicious positions as per astrological determinations, they set the date for the raja's daughters' nuptials, and said, 'The coming Monday will be most auspicious and favourable for the betrothal of your four beloved daughters.'

Immediately, Baidar Bakht sent for his officers and ordered, 'Prepare jewellery and dresses for my beloved daughters' wedding.'

Within three days all the jewellery and regal clothes were readied as ordered by the raja, and four litters were prepared at an expense of four lakh gold pieces for the conveyance of the princesses. On the Monday suggested by the astrologers and philosophers, the raja had his daughters dressed and caparisoned in finery and jewellery and sent off to Kevan Shah in the litters with great pomp and ceremony. At the moment of their parting, the raja was overcome with fraternal love, and broke into uncontrollable sobbing. Seeing the raja crying, all those gathered also became tearful, and with the departing of the princesses, the house rang like a house of lamentations.

After seeing them off, Raja Baidar Bakht sat dejected and forlorn on his throne, and said to those present, 'I was bestowed these daughters from God after much pleading and begging. And I am telling the truth when I say that I raised them with greater care and indulgence than one lavishes on a male child. No sorrow touched me from the day they were born. I know that a father cannot keep a daughter under his roof forever, but there is no putting out the fire of grief consuming my heart. I never realized that my daughters would leave to settle another's home, ravaging mine.

'Be that as it may, it is now my desire to renounce all worldly things, and spend the rest of my days in prayer and reflection, without thinking about them ever again.' Much did Baidar Bakht cry and lament, in this vein. Finally, with people continuously consoling him, his grief was somewhat allayed.

The narrator recounts that when the four litters arrived outside the royal palace with great pomp and majesty, the messengers brought Kevan Shah the news. The king said to vizier Khiradmand, 'Take a procession of troopers to greet them, and conduct the conveyances of the four princesses to separate palaces.'

As ordered, the vizier greeted the brides and conveyed them to separate palaces.

In the evening, when the silver cloth–clad bride of the sky arrived in her resting place, the king gave orders, 'Prepare my bed in the palace where Queen Dil Aaram is lodged.'

It was made ready as the king had ordered. The king happily had his repast, and fresh and spry, entered the palace. He sat on the bed beside Dil Aaram, and said to her, 'My queen, by the Grace of God I possess all the world's choicest things, and thousands of pretty and beautiful girls respectfully attend on me. I only married you to ask you a single question.'

She answered, 'Pray say what it is that you wish to ask.'

The king answered, 'It has been five days now since I displayed the headless corpses of two women outside the magistrate's hall. Whenever anyone made a comment about them, I was informed of it. Then you and your sisters arrived there in men's clothing, and you said, "These girls knew well how to tinge their teeth with missi." I desire to know how you learned that they stained their teeth, as the corpses were headless.'

Dil Aaram laughed merrily upon hearing this, and said, 'O Refuge of the World! For making such a small query you went to such great lengths, and also made our existence miserable by stopping us from the pleasure of the hunt and chase, and of watching sights and spectacles of the world. What eluded you was not all that difficult to deduce.'

The king said, 'Very well. Pray explain to us.'

Dil Aaram answered, 'O Refuge of the World, if a woman is slovenly her fingers remain stained from the application of missi. But the meticulous one removes the stain with some sour substance. As the girls' fingers did not show any stains, and there was a tinge of blackness in their blood, I concluded that they were meticulous in the application of missi.'

Her words proved to the king that she was very wise. Kevan Shah took Dil Aaram into his arms and spent all night in pleasure-seeking.

When it was morning and the world-illuminating sun bathed the expanse of the world with its light, the king rose from a peaceful sleep, bathed and dressed, and busied himself with the affairs of the state, while looking forward to the evening.

When it was evening and the Emperor of the Sky retired to its private chamber after tracing its path in the heavens, the king ordered: 'Arrange all the paraphernalia of conviviality tonight in Dilruba's palace.' As per the king's orders, the arrangements were made, and after having his repast, the king arrived in Queen Dilruba's palace.

He took a seat beside Dilruba, and said to her, 'O Queen, the other day two headless corpses were displayed outside the magistrate's hall, and you and your sisters arrived there and commented upon the corpses thus: "They lined their eyes with lampblack with great finesse." As you could not see their eyes, how did you learn of their skill in the application of lampblack?'

Dilruba answered, 'It is not at all difficult to guess. When women line their eyes with lampblack, their eyes tear up and lampblack flows out of their eyes, with the tears. A slatternly woman wipes it off with the skirts of her dress. A meticulous one, however, wipes it away with the hem of her peshwaz.[12] Since I saw the lamp-black stain on the hem of their peshwazes, I commented that they knew how to line their eyes with lampblack.'

Very well pleased with her answer, the king pulled Dilruba into his lap and retired for pleasure-seeking.

When the Emperor of the Heavens arose from his sweet slumber and sat on the throne of sky to give audience, Kevan Shah too, came out of Dilruba's palace and gave audience, and busied himself with the affairs of the state, in which he passed the day.

In the evening the king arrived in Queen Zaibunnisa's palace and reminded her too about her comment about the headless corpses and asked her, 'How did you know about their long hair since the corpses were headless?'

Zaibunnisa answered, 'There was nothing to it. The backs of the corpses glistened with oil down to the hips. That was the reason I said that they had long hair.'

The king was delighted by Zaibunnisa's reply and lay down with her on the bed of pleasure.

When the Emperor of the Heavens, sporting his golden crown, sat on the throne of the skies, the king left Zaibunnisa's palace and held court.

As the day ended, he arrived in Farkhanda's palace and after sitting down, asked her, 'O Farkhanda, I heard what your three sisters said, and found it creditable. I am now curious to know what you have to say. Tell me what you meant when you commented that "They did it, but knew not how"?'

Farkhanda replied, with hands joined together in submission: 'O Refuge of the World, the three things deduced by my sisters were easy to guess. My sisters are simple for readily sharing their method of deduction with you. This slave girl of yours, however, has a condition. If you were to fulfil it, I shall reveal the truth of the matter to you.'

The king asked, 'O Farkhanda, tell me your condition.'

12. Peshwaz: A formal dress gown for women that reaches a little below the knee.

Farkhanda replied, 'O Refuge of the World, if you were to fetch forty pitchers of water to sprinkle the ground around my bed, you shall learn the reason for my comment. Afterwards, whatever demands you make of this slave girl, she will carry out without flinching. But without your fulfilling this condition, this slave girl shall not come near you.'

The king was extremely displeased when he heard this, and said, 'O Farkhanda, the condition you set is beneath the dignity of kings. Should you ask for it, I'd have a thousand sheepskins full of rosewater and willow flower essence sprinkled around your bed. It is not possible, however, for me to fill up and sprinkle forty pitchers of water with my own hands.'

Farkhanda answered, 'You would accept the condition, should you wish to please me and desire that I willingly lie with you. If not, I am ready to submit my neck.'

Her words vexed the king and he spent the whole night arguing with her. He tried to reason with Farkhanda but was unable to sway her. In the morning he said to her, 'O fool! You may still desist from your caprice. Nothing has yet been lost, but once things get out of hand there will be nothing to gain except remorse, and you will wring your hands with compunction.'

Farkhanda replied, 'Pray don't be sparing, and expose this slave girl to the worst punishment you can think of. I will stand by my word, and happily embrace the consequences.'

After this exchange the king angrily left the palace, came to his public hall of audience, and said to himself: 'I must visit such severe punishment on this deceitful strumpet that she learns the value of harmony, feels contrite about her behaviour, prostrates her head before me, and feels the brunt of defying me.'

Thus resolved, the king sent for the superintendent of the buildings, and ordered: 'Construct a brick building surmounted by a dome in the middle of the river within three days.' The superintendent of the buildings had the domed structure constructed within three days, and informed the king.

The king rode with Farkhanda in a pleasure-boat and reached the building. He put a purse of a thousand gold pieces before her, and said, 'I am leaving on a campaign and shall return to the city in a year's time. It is incumbent upon you to spend five hundred gold pieces from this purse without breaking the seal on it, and save the other five hundred. You must also, within this dome, give birth to a son who is my legitimate child.'

Farkhanda made an obeisance and submitted, 'Very well, you may leave.'

Fulfill your wishes, and slay me
But I am blameless, truth be told

After giving her his commands, the king locked the door, and gave these orders: 'Everyday in the afternoon a eunuch must bring her an ewer of water with two pieces of barley bread and lower them from the skylight; besides this she may not receive anything.'

Thus ordering, he closed and locked the door of the dome, put the key in his pen box, and left, reciting this couplet:

'May you abide, while I depart
Carrying away a singed and marked heart.'

FOURTH STORY: OF THE MERCHANT DANISHMAND ARRIVING IN KEVAN SHAH'S LAND; OF FARKHANDA COMING OUT OF THE DOME, AND MAKING THE KING FILL UP FORTY PITCHERS OF WATER

When Kevan Shah entered his palace after imprisoning Farkhanda in the dome, he summoned the head steward and ordered him to dispatch the baggage-tent westwards without delay, and commanded the supervisor of the kettledrums to beat the march. The tent-keepers dispatched a hundred carts filled with baggage tents, and speedily moving, set up camp three kos from the city.

In the evening, when the bugles announced the beginning of the march, Kevan Shah came out of the city riding a mule-borne litter, with the viziers, office bearers, and functionaries riding along, and entered the royal pavilion with great pomp and ceremony.

Early in the morning, when the Journeyman of Heavens emerged from his pavilion of light and started his trek across the sky, the king also set out. In this manner, he made short stops of two to four days' duration along the way, to divert his mind. When he thought of Farkhanda, he would recite these verses:

Why should I repent what I did
Whatever I did was well justified

The narrator informs us that, meanwhile, Farkhanda remained a prisoner under that oppressive and dark dome, and hoped for the year to come to an end, and her wishes to be fulfilled. She bore with equanimity the suffering fate had apportioned her. Her days passed in torment and she bided her time under the dome in silence, reflecting on God, and reciting:

'I have given over my affairs to the munificent God
Let us see what His benevolence proffers'

'O God I wish that my word prevails. There is none here who can offer me succour except You. I invoke Your aid to not let me lose face.

'O helplessness, may I become your sacrifice
You alone hold my hand in difficult times'

Sometimes, restive from her oppression, she would intone these couplets:

'Shedding tears is now my eyes' occupation
The eyes God gave me have become seeping wounds
My prayers wander, and do not find their mark
Why has the door of divine acceptance been walled up?
The flame develops and rises from the heart's burning
The house was burnt down by the house lamp.'

One day as she recited these verses, Farkhanda's prayers were successful, and God granted them His approval. Her hopes were fulfilled as a merchant from a foreign land arrived, and his boats sailed close to the dome which was built in the middle of the river.

Farkhanda was looking out at the river from the skylight through which she received food and water, when she beheld a rich merchant seated on the roof of his pleasure-boat. A steward stood before him, shielding him from the sun with a pankha. Some of his boats had sailed past the dome, and others were coming up in their train.

Farkhanda reckoned that his pleasure-boat would go past the dome, and at once she thought of a stratagem to put into action. She broke one of the clay bowls in which water was brought her, and picking up a shard, wrote on it with a piece of coal, as follows:

'O merchant! Since the time God Almighty laid the foundation of Creation, he has yet to make someone as beautiful as me. Through an accident of fate I have been imprisoned in this dome, and it has been as if God Almighty has interred me alive. If you wish to have me, you must hire a mansion near the riverbank, and from there run a copper aqueduct to the dome to break me out of here. Then you and I can bide our time in pleasure-seeking, and fill the goblet of hope with the wine of fulfillment.'

Thus inscribing the piece of the clay, she threw it towards the merchant's boat from the skylight. The merchant, whose name was Danishmand, marvelled when the piece of clay landed near him. He said to himself: 'Whence has this clay piece come, since the riverbank is not close by?' After considering the matter, he realized that the clay piece must have come from the dome he had espied. He picked up the piece, and upon perusing it, fell victim to love's arrow which shot right through his heart.

Danishmand said to himself: 'Until I have secured this damsel, I will not touch food or drink. I should think of some subterfuge to gain possession of her.'

Thus resolved, he moored his boat on the other side of the river, hired a mansion appropriate to his status, and had all his goods and merchandise unloaded and stored therein.

The following day he summoned several braziers from the city and met them in a separate house. After tempting them with the promise of riches, he informed them of the secret commission, and said to them: 'If you were to speedily and successfully carry out this work for me, I will reward you so richly that you will be liberated from worry for the rest of your lives.' Tempted by the promise of the rich reward, the braziers agreed to carry out the difficult task, and said to him, 'We are willing to perform this labour, and leave the compensation to your munificence.'

As requested by the braziers, Danishmand purchased and handed them a hundred maund's worth of copper sheets, and also identified the place where the aqueduct was to be constructed.

With much hard labour, the braziers prepared copper cylinders and, over a period of five days, laid them underwater from the river bank to the floor of the dome.

Then they said to Danishmand, 'If you give the order we can break through the dome's floor.'

Danishmand said to them, 'Break open the dome floor and clear a passage inside the copper cylinders wide enough for a person to pass.'

When the labourers started hammering at the floor of the building, Farkhanda reckoned that it must be the merchant who had gone to all the trouble and expense to liberate her. She hid herself in a corner of the dome and waited.

After finishing the work, the labourers informed Danishmand. He was very pleased at receiving the news and sent away the workers after giving them a rich reward. He then sent a shrewd woman with a message for Farkhanda that read: 'I undertook all the hardships and trouble in compliance with your wishes. In my desire for you, I had this aqueduct prepared speedily. It is now incumbent upon you to allow me to place your feet upon my eyes, and reward this devotee by granting him the fruit of desire from life's tree.'

When the woman gave Danishmand's message to Farkhanda, she laughed and said to the former, 'You must return to Danishmand and bring me clothes and jewellery to wear.' That woman returned to the merchant with her message.

Danishmand was beside himself with joy when he received the happy message, and hastily arranged for a fine dress and costly jewellery to be delivered to Farkhanda in a salver through that woman.

When the woman arrived carrying the salver with the dress and jewellery, Farkhanda bedecked herself and set out with the messenger through the aqueduct to meet the merchant.

Danishmand was overjoyed when he heard the news of Farkhanda arriving. He had carpets laid out for her, and he himself sat with great pomp on a throne, wearing a fine dress and costly adornments.

Upon seeing Farkhanda, he devotedly rose from the throne. She approached and said to him: 'Dear father! Pray accept the greetings from your slave girl.'

Dumbfounded at her words, Danishmand said to Farkhanda, 'O good woman, I underwent all this trouble at your command, and spent untold riches, nursing the hope of fulfilling a secret desire. I never suspected that you would declare me your father and slip out of my hands. Indeed, the saying is true that a fool is the one who hastens into action; wise the one who carefully considers before acting. Had I not hurriedly fulfilled your wishes, but incrementally doled out favours, I would not have looked a fool. Now you may do as you please.' Thus speaking, he recited the verse:

Alas, when you find association with me beneath you
Why shouldn't my body find life's robe suffocating?

Farkhanda listened to his account, then said: 'O merchant, I am the king's wife. He imprisoned me in this dome and left on a campaign. Did you desire to break me out of the dome and violate my honour? Has life become such a burden to you that you entertained such thoughts? And do consider why someone like me, who refused the king himself without his first fulfilling my conditions, and is ready to wager her life rather than take the easy course, would grant you any favours. You would do well to follow my commands and spend your gold as I tell you. After the year is over and the king returns from the campaign, I shall return you all the gold that you would have spent by then, with a fourfold profit. Defy me and you will come to a bad end.'

Upon hearing this, Danishmand resigned himself to his fate, and reckoned that he had received his just deserts. He said to Farkhanda, 'Very well. Your slave shall do as you tell him.'

Farkhanda said, 'O merchant, first you must depute a woman to receive food and water from the eunuch every afternoon at the dome. But she must never utter a word. Next, you must find and purchase, however you may, thirty attractive and beautiful slave girls who resemble me. Then I will have further orders for you.'

Following her commands, Danishmand deputed a woman to receive food and water from the eunuch at the dome every day. After five days' search, he was able to purchase thirty beautiful and attractive slave girls who resembled Farkhanda. Having accomplished this, he said to Farkhanda, 'I await further orders.'

Farkhanda said to him, 'O Danishmand, now let us move to where the king is camped.'

As instructed, Danishmand ordered his goods loaded up, and leaving behind a few men to guard the mansion, set out with Farkhanda and the thirty slave girls. After some days he arrived near the royal encampment, set up his camp, and unloaded his goods. Farkhanda with the thirty slave girls lodged herself in the women's quarters, and passed the night in comfort and safety.

The following day Farkhanda said to Danishmand, 'You must present yourself before the king and take along a salver of priceless jewels as offering. When you are presented before him, offer salutations according to courtly etiquette, and present this salver as an offering. When the king asks you your business, tell him that you have come from a distant land to sell your wares in His Honour's dominions and have all kinds of merchandise with you, and that you desire an opportunity to present it before His Honour, so that he can purchase whatever he finds to his liking.'

Danishmand listened to the instructions given by Farkhanda and headed for the king's camp. Upon arriving at the abode of felicity, he gave his particulars to the entrance guards. The royal servants went before the king and informed him that a merchant from some foreign land had arrived at his felicitous abode with news of all kinds of merchandise.

The king ordered, 'Send him into our presence.'

Upon presenting himself, Danishmand made his salutations as instructed and presented his offering. The king accepted the offering, was pleased with Danishmand, and asked, 'Whence have you arrived and what is your business here?'

Danishmand replied as Farkhanda had instructed him.

The king said, 'Consider this as your home, and do show us all that you have brought so that we may purchase the merchandise.'

Danishmand answered, 'Kindly allow your devotee the freedom of your court, so that whenever he arrives, he may be allowed into your presence without let.'

The king announced, 'Let no one obstruct him from presenting himself before us.'

After making his request, Danishmand took his leave of the king, and upon returning home, gave an account of his visit to Farkhanda.

The following day Farkhanda said to Danishmand, 'Go before the king again today and take along all kinds of rare merchandise you have, and do not accept money for anything the king chooses.'

As per Farkhanda's orders, Danishmand took all the merchandise before Kevan Shah, and presented it to his exalted gaze. The king chose a few objects after inspection, and said to Danishmand, 'Pray take your price from the royal treasury.'

Danishmand submitted, 'Your slave will not accept any payment. By the grace of Your Honour this slave has everything in this world and does not lack for anything.'

The king was very pleased to hear this and reckoned that the merchant had come to him in hope of some personal favour, and that he must fully indulge him at the appropriate time.

After presenting the goods before the king, Danishmand returned to the camp and narrated the whole account to Farkhanda.

On the third day, Farkhanda said to Danishmand, 'O Danishmand, go before His Honour and when taking your leave of the king, submit respectfully to him that you, his devotee, are desirous of making preparations for a feast for the king, so that His Honour may set his august foot in your home and illuminate your humble abode. Tell him that you will then present before His Honour all you possess; that you own thirty graceful and beautiful slave girls whom you have gathered at great expense, and you would like to display them before the king and, should it please him, he may buy any of them; and that you have a daughter who has come of age, and that it is your desire to make His Honour an offering of her, too.'

After receiving these instructions, Danishmand presented himself before the king and made his submission, as Farkhanda had taught him. The king was very pleased to hear Danishmand's request, and said, 'O Danishmand, even though it is indecorous for kings to visit the homes of commonality, we accept your invitation, as your pleasure is paramount to us. Let us know when you wish us to visit your abode.'

Danishmand said, 'I would be grateful if Your Honour would confer a pavilion upon me.' The king ordered the supervisor of the baggage train to provide a pavilion to Danishmand and set it up wherever he desired.

Then Danishmand said, 'Should it be Your Honour's pleasure, you may visit this devotee's humble abode tomorrow.'

The king accepted Danishmand's invitation, who then took his leave of the king and returned to the camp, and narrated the whole account to Farkhanda.

She said to him, 'O Danishmand, before the night is over you must get readied for the slave girls thirty dresses in different colours, adorned with gold lace edging, spangle-studded ribands and fretted gold thread lace. Arrange, as well, a set of jewellery for each slave girl that compliments the colour of her dress.'

Before it was daylight, Danishmand provided the thirty dresses and sets of jewellery for the thirty slave girls as Farkhanda had ordered.

The following day the royal pavilion was furnished with a colorful carpet, and flower trays, a betel-box, and perfume box were placed next to the throne. The cooks were ordered to prepare many courses of delicious food.

In the afternoon, the king arrived at Danishmand's camp in a mule-borne litter. Danishmand greeted him and made an offering of a salver of jewels. The king took Danishmand with him and went and sat on the throne.

Afterwards, Danishmand went to Farkhanda and said to her, 'The king has arrived. Tell me what to do next.'

Farkhanda sent Danishmand off with instructions, and he soon returned to join the king.

Farkhanda now had a slave girl made ready in a red dress, and had her decorated and adorned with jewellery. She gave the woman a betel-box containing betel-leaves flecked with gold, and told her to present herself before the king, make a salutation, and stand reverentially before him. The slave girl went out to the royal pavilion as instructed.

When the king saw the slave girl, he was baffled and imagined that Farkhanda had come out of the dome. Staring, he sat up attentively on the throne, and said to the merchant, 'O Danishmand, is this your daughter?'

Danishmand answered, 'O Refuge of the World, she is a mere slave girl. What made you think she was my daughter? How could she be my daughter's match? My daughter is in the female quarters.'

The king marvelled upon hearing this, and said to himself: 'If the merchant's slave girl is so beautiful, how much more beautiful will his daughter be!'

After some time Farkhanda dressed a second slave girl in a light green dress, bedecked her elegantly with emerald-studded gold jewellery, and sent her into the king's presence with a flower tray.

The king again felt disquiet at the sight of the new slave girl, and asked Danishmand, 'Is this girl your daughter?'

Danishmand answered, 'O my Lord and Master, what is it you say! How could this slave girl be my daughter's equal?'

The king fell silent.

After some time Farkhanda sent out another slave girl into the king's presence, this time wearing a saffron dress and holding a rose water sprinkler.

The king was startled again when he saw her and made the same query of Danishmand. The merchant replied to him as before.

Farkhanda kept sending out slave girls at regular intervals after dressing and adorning them and giving them something to carry before the king. Each time, the king marvelled at the sight of them, and kept asking Danishmand about them, and the latter returned the same answer.

When all thirty slave girls had been presented before the king, he looked at each of them with desire, and recited this couplet:

I knew that there is no pleasure in a lover's destiny
But I was helpless as I had no power over my heart

He said to himself: 'While I mourned one Farkhanda, God Almighty has conferred thirty Farkhandas upon me.'

When Danishmand saw the king in this state, he excused himself and went into the women's quarters and told Farkhanda about it. Whereupon Farkhanda dressed herself in white, and adorning herself with colorful gems and jewellery, stepped into the king's presence with great delicacy. The king was crestfallen when he beheld Farkhanda, and rose to greet her. He held her hand and said, 'O Farkhanda, tell me truthfully, how did you manage to come out of the dome, and find your way here?'

Farkhanda said, 'O Refuge of the World, I do not understand what you mean. My name is not Farkhanda and I have no association with any dome. Indeed, I do not know any particulars of a dome or anyone named Farkhanda.'

The king was embarrassed to hear this, and said to himself: 'She is not Farkhanda, after all. God has the power to create a hundred people having the same face. Indeed, Farkhanda has no wherewithal to break free from the dome.'

Convinced, the king held Farkhanda's hand and led her to a seat, and asked her, 'Tell me your name.'

Farkhanda answered, 'This humble servant of yours is called Zahra, and I am the daughter of Danishmand the merchant.'

The king's heart filled with desire, and he said to himself: 'I must take her to bed and ravish her.'

Farkhanda guessed what was on the king's mind, and said to him, 'O Refuge of the World! What is the hurry? I am available to you along with the thirty slave girls. Come night, you may fulfill all your heart's desires.'

The king answered, 'O Zahra, I do not have the patience to wait till nightfall. Let what must happen come to pass now.'

Farkhanda said, 'O Refuge of the World, this slave girl has one condition. If you were to fulfill it, you may do as you desire with this slave girl.'

Kevan Shah was greatly surprised to hear this, and said to himself: 'O God, it is a marvel that all women apportioned to me are cast from the same mould. Farkhanda was imprisoned because of her setting a condition. Let us see what this woman says.'

He said to her, 'O Zahra, name your condition!'

The false Zahra replied, 'O Refuge of the World, the condition is that you must send for two horses from the stable. Both you and I will mount and race them, and the one who gets ahead will be the winner. Should I win, I will receive five lakh gold pieces from you, and should you win, I will surrender myself to you.'

The king was very pleased upon hearing this, and said, 'Arrange it when you please.'

I have now become familiar with all
And they have all been proved self-serving

The false Zahra answered, 'This slave girl would have it now.'

The king sent for the equerry and whispered to him, 'Saddle up and bring two horses right away. Make sure that one of the horses is beautiful and fleshy, and fitted with a colorful golden saddle. Search the stable and select a horse whom a short gallop would tire out, one that is unable to go a long distance. And bring another horse that looks lean but is capable of galloping over long distances, and put an old saddle on him.'

After giving these orders to the equerry, the king said to himself: 'When the two horses are brought, I will mount the lean horse and make her sit on the fleshy horse. In the horse race, I will take the lead and she will be left behind. Thus, I will win her.'

The equerry brought the horses while the king was thinking these thoughts and reciting the couplet:

'In time my well-statured beloved would become a calamity
When she steps forward the Day of Reckoning will be ushered in'

The king said, 'O Zahra, I will ride this lean horse while you ride this beautiful horse.'

Farkhanda answered, 'O Refuge of the World, this slave girl would never be guilty of such impudence as to ride the better and more expensive horse while Your Honour rides a lean and worthless horse.'

Thus speaking, she quickly mounted the lean horse. The king was astounded, and said to himself: 'This woman is a great trickster. Why did I put myself to this trouble? I lost five lakh gold pieces for nothing.' Powerless to do anything about it, the king sat on the fleshy horse and both of them whipped their horses.

When Farkhanda gave the horse a cut of the whip her horse galloped away and covered a great distance in no time, and the king's horse lagged behind because of its weight. When Farkhanda had put a distance of a kos between her and the king, she left the open field and rode off into the forest. While the king kept trotting, whipping his horse and pounding forward, Farkhanda disappeared from his sight into the trees.

When Farkhanda entered the forest, she saw a beautiful young woman, wearing rough, old clothes, sitting beside a well and crying, with an empty pitcher and rope lying in front of her.

Farkhanda approached and asked her, 'O woman, who are you and why are you sitting here so forlorn?'

The woman answered, 'How will it benefit you to know my story?'

Farkhanda said, 'Although I may get no benefit from asking it, one human being can share his pain with another.'

That woman replied, 'My pain is not one whose details can be shared.

'To whom should I open my heart, for I have no consoler
I opened myself to my heart once, it has now become closed
The eyes are flooded and the heart burns
What injustice that my house burns in rain'

'O rider, it would be better if you do not ask me my circumstances. My village is far away and I have come here to fetch water at my mother-in-law's command. Even though I lack the strength, yet I bear the burden God has apportioned me, and thank Him every moment.'

Farkhanda said, 'O woman, I know that you have suffered some pain. I am going to make you an offer, and I wish you to kindly accept it, because it will help both of us.'

The woman asked, "What is it that you ask?'

Farkhanda answered, 'Take off and give me the clothes you have on, and put on my clothes and jewellery instead, and hold my horse's reins and take him home as well, and do with these things as you please.'

That woman asked, 'My good woman, what do you get by giving me such riches for these poor clothes? I do not wish to invite trouble by returning home with your fine clothes and jewellery. I will happily give you my clothes if they can benefit you, but I do not wish to have yours.'

Farkhanda laughed, and said, 'O fool! Have not the least fear. Nobody will question how you came into possession of these clothes. All these things are my own property, and I am willingly offering them to you.'

That woman was finally satisfied by Farkhanda's words. She took off her clothes and gave them to Farkhanda. Then Farkhanda quickly took off her clothes and jewellery and gave them to the woman, and donned the woman's clothes herself, and also gave the horse to the woman.

Holding the clothes and jewellery under her arm, and leading the horse by its reins, the woman disappeared into the forest. Farkhanda sat beside the well, placed the pitcher before her, and started crying. She smeared a little dirt on her face and drew her veil across her face.

Meanwhile, the king arrived near the well, tracking the hoofprints of Zahra's horse, and saw that she was not to be seen anywhere. Despairing, he asked the woman sitting there, 'O woman, did you see any rider pass here?'

She answered, 'I am caught up in my own worries; I do not know of any rider.'

The king felt confounded and said to himself: 'Zahra tricked me and God alone knows where she has disappeared. Had I known that she would slip away from my hands like this, I would never have made a wager with her.'

The king tried to track the horse's hoofprints but he could not find them because of the dense grass. He lost all hope of finding Zahra, and recited the quatrain:

'The one who knows that the worthless world is transient
For him life is a tale to be enjoyed
Only he can ford the sea of truth
Who thinks of life as nothing more than a bubble'

Then the king asked the woman sitting beside the well, 'O woman, why are you sitting here crying?'

Farkhanda answered, 'You would do well to return whence you have come. What business do you have asking about my circumstances?'

The king felt desire stirring within, and said to himself: 'I must somehow find out whether this woman is young or old.' With that in mind, he dismounted and stood beside the well. Then he lifted up her veil and said to her, 'O woman, why do you cry?'

Upon lifting the veil, the king saw a face that was beautiful as the moon. He was stunned to behold her beauty, and said to himself: 'God's wondrous Nature be praised, for hiding a jewel in rags, and bestowing such beauty even to the poor. I must find a way to take this woman to bed. It is likely that, tempted by a little gold, she will consent to it.'

He pressed the woman again, and said, 'What trouble has befallen you? Share it with me.'

Farkhanda said, 'My good fellow, I was married a year ago, and until today I had lived in my father's house. Today my husband brought me to his family home. It is a custom in my in-laws' family that when a bride visits the house for the first time, she must, before entering the house, go to a well outside the community, and fill forty pitchers of water and sprinkle them around the well as an offering to saints. I came here thus to perform the ritual, and now wonder how I will ever be able lift the heavy pitcher from the well and sprinkle water with it. That is the reason I bemoan my fate.'

The king said, 'I do not see anyone here. If you were to lie with me, I will fill up the forty pitchers and sprinkle water with them.'

Farkhanda said, 'I do not see any harm in that.'

The king was mightily pleased to hear this. He immediately tied up the skirts of his robe around his waist, filled up a pitcher from the well, and said to Farkhanda, 'Keep count while I will fill up the pitchers and sprinkle water.'

Farkhanda agreed to do this.

The king busied himself filling the pitchers from the well and sprinkling the water around it, while Farkhanda kept count. The king filled up thirty-nine pitchers with water and sprinkled them around the well. When he began filling the fortieth pitcher, Farkhanda escaped from there without the king noticing.

After filling up the fortieth pitcher, when the king looked towards Farkhanda, he found the woman had disappeared. Surprised and confounded, he searched for her in every direction, and said to himself: 'I am singularly unlucky, in that I lost Farkhanda to the prison dome, Zahra to the forest, and when in my despondency I decided to console myself with a lowly woman, she too has disappeared after making me fill up forty pitchers.'

Thus speaking to himself, he rode home, after sadly reciting these verses:

I am not fated to behold my beloved
Only God in his power can grant me sight of her
If my beloved would come and spend a night with me
I would distribute sweetmeats in the name of saints on Thursday eve

Farkhanda, having deceived the king, returned to the camp.

FIFTH STORY: OF FARKHANDA LYING WITH KEVAN SHAH AND BECOMING PREGNANT; OF HER COMING OUT OF THE DOME AND BIDING HER LIFE IN PLEASURE WITH THE KING, AND REWARDING DANISHMAND

The next day Farkhanda said, 'O Danishmand, arrange for men's clothing for me, and get me a fine Arabian steed.'

Danishmand did as Farkhanda had ordered. He provided the clothing and bought an Arabian horse for five thousand gold pieces.

On the third day, Farkhanda put on men's clothes and decorated herself with arms and armour. Holding a lance, she rode out by herself.

Perchance the king was looking out at the river from the window of his fort. Farkhanda positioned herself before the window and lunged her horse, moving him with her lance. When the king beheld the sight, he became enamored of the rider, and said to one of his troopers, 'Call the horseman lunging the horse.'

The trooper approached Farkhanda, made his salutation, and said, 'Our king wishes to see you.'

In obedience to these orders, Farkhanda went into the king's august presence, and made her salutations as per royal etiquette.

The king said, 'Sit and tell me about yourself, your name, who you are, whence you have come, and your business here.'

Farkhanda answered, 'O Refuge of the World, I am a traveller and have arrived from a far-off land. My name is Farkhanda Bakht and I am in search of employment. I will go wherever fate takes me.'

The king felt as if Farkhanda herself had come out of the dome. Then he realised it was not possible for her to break free, and nobody would dare help free his prisoner. He told himself he must attribute it to God's wondrous, boundless nature that there were hundreds of people who had similar features. He also considered that Farkhanda was a woman and the person before him was a man. He told himself that had the horseman been a woman, he would have added her to his harem as well, and been compensated for his longing for Farkhanda and Zahra and the grief at their loss. He decided that he should employ the man until the year of Farkhanda's incarceration was over, to find some solace looking at his face.

Thus decided, he said to the rider, 'O Farkhanda Bakht, if it is employment you seek, what would be better than you entering into our service?'

Farkhanda answered, 'Very well! Your slave is willing.'

The king was very pleased by the answer, and said to himself: 'I am indeed lucky that God granted me this boon.'

Farkhanda, too, made such captivating discourse that the king fell into her snare of deception. In short, the day passed in this manner, and when it was evening, the king said, 'O Farkhanda Bakht, I wish that the two of us may have supper together.'

Farkhanda answered, 'How could this slave dare share food with His Highness?'

The king answered, 'There is no harm in it. I am deeply enamored of you, and it is proverbial that love overrides all relationships of master and servant.'

Farkhanda answered, 'Your humble servant has no merit except what His Highness graciously sees in him.'

The king ordered food to be served and, holding Farkhanda's hand, sat before their repast. They had dinner together.

When some hours of the night had passed, Farkhanda said, 'Now your slave must beg his leave. I shall present myself again tomorrow.'

The king's heart became disconsolate when he heard this, and he said, 'Should you wish, you could spend the night here.'

Farkhanda answered, 'Should Your Honour wish to keep me in his employ, I will remain in your service all day long, but return home at night.'

The king said, 'O Farkhanda Bakht, even though my heart is sorrowful at the thought of you leaving, I do not wish to make you unhappy.'

We shall judge of your promise of union
Should I still have life till the end of day

Upon hearing this, Farkhanda rose and made her salutation. She took her leave from the king and went home. The king became sorrowful at her departure and spent the night tossing and turning, reciting these verses:

'Those who fall in love with travellers
They spend all their lives crying
Come quickly, for the heart is restive
And all that you say like candied sugar
My heart is entangled in your locks
And now it cannot escape, it is a narrow lane'

When it was time for morning prayers, and the sun, beloved of the heavens, emerged from his pleasure chamber, sporting golden headgear to show himself to his lovers, Farkhanda again put on men's clothes and prepared to present herself before the king.

The king had spent the night lamenting and crying, and was sitting, looking out for Farkhanda Bakht, when he arrived and made an obeisance. The moment the king saw him, he sat up restlessly, and recited:

From the time I became desirous of your sight
I earned disrepute in the world and infamy,
and became ignominious
Without seeing you I am always in the danger of dying
Always drawing pain and suffering in your separation

The king held Farkhanda Bakht's hand and made him sit beside him.

Farkhanda said to herself, 'The king has become besotted with me.' She talked to the king even more indulgently.

After they had passed the day happily, the king asked, 'O Farkhanda Bakht, do you play chausar?'

Farkhanda answered, 'Your Honour, your slave has some little familiarity with the game.'

The king ordered the chausar board to be brought, and threw the dice.

Farkhanda said, 'Your Honour, would we be playing the chausar game for mere entertainment?'

The king replied, 'You may set a wager if you wish.'

Farkhanda said, 'Any stake less than one lakh gold pieces would be worthless.'

The king said, 'I accept! But you must also pay up if you lose.'

Farkhanda said, 'Should I lose, I shall not set foot out of the palace until I have settled with you, and should I win I will demand to be paid on the spot.'

The king replied, 'I accept these conditions.'

The two of them started playing chausar. They first played a game of three rounds. Farkhanda lost on purpose. The king was delighted, and he said to himself: 'God fulfilled my desire without any effort on my part. Until I have recovered the amount from him, I will not give him leave to depart.'

While the king was engrossed in these thoughts, Farkhanda won the next three rounds, and afterwards won six games of three rounds each from the king. Then she got up and said, 'O Refuge of the World, it is late at night. Yours truly must now beg your leave. Kindly order the eighteen lakh gold pieces to be brought, and let me go.'

The king answered, 'It is not safe to take the payment in the night. Take it tomorrow in the morning when you arrive at the court.'

Farkhanda answered, 'A gracious man does not break his promise. Had I lost, you would not have let me return home.'

The king answered, 'It is unlikely that the royal treasury will have eighteen lakh gold pieces to pay at this hour. You will be paid tomorrow upon arrival. You will have reason to complain if I refuse then.'

Farkhanda remained silent.

The king realised that Farkhanda had become unhappy. He said, 'O Farkhanda Bakht, the treasury does not have eighteen lakh gold pieces to pay you at this moment. Tell me what I can do to make you happy.'

Farkhanda answered, 'If you were to give me your signet ring to keep for the night, it would satisfy me.'

The king was blinded by love and did not pause to consider the consequences. He hurriedly took off his signet ring and threw it before Farkhanda. She took the ring and went home.

After arriving home, she said to Danishmand, 'I am now going to the city and will return before daybreak.' Then she spurred the horse and within three hours she travelled forty kos to the mansion, returned to the dome through the aqueduct, took out five hundred gold pieces after breaking the seal on the purse given her by the king, and with the signet sealed the other five hundred as before. She returned to the mansion again through the aqueduct, and then rode back, returning to Danishmand's camp before daylight.

In the morning she changed her clothes and returned to the court. The king was delighted to set eyes on Farkhanda Bakht, and they passed the day in pleasantries. In the evening the king ordered food to be served for them, and later, the two sat down to play chausar again.

Farkhanda began losing on purpose, to the extent that the king recovered the eighteen lakh gold pieces he had lost the previous night, and now it was she who owed him eight lakh gold pieces.

Then the king said, 'O Farkhanda Bakht, it is now late at night. We shall play again tomorrow.'

Farkhanda said, 'Your humble devotee now takes his leave. I shall return tomorrow.'

The king said, 'I will not give you leave until you have paid the eight lakh gold pieces. Furthermore:

> *'Stay the night since you are already here*
> *The night of lovemaking is better than the night of prayers'*[13]

Farkhanda answered, 'If that is your wish, so be it. I am helpless in this matter.'

The king ordered, 'Put a bed beside mine for Farkhanda Bakht.'

At his orders, the royal servants brought a fine bed with jewel-encrusted legs, and placed it near the king's bed. Then the king rose, and Farkhanda rose too, but said with a grimace,

'I am now in your debt, and must do as you tell me.'

The king reckoned that Farkhanda Bakht was displeased. He said, 'O Farkhanda Bakht, do not take offence at this. I have not kept you

13. Night of prayers: The night of blessings.

here because of the debt. It is on account of you yourself, who bring such joy to my heart. What is gold in comparison?

I am sick with love, let us see what happens
It is a terrible malady, let us see what transpires'

Upon hearing this, Farkhanda went and sat on the bed.

The king said, 'O Farkhanda Bakht, God with his munificence brought you close to me, but what great injustice it is that he made you a man.'

Farkhanda realised that the king was badly smitten by her and the arrow of her love had shot through his heart. She replied softly thus: 'O Refuge of the World, I can sense the stirring of your feelings and your graciousness towards your slave. It is therefore only right that I do not keep my secret from you, and tell you the truth about myself.'

The king sat up when he heard this and listened with great engrossment.

Farkhanda said, 'O Refuge of the World, beside this city is a habitation where a wealthy merchant lives whose name is Malik Feroz. I am his daughter, and my name is Gul Rukh. I am unmarried and I am very fond of hunting and chase. Every morning I sneak out on horseback in men's clothes and return in the evening. It was an accident of fate that I met you. The rest is in your hands.'

The king jumped with joy when he heard this, and picked Farkhanda up in his arms. Farkhanda kept saying, 'No! No!' but he did not desist.

It is said that cotton and fire cannot be gathered together, and a woman cannot prevail against a man. In the end, the fire of concupiscence consumed the king's mind, and he could no longer make conversation, and ravished her. Farkhanda who had a delicate form, could not bear the shock and fell into a daze and recited the couplet:

'I let you prevail and caused my destruction
Release my hands as I am become your sacrifice'

After relieving himself, the king picked up a rosewater sprinkler and sprinkled rose water on her face. She came to and spent the rest of the night crying and weeping.

In the morning Farkhanda left the king's side and, as she was leaving, secretly took the king's handkerchief. Then she mounted her horse and returned home.

It so happened by God's Will that a full three months had passed from the day the king had incarcerated Farkhanda in the dome, to the day he bedded her, imagining her the daughter of the merchant Malik Feroz. From lying together that night, Farkhanda was impregnated by the king's seed.

Farkhanda realized she had accomplished what she set out to do and it would be purposeless to remain there any longer. She said to Danishmand, 'It would be better to load up and depart for home.'

As instructed, Danishmand had all their luggage and goods loaded up, and left for the city with Farkhanda and the thirty slave girls. They arrived on the fourth day at his mansion.

Once there, Farkhanda said to Danishmand, 'I shall now return to the dome. You must remove the aqueduct. The king had promised to return in a year's time. Three months have passed from that period and nine remain. After they are over, the king will arrive in the city and bring me out of the dome. At that time, I will satisfy the king's conditions, and then send for you. I will then do for you all I can. But you must make sure not to leave this house until I come out of the dome and summon you. You must wait for me here and not let go of equanimity.'

After communicating this to Danishmand, Farkhanda returned to the dome through the aqueduct and started living there as before.

Danishmand sent for the same braziers and made them remove the aqueduct and repair the floor of the dome so that nobody could tell that it was ever breached.

• • •

After Farkhanda left the king's side and returned home, Kevan Shah awaited her arrival all day. He did not touch food and spent the whole night crying for her. The memory of her made him inconsolable, and he recited these verses:

'My beloved did not come, long did I await her
And all my sighs had not the least effect
When will the salve come to sooth my heart's pain
My beloved was beside me once, when will the next visit be

The restive pupil looks out my eye's window
To search for and await the beloved
The one whose forehead is august like Jupiter proved for me inauspicious like Saturn
When will it blossom, the balsam flower of the garden of love?'

He spent the next few days waiting for her and suffering pangs of longing. When there was no sign of her even after ten days, he steeled his heart, cursed her inconstancy, and recited this couplet:

'To the world you have only slain Sauda[14]
Only Sauda's heart knows how terribly you killed him'

He said to himself: 'Had I known that the faithless creature would disappear after merely spending a day with me, I would never have become attached to her, and my heart would not have suffered in remembrance of her.'

Conversing thus with himself, he summoned the supervisor of the kettledrums and ordered him to beat the orders for the return march, and to send the baggage-tent towards the capital of his kingdom.

As per his orders, the royal stewards took the baggage tent ten miles towards the capital. Four days later, the king entered his palace and awaited the completion of Farkhanda's imprisonment.

Farkhanda, meanwhile, kept living in the dark dome, and received the food and drink brought by the eunuch, and passed her days as best she could.

Finally, it was a year since she had been incarcerated. One day, Farkhanda's labour pains started, and she spent the night in agony and solitude. The next day, in the afternoon, a son as beautiful as the moon was born to her.

When the eunuch brought her food, he heard the sound of a child crying. He was greatly surprised at this, and said to himself: 'O God, how has a child been conceived inside prison?' Worried, he rushed to the king and said,

'O Refuge of the World, a child can be heard crying inside the dome.'

14. Sauda: The takhallus (nom de plume) of the poet Mirza Muhammad Rafi Sauda (1713–1781)

The king marvelled upon hearing this, and hastily arrived at the dome in a pleasure-boat. When the door of the dome was opened, he found Farkhanda sitting with an infant boy in her lap, with all the signs of a woman who has recently brought forth a child manifest upon her face.

The king angrily asked Farkhanda, 'O shameless woman, with whom did you have this child?' Then he saw the purse of gold and became further enraged, and asked, 'O Farkhanda, tell me truthfully, whose child is this, and where did you spend the five hundred gold pieces?'

Farkhanda laughed, and said, 'O Refuge of the World, this child is yours, and it was I who took out the gold from the purse. Your anger is unjustified without first enquiring into the matter. If you were to sit peaceably, I will narrate to you all that has passed.'

The king was somewhat mollified upon hearing this. He sat down and said to her, 'If you wish to live, you must truthfully tell me everything, or else it will not bode well with you.'

Then Farkhanda narrated everything as it had happened, from her coming out of the dome, sending the slave girls before the king, mounting the lean horse, making the king fill up the pitchers, playing the games of chausar with him, obtaining the signet ring, and the king bedding her. She reminded him of all that had passed, showed him the handkerchief she had picked up from his bed, and the clothes she had worn.

Then she said to the king, 'When I commented about the headless corpses that they did it, but knew not how, I meant that, had those two women been wise, they would not have drowned themselves in the river of sin and lost their lives.'

Upon hearing her account, the king was most pleased, and believed all that she had told him. He took Farkhanda's hand in his and asked her to excuse his conduct. He came out of the dome with her and returned happily to the palace on the pleasure boat.

Then Farkhanda spoke, with hands folded at the waist, 'O Refuge of the World, there is a merchant in this city because of whom your slave girl was able to play all her deceptions until she returned to your august feet. I have made him my father, and he spent his riches liberally at my behest. You must restore to him the amount he has spent with a fourfold profit, and reward him further for his most excellent service.

The king said, 'Send for him.'

As per the king's order, Farkhanda sent for Danishmand. At the summons he presented himself before the king and made an obeisance. The king showed him much favour, and paid him the amount he had spent at Farkhanda's instructions with a fourfold profit. He gave him as well a ministerial robe of honour, as was his due. Then the king recited this couplet, and bided his time with Farkhanda in great pleasure and comfort:

'Summon my soul, O God, but not on the night of union
Lest I should see a night of separation from my soul.'

End

CULMINATORY VERSES

The story of Farkhanda I have told
Do not consider it fiction, it is all true
Great reserves of my heart in its telling I spent
Much pleasure in its narration to discover
I named this story Four Flower Gardens
For autumn to forever keep away from it
Be assured that anyone who listens to it
Will offer the author rapturous praise
And here the story comes to its end
Be it in the name of the Holy Prophet.

Qissa 2

The Adventures of a Soldier

A First Translation of Khushdil Kiratpuri's
masnavi *Qissa Sipahizada*

AUTHOR'S PREFACE

May God grant me the capacity to narrate, in order for me to write a new qissa. May it be a fresh tale and an original one, whose writing may commit my name to posterity. Whoever reads it should find in it happiness and joy, and remember me with kindness. May this story find renown, and there be none who finds fault with it. Should a learned one find some error or flaw, however, he may freely suggest improvements and emendations. Far be it from me to claim that my qissa is flawless; it could be replete with shortcomings.

Kiratpur has been my home for a long time, where I live inebriated on the wine of love. Fate drives me all over the land, in different cities, places, and countries. Wherever I behold someone beautiful I become that garden's lovesick nightingale. Like the heavens which remain in revolution ever, I, too, Majnun-like,[1] tarry all over the land; now in Delhi, now in Lahore, sometimes in Kashi, and sometimes in Ayodhya or Bijnor. Fond of the remembrance of the doings of love, these matters are my life and my engrossment.

Given as I am, wholly to love, this is, in fact, not a qissa about love. For this here is a wondrous tale, and an extraordinary and marvellous story. While it makes mention of love, its account is a little removed

1. Majnun: A legendary Arab lover. Protagonist of the legend of Laila and Majnun.

from the usual amorous encounters. I endeavoured to versify it and hope that the result of my effort will find favour with all.

I shall now relate this qissa as I heard it narrated by Bhikari Das Bijnori. May the pen show its cunning in recounting it, and consign it to paper more or less as it was told. Should the subject of the verses be not grand, may they be not devoid of eloquence. May I write in clear language that everyone may readily understand. And may it be brief, for I tend towards brevity, not preferring an overlong narrative.

THE ADVENTURES OF A SOLDIER

There lived in some town a handsome young man who was both clever and adroit. He bided his time happily and comfortably at home, and did not have to step out of his house to make a living, as he had enough to live on. He loved his wife and son, and was unencumbered by any worries.

After a long time had passed in this manner, his prosperity began to wane and all his wealth was slowly spent as he continued in his old fashion. Beset by penury, he finally decided that he must find some employment, as it would not bode well to continue sitting idle at home. He set out from his home and arrived at a provincial court and entered into service.

But it was an unhappy place, and all who served there were miserable. None who entered the service at the court received their wages without ado. The employer had a proclivity for incurring debt, and owed arrears in perpetuity. The master's natural tendency was further compounded by his looming poverty.

The young man suffered great hardships in his service. After many months had passed, he finally demanded his wages. Upon this, his master said to him, 'Do not worry about your wages, soldier! What great calamity has afflicted you that you need the money? The coffers are presently empty and we cannot satisfy your demand for payment. But revenue collection will soon begin, whereupon all your arrears will be cleared. Have no worries and do not make demands. In time, you will receive your wages, without having to ask for them.'

The soldier resolutely slapped his upper arm, and announced, 'Very well, then I must leave your service! I have no desire to stay, as there are no means of subsistence. When a servant is unable to obtain his wages, how is he to make a living? I shall go to some other town where, by the beneficence of God, I will find other employment. You must now give me leave, and settle my dues. I am leaving your service and you must pay me every last cowry[2] owed. I had better get my payment full and entire, or I will show you such a fine spectacle that you will remember it all your living days.'

2. Cowry: A small seashell once used in India as the smallest unit of currency.

When the soldier made these threats, his master realized that until the soldier's demands were met in full he would not let him have any peace, and he must somehow settle the man's dues and send him off. But there was no money to speak of, and he wondered how to resolve the situation. He said to the soldier, 'I have never seen a person as wicked as you. You are already tired of service when you have not even worked a year. You leave without reason and show insolence. As God is my witness, there is not a single cowry in the coffers. But no matter, I give you a bull to address your grievance. I have no gold or cash to give you; take the bull in lieu of wages and be gone!'

Already loath to serve him further, the soldier was only too glad to leave with the bull.

. . .

It was a prize bull, young, strong and massively built. The soldier saddled it up and set out for his home, astride the bull. He told himself that although he had had a wretched time of it in his master's service, he was lucky to have received this fine bull, and if he were to sell it, it would fetch him at least sixty rupees.

As he was making his way through the woods having this conversation with himself, he came upon two men. They were two thugs, brothers called Ameera and Muneera, whose profession was brigandage. They circulated without, to ply their trade, while their father guarded the house, situated close by in the woods. Sighting the bull, the thugs said in their hearts that it would be a very fine thing if they could snatch that splendid bull, but it did not seem an easy proposition as the soldier was well armed. They decided that it would be best to resort to stratagem to get the bull from him. They said to him, 'Where did you find this fine bull? We are happy to buy it from you if you wish to sell, and pay you whatever amount is agreed between us.' The soldier replied, 'Very well! I am happy to sell if you wish to buy the bull. I will sell it to you for sixty rupees.' They answered, 'We do not think the price will be agreed in this manner. Let a third party name the price. Let us go onward and we are sure to find someone. Whatever value he determines will be decided as the bull's price.' The soldier said, 'Very well! Let us do that. You may pay whatever is declared the price by a third party. The city is not too far, either. I will get a fair price for the bull there.'

The thugs tricked the soldier with their talk, and brought him by deception to their house. The soldier only realized that they were thugs when he arrived at their doorstep, and reckoned that his life and possessions were now in peril. He wondered how he would escape with his life, having landed in their trap.

The father of the thugs was beside himself with joy when the soldier arrived there, and said to the thugs, 'What a fine youth has come here astride a bull.' His sons replied, 'Let us tell you why we have come here. This soldier wants to sell his bull to keep the wolf from the door, for poverty is a terrible foe. We will purchase his bull at a price that you suggest. Do now inspect the bull and set its price. We will accept the value you set and bind ourselves by your decision.'

The old man replied, 'I have regarded the bull and reckon its price at six takas.'

Hearing the price, the soldier left his bull with the thugs, and started from there, saying, 'I go home now, as I had agreed that I would accept whatever is reckoned as the bull's price, by a third party.'

When he arrived home he told everyone: 'I had entered someone's service, but left it as I was unable to subsist on it. I was given a bull in lieu of wages, but on the way I met a pair of thugs who took it by artifice and without fair compensation. It was a wicked deception they played on me, and I am sure to revisit them and find a way of recouping my loss.'

. . .

After some days, the soldier dressed himself as a woman and adorned himself so that anyone who beheld him became enamoured of the woman's looks. Arranging for an elegant palanquin for conveyance, and skillful palanquin bearers, he set out for the domicile of the thugs. As he approached their house, the soldier said to the palanquin bearers, 'Put the palanquin down, and return home. All kinds of danger surround me, but God Almighty will be my protector.' Putting the palanquin down, the bearers immediately returned home.

After some time had passed, the soldier sighted the two thugs. When they beheld a palanquin in the woods, they rushed towards it, and pulled up its curtain. Their joy knew no end upon finding a woman inside. They asked her, 'O good woman, tell us whence you have come, and how you happen to be here. Truthfully tell us all that passed with you, and do not hold back anything.' She answered, 'How to tell you of my circumstances! It is, indeed, a strange and extraordinary story. Hear that my husband wedded me from my parents' home, and then brought me into these woods, where, horror of horrors, he took off all my jewellery, and ran off with it. After he was gone my palanquin bearers also left. Never did I give the least offence to my husband, and do not know what made him so vexed with me, to act thus. He left me in this godforsaken place, and I have no idea which way he went. I find it difficult to tell anyone these circumstances, as I have never even set foot outside my house. I have been left alone and unguarded in these woods. God alone is my support. I am worried about my life and God knows what will become of me. I curse my husband, a villain the like of whom never drew breath!'

Ameera and Muneera replied, 'We now go to find him, and will bring him to you.' Tempted by the bride's mention of the gold and jewellery taken from her, the two thugs carefully searched all the nooks and crannies of the woods but did not find anyone. They returned to the false bride, and said, 'We searched every inch of the woods but did not find your husband. Indeed, it is a flint-hearted man who deserted you in this manner. You should not expect him to return, and look upon us now with eyes of favour. We will make our utmost effort to seek your pleasure, and do everything to bring you cheer. Your husband committed a vile deed, and you must never utter his name again. He was loath to be with you, and you must not search for him either. Now we wish to ask if you would be amenable to living with someone who will keep you?'

The false bride made sheep's eyes at them with much coquetry, and said, 'I find myself utterly helpless. What else is there for me to do except live with whosoever shall have me? If I were to refuse your proposal, where would I go? Indeed, whoever agrees to keep me will be doing me a great kindness.'

When the two wretches saw the false bride's flashing kohl-lined eyes, they fell head over heels in love with her. Ameera said, 'You should stay with me.' Muneera said, 'You should live with me. I will do everything to make you happy, as I am besotted with your airs.' Ameera said, 'I intend to serve you faithfully. I shall obey your wishes and render my service with all my heart and soul.'

As they started arguing amongst themselves, the false bride said, 'Does anyone else live with you in the house?' They answered, 'Our respected father lives with us.' She said, 'Do not argue here, but take me to your home. You must accept whatever your father decides, and act accordingly.'

The two of them agreed to this, and carried her palanquin home to their father. The false bride made sheep's eyes at the old man when he looked at her, and put him under her spell.

The thugs said to their father, 'We found this woman in a precarious situation, as her husband has deserted her, and she has nowhere to go. She wants to live with us, and we have brought her here so that you may decide if she should live with me or my brother. She will live with the one in whose favour you decide.'

The old man, whose desire had been awakened by the false bride's glances, said to them, 'My sons, what can I say! Now that you have brought her here, there will be someone to cook for me. If she were to live with either of you, however, she would be of little use to me. My sons, why don't you do that which will ease the burden of cooking for all of us? It is my decision that she will stay with me, and I reckon she will be happy and content with that. This will be for the best, and the two of you now will do well not to touch her.'

The sons were confounded to hear their father's words, but could not prevail against him, and remained silent. When the false bride started living with their father, the thugs gave up all hope.

The father of the thugs doted on and worshipped the false bride, and fed her all kinds of choice and wondrous food, and all manner of marvellous delicacies. He disclosed to her the location of all the gold and jewels and pearls and other valuables kept in the house. He would say to her: 'You are now the mistress of the house; all the gold and jewels are now in your charge. Thank your lucky stars, my dear, that my sons brought you here. You would not have survived alone in the woods, and would have wandered about in distress. Had you tarried there longer, some lion would have made a morsel of you. And if you had died thus from the dictates of fate, you would not have found someone like me. Do reflect in your heart and consider how much I love you. What else should I show you from this house, where untold amounts of silver and gold are amassed? You should give thanks continuously to the Almighty that you found a house such as mine. Freely eat all you like, and play the dhol and sing, if you please. Any kind of dress can be sewn for you, should you desire. You may put on gold cloth, covered in which you will look like a fairy, or make a bodice of your choice. You have only to say the word and I will have bangles and nose-rings made for you on the instant. Sport a nice nose-ring, and do not leave your ears unadorned either. I will order you a fine anklet, whose tinkling can be heard from afar. Do not act bashful towards me, for this house now will be your home for a lifetime. You know I have business with you, and you with me. Do not shy away from me. I am mindful that you are the daughter of a noble family, and have not lain with a man. I know you are full of modesty in all things, and it is from shyness that you do not uncover your face. It is again from modesty that you say such few words. But how should I derive satisfaction from that, after having seen your coquette's eyes?'

The false bride said in soft tones, 'Why are you in such a great hurry? I have been here just a few days, and modesty holds me back. Think you that I do not long for a lover's embrace? I am only too eager for its pleasures!'

In short, the false bride made such talk, and the old man believed everything without the least suspicion. Whenever his sons were away, he would find an opportunity to touch and caress the false bride, who always acted bashful. Then he began taking greater liberties and tried to lie with her.

Finally, the false bride said coyly to him, 'I thought you had more sense! Until I am properly betrothed to you, it is not seemly for you to touch me.' He answered, 'Why don't you make the arrangements then, since everything is at hand? Do organize the ceremony to your satisfaction, as you have full charge of the house.' The false bride replied, 'Come Friday, send someone to the city to bring the qazi. Once he has recited the marriage vows, nothing else will be required. Let me first become your lawfully wedded wife, then you may have your way with me.'

Upon hearing this, the old man was beside himself with joy. He sent for one of his sons, and told him to go to the city on the Friday and bring the qazi with him.

On Friday, Ameera headed for the city to bring the qazi, as per his father's orders. When he was gone some one kos[3] from the house, the false bride said to the old man, 'A great pity, that when arranging for

3. Kos: A measure of length equal to about two miles.

the qazi, we forgot all about batashas[4] and paan. The qazi will not be pleased when he finds them missing. Without these refreshments present, he will leave in anger.' The old man said, 'Yes, my soul, you are right! We need both batashas and paan. Muneera is in the house and he will go and fetch them.'

Upon hearing this, Muneera too left for the city to bring what was needed.

When only the old man was left in the house with her, the false bride said, 'Now that the qazi will be coming, I must bathe and get dressed. Go and sit outside the house for some time. Once I am finished, I will call you inside.' When the old man went out of the house, the soldier took off his womanly garb. He put on men's clothing and gathered the money and gold and jewellery in the house into a bundle, and after decorating himself with weapons, stepped out. He went forth in that array to the old man and made a bow to him, and asked, 'Tell me, old man, was my bull worth six takas?'

Shocked beyond belief, as the old man marvelled at his bride's transformation, the soldier weighed his staff and gave the old man a fierce beating, landing powerful blows on his head and back. The old man's back swelled up from the beating, and his head started bleeding. After he had fallen unconscious, the soldier tied him up with a strong rope, and hung him upside down in the nearby well. Then, carrying all the loot, he sped away, looking neither left nor right, and did not stop until he had reached home.

Meanwhile, Ameera and Muneera brought the qazi and the batashas and paan. When they did not find the old man in the house, they wondered where he had gone, and after searching everywhere, said to themselves, 'God knows where the two of them went. Where should we search for them now, as we have looked both within the house and without?'

The qazi asked them, 'How old was the girl?' They said, 'She must be fourteen or fifteen years old.' The qazi replied, 'Then you might as well give up on your search! Knowing what I do of these matters, it would be well-nigh impossible to find them now. Your father was a wise man and he realized that a qazi would never consent to marrying an old man like him to a nubile girl, and would give her in matrimony to one

4. Batasha: A sweetmeat.

of his sons, instead. I swear by God it was this realization that made him abscond with the girl. Take my advice now, and stop searching for him, as you will not find him. I will also head back now, as there is no doubt in my mind as to what transpired here. But do me the kindness of fetching me some water to drink from the well.'

When the thugs went to the well to fetch water, they looked inside, and lo and behold, what did they see but their dear old father hanging upside down. They quickly pulled him out of the well and carried him home and lay him on the bed. Alarmed by the scene, the qazi exclaimed, 'There is no power, nor strength, except by Allah,' and left in haste.

The thugs were devastated to see the marks of a beating on their father's body. They massaged him so that he would return to consciousness and recover his power of speech. They rubbed his head and feet and brought him a fistful of earth to smell. When the old man regained consciousness, they asked him what had transpired. He said, 'What do you know! The one you brought home, imagining to be a woman, was not one! Have you not eyes to see and verify? It was no woman, but the man with the bull! He dragged me and savagely beat me with his staff. He was the one who hung me upside down in the well. My back is hurting terribly from the shock.'

When his sons heard the old man's account, they were miserable, and said, 'We will chew him up alive if we find him anywhere. Our hearts will not be consoled until we have apprehended him. As God is our witness, if we manage to lay our hands on him, we will teach him the meaning of deception.'

Then they checked the house and did not find any gold in the place where it was kept. Not only gold, but the jewellery and weapons, including the dagger and the arrows and quiver, were also gone. Seeing their house empty of all valuables, they struck their heads against the walls in anger and frustration but could do naught about it.

. . .

Having related all that passed with the thugs, let me now give an account of the soldier. After spending three days at home, and not sharing his adventures with anyone, he put on old clothes to appear destitute, and effected such a humble manner that let alone the thugs, even their preceptor would not recognize him. He planned to revisit the thugs and procured a quantity of medicines before heading to their dwelling without the least apprehension. He arrived at the well in which he had hung the thugs' father. He bathed, marked his forehead with red sandalwood powder, and started praying with great absorption and devotion.

Before long, the two scoundrels Ameera and Muneera arrived. They sat opposite him and began conversing with him. They asked, 'Venerated sir, whence have you come, and where do you plan to go from here? Tell us about your trade and occupation.' He answered in a voice heavy with sadness, 'I am a poor, destitute Brahmin. I know many a trade and have set out from home to go wandering wherever work takes me. I am a healer and if I come across someone who is ill or in pain, I bring them relief. I know the science of medicine and can diagnose maladies. I know astrology and the holy books,[5] and am an adept in the secrets of herbs. I am knowledgeable, too, about omens, and can tell the good ones from the bad. In short, I am a master of every art, but my situation was unsustainable, as I was plagued by destitution. I have therefore set out in search of work.'

The thugs said to him, 'If you are indeed a master of all these trades as you claim, you should sojourn with us for some days, and lodge and board freely. Our father is unwell and suffers terribly with aches and pains. Do examine him to diagnose his condition and make your prognosis. Come with us to our house, and we will be forever in your debt, and follow your word.' The false healer said, 'It is indeed what I desire, for I am ever looking for patients to treat. I set out from home in order to earn a living with my art. Only after I have shown you my art can I expect to receive some recompense from you. Have no worries if your father is unwell, for I am now responsible for restoring him to health.' Thus speaking, he accompanied the two brothers, and they went forth hand in hand.

The two thugs led him to their house, and sat him with great respect on the bed where their father lay indisposed. They said to their father, 'Pray have a look at the one sitting beside you on the bed. Our good fortune has led him here, and you will regain your health through his ministrations. He is a past master in medicine and a veteran healer. He has mastery over the healing arts, and is an adept in many skills

5. Holy books: The word used in the source text is *shastras*.

besides. In short, there is no end to praising his talents. You should now seek a cure for your condition from him.'

Hearing this, the old man was beside himself with joy. He raised his hands in salutations, and said, 'If you indeed have such art, my good man, then my whole house will become your sacrifice. It was well that you arrived here. Pray heal me now with your treatment, O kind Sir. If you were to do that, you will find all that you seek from my home.' The false healer said, 'By the grace of God,[6] I am such a healer that every malady flees before me. Once I start treating you, not even a trace of your present condition shall remain. Now, extend your hand and let me take your pulse to diagnose whether you have fever or shivering or constipation.' The old man said, 'You may ignore the pulse and inspect my body. There is no internal malady that afflicts me. All that I suffer from is manifest on my body. Pray examine my wounds and give me some medicine to heal them.'

The false healer began examining him, and after a thorough survey of his wounds, said to him, 'I have examined you and your body is badly swollen. I also came upon a wound to your head that seems to have been incurred by a blow. Or else you were in a fight and received these injuries from it. Tell me what enemy attacked you, or whom you fought.'

The old man said, 'Now I know that I am in expert hands. Indeed, you are a wise man who, from just a few marks, has reckoned all that is wrong with me. It is true, indeed, that these wounds were inflicted on me by an enemy. I cannot give the whole account but will summarize it for you: A young man had a bull to sell and he asked me to name the price. When I named six takas as the bull's price, he left the bull here and went away. Later, he returned disguised as a beautiful woman and played a great deception upon us. I did not have the least misgiving, and immediately fell in love with her.

CAP-A-PIE

'Who can give an account of his beauty! He was delicate-bodied and the very image of a houri. His luminous visage put to shame the full moon.

6. By the Grace of God: The word used is Har which can be generally translated as Lord, as used in the present context, or specifically translated as Vishnu in a more restricted sense.

Dark like the Night of Destiny[7] were his locks. Had Zulaikha[8] seen his moon-like face, she would have entirely forgotten Yusuf.[9] When his cheeks dewed it looked as if a rose's face was drenched with dewdrops. The sight of his spikenard locks alone snared the heart in his love's trap. His locks were dark and redolent, from which Tartary's musk deer could borrow fragrance. A heavenly scent wafted from them which perfumed the core of my soul. His forehead was a talismanic silver tablet whose refulgence would even blind the eyes of houris. The assemblies of heaven were thrown into disarray if a frown creased his brow. When he displayed his forehead's mirror, the reflecting mirror itself gazed upon it wonderstruck. His brows were the opening couplets of a book of wonders, and his ears the shops of excellence. His brows were wondrous, his eyelashes arrows in flight, which every instant sought the heart to make it their prey. None who became their prey survived. The moment his brow moved, lightning struck. Sameri's[10] magic was envious of his spellbinding eyes; even the deer have not such a haunted look in their gaze. Intoxicated, cruel, and heart-afflicting were his eyes that made even the languorous-eyed narcissus[11] more languid. His small mouth's virtue was its narrowness, which put even the aperture of a rosebud to shame. His lips were of a brighter hue than the ruby, made further captivating by the application of the missi. Even the pearls from Aden could not match the brightness of his teeth. I may justly say that they were like thirty-two bright stars of a constellation. God Almighty, what sweet discourse he made! His speech was like the scattering of pearls. How to praise the apple of his double chin, for nobody has the words to adulate it. Every lover can sing the praise of his neck though, a sweet burden on his shoulders like a wine ewer. With the wine of pleasant thoughts it was filled, and cast by God in the mould of light. On the subject of his waist, however, I offer vigorous praise as it was thinner than a strand of hair; despite its best efforts the intellect could find no clue to the art of its making. If his navel was like the whirlpool of the sea of beauty, his arms were translucent like crystal. His henna-dyed hand was the image of corals, but in fact it was dyed with lovers' blood. His white fingers were like five tapers jointly emanating light. The beautiful whiteness of his

7. Night of Destiny: The holy night of Shab-e Qadr commonly believed to be the twenty-seventh night of the Islamic month of Ramzan.

8. Zulaikha: Potiphar's wife.

9. Yusuf: Joseph.

10. Sameri: A magician who according to legend made the golden calf.

11. Languorous-eyed narcissus: A metaphor for the beloved's spell-binding glance.

> fingernails was manifest to all: some were shaped like the crescent, and some like the full moon. With his lovely stature he delighted hearts and made the box-tree envious. Had that flower-like beloved ever stepped into the garden, the nightingale would not have looked at the rose twice. He taught a beautiful gait to the rock partridge, and with his comely ways enchanted the fairies. When he was cruel to his lovers, their hearts forthwith left the cage of their breasts. The pink dupatta on his head showed his lovely face to advantage. Was it a gold-laced hair-ribbon or snakeskin with which he tied his hair? When that jasmine-bosomed beloved washed and donned a bodice, it seemed to reveal all. How his back twisted and turned as he went about his house chores. His pajama of floral silk cloth made the spring garden's colours envious. The shoes with silver-work he wore made the sky scatter down stars in sacrifice. Sometimes, when he glanced from behind the veil, the hearts of lovers were rent asunder. Sometimes, when the wind blew away his veil, he would draw it down with great shyness and modesty. How captivating were his glances, and how marvellous his ensemble and attire. He had the finest traits of beloveds.

'He came to our house and began living here, and learned all the secrets of the household. He behaved so coquettishly with me that I held him dearer than my own life. After many a day, finding me alone at home, he found his opportunity and beat me so savagely that I was brought to death's door. I can describe it no further, and it is better to maintain silence now. He gathered all the silver and gold from the house, and absconded with it whence he had come. In short, I was first beaten to within an inch of my life, then my house was pillaged.'

The false healer answered, 'It was a terrible thing he did, inflicting such suffering upon you. However, you too were unfair to him in pricing his bull at six takas. As far as I see it, both of you are blameworthy in the matter, but you are the best judge of your situation.'

Then the false healer prepared a balm, applied it on the old man's wounds, and began the application of poultices. He applied turmeric paste on one part of his body, and another pain-relieving concoction of herbs on another. In this manner he ministered to him continuously. At times he would apply heat to his body and at times massage him with heated oil and butter. At times he would forbid him from having ghee with his food, and at other times he would mix butter in his lentils. At times he gave him the moong lentils to eat, and at other times fish curry. Some days he told the old man to eat rice with milk, and on other days prescribed him chicken.

As the old man's condition started improving with every passing day, he praised the false healer, and said, 'My dear man, you well know how to treat maladies and ailments. Indeed, you are the teacher of all healers. You have healed me with your ministrations, and I have not the words to thank you. I have fully regained my health and, if you allow, will now go to bathe in the Ganges.' He replied, 'Do not think that you are fully recovered. Some small measure of your affliction yet remains. Take the medicine for a few days more. I will bathe you myself when you are ready. I will not permit you to bathe, however, until you are fully well. There is another medicine I have to give you, which will restore your youth to you. However, it has to be obtained from the bazaar. Please send for what I will now prescribe, and take it with milk. God willing, you will acquire such potency from it, that it will become the talk of town. Have no worries! You will be so well pleased by it that you will never forget me. If I were to go myself to get the medicine from the market, however, there is no knowing if I will be able to return. Some patient or the other is sure to sight me there, and they will detain me and not let me return.'

The old man prostrated himself at the false healer's feet, and said, 'Please give me such medicine that I become youthful again. Do me the kindness that my body retires all signs of eld and becomes brimful with youth. You do not have to go to the bazaar yourself to get the medicine. My son Ameera will fetch what is required. It is not my wish that you inconvenience yourself by making the visit.' The old man sent for Ameera and asked him to get the medicine from the bazaar.

Ameera left home to get what the false healer had requested. After he had been gone for some time, the false healer said, 'I have remembered another medicine that too must be sent for.' As Muneera was present, he was dispatched to get it, and he too went away.

When the old man was left alone in the house, the soldier girded himself, and knowing the place where gold and jewellery were kept, helped himself to all that remained. Then presenting himself before the old man, he made a bow, and asked, 'Tell me again, was my bull worth six takas?'

Upon seeing and hearing this, the old man's senses deserted him. The soldier picked up a shoe and began belabouring him, raining blows on his head with such plentitude that the old man lost all count and number. Finally, when he had lost consciousness, the soldier quietly slipped out and headed home.

By the time he reached his house, Ameera and Muneera also returned to their home. Finding their father in a sorry state, they said to him, 'Tell us what passed with you. Speak to us and tell us how you lost consciousness and your power of speech. Where is the healer who uttered the holy names with every breath? We do not see him around.'

After the old man had regained consciousness somewhat, he said, 'How to tell you of what passed with me! The one you brought here thinking he was a healer, turned out to be the same villain. It was the man with the bull! The moment your backs were turned he lost no time in plundering the house. Then that wretch kicked me and beat me with a shoe. He did not stop hitting me until I lost consciousness. Where should I go, because he will not let me live here in tranquility! He has made my life a misery and will not let me have any peace. Alas for the cunning disguises he appears in, and alas for the wicked deeds he performs. The day you brought this bull here was the day you prepared my grave. Now he is after our blood, and there is no knowing how we are to find reprieve from his viciousness. I well know he is after my life. Tell me, where must I go to be safe from his hands? If he visits here again, my heart will burst.'

His sons replied, 'If he shows his face again, we will behead him on the instant. We will never forget his tyranny and the vicious way in which he treated you. No matter what disguise he takes on now, we will not allow him to escape with his life. We will remain alert and on the lookout for him. We will be watchful and vigilant. Sooner or later, he will fall into our hands. We won't leave the house now, and will lie in wait for him for some days. He has already come twice, and it is a sure thing that that wily man will make another visit.' After making these fulminations and claims, they fell silent.

• • •

Now hear of the soldier, and what he did in the meanwhile, after reaching home. He began ordering meals and fruit and sweets from the bazaar daily. Sometimes, he would make halva, eat it himself, and share it with others. Sometimes, he would mix butter and sugar in rice and devour it.

As he started spending money liberally, his two neighbours, who were brothers, were consumed with jealousy. They noticed the change in his circumstances, and wondered at his turn of fortune. They said to him, 'How did you come into all this gold? You spend it in a hundred ways; indeed, nobody spends so freely as you. You seem to be both wealthy and sagacious. Now that you are well-off and free of financial worries, pray have a care for our situation, too. We are in difficult circumstances and our situation constantly oppresses us. Earlier, you had told us that you received a bull in wages which you sold to someone along the way but did not receive payment. Tell us now from where have you earned the wealth that you have brought from your travels.'

The soldier answered, 'Indeed, I had told you the truth when I said that I did not receive payment for the bull. But when I visited the buyer, he gave me some money. He is a noble soul, I believe, and entertains nothing but good wishes for me. Whenever I visit him, he gives me a little something, by way of spending money. His two sons, however, are vicious creatures. When I visit their house for the money due me, those ill-starred ones start croaking. The father is a most reasonable man and pays me dutifully, and I cannot praise him enough, for it is difficult to do justice to his virtues with my encomiums. Now you know that which you did not know before: that it is on account of the old man that I have the means of sustenance. In fact, I would suggest that you, too, accompany me when I go the next time, as the place is familiar to me. You're sure to receive a little something from the man.'

Upon hearing this, his neighbors were delighted, and said to him, 'We will do as you tell us. You will do us a great kindness if you take us along on your next visit.'

The soldier did not disclose the truth to the neighbours, and took the brothers along. As they approached the thugs' house, the soldier pointed it out to his neighbours from afar, and said to them: 'Go with haste now, and call out at the door: Is there anyone at home? We have come on business. If those idiots ask your name, tell them you are the soldier with the bull. If you only find the old man at home, he will show you much kindness. He will treat you as honoured guests and prostrate himself before you in service. If you find his sons at home, however, they will show belligerence. At the sight of them you must run as fast as you can, and never look back until you have reached home. You must not stop there even for an instant, for if you were to do so, you will get the beating of your life. But then again, you're not such weaklings as to be easily beaten up by them.'

In short, the two brothers went and called out to the thugs as instructed by the soldier. Both Ameera and Muneera were at home, and they immediately stuck their heads out and asked, 'Tell us your name.' The brothers replied, 'It is the soldier with the bull.' The moment Ameera and Muneera heard these words, they rushed out of the house. Seeing them come running, these two made to run away. But the thugs apprehended them. They came to blows, and all of them got a good knocking, as each gave the other his worst.

The soldier, who was watching the scene from a safe distance, took another path to the thugs' house, and rained blows with a shoe on the head of the old man, until he fell unconscious. Then he unfastened his bull from the house, and boldly headed back home.

After a while, the thugs returned home, wiping themselves and dusting off their chests from the scuffle. When they saw their father lying unconscious, they asked, 'Tell us why you are so quiet. We left you all sound and well. What happened to you during the short period that we were away?'

The old man finally came to, and replied, 'Why did you think I was unconscious? It was because my head was again hammered with shoes. The moment you left the house the same soldier arrived and gave me a thrashing. After beating me, he mounted his bull and sped away, without looking left or right. God knows where the two of you were gone when he played this vile hand with me.'

His sons answered, 'How did he manage to come here, as we fought him off and drove him away? And why did you not call for help? He would surely have died at our hands if you had. We would have put him to death right here in the house, and earned renown for both you and ourselves.' The old man answered, 'You are only good at making empty boasts. Had you been capable, I would not have been treated so ill at his hands. It is a good thing that he took away his bull, for it was cursed. From the day we brought it to this house we saw nothing but ruin. We may have lost the bull, but we escaped with our lives, as that wily man will now have no reason to return. Now that he has plundered the whole house, we shall be rid of him.'

In short, after making this speech with a wounded heart, that malevolent old man became silent.

. . .

Having narrated all there was to tell of the thugs, let me return to the soldier. When he returned home with the bull, the two neighbors who had accompanied him, said to him, 'Ah! Where did you disappear? Two villains accosted us, beat us mercilessly, and rolled our honour into the dust. With great difficulty, we escaped with our lives from their clutches, and returned home.'

The soldier answered, 'I had already told you that his sons are baleful. They could not have missed this opportunity to accost and attack you. I visited their home but did not receive any payment this time. Not seeing any payment, I unfastened the bull from the halter and took him away. I will now sell him as soon as I find a buyer. When I receive payment for the bull, I will give you a little.'

. . .

Now O Khushdil, it is time to become quiet, as you have spoken much and must now observe silence. The story has ended, in whose narration you have scattered pearls.

End

Qissa 3

Chhabili the Innkeeper

A first translation of *Qissa Chhabili Bhattiyari*[1] by unknown author from the Urdu

KING SIKANDAR SHAH BECOMING A MENDICANT AND RECEIVING ANNUNCIATIONS ABOUT AN HEIR

Narrators of chronicles thus recount this colourful tale, that in the city of Delhi there was a king named Sikandar Shah who was as liberal as Hatim Tai,[2] as just as Naushervan,[3] and the possessor of as great a fortune as Qarun.[4] What he did not possess was an offspring.

One day the king was sitting in his private hall of assembly when he saw a sweeper approach looking at him. But when their eyes met the sweeper did not salute the king and went away with knitted brow, after casting a dejected look at him.

The king said to himself: 'I am the king of this dominion. If someone sees my face in the morning he has an auspicious day. Why then did the sweeper not salute me, and go away downcast and frowning? What blemish did he see in me?'

After duly considering the matter, the king said to himself: 'Except for my being childless, there does not seem to be any flaw in me. Mayhap the thought that he had seen a childless person's face in the

1. *Qissa Chhabili Bhatiyari.* Printed at Muir Press, Delhi (n.d.).
2. Hatim Tai: An ancient Arab chieftain renowned for his liberality.
3. Naushervan: An emperor of the Sassanian dynasty.
4. Qarun: The Korah of the Old Testament, known for his great wealth and avarice, is mentioned as Qarun in the Quran.

morning made the sweeper doleful; perhaps he feared that it might bode ill for him, and God forfend that he get into any argument that day.'

The king considered that his father had kept his grandfather's name alive, while he himself kept alive the name of his father; but there was no one to carry forward his name. He told himself that a life of mendicancy would be preferable to kingship such as his. The king went into the palace and, taking off all his royal vestments, tore a mantle and put it around his neck to clothe himself. The news that the king had put on beggarly clothes caused an uproar in the city. All those who heard about it or saw him in that state, accompanied the king in wonderment, and his servants, nobles, and high officials followed him alongside.

When the king came out of the city, those present asked him, with hands folded respectfully at the waist: 'What passed in Your Honour's heart that you decided to take up mendicancy?' The king answered, 'It would be a shame if I continue with the burden of kingship, as I have no heir to my crown and throne.'

The king said to his vizier, 'O vizier of wise counsel, you should return to the city and assume the title of king, while I follow the way of mendicants on the path of God.'

The vizier answered, 'I shall be your stirrup fellow, as I have eaten Your Honour's salt.' The king repeated what he had said before, saying, 'It is my wish that you ascend the throne and start minding the welfare of the subjects.'

In the end, the king sent back the vizier and all others to the city, and headed alone into the forest. After travelling for some hours, he sat down in the afternoon in the shade of a tree, sorrowful and despondent.

God was pleased with the humility the king had shown in choosing the path of mendicancy. At His command a venerable personage in a faqir's guise appeared before the king, and asked, 'Why do you look so sad and downhearted?' The king heard the question but did not make a reply. When the faqir asked the same question of him a second time, the king replied in vexation, 'What business is that of yours? Go on your way! You cannot grant my wish even if I were to tell you.' The faqir said, 'Tell me your wish. I shall pray to God and intercede on your behalf to have your wish granted.' The king said, 'I have no child, and am unable to have one.'

Upon hearing this, the faqir prayed and said, 'You may now return to the city and lie with your wife. She will become pregnant, and after nine months a boy will be born to you.' The king was delighted to hear these annunciations from the faqir, and took his leave and returned to the city and entered his palace. He cast off his beggarly clothes and put on regal vestments.

The entire city learned that the king had returned to the palace. Upon receiving this news, a joyous tumult rose from the house of every noble and officer of the court, and alms were distributed. All the women in the palace sent the king offerings of cups of oil embedded in pulses.[5]

The following morning, the king held an open court, to which the nobles and officers arrived, bearing offerings. The king happily received them, and conferred upon each of them a robe of honour according to his station. Joyous gatherings were held in the city, and the king busied himself in minding the affairs of the kingdom as before.

OF A SON BEING BORN TO THE KING AND HIS GROWING UP AND RECEIVING AN EDUCATION

It so happened that one day while the king was holding court, the midwife presented herself and announced that a son had been born to the king. Upon hearing these glad tidings, the king was beside himself with joy, and he richly rewarded the midwife, conferring estate and elephants and horses upon her. All the naubat-khanas[6] in the city played festive music, and the populace exchanged congratulations and salutations on the birth of the prince. The king sent for the fortune-tellers, who made their calculations based on the moment of the child's birth and announced, 'Your Honour, the prince has an auspicious destiny. He will be an emperor.' The king rewarded the fortune-tellers and sent them away.

He named his son Zaman Shah, and midwives and nannies were appointed to care for him. The prince grew up, and when he was five an instructor was appointed to teach him. Within a period of seven years, the prince had acquired education in all branches of knowledge.

5. Cups of oil embedded in pulses: When someone returns from a journey or convalesces, he is shown his face in a cup of oil embedded in maash pulses as a ritual.

6. Naubat-khana: Music chamber where drums, cymbals, and pipes are played.

The instructor presented the prince to the king, and said, 'The prince has been educated in all branches of knowledge.'

Upon quizzing the prince, the king indeed found him well versed in every branch of knowledge. He was very pleased, and rewarded the instructor with an estate, riches, and a robe of honour, and sent him away.

The prince made an obeisance to the king and submitted: 'You conferred estate and riches on the instructor, but Your Honour did not confer anything on me. What is the reason for that?' The king happily replied, 'This entire land and all the wealth it contains belongs to you. You are its master.' Upon hearing this the prince did not make further comment.

OF PRINCE ZAMAN SHAH GOING HUNTING AND MEETING CHHABILI THE INNKEEPER

One day, some years later, the prince presented himself before the king, saluted him, and said: 'Your Honour, your devoted slave feels restive from sitting idle. I hope you will grant this humble creature permission to take a horse and go hunting.' The king immediately ordered the keeper of the royal stables to give the king's own stallion to the prince, and said to the prince, 'You may hunt all day, but do return home in the evening.' The prince made an obeisance after receiving permission for the hunt. He happily mounted the steed, and taking his servants along, headed for the hunting grounds.

The prince would hunt during the day, and return home in the evening. For four months the prince followed this routine.

One day the prince was returning from the hunt when he crossed paths with a woman filling up water at a well. The moment their eyes met the prince fell unconscious at the sight of her beauty. When his servants noticed his state, they helped him down from the saddle. After some time, the prince regained consciousness and told the servants to proceed onwards to the city, and that he would follow in due time. The prince kept one servant with him, and after the others were gone, he said to the servant, 'Follow that woman and find out where she lives, and her name and her caste.'

The servant followed the woman as instructed. As he neared the city, he saw her go into an inn where an old woman was sitting. The servant said to the woman, 'Dear Mother, what is the name of the woman who brought the water?' The old woman replied, 'Her name is Chhabili, and she lives in the inn opposite mine.' The servant returned to the prince and gave him this information. The prince said to him, 'Take me to the house of the innkeeper.'

The servant led the horse to the inn. Seeing them, the female innkeepers began calling out to the prince: 'O soldier, come to my inn. It is breezy. Come and sit under the shade of the neem tree on a nice charpoy.' Every one of them sang the praises of their respective inns in their own way. The prince said to the servant, 'I have no business with the others. Take me to the inn of the same woman.' The servant took the prince to the inn where Chhabili lived.

Chhabili's mother-in-law called out to her, 'Chhabili, my daughter, come! A soldier has arrived. Bring out a charpai for him.'

Chhabili brought out a charpai for the prince and said to him, 'Respected sir, sit down and make yourself comfortable.' Pleased to hear that the prince dismounted and sat on the charpai. Chhabili washed the prince's hands and feet with warm water, and said to the servant, 'Fasten the horse to the neem tree, and put some grass before him.'

The prince asked for water to drink and Chhabili brought cold water for him. The prince drank it and was happy. Then, with her hands folded at the waist, she asked, 'What food would you like to be prepared for you?' The prince took out a gold piece and gave it to Chhabili, saying, 'Have some fine and rare dish prepared for me.' Chhabili took the gold piece to her mother-in-law. She told her that the soldier had given it to her and asked for some fine food to be cooked for him.

Her mother-in-law said, 'There are just two men and a horse to feed, and he gave you a whole gold piece? Go back and find out how many are in his party for whom the food should be prepared.' Chhabili returned to the prince, and asked him about the number of people for whom food was to be prepared. The prince answered, 'Prepare food for two people and feed the horse. The rest you may keep.' Very pleased to hear this, Chhabili went back to her mother-in-law and reported that he asked her to prepare food for two people and feed grain to the horse, and that the rest of the money was hers to keep.

Chhabili's mother-in-law said to herself: 'He seems to be a very wealthy man to have given a whole gold piece for a meal for two.' She prepared a gilauri[7] and told Chhabili to take it to the soldier. Chhabili brought the gilauri to the prince, who took it and took out two gold pieces from his purse and gave them to her.

Chhabili's mother-in-law now reckoned that the soldier had fallen in love with Chhabili. After a while, she prepared another paan[8] with silver foil and sent it with Chhabili to the prince. She brought it to the prince and said to him, 'Respected sir, please have this paan.' The prince said, 'Come closer.' When Chhabili drew near, the prince held her by the hand and seated her on the charpai.

Chhabili humbly said to him, 'It is not my place to sit next to you.' The prince said, 'You are allowed to sit here. Have no fear.' Then Chhabili sat beside the prince, and she said to him, 'First you must promise me that, for as long as you are in Delhi, you will lodge at my inn. And that you will have eyes for no one but me.' The prince promised and swore to it. Then Chhabili and the prince happily conversed together. The servant drew a curtain in front of the quarters and the prince took Chhabili in his arms, lay down with her, and derived the pleasure of life from her.

The lips met lips, and the bodies embraced
The hearts joined together, as did the mouths

The prince was busy in pleasure-seeking when his servant called out, 'It will be evening soon, Your Honour!' The prince got up when he heard this. Chhabili asked, 'Where are you going?' He answered, 'I am going home.' She asked, 'What preparations should be made for your meal?' The prince answered, 'I shall have food upon reaching home.' Thus speaking, he mounted his horse and, with his servant alongside, headed back to the palace.

Chhabili stood watching him as he left. When he was lost to sight she returned to her mother-in-law and handed her the five gold pieces which the prince had given her upon leaving. These her mother-in-law kept, and made much of her.

The following day the prince forbade all the servants from accompanying him on the hunt, and said to them, 'It becomes very difficult to find quarry in the presence of a crowd. I shall only take along one servant.'

7. Gilauri: A presentation of betel-leaves.
8. Paan: Betel-leaf.

Thus, taking along the servant who knew his secret, the prince returned to Chhabili's inn. She came and sat next to the prince, and when it was afternoon the two of them took a meal together. Afterwards, Chhabili prepared a paan and gave it to the prince, who took it and ate it. After some time, the two of them retired to bed, while the prince's servant kept guard. They passed the whole day in pleasure-seeking.

When evening drew near, the prince mounted his horse and, taking the servant along, retired to the palace. In this manner the prince visited Chhabili every morning and spent the whole day with her in pleasure-seeking. In the evening he returned to the palace. He followed this routine for a long time, and gradually the whole city came to know that the prince was in love with Chhabili and spent all day with her.

OF THE KING LEARNING ABOUT PRINCE ZAMAN SHAH FALLING IN LOVE WITH AN INNKEEPER

One day, a servant went before the king's vizier and gave him a detailed account of the prince and his routine. Upon hearing that, the vizier condemned the prince's actions with regret and considered sharing the news with the king. He reckoned that if he did not tell the king, and the king learned it from someone else, it would not bode well for him. He decided it would be opportune to broach the subject with the king when he was alone and in good humour.

It so happened that one day the king was enjoying a pleasant moment in his private chambers when the vizier presented himself, made an obeisance, and said, 'If Your Honour would spare my life, I beg to make a submission.' The king asked, 'What subject do you wish to broach that you ask me to spare your life? Very well! Your life shall be spared.'

Then, with his hands folded at the waist, the vizier submitted, 'The prince has fallen in love with an innkeeper. He visits her every morning on the pretext of going for the chase and, after spending all day with her, returns in the evening to the palace. The prince has forbidden other servants from accompanying him, and takes along only one attendant from his private retinue. Pray tell me, what is to be done?'

Upon hearing this, the king went into a towering rage and his face turned crimson with anger. He said to the vizier, 'O shameless man, you deserve to be beheaded, but I am helpless as I gave my word to spare your life. What can I tell you now? You ought to have taken care of this business much earlier. As the saying goes, 'One ought to kill the cat on the first day'. Go away, O Vizier, and you will attend to this matter if you know what is good for you.'

The vizier rose and left after making an obeisance. He gathered all the nobles and ministers attached to the court and sought their opinion regarding the prince. Everyone came to an agreement that the prince should get married, so as to drive all thoughts of Chhabili from his heart. Once married, he would spend time with his wife in pleasure-seeking, and would not think of leaving home, since what he desired would be available to him at home.

Finally, the vizier presented himself before the king, and said, 'O Refuge of the World, if my life is spared, I beg to make a submission.' The king said, 'Speak!' With his hands folded at the waist, the vizier said, 'Your Honour, the prince should be married off so that he stops longing for Chhabili.'

When he heard this, the king answered, 'Very well, but know that if we arrange his marriage, and he does not like his wife, it will be the same as his remaining unmarried.'

The vizier made an obeisance and took his leave. He returned to the court and sent for all the kutnis[9] in the city, and said to them, 'I have an assignment for you, and if you carry it out to my satisfaction, you will be rewarded higher than your expectations.'

The kutnis, folding their hands at the waist, spoke, 'We will put our hearts and souls into the work. Pray tell us, Your Honour, what we have to do.' The vizier gave the whole account of the prince, and said to them: 'By the order of the king you must bring portraits of all the young and beautiful girls in the city and neighbouring areas.' He dispatched a painter with each kutni to help in the assignment.

Every kutni said to the painter accompanying her, 'Fill up a tray with water and put it by the wall of the house. I shall bring the girl to the roof on some pretext. When she looks down to see the spectacle,

9. Kutni: A name given to older women who acted as spies and carried out assignments on payment.

her image will be reflected in the water and you may draw it.' The painter did as he was told, and after some time made a portrait of the girl from her reflection in the water.

Thus all kutnis obtained the portraits in this manner, and submitted them before the vizier. Within a few days a large number of portraits were gathered. The vizier now sent for the mason and instructed him to construct two parallel walls flanking a thoroughfare at a particular spot. As ordered, the walls were immediately constructed, and the portraits of all the girls were affixed to them. On his way to the palace the prince passed between these walls, and upon regarding the portraits, said to himself, 'There is no one here who can be said to equal Chhabili's beauty.' In this manner the prince passed daily before the portraits, but none of them caught his eye.

OF PRINCE ZAMAN SHAH EXPRESSING A DESIRE TO WED BICHHITTAR KUNWARI

One day a kutni brought the portrait of a landowner's daughter to the vizier. He had it affixed to the wall as well. When the prince passed by as usual, glancing at the portraits, his eyes fell on the portrait of the landowner's daughter and he involuntarily said, 'It would be most wonderful if I could have her for my wife.' Then he entered the palace.

When the couriers deputed there by the vizier heard these words, they went before him and said, 'The prince said such-and-such words looking at the new portrait that was put up on the wall yesterday, and regarded it for a long time.'

Upon hearing this, the vizier sent for the kutni who had brought the portrait and asked her, 'Who is the girl in this portrait?' She answered, 'She is Bichhittar Kunwari, the daughter of landowner Maan Singh of Chaudheer.' The vizier richly rewarded the kutni, and going before the king, gave him the whole account.

The king said, 'I shall hold an open court on the night of the full moon. You may announce it to the whole city. And remind me of the matter when landowner Maan Singh comes to court.' Upon the king's orders the vizier had it announced that the king would be holding an open court. On the night of the full moon, all the nobles of the city and landowners from the environs presented themselves. All of them made offerings to the king, which he accepted, and granted them estates according to their stations.

Later, Maan Singh's son, Thakur Singh, made his offering. The vizier made a sign to the king to remind him. The king said, 'Why didn't Maan Singh come today.' Thakur Singh answered with hands folded at the waist, 'He is at home.' The king said, 'Send for Maan Singh.'

At the king's orders the couriers rushed to inform Maan Singh that he had been summoned by the king. He felt anxious at the news, and said to himself: 'I am a lowly man. Until today the king has never summoned me. What could be the reason that he has done so today? May God keep me in His protection.' Wondering and anxious, Maan Singh arrived at the court and stood humbly before the king, hands folded at the waist. The king asked him to approach and said, 'Maan Singh, you have something that I need. If I ask you for it, will you give it to me or not?' He replied, 'Your Honour, what is this thing which I have? If Your Honour would care to name it, I will present it to you without hesitation, and never deny possession of it to you.' The king said, 'Marry your daughter to my son.' Maan Singh replied, 'I accept, but I request time to seek the advice of my wife and older brother in the matter.' The king accepted his request and said, 'You may go right now and bring me a firm answer. I shall await your return.'

Maan Singh rode back to his house and went to his wife. She asked him, 'I hope everything is well as you had an audience with the king?' He answered, 'All is well, but the king has asked for our daughter's hand in marriage for his son, the prince. I have come to seek your advice in the matter.'

She asked him: 'What did you say in reply?' He answered, 'I accepted the request but told the king that my approval depends on my wife's and older brother's consent.' His wife said, 'You did well to accept. Landowners often present their daughters to the king and give them away in tribute. Moreover, we would have to marry her off one day. It was good that the king asked for her hand for his son by himself. Now he will remain forever indebted to you.' Maan Singh then sent for his older brother and sought his advice. His brother endorsed as well what his wife had told him. Then Maan Singh went to his daughter. She was playing with other girls, and stood up when she saw her father enter. He said to her, 'My daughter, the king has asked for your hand in marriage for his son, and I have given my consent. What is your wish in this matter?' She answered, 'You are my lord and the decision is entirely yours to make.'

Maan Singh was very pleased with her reply. He immediately rode to the court, where he presented himself before the king, and said, 'I have obtained my wife's and older brother's approval. But if Your Honour would grant me two wishes he would be showing utmost indulgence to his slave.' The king asked, 'What are these two wishes? Tell me.'

Maan Singh answered, 'My first request is that the wedding ceremony be held according to Hindu custom. And the other is that Your Honour's son should wed my daughter at my village in Chaudheer.' The king said, 'I grant both wishes.' Then the king conferred a very expensive robe of honour on Maan Singh and the court was adjourned.

Maan Singh arranged for the letter appointing the date and time of the nuptials to be drawn and sent it to the king. The king told the vizier and divan[10] and other court officials to arrange everything for the ceremony according to Hindu custom.

A carpet was spread and festive powders of abir[11] and gulal[12] were sprinkled and a seat was placed within. The pandits and astrologers came, and upon determining an auspicious moment for the nuptials, asked for the prince. The king immediately sent for the prince by messenger. Upon receiving his father's summons, the prince rose and left with the messenger. The astrologers then gave the letter appointing the time and day of the nuptials into the prince's hand. They sat him on a seat, and carried out all the rituals according to Hindu custom.

The prince brought the letter to the palace to his mother and put it in her lap. Cries of 'Congratulations!' and 'Felicitations!' rose from all corners of the palace, and the female attendants began singing.

OF CHHABILI LEARNING OF THE PRINCE'S IMPENDING BETROTHAL TO BICHHITTAR KUNWARI

After the prince left, Chhabili wondered why the king had suddenly sent for him that day, and the possible reason. A little while later, she

10. Divan: An officer of the state.
11. Abir: A red powder for festive use.
12. Gulal: A red powder for festive use.

sent for a maidservant, and instructed her, 'Go to the palace and find out why the king summoned the prince today.'

When the maidservant arrived at the gate of the city, she heard the sound of music. When she arrived at the threshold of the palace she saw a crowd of women, and heard the uproar of congratulations, and strains of such beautiful singing as to defy description. She asked a woman, 'What is the occasion, that there is singing in the palace?' She answered, 'It seems that you are not from the city.' The maidservant answered, 'I am from the village.' She replied, 'The letter giving the appointed day for nuptials was delivered to Prince Zaman today. He will take out the wedding procession on the given day, for which celebrations are being made.' The maidservant returned with this information and gave the whole account to Chhabili.

The following day, when the prince sat on the bed beside Chhabili, she said to him, 'O Prince of the World, I hear that you are getting married.' The prince answered, 'Yes, some people say that. We shall see!' Chhabili asked, 'Will you take me to your wedding, or not?' The prince replied, 'I swear that I will take you with me, as I will be too restless without you.' Chhabili did not say anything further when she heard this.

After many days, the prince was sent into seclusion for the ceremony of maiyoon,[13] and his movements were restricted. On the day of the wedding procession, Chhabili sent her maidservant to the prince. She said to him, 'Chhabili has sent a message that you have already forgotten her, and asks whether or not you remember your promise, and enquires how you will take her to your wedding ceremony.' The prince told the maidservant that he would send a palanquin with some soldiers for Chhabili, so that she may ride along in the wedding procession.

The maidservant brought the prince's answer to Chhabili. She sent the maidservant back to the prince to tell him that she would not be accompanying in the palanquin because others in the wedding procession would learn that she was travelling with them and would laugh at her and say that Chhabili had come to perform her paramour's nuptials. She said that she would travel on a camel in the luggage train to avoid recognition.

13. Maiyoon: A ceremony that takes place a few days before the wedding in which the bride and the bridegroom are dressed in yellow clothes and sent into seclusion for a few days.

The prince said to the maidservant, 'Chhabili may come along however she pleases; I am agreeable to it.' When the wedding procession started from the city the prince sent a camel for her from the luggage train with a few soldiers. Chhabili quickly sat on the camel and joined in the wedding procession.

After two days the procession arrived in the village of Chaudheer where it was conveyed to a large, elegant garden. Maan Singh hosted the wedding guests and celebrations took place all night long. The prince performed all the pre-wedding rituals according to the Hindu custom and then returned to Chhabili to spend time with her.

The thought passed Chhabili's mind that after he was married, it was likely the prince would stop coming to see her, and she must ensure that this would not be the case. She said to the prince, 'I hear that the woman to whom you are getting married is ugly. But my heart is not convinced. I need the evidence of my own eyes to believe it. Therefore, I am going to visit the house of your wife-to-be.' The prince replied, 'How will a woman like you gain entry into the house? How will the guards let you pass?' Chhabili answered, 'I will find a way so that nobody will be able to stop me.' Hearing her reply, the prince did not say anything further.

Chhabili summoned the female garden-keeper and gave her a rupee and said to her, 'Make me a garland of flowers having the finest perfume.' The garden-keeper prepared the garland and presently brought it to Chhabili. She put the garland in a basket, covered it with a gold brocade kerchief, and taking two torchbearers along, headed for Maan Singh's house.

When she arrived at the door of Maan Singh's house, the guards barred her way, and asked, 'Who are you to attempt entry in the middle of the night?' Chhabili replied, 'I am the king's garden-keeper, and have prepared and brought a garland at the king's orders. It is to be worn by the bride and bridegroom at the time of their wedding vows.'

One guard said, 'There will be no entry without permission.' Another guard said, 'Fellows, let her go inside. She is the king's garden-keeper.' At these words nobody stopped her, and Chhabili went into the garden.

She saw Bichhittar Kunwari sitting on a bed and women crowding about her. One was singing, and another playing music; one attendant was standing at hand, holding the perfume box, while another had the paans made into gilauris; one carried cardamom, another moved the fan, and yet another stood with the betel-box.

Seeing these arrangements and beholding Bichhittar Kunwari's beauty and grace, Chhabili was stunned. She forgot all about the garland she had brought and became so miserable that although she had placed the basket on the floor before the bride, she could not bring herself to put the garland around her neck. The bride's mother said to her, 'What kind of garden-keeper are you that you do not put the garland around her neck at this time of happy omen and put it on the floor?'

Chhabili answered, 'Until recently she was a landowner's daughter, but now she is to become a princess. I do not dare raise my hand above her head.' Thus speaking, she put the garland around Bichhittar Kunwari's neck. At that moment Bichhittar Kunwari's mother put many a silver and gold pieces in the skirts of Chhabili's dress.

Seeing Bichhittar Kunwari's beauty, Chhabili broke down crying and the bride's mother said to her, 'O wretched garden-keeper, why do you shower my door with tears at this auspicious hour?' Chhabili replied, 'Mistress, I am not crying. My eyes are smarting from the lamps' smoke. That is the reason they water.' The bride's mother said, 'What do you burn in your house lamps?' She answered, 'In our home we burn itr,[14] which is fifty rupees a tola.'[15] With that, Chhabili took her leave, saying that she had to return before it was morning. The bride's mother said, 'Very well,' and Chhabili departed carrying her basket.

OF CHHABILI SECURING A PROMISE FROM THE PRINCE OF NEVER LOOKING AT BICHHITTAR KUNWARI

On her way back to the prince's camp, Chhabili thought that she must devise a plan which would ensure that her relationship with the prince was not hindered by his marriage. With this thought she removed the silver and gold pieces from the basket and replaced them with some grains she picked on the way.

Upon her return, Chhabili presented a much troubled face to the prince. The prince, who had spent a long time waiting for her, asked,

14. Itr: An oil-based perfume.
15. Tola: A unit of weight.

'Chhabili, is all well? What is the matter with you?' She answered, 'O Prince of the World, pray ask me no more, as it is something I cannot divulge.'

When the prince insisted on knowing, Chhabili said, 'You are not going to believe what I have to tell you!' The prince answered, 'I have complete faith in you.' Then she said, 'The woman to whom you will soon be married is so hideous and frightening that she would strike terror in a man's heart. My senses are still in disarray from the sight of her. It seems that in marrying you off to the landlord's daughter, the court officials hatched a conspiracy to kill you. They knew that the king would not spare them should any plot on their part become known, so they decided on this scheme so that you die instantly upon beholding her face.' The prince said, 'O Chhabili, tell me some way that I can be rid of this monster. I cannot turn back, as my respected mother has accompanied me here. Find a way to save my life.'

Chhabili said, 'There is nothing to be done, as you will have to look at your wife.' The prince again asked her to find some way of saving him. Chhabili said, 'If you swear to do as I say, I will tell you a way to save your life.' When the prince had sworn to do as she told him, Chhabili tore a band from her dupatta, wrapped it around the prince's eyes, and said, 'Should anyone ask you why it is wrapped around your eyes, you must tell them that your eyes are hurting. That way you will be saved her sight and will not die from looking at her.' The prince agreed to do as Chhabili suggested, and kept the band on his eyes and made groaning sounds, pretending to be in pain.

Chhabili said, 'O prince, give me leave as I must return to my home in Delhi.' The prince said, 'You can go in the morning.' She answered, 'My heart sinks whenever I think of her horrible face. Give me leave to depart so that I may return home.' The prince was unable to refuse and gave her leave to return. He sent her off on a camel accompanied by some soldiers and two torchbearers, and instructed the soldiers to return after conducting her safely to her house.

Meanwhile, the prince pretended that his eyes were hurting. 'Ah! Ah!' he groaned when the king and the court nobles and astrologers came to take him to walk around the sacred fire with the bride. He accompanied them and ascended to the nuptial bower. The pandit said to him, 'O Prince of the World, open your eyes.' He replied, 'My eyes are hurting badly and they smart from the lamplight. That is why I have wrapped a cloth band around them.'

The pandits finally led the bride to the prince and placed her hand in his. They made seven rounds of the sacred fire and performed other ceremonies adhering to Hindu custom.

After three days had passed, Maan Singh prostrated himself before the king, and said, 'I am most unworthy, but do accept my daughter as your slave girl.' The king raised and embraced him, and offering words of praise, said, 'You are a most worthy man.'

Bichhittar Kunwari's dowry was loaded onto camels and sent to Delhi, and Maan Singh offered robes of honour to all nobles and ministers of the king's court. Alms were distributed in such abundance among the poor and destitute that all of them became free of want. When it was time for the bride to be sent off to her new home, and her palanquin was placed at the threshold of the house, cries of grief rose from Maan Singh's household.

The prospect of a father's separation from his daughter
Why should not one ceaselessly cry on such an occasion?

In short, Maan Singh saw off Bichhittar Kunwari, and her wedding procession began the return journey to Delhi with great fanfare, arriving there in four days. The prince remained blindfolded throughout the night, and entered the palace too with the blindfold on.

On their first night together, Bichhittar Kunwari put on the sixteen adornments[16] and came to where the prince lay. She saw that he lay blindfolded on the bed. She stood by the bed for four hours. Finally, she asked the prince, 'O Prince of the World, where should I sleep?' The prince answered, 'You may lie at the foot of the bed.' Hearing this indifferent reply from the prince, Bichhittar Kunwari felt dispirited, and lay at the foot of the bed, waiting all night for the prince to speak to her. Her whole night passed in this hope. At the time of the morning prayers, the prince left their chamber, and only upon arriving at the threshold of the palace did he remove his blindfold and put it in his pocket. Then he headed to Chhabili's inn.

16. Sixteen adornments: Sixteen cosmetics, unguents, and implements which complete a woman's makeup. They are: miswak (stick for brushing teeth), manjan (tooth powder), surma (antimony), missi, ubtan, chandan (sandalwood powder), nil (indigo), itr (perfume), kanghi (comb), tel (oil), mehndi (henna), surkhi (rogue), paan, bindi, phool (flower), libas (dress).

Chhabili asked him what had transpired at the wedding and on the first night. The prince gave her a full account and told her that he had not taken off the blindfold for a moment since she had put it on, and only removed it that morning. Upon hearing this, Chhabili was very pleased, and said to herself: 'My ploy has worked very well!'

In short, every night thereafter, the prince slept on his side with his back turned to Bichhittar Kunwari. Every night, she asked him where she might sleep, and he would tell her to lie at the foot of the bed. She would keep quiet and go to sleep as instructed. In the morning, when the prince woke up, he went to see Chhabili and spent all day in pleasure-seeking with her. Upon returning home in the evening, he would put on the blindfold.

OF BICHHITTAR KUNWARI LEARNING ABOUT PRINCE ZAMAN SHAH'S RELATIONSHIP WITH CHHABILI

When months had passed in this fashion, Bichhittar Kunwari said to the female attendant sent for her by her father, 'I will give you an assignment if you will carry it out.' She answered, 'O lady, I am your slave girl and have eaten your salt. Whatever you order me to do, I shall carry it out with all my heart and soul.' Then Bichhittar Kunwari narrated all that had passed between her and the prince, and broke down crying in the telling. Her female attendant also cried with her. After a long while, Bichhittar Kunwari stopped crying and said to the maid, 'Tomorrow, dress up in man's clothing and follow the prince. Learn all there is to know about his doings, and bring me a report.'

Early the following morning, the female attendant dressed herself up in men's clothing and sat at the threshold of the palace. As was his custom, the prince, upon waking, went to meet Chhabili, and the female attendant followed him. When the prince arrived at Chhabili's inn, the female attendant enquired about the prince from the innkeeper. She told her that the prince and Chhabili had been friends for ten years and that the prince visited her daily and returned to the palace in the evening. After learning all the details, the attendant returned to the palace and reported everything to her mistress.

Bichhittar Kunwari remained quiet that day but the following morning, at the time of the morning prayers after the prince had left, she went to see her mother-in-law and stood before her after making an obeisance. Her mother-in-law rose and embraced her, seated her beside herself and asked, 'What brought you here today, dear daughter-in-law?' Bichhittar Kunwari answered, 'I have come to make a submission; if you would allow it and not take offence, I will make it before you.' Her mother-in-law said, 'Speak freely.' Then Bichhittar Kunwari said, 'O dear mother, what is wrong with the prince's eyes that they hurt still and have not healed? What is the truth behind that?' Her mother-in-law answered, 'O daughter-in-law, for the last ten years the prince has been in love with Chhabili the innkeeper, and he spends all day with her. Maybe Chhabili has ensnared the prince in some deception, and he has fallen for it and in consequence neither opens his eyes nor looks at or addresses you.'

Bichhittar Kunwari said, 'If you give me permission, I can bring the prince around in no time.' Her mother-in-law said, 'My daughter, what could be better? As the proverb says, the blind man needs naught else but seeing eyes. Go and do what you must. You have my permission.'

Bichhittar Kunwari made an obeisance to her mother-in-law and returned to her quarters.

OF BICHHITTAR APPEARING BEFORE THE PRINCE AS A CURD-SELLER

Bichhittar sent for her female attendant and said to her, 'Go to the house of Raju the curd-seller. Give her a gold piece and ask her to give you her clothes, a new clay pot filled with fresh curd, and her cloth ring for carrying the pot. Fetch these things from her and return soon.'

The female attendant gave the gold piece to the curd-seller who handed her all the items requested of her. The attendant brought them and put them before her mistress.

Bichhittar Kunwari took off her clothes and dressed herself in the clothes of the curd-seller. Then she placed the cloth ring on her head with the clay pot on top, and holding the weighing scales and weights, she went before her mother-in-law and said, 'My good woman, I have delicious curd to sell. Won't you buy some?' Her mother-in-law looked at her and said, 'O curd seller, where do you live?' She answered, 'I have lived with Your Honour for a while.' She asked, 'Have you ever brought me any curd before?' Bichhittar Kunwari answered, 'No.'

Her mother-in-law tasted the curd, and said, 'You may bring us curd every day.'

Then Bichhittar Kunwari smiled and said, 'It is I, Your Honour's daughter-in-law, and I am headed to see the prince. I just came to let you know about it.'

Her mother-in-law said, 'Now I am certain that you will be able to free the prince from Chhabili's deception.' Bichhittar Kunwari rose and offered salutations, and said, 'It shall be so with the prayers of my elders accompanying me.'

When Bichhittar Kunwari reached the gate of the palace she instructed the guard to not let anyone enter her quarters until she had returned. Then she arrived outside Chhabili's inn and began calling out, 'Curd! Buy fresh curd!'

Hearing her call the prince looked out and beckoned her over. Seeing the curd-seller's beauty and loveliness, the prince became enamoured of her, and said, 'Allow me to taste some of your curd.' The curd-seller put down the pot of curd before the prince. Then Chhabili cast an angry glance at her.

The prince asked the curd-seller, 'How much is it for the whole pot?' She answered, 'O Prince of the World, it will cost you a hundred thousand copper coins.' Chhabili said, 'Are you selling yourself or the curd?'

The prince said to the curd-seller, 'Let me taste some.' When he tasted the curd, he found it delicious and sweet.

The prince praised the curd to Chhabili, and said to the curd-seller, 'I do not have a hundred thousand copper coins with me to give you. I will pledge something of mine with you instead. Tomorrow you may bring some more curd and collect two hundred thousand copper coins for both days' payment, and return my property to me.' The curd-seller said, 'Very well!'

The prince took off his pearl necklace and two jewel-studded armlets and gave them to her. She gave the pot of curd to the prince and took the jewellery and turned to go.

She had gone a few steps when the prince started praising her beauty before Chhabili. She answered, 'O Prince, how can one have any faith in these people? They will transfer their loyalty to whomsoever pays them the highest price and submit to their pleasure.' Overhearing these words, the curd-seller turned back and said to Chhabili, 'Such must be your custom, but it is not ours. It is you who do the bidding of anyone travelling alone at night, and lie down with whomsoever pays you more.'

Chhabili was enraged upon hearing these words from the curd-seller. Noticing her anger, Bichhittar Kunwari could not hold back and said, 'O Chhabili, being an innkeeper, it does not behove you to sit beside the prince. Get up! A vulgar woman like you must not come near him.'

Hearing the two of them argue, the prince turned to Chhabili and said, 'You should go away now.' Chhabili was chagrined at these words and left the prince's side. The curd-seller felt delighted at this, and headed out. The prince, who had become enamoured of her, thought of asking for her address and whereabouts so he could later find her, and called out to her as she was leaving. Hearing his call, she returned and said, 'What can I do for you?' The prince asked, 'O curd-seller, where do you live?' She answered, 'I live at the famous tavern of Bed's Foot.' Then she left, and upon returning to the palace, removed the curd-seller's clothes and put on her royal vestments.

After she had left, the prince asked his attendant to bring him his horse. Chhabili said to him,

'O Prince of the World, it is still some hours to sunset. What will you do upon returning home so early?' The prince answered, 'Today I plan to go sightseeing at Chandni Chowk as I have some business there.' Thus speaking, the prince mounted his horse and rode away to Chandni Chowk.

The prince saw an old man pass by and told his servant to find out the directions to Bed's Foot tavern from him. The servant approached the old man and asked him about the tavern. He answered, 'My good fellow, in all my many years I have neither heard of nor seen the Bed's Foot tavern. Ask someone else, who may know.'

Seeing a soldier pass by, the servant asked him, 'O soldier, do you know where Bed's Foot tavern is and how to get there?' The soldier thought that he was either joking or mocking him, and answered, 'O idiot, neither you nor your father could have ever found accommodation at the Bed's Foot tavern, so why do you ask me its address?' The prince overheard the soldier's reply and instructed the servant not to make further enquiries. Thereafter, he went for a promenade in the garden and when it was evening, he returned to the palace with the blindfold on, and as was his custom slept on his side of the charpai.

Bichhittar Kunwari again put on the sixteen adornments and greeted the prince and stood waiting for hours beside the bed. When the prince made no reply, she helplessly asked, 'O Prince of the World, where should I sleep?' As usual, the prince answered, 'Lie at the foot of the bed.'

Bichhittar Kunwari said to herself, 'This ignorant idiot still has not understood a thing.' That night, too, she slept at the foot of the bed.

OF BICHHITTAR APPEARING BEFORE THE PRINCE AS A NOBLEMAN

When it was morning, the prince went to visit Chhabili at the inn as was his custom. Bichhittar Kunwari sent for the keeper of the household and told him to go before the king and request on her behalf a horse with a fine saddle, as well as other paraphernalia of hunting, including a musket and sword. The moment the keeper of the household conveyed Bichhittar's request, the king ordered the superintendent of the stables to saddle up his own hunting steed and give it to the keeper. He also ordered the superintendent of armoury to provide the keeper with any weapons he may require. The keeper brought all the things and presented them to Bichhittar Kunwari. She put on men's clothes and sporting five weapons,[17] rode to Chhabili's inn and stopped at its threshold.

The prince had deputed a doorman to secretly alert him upon the arrival of any trooper or king's agent. As Bichhittar tried to enter the inn he asked, 'Where have you come from and where do you wish to go?' She answered, 'I have come to meet Prince Zaman Shah.' The doorman said, 'Pray sit here and I will announce you to the prince. What is your name?' She answered, 'My name is Bichhittar Shah.'

The doorman went before the prince and told him that Bichhittar Shah had come to meet him. The prince said, 'Go and tell him that a few hours now remain until the end of day and I will not receive any visitors. He may come tomorrow morning.' The doorman conveyed the message to Bichhittar Shah. Upon hearing it, she gave him a few cuts of the whip. The doorman went crying before the prince, and said, 'For no fault of mine and without cause Bichhittar Shah whipped me.'

17. Five weapons: Sword, shield, spear, bow, and arrows.

Upon hearing this, the prince was enraged and dressed and armed himself, and said to the doorman, 'Tell me who whipped you and I will behead the fellow.' Talking thus amongst themselves, they came to the inn's entrance. There, the prince laid eyes on Bichhittar Shah and was instantly enamoured of his beauty, and said to himself: 'God's providence is boundless. Verily, one cannot tell whether the curd-seller I saw yesterday was more beautiful, or this young man.' The prince had completely forgotten his anger. He approached Bichhittar Shah and, greeting him, walked with him.

Bichhittar Kunwari said to herself, 'He is my husband. I should not be mounted while he accompanies me on foot. I should dismount and let him sit on the horse.' Then Bichhittar dismounted and told the prince to sit on his horse. The prince asked him why he had dismounted and told him to return to the saddle. While they were having this conversation the prince's horse was brought by his attendant, and both of them rode out to hunt.

When they had come far from the city, they sighted a deer. The prince drew an arrow from the quiver and shot it, and Bichhittar Shah shot an arrow as well. Pierced by the arrows, the deer ran into an indigo field, and fell down, injured. The prince chased the deer and found it had fallen in the indigo field. The prince dismounted to slaughter the deer. As Bichhittar Shah tried to dismount, he cut his foot on the knife and it began to bleed. Prince Zaman Shah tore up his headgear to bandage the foot, and was grieved at the young man's pain, and said to him, 'O Bichhittar Shah, it seems to me that it is not your foot but my heart which has been lacerated and wounded. It is as if it is not you who is hurting but I.' Bichhittar Shah said, 'Do not think so much of it. Such injuries are common during the hunt. Do not worry about it.' Thus speaking he sought to slaughter the deer, but Zaman Shah told him, 'I will slaughter the deer. You must not do it. You are injured.'

Then Zaman Shah slaughtered the deer and gathered the meat, and together he and Bichhittar Shah headed back to the city.

On the way back, Zaman Shah asked, 'O Bichhittar Shah, how is the pain now?' He answered, 'O Prince of the World, I am feeling slightly better.' The prince asked, 'Where do you live?' Bichhittar Shah answered, 'My house is in Delhi in the Bed's Foot tavern.' The prince said, 'Yesterday I met a curd-seller at the inn who also lived at Bed's Foot tavern.' Bichhittar Shah replied, 'She lives under my house.' The prince said,

'God has gifted the curd-seller with such perfect beauty that it is beyond praise.' Then the prince said, 'I will accompany you to your home, and tomorrow you can accompany me to mine.' Upon hearing this, Bichhittar remained silent and did not answer. Then she conversed with the prince so that their journey would pass pleasantly.

When the gates of the city appeared in the distance, she said to herself: 'We are approaching the city and this ignorant man will follow me and if I were to allow it, it would reveal my secret. I must use subterfuge and cunning to be rid of him.' With this in mind, Bichhittar said to the prince, 'O Prince of the World, do show me your horse's gaits and gallop.' The prince made his horse gallop and showed off its gaits. Bichhittar praised the horse's speed and trot, and said, 'Now it is my turn to show you my horse's gaits and gallop.' Thus speaking she galloped away and did not stop until she had entered the doors of the palace. She quickly dismounted and went into her quarters where she changed into women's clothes.

Meanwhile, the prince waited outside the city for Bichhittar Shah to return so that he could accompany him to his house. When a long time had passed and Bichhittar Shah did not return, the dejected prince returned to the inn. Chhabili brought warm water and washed his face and hands. Then Chhabili sat beside the prince and began speaking words of love. But the prince did not seem to find them amusing or distracting that day.

Chhabili said, 'O Prince, why are you sad and despondent? Say something.' The prince replied, 'There is nothing to say, Chhabili. Today Bichhittar Shah accompanied me on a hunt. On the pretext of showing me his horse's gait he galloped away into the city and did not return. His visage is impressed upon my eyes. O Chhabili, he is such a handsome man that I cannot describe his beauty. Had he asked me to pay him five hundred rupees daily for the privilege of seeing him, I would not have refused. But what grieves me is that he did not take my leave, for I would never have allowed him to be separated from me.'

Chhabili said, 'O Prince of the World, these days your heart has become inconstant, and you very easily become enamoured of women and men. Do not become downcast. When you have money, scores of men wish to serve you.'

It was soon evening, and the prince rode back to the palace where he took out the blindfold from his pocket and put it on before entering his quarters. After he had eaten, the keeper of the household led him by the hand to his bed. The prince lay down and turned onto his side.

OF THE PRINCE LEARNING ABOUT BICHHITTAR'S BEAUTY

Bichhittar Kunwari put on the sixteen adornments and strung pearls in her hair and came to the prince. After she had stood waiting fruitlessly for several hours, she dejectedly asked the prince, 'Where should I sleep?' The prince replied, 'Lie somewhere at the foot of the bed.' When she heard this a great sadness overcame her, and she lay down at the foot of the bed to sleep.

Meanwhile, the prince thought that his wife must be wondering how he was able to sleep peacefully all night long, and not complain about his eyes hurting. He started groaning and said, 'Put out the candle, its light hurts my eyes.' Bichhittar groaned in reply, saying, 'Ah, ah, my foot hurts. I can't get up.'

At these words the prince got angry and sat up in bed and said, 'O shameless woman, let me examine your foot to see what injury it could possibly have received, as it is either on the bed or the carpet all day long.' Bichhittar answered, 'And how is it that your eyes are paining? Don't they hurt daily when you go hunting? How are you able to hunt with your eyes in such a terrible state?' Then she called out for an attendant to bring her a taper. The attendant presently brought one.

Bichhittar Kunwari untied the prince's blindfold and said, 'Let me see if your eyes are hurting.' The prince replied, 'Let me see if your foot is injured.' Upon that, Bichhittar removed the bandage and showed him her foot. The prince asked, 'How did you injure yourself?' She replied, 'I had gone hunting today with Your Honour, and you had bandaged my foot with a piece torn from your headgear; do you recognize it?'

Then Bichhittar said, 'It was I who met you at the inn dressed as the curd-seller, and you still owe me for the curd.' The prince said, 'I had pledged something with the curd-seller.' Bichhittar answered, 'It is all here: your pearl necklace and the jewel-studded armlets,' and thus saying, she put these before the prince. The prince first felt the necklace and armlets with his hands, then with his back turned to Bichhittar, opened his eyes to inspect them and found the pearl necklace and armlet he had given her.

Now the prince turned to look at Bichhittar Kunwari and was stunned by her beauty and comeliness and wished to bed her. But Bichhittar drew a dagger and with its point pressed against her bosom, said to him, 'O Prince of the World, even though I am your wife, I will never lie with you until you do as I tell you. And if you were to force me I will put out my life with this dagger.' The prince said, 'Speak and tell me what you wish.'

Bichhittar answered, 'The way Chhabili has tormented me, I will only be pacified if she is buried waist-deep in the ground, and riddled with arrows in retribution. Then I will be your slave girl and you may do with me as you please.'

OF BICHHITTAR KUNWARI WREAKING VENGEANCE UPON CHHABILI

The prince waited impatiently for morning. When it was daytime, he put on his court attire and went to take his seat at court. All the nobles and ministers were in attendance, and they were greatly pleased to see the prince realize his responsibilities and join them. The king, too, was very glad to see the prince at court.

The prince consulted the viziers about Chhabili, and sent soldiers to arrest and produce her before him. When the soldiers brought her, the prince said to them, 'Make her stand at a distance from me, lest her love should again overpower my heart.'

Thereafter, the prince consulted with all the court nobles about a suitable punishment for Chhabili. They all advised him to exile her from his dominions.

Bichhittar Kunwari had sent a few eunuchs to keep her abreast of everything that was spoken at court. When she learned that Chhabili was to be exiled as punishment, she forthwith sent a messenger to tell the prince that Chhabili must be buried waist-deep and the prince himself must riddle her head with arrows until she was dead; if he was not agreeable to this, then she would put out her life. Powerless to act otherwise, the prince had Chhabili buried waist-deep and shot arrows at her until she was dead. Then he ordered her corpse to be buried.

The prince then left the court and returned to the palace and waited for evening. When it was dark, the prince had dinner and happily retired to bed. Bichhittar Kunwari put on the sixteen adornments and came to the prince. Seeing her beauty, he felt a terrible longing for her and took her in his embrace and spent the whole night seeking pleasure of her.

When it was morning the prince took a bath, put on royal attire and attended the court. He spent his days minding the affairs of the state and in the night busied himself in pleasure-seeking with Bichhittar Kunwari.

Many years passed in this fashion. Then the king abdicated in favour of his son and the prince ascended the throne and put on the crown of kingship. Zaman Shah busied himself in dispensing justice and all his subjects bided their time in peace and happiness, from his justice and equity.

End

Qissa 4

Azar Shah and Saman Rukh Bano

A first translation of Mehr Chand Khatri Mehr's *Nau Aaeen-e Hindi*

AUTHOR'S PREFACE

We have no power to offer Your eulogy and praise
O Lord, you are the Master of the Earth and Heavens

It is beyond the scope of a humble man to praise the Creator of the Universe.

Swift of wing are the birds of imagination and fancy
But even they cannot take God's scope and measure

These days it is common to find Englishmen with an interest in learning the Hindustani language—but in the past no such interest existed in Hindustan, the image of Heaven (may God Almighty preserve it in peace and welfare until Judgment Day), and therefore no master authored a book of prose in this language. In the past days Ata Hussain Khan Murassa Raqam[1] adapted the qissa of the four dervishes from the Persian into Hindi[2] and gave it the title *Nau Tarz-e Murassa* [A New Ornate Style]. And verily it is a new and ornate style. But being composed in the Rekhta language, using difficult words and ornate phrases, it did not find favour with Englishmen.

1. Ata Hussain Khan Murassa Raqam: Author of *Nau Tarz-e Murassa*, a famous qissa.
2. Hindi: One of the names given to Urdu in the nineteenth century.

A receiver of favours from the Almighty's court, this humble man from Lahore, Mehr Chand of name, belonging to the Khatri Chopra clan, and having the pen name Mehr—whose food and drink is apportioned at the Fatehgarh camp in Farrukhabad—is blessed to be in the retinue of Baron Cowley,[3] a man matchless in liberality and manliness.

In generosity the equal of Hatim[4]
In bravery superior to Rustam[5]
O Lord, Mehr prays that
He may abide in grandeur and majesty always

The reason for authoring this book is that this source of beneficence took a fancy to the Hindustani language as well, and despite my research, a book of prose, that could be an exemplar to teach Hindi language's common discourse, was not to be found.

Even though this unlearned man lacks any excellence, at the request of that mine of bounteousness and sea of generosity I wrote the qissa of Azar Shah and Saman Rukh Bano to fulfil the present need, in a chaste and simple language that even the common man can understand, and have given it the title *Nau Aaeen-e Hindi* [A Fresh Hindi Style].[6] I plead to noble-natured learned readers that should they find any errors and omissions, they ought to avoid fault-finding, and with rectification conceal them.

If [this qissa] is entirely filled with omissions and errors
I yet have hopes of forgiveness from men of fortitude
The invisible speaker asked me to make its chronogram[7]
"Narrate with dispatch O Mehr, this qissa."[8]

3. Baron Cowley: Henry Wellesley, 1st Baron Cowley (1773–1847), an Anglo-Irish diplomat and politician who was posted in India in the late eighteenth and early nineteenth century.

4. Hatim: A historic figure from the Tayy tribe in sixth-century Arabia, known for his liberality. Protagonist of *Qissa Hatim Tai* in Persian and Urdu.

5. Rustam: A legendary hero from Persian mythology, known for his great strength and bravery.

6. *Nau Aaeen-e Hindi*: A Fresh Hindi (Urdu) Style. The title of the present book.

7. Chronogram: A combination of words or verse the value of whose letters determine the year of a work's completion.

8. *Narrate with dispatch O Mehr, this qissa*: The numeric value of the line in Urdu amounts to 1218 which is the commencement year (1218 AH/1802 CE) of the tale.

FIRST TALE

The beginning of the story of King Azar Shah; Of his deciding to become a beggar from grief at his childlessness, and meeting an old man; Of the old man giving injunctions to Azar Shah and returning whence he had come

In the lands of Hindustan, the image of Heaven, there lived a king, Azar Shah of name, who was renowned in the world for his equity and justice. But he had no son who could carry forward his name. For this reason, he remained downhearted, and served the devout faqirs faithfully, perchance to have his ardent wish fulfilled by the prayer of one favoured by God. A long time passed in this state and his heart's desire remained unfulfilled.

One day in the middle of the night it occurred to the king that he had wasted a good part of his life in idleness: He had no heir to inherit his wealth and dominion, and with human existence there was no telling whether or not one would draw the next breath.

Life is like a bubble, the duration of a breath
Why should one bother even opening the eye to take notice
Life keeps moving constantly forward like flowing water
What is there in such existence, O Mehr,[9] for one to take pride?

He reckoned that it would be preferable to retire to a forest and devote his remaining days to God Almighty's worship. Thus deciding, he took off his crown, dressed himself in beggarly clothes, and headed for the forest without apprising anyone of his decision. He had travelled a few kos[10] in one direction when he came upon a wilderness, and beheld a hunch-backed, green-clad old man with a flowing white beard coming towards him, walking slowly, with the aid of a staff, on account of his advanced years. He approached and said: 'Peace be upon you, O Azar Shah!'

Azar Shah returned his greeting, and said: 'O old man of enlightened heart, in your advanced age, which I reckon to be over a hundred years, and a state such that you are unable to take a step without the aid of your staff, why do you roam this dangerous forest in the middle

9. Mehr: The nom de plume of the present book's author.
10. Kos: A unit of measurement approximately equivalent to two miles.

of the night, unless you are the holy Khizr,[11] come to guide the lost on their path?'

The old man answered: 'My dear fellow, I am neither Khizr nor Ilyas.[12] I am an ordinary person who, believing the world to be an impermanent abode, has spent eighty years of mortal existence in the middle of a desolation that lies some forty kos from here. In an earlier time, I was a thug and killed travellers through deception and deceit, robbing them of their goods and chattels. For twenty years that remained my trade. One day perchance, I came upon two well-to-do young men between the ages of twenty and thirty years along my path. I believed that they were some jeweller's sons and would of a certain be carrying jewels, and killed them by deceit. Upon searching them, however, I found no valuables on their person, beside the clothes they wore.

'I felt great remorse at killing them, and swore that I would forever renounce my profession. I headed for home at that very moment. I felt anxiety that I did not know any trade except banditry, and wondered how I would provide sustenance for myself.

'As I went forth, I came upon a huge snake that was unable even to move on account of its great weight, and lay mouth open on the forest floor. I marvelled at the sight and said to myself: "This creature cannot even stir from its place. Let us see how food reaches him, as he cannot survive without nourishment."

'I was engrossed in these thoughts when a herd of deer galloping at the speed of wind arrived, with a lion in pursuit. Taking the huge snake's open mouth to be a hilly pass, the deer ran inside it to take refuge from the lion. The snake immediately shut its maw and swallowed the entire herd of the deer as a single morsel. The snake then raised its head to the heavens and by God's grace a cloud formed in the sky upon the instant, and it began to rain heavily. The snake drank the water and rested, and the disappointed lion returned to the forest.

11. Khizr: A holy character known to help those in distress, and who appears to those who have lost their way on their journey. He is described as an old man dressed in green.

12. Ilyas: Ilyas appears in the Quran as God's prophet. In qissa literature he is described as Khizr's brother, and someone who helps those in distress.

'Upon witnessing this, I proclaimed: "All praise to my Lord's grace that the powerful lion strove so mightily but received no fruit, while an immobile creature His Lordship fed in this manner."

The prospect of researching Your mysterious ways
Is an idle thought I dare not entertain

'O Azar Shah, from witnessing what passed with the snake, the anxiety about finding the means of sustenance, which had beset me, was put to rest by a certainty that the One who has given me life will also provide for me. This couplet came to my lips:

The decree of fate is irrevocable
Fughan[13] *purposelessly sought recourse in strategy*

'That very instant I renounced my love of all worldly possessions and relations, and retreated into the forest. Now I eat what I receive by the end of the day, to keep body and soul together, and spend the rest of the time on my devotions to the Creator.

'At this time, the holy Khizr sent me here to dissuade you from becoming a mendicant on account of not being blessed with a child. You must banish this idle thought from your mind. You are destined to have a child, not from your wife Zalala but from the daughter of the King of Tartary, Princess Saman Rukh Bano, who is peerless in comeliness and beauty.

Unjust is the one who compares her with the moon
Pock-marked is the moon's face, and hers unblemished

'If you were to marry her, you will have a child.' Having conveyed this message from the holy Khizr, the old man said: 'O Azar Shah, you must return home now while a little of the night remains. If you return in the morning, all your servants and retainers, upon seeing you in this garb, will think that you have lost your sanity, and the whole world will laugh at you.' Thus speaking, the old man went away whence he had come.

13. Fughan: The takhallus (nom de plume) of the poet Ashraf Ali Khan.

SECOND TALE

Of King Azar Shah falling in love with Saman Rukh, King of Tartary's daughter; Of his returning home and penning a letter and sending Vizier Khajasta Rai to Saman Rukh's father; And of King Azar and Princess Saman Rukh getting married

The narrator recounts thus that Azar Shah fell in love with Saman Rukh from merely hearing of her beauty. He turned back, and retracing his steps, returned to the palace and lay down to sleep in his bed, without informing anyone of his return or earlier excursion.

After court was held the following day, the king gathered his ministers, counsellors, and strategists, and narrated all that had passed in the night, and of his falling in love with Saman Rukh.

Vizier Khajasta Rai made an obeisance and submitted: 'From the lands in the East to the West, there is none among the monarchs of the world who does not bow his head in submission at Your Honour's doorstep. As a first step, someone from Your Honour's court, lofty as the heavens, should go to Saman Rukh's father as an envoy. In all likelihood, he will consider it a signal honour and never refuse his daughter's hand in marriage. But should monarchical conceit sway him otherwise, the means of war and combat may be employed as needed, to obtain the desired outcome.'

The king found favour in the advice and said: 'O Khajasta Rai, who could be more suitable than you to take the embassy?' Khajasta Rai bowed, and said: 'Your obedient servant shall do as you command.' The king ordered the royal secretary to immediately compose a letter addressed to the King of Tartary, and sent Khajasta Rai bearing many presents for the king from his land.

. . .

LETTER

After praise to the Administrator of the World—who lit up the day with the sun and gave light to the night with the moon—the essence of the friendship of supporters is manifest[?], and while serene relations, camaraderie, and friendship have long held between us, epistolary correspondence has altogether ceased, and the exchange of letters and communiques has stopped. Those who view and judge things superficially and from appearances, derive inauspicious interpretations of the most tranquil and loving of relations without caring to delve into the truth of the matter. There is nothing more precious than amity and fidelity—and it is most praiseworthy among kings, the favoured ones of the court of heaven—as it engenders peace and comfort for God's creatures. Thus, in order to strengthen the bonds of affinity and union, and augment the durability of the links of love and affection, the cream of my nobles, Khajasta Rai, has been given sanction to present himself before you with a highly confidential matter entrusted to him. He will communicate it to you during a private audience. It is my earnest hope that the henna of approval dyes the hand of the bride of hope, the wish expressed attains a favourable reply, and the tradition of letters and communiques is resumed between the present parties in the future.

May Love's domain forever prosper
The letter ends here. Salutations!

. . .

At long last, after travelling for many days and traversing the stages of the journey, Khajasta Rai arrived in Tartary. The King of Tartary wondered about the reason for his arrival, as no ambassador of the Emperor of Hindustan had ever presented himself in his lands until that day. He was still conferring with his courtiers when the announcer of petitions arrived and said: 'The ambassador of the Emperor of Hindustan has arrived to present himself in Your Honour's service.' He said: 'Show him in!'

Khajasta Rai presented himself before the king and made an obeisance as per the decorum of plenipotentiaries. He handed him King Azar Shah's missive, presented the gifts, and made a verbal submission suitable to the occasion. The king learned the petition made in the missive, and said with great joy: 'I hereby accept all that Azar Shah has written. Do stay, however, for a few days so you may recover from the fatigue of the journey. We shall send you off after two months.' Khajasta Rai was very pleased to hear the auspicious words, and respectfully folding his hands, submitted: 'As it may please Your Honour! Your slave shall be loyal, devoted, and obedient to your wishes.' He then kissed the ground before the king, and returned to his camp.

The king turned to the minister who stood on his left and said to him: 'For as long as Khajasta Rai is our guest, the officers of the court must not be negligent in the duties of hosting and entertaining him.

The entire expense and payables for him and his entourage shall be borne by the royal treasury. And do arrange speedily all the necessities for a wedding ceremony.'

The royal retainers attended to Khajasta Rai's every need as ordered, and within a few days they provided all the material befitting a royal wedding. Then the king had Princess Saman Rukh put on her wedding finery. He arranged many slave girls, beautiful as the sun, to accompany her, and pretty slave boys to attend upon her, and thus escorted, sent his daughter off with Khajasta Rai.

He gave in dowry a thousand fleet-footed horses with golden accoutrements, elephants tall as hills, countless objects and wares, innumerable gifts, and many elephant-loads of treasures, and said: 'O Khajasta Rai, convey this message of humility to Azar Shah that although the gifts sent may not be worthy of His Eminence, we send Saman Rukh to his service in accordance with his wishes.'

Khajasta Rai answered with words befitting the occasion and sought leave to depart. The king bestowed a seven-part robe of honour on Khajasta Rai, along with a golden ornament for his turban, a pearl necklace, and a number of elephants and horses. He conferred five-hundred robes of honour on Khajasta Rai's companions, according to their station, and then bid farewell to the retinue with tear-filled eyes.

. . .

Khajasta Rai crossed the stages of the journey, escorting Saman Rukh, and arrived in his land.

There was a garden situated outside the city that was called the Garden of Desire, where every tree was laden with ripening fruit. Many kinds of birds chirped, perched on the tree branches. The place presented a vision of spring that overwhelmed the mind. Khajasta Rai camped there and sent notice of his arrival to King Azar Shah.

The king was delighted to receive the happy tidings, and festive notes were played through the length and breadth of the city. Carpets were spread out in the city, lamps were lit, and Azar Shah, accompanied by his vizier and some commanders, bent his legs towards the Garden of Desire.

Upon receiving news of the king's approach, Saman Rukh instructed her servants to spread a carpet made of gold brocade from the entrance of the garden all the way up to the fortifications of the city. She told them that after Azar Shah had passed over it to arrive in the garden, to distribute the carpet and all the furnishings, to beggars and the destitute, in alms. Then she ordered the pari-like[14] slave girls to make ready salvers of jewels to scatter as the sacrifice of the king, and they carried out her orders. Saman Rukh then placed three thrones for the king, of which one was made of emerald, another studded with rubies, and the third made of gold, enchased with many kinds of jewels. A costly carpet covered the garden's expanse from end to end.

Upon arrival, King Azar Shah first embraced Khajasta Rai with great honour, and conferred upon him royal accoutrements, including his turban, girdle, dagger, sword, and the fleet-footed charger along with its gold-worked saddle that he had inherited from his father, and with great affection said: 'The matter would not have been resolved so amicably had you not taken the responsibility upon yourself to see to it.' Khajasta Rai made an obeisance and replied: 'All of it came about from Your Honour's august fortunes. If your devoted servants are called upon to sacrifice their lives in carrying out your wishes, we shall never flinch.'

The king was very well pleased to hear this expression of Khajasta Rai's devotion, and headed into the garden. Saman Rukh's slave girls offered salvers of pearls, rubies, and emeralds as the king's sacrifice and then distributed them as alms. Within the garden of desire, Azar Shah found the walls and entrances covered with gold and jewels, and beautiful carpets laid everywhere. He was enthralled by the sight of these luxuries. Farther down, he found himself in an apartment where a beautiful damsel was seated on an enamelled throne surrounded by pari-like slave girls, who stood by respectfully with hands folded at their waists. Thrones made of emerald, studded with rubies, and worked in gold were stationed there. At the sight of Azar Shah, Saman Rukh drew her veil across her face, stepped down from her throne, and gestured to her slave girls to guide the king to his throne.

After taking a seat on the throne, the king commanded the royal servants: 'Proceed with the wedding festivities!' Khajasta Rai forthwith arranged an assembly of the high officers of the kingdom and sent for the qazi.[15]

14. Pari-like: As beautiful as the pari, a fairy-like creature of Indo-Iranian mythology.
15. Qazi: A religious official who supervises the betrothal.

The tongue has neither the power nor the expression to praise the resplendence of the ceremony and wedding procession, or to eulogize the arrangements and decor of the assembly from which even the sun and the moon wished to learn excellence; or how Venus and Jupiter sought just a glance of the comely, moon-like beauties present at the assembly. All the paraphernalia of the wedding being present, the officers responsible for observance of the holy law held the nuptials of Saman Rukh and Azar Shah, uniting them with a conjugal bond. First Khajasta Rai presented two precious rubies by way of felicitations, and then the rest of the ministers made their offerings in their turn.

The king conferred robes of honour on each, according to his station. Thereafter, in accordance with the convention, Saman Rukh was carried in a golden, jewel-studded palanquin into the city to the playing of happy and festive music, and was conveyed to the palace where other wedding rituals were performed.

Thereafter, Khajasta Rai's wife presented herself in service to Saman Rukh Bano and offered a pair of rubies. The queen of the world showed her signal favour by accepting her offering, and conferring upon her a resplendent robe of honour along with her burqa, a gold chair studded with jewels, a pearl necklace, and a white elephant from her dowry, along with its golden saddle and jewel-enchased golden howdah; and saw her off with honour. Khajasta Rai's wife made her salutations and left, and on her way scattered fifty purses of gold coins to beggars and the destitute as a sacrifice of Saman Rukh. Then the wives of the king's nobles and officers presented themselves in the queen's service, and made their offerings. The queen of the world rewarded each of them according to their station, and gave them leave to depart.

Azar Shah presented all the officers of the court with robes of honour according to their station, and opened the treasury to provide alms, charity, and largesse with such open-handedness that nobody was left with want in his heart.

Having supervised the distribution of the alms and riches, His Highness returned to the palace in the afternoon. Saman Rukh drew her veil across her face at the sight of him. The king approached her and lifted her veil. He noticed her face dewing, her heart racing, and the damsel feeling oppressed by the heat. Azar Shah dried her face with his handkerchief and embraced her and after kissing her many times on her lips and cheeks, said to her:

'To behold you, that is what I desire
To not open my eyes without you, that is what I desire'

She replied shyly, in whispers:

'Indeed, all your prestige is what my love has bestowed'

The two of them then bided their time exchanging words of love and affection. When a little time remained before the break of day, King Azar Shah stepped out of the palace and received the salutations of all present. At the close of the day the king ordered a dance assembly to be organized, and along with his commanders and viziers retired to a separate chamber and became engrossed in viewing the dance recital.

THIRD TALE

Of King Azar Shah's first wife Zalala casting a spell of madness on Saman Rukh; Of Khajasta Rai bringing Sheikh Sanaan from Qandahar to cure Saman Rukh; And of Sheikh Sanaan summoning his two disciples, Dana Dil and Roshan Zameer

It is related that when Zalala—who was Azar Shah's first wife—heard of Saman Rukh's arrival, she let out a sigh and said: 'One must find a way to make the king vexed with Saman Rukh, otherwise he will spend all hours of night and day with her.'

That wretch had a stone of such power that if one ingested its particles admixed with water, one immediately became insane. That vicious woman rubbed that stone to obtain its powder, gave it to a woman promising her twenty thousand rupees, and said to her: 'However you can, make Saman Rukh drink this admixture.'

Driven by avarice, the woman put that in a sherbet, and took it to Saman Rukh. After making some deceitful prattle, she made Saman Rukh drink the sherbet as a potion of auspiciousness. Immediately upon drinking it, Saman Rukh developed goose pimples all over her body. After some time had passed, her vision became blurred and her heart began palpitating. She lay herself down in bed uneasily, and called out to her slave girls: 'I feel nauseous, and I cannot find the strength to rise and sit up in bed. God knows what it is!' They brought her a betel-leaf prepared with green cardamom and cloves, but her condition steadily worsened.

In the evening, Azar Shah returned to the palace from the dance assembly. Seeing Saman Rukh lying in bed, he enquired after her. She narrated all that had passed with her and said: 'I was well the first three parts of the day, but God knows what happened to me towards the end of the day that my condition has continuously worsened.' Even as she finished speaking these words, she went into a fit of senselessness and began uttering absurdities.

Azar Shah grieved to see Saman Rukh in that state. His Honour summoned the royal physicians and gave them the particulars of her condition. The physicians treated her according to their diagnoses, but it did not improve her condition in the least, nor did any physic help her. Then the king sent for the wizards and exorcists, lest the queen had fallen under the influence of some jinn or pari or dev.[16] Even though they used fumes, burnt paper wicks written with spells, and chanted spells to invoke the presence of the possessor, it had no effect. Her condition worsened from moment to moment, and the fits of insanity became aggravated.

The physicians and wizards made an obeisance to Azar Shah and submitted: 'We have done all we could, but the queen has not responded to the treatments. God alone knows the cause of her illness; it is beyond our comprehension. However, a great wonder-worker by the name of Sheikh Sanaan lives in Qandahar who remains engrossed in prayers and devotions to God night and day. We are certain that if he could be persuaded to visit and suggest a cure, it would prove successful.'

Upon hearing this, the king said to Khajasta Rai: 'Depart now and take my entreaties before that pious man, and plead with him so that he may find it in his heart to grant us a visit.' Khajasta Rai forthwith set out for Qandahar, and after travelling for many days arrived there and met Sheikh Sanaan. He related Saman Rukh's condition before him, and said: 'You would do us a great kindness if you were to grant her a visit.' The Sheikh replied: 'For twenty years I have stayed in this place engrossed in my prayers and devotions. I cannot leave this place.' Khajasta Rai entreated and pleaded with him, and said: 'O Venerated Sir, your visit will resolve this matter. If you could find it in your heart to grant it, it would be an act of benignancy.' Upon these words the

16. Dev: A demon of Mount Qaf.

Sheikh's heart was moved, and he said: 'If my visit will help her condition, I am willing to accompany you. Stay here for another two days, and on the third day we will depart.'

Khajasta Rai was very pleased at the outcome, and stayed there. Sheikh Sanaan departed with Khajasta Rai as he had promised, and after some days arrived near Azar Shah's kingdom. The king received him at the gates of the city, conducted him into the city, and seating him with great honour, described Saman Rukh's ailment.

Sheikh Sanaan reflected awhile, then said: 'I have two disciples: the one named Dana Dil has taken my leave and journeyed to the south, and the other named Roshan Zameer has gone to the north. If they were here, Saman Rukh could have been speedily cured, as the two of them are highly proficient in curing such cases.'

Azar Shah said: 'Now, pray be so kind as to send for them.' Sheikh Sanaan wrote out separate letters to his two disciples. The king dispatched one of his courtiers with the letter to Dana Dil to the south, and another with the missive to summon Roshan Zameer from the north. Both disciples of Sheikh Sanaan accompanied the king's courtiers upon receipt of their master's letter, and after some days presented themselves before him.

Sheikh Sanaan described Saman Rukh's condition to them, and asked how she could be cured. The two of them reflected in their hearts, then said: 'O Master, she is under some conjurer's spell, and no medicine will cure her. But we prescribe that choice stories and fine anecdotes, and rare qissas and dastans be narrated before her which will engross her heart, and dispel her derangement.'

The Sheikh replied: 'Who better to narrate them than yourself. Narrate before us what you have witnessed and heard.'

Dana Dil said: 'A secluded apartment should be arranged where Azar Shah and Saman Rukh and yourself are gathered together, so that this slave can narrate what he has witnessed and heard.'

Azar Shah forthwith arranged a secluded apartment where no one was allowed entry, and had Saman Rukh put behind a curtain. Like the four elements, all four of them sat on a royal carpet opposite the curtain.

Then Sheikh Sanaan said: 'O Dana Dil, you may now begin relating what you find suitable for the occasion.'

FOURTH TALE

Of Dana Dil narrating the tale of Malik Muhammad and Giti Afroz before Saman Rukh, relating how Malik Muhammad fell in love with the pari Giti Afroz; And of Giti Afroz turning him into a pigeon, and of his returning to human form through Vizier Danishmand's ministrations

It is related that Dana Dil began his narration with his master's permission thus:

'Hear, O Queen of the Heavens, that among my relations was a man named Malik Muhammad who was forever travelling to foreign lands and cities, and often spent his nights in hills and deserts.

One day fate took him to the land of Babylon. Outside the city walls was a beautifully constructed marble pond brimful with sparkling water. Beside it was a small garden patch that was tastefully laid out and in which fruit trees stood, laden with fruit of many kinds. Numerous kinds of flowers were planted at the edge of the garden, and nightingales, doves, and many other colourful birds sang, perched on the tree branches.

MASNAVI

Flowers were in bloom everywhere, and in every garden patch
The song of nightingales issued from all directions
Water flowed in the streams which lined the garden
Everywhere one heard the cooing of doves
Cypresses bordered the garden in such fine array
One involuntarily called out: Praise the Lord! Praise the Lord!

Upon beholding the beauty and artistry of the garden, Malik Muhammad recited this couplet:

This must be the Garden of the World's Creator
Or the Garden of Paradise on Earth

Malik Muhammad promenaded in the garden all day. When it was evening, he partook of some fruit from the trees to allay his hunger. He drank water from the pond and at night stayed in that charming place.

In the middle of the night a commotion and tumult reached his ears and his eyes opened. He beheld in the heavens countless torches burning, in whose light a throne was flying across the sky, surrounded by thousands of paris and parizads dressed in brocade and gold cloth.

Malik Muhammad wondered what mysterious event it was that he had witnessed, and lost all sleep. When it was morning, he went into Babylon and asked people there about the marvellous sight he had seen the previous night, and enquired the name and rank of the one sitting on the flying throne.

Those who knew the truth of the matter said to him: "O young man, do not dwell upon this matter. The one you saw was Giti Afroz, the daughter of the king of paris. She has become estranged from her father and constructed a palace and set up residence in the nearby hills. If a human being so much as sets foot there she turns him into an animal."

Upon hearing these words, the desire to see Giti Afroz only grew stronger in Malik Muhammad's heart. He said: "It is preferable to be in her company even as an animal," and immediately set out for the hills. Upon arriving at the palace of the pari he found the gates closed. Malik Muhammed announced his arrival, and at the command of their princess the paris opened the gates.

As he stepped indoors, Malik Muhammad saw all the walls and entrances of the palace adorned with gold cloth, a royal carpet spread across its length and breadth, and a beauty resplendent like the full moon sitting on an emerald throne.

MASNAVI

How to describe her pretty face and features
The tongue has no capacity to sing their praise
Straight-statured like the cypress, mouth like a rosebud, eyes like narcissus
Jasmine-faced, rose-bodied, she was the envy of the garden
Her locks thus covered her cheeks
As if night and day had become merged
The moon paled in comparison before her resplendent face
Her refulgent beauty mortified the sun
Every part of her being was a marvel
Suffice it to say she was a marvel cap-a-pie

Thousands of parizads stood alongside her like stars beside the moon. Malik Muhammad's senses were overwhelmed upon beholding her beautiful visage, and he fell down in a faint. The parizads sprinkled his face with rose water, which restored him to his senses.

Giti Afroz asked him: "Who are you, O human, and what has brought you here?" Malik Muhammad was still so engrossed in her beauty he could make no reply. Seeing that he was enraptured by her beauty, Giti Afroz pointed him towards a gold chair that lay near the throne. Malik Muhammad was delighted to receive this favour. He sat there and gave her an account of spending the night in the garden and how it had led to his presence before her. Pleased by his account, Giti Afroz conversed with him at length. Then she ordered a parizad named Rooh Afza to serve them, and she brought forth a bottle of wine and poured two cups for Giti Afroz and Malik Muhammad. When she was intoxicated, Giti Afroz said to Malik Muhammad: "If you wish I could confer the cupbearer Rooh Afza upon you." Malik Muhammad answered:

Except you, I have business with none
I seek you, why would I look at another

Giti Afroz said to him: "O Malik Muhammad, I also wish to keep you with me. But human beings have no patience; they come to grief on account of their lack of restraint and then calumniate us. That is why I confer Rooh Afza upon you. You may now take pleasure of her company."

He replied: "I have no business with another."

If my wish were to be granted, I would arrange
For you to be beside me, and to behold you night and day

While they conversed together thus, the day came to an end. At night, Giti Afroz gave orders that Malik Muhammad's and Rooh Afza's beds be placed together. But Malik Muhammad did not accept the offer, and replied: "O beloved, I am satisfied even to behold you from afar."

Upon hearing this, Giti Afroz arranged her and Malik Muhammad's beds to be placed on either side of a pool in the courtyard. Malik Muhammad spent the night with great difficulty, in an endlessly restive state.

The following day a royal assembly was arranged beside the pool, and a dance recital began, and the cupbearer Rooh Afza handed them cup after cup of wine. Finally, his desire and love for Giti Afroz overpowered Malik Muhammad and he threw himself at Giti Afroz's feet. She said: "O Malik Muhammad, beware, lest you should commit any impropriety and be turned into a beast. Then it will be very difficult to return to human form!" For the moment, Malik Muhammad became somewhat composed and restrained himself.

But when does a lover have peace! After some time, one of the parizads brought a rose and Malik Muhammad took it from her hand and offered it to Giti Afroz. When she stretched out her hand to receive the flower, Malik Muhammad caught it in his, and kissed it.

Giti Afroz was incensed and said: "O damned pigeon, I did warn you that humans, with their lack of self-restraint, have no place in our company!"

Immediately at her words, Malik Muhammad rolled on the ground and turned into a pigeon; flew up and perched on the balustrade of the palace. All day long he kept flying within sight of Giti Afroz, but that cruel creature showed him no pity.

Helpless, Malik Muhammad flew from there to his home on the following day. His servants caught him, taking him to be a wild pigeon. One of them picked up a knife, intending to slaughter him. But another fellow said: "O Friends, one pigeon will not satisfy our hunger. And, for a long time, we have not received any word of our master, Malik Muhammad. God knows where he is. Let us release this pigeon as a sacrifice for our master. The other day Danishmand, who is our master's uncle and the king's vizier, asked me news of him. I replied that it's been a month since our master has been gone, and we have no news of him. Vizier Danishmand then said: That wretch was very fond of roaming in lands and cities and hills. One hopes he has not gone towards the pari's palace, for she transforms all who go there into animals. If he has indeed gone there, and returns in animal form, do inform me, as I have a lincture which will immediately restore him to human form." Upon hearing this, the servants released the pigeon as a sacrifice of their master.

Malik Muhammad gave thanks to God upon his release from their clutches, and flew away to Danishmand's house.

The vizier was seated on his throne, occupied in the business of the state, and a crowd of people stood there awaiting his attention. When Malik Muhammad came flying in and landed in his lap, all those present marvelled at the pigeon landing in the middle of the crowded assembly, as the birds were known to avoid even the shadow of humans.

Danishmand reckoned upon reflection that Malik Muhammad had been turned into a pigeon by the paris, and that was why this pigeon came to him—for there was no reason a wild animal would approach humans on its own. Once he realized this, Danishmand sent his eunuch Kafur to bring the small jar of lincture. He put some of it into the pigeon's mouth, whereupon it rolled on the ground and returned to human form as Malik Muhammad.

Danishmand embraced Malik Muhammad and forbade him from ever going back to the hills. Malik Muhammad replied: "There is no reason why I would ever visit that place again." Then he took leave of his uncle and returned home.

All of Malik Muhammad's servants and attendants were very pleased at the sight of their master. They asked him where he had been all those days. Malik Muhammad answered: "It seems that devotion and fidelity ends with you, since you sharpened a knife to slaughter me! I had some days remaining to my life that I escaped your clutches."

All of them were greatly surprised to hear this, and said: "O Master, what is it that you say?! We are loyal to you, and true-hearted, and would not dare commit such a transgression. Where a drop of your sweat falls we are ready to spill our blood!"

Then Malik Muhammad narrated the account of his becoming a pigeon and returning home. They were mortified and ashamed at their actions, and everyone commended the person who had persuaded them to release the pigeon, and Malik Muhammad also gave him a reward.

For some days afterwards, Malik Muhammad bided his time at home in great comfort and luxury.'

FIFTH TALE

Of Malik Muhammad returning to the hills to revisit Giti Afroz; Of her turning Malik Muhammad into a waterfowl, and of his uncle Vizier Danishmand returning him to human form

Dana Dil said: 'Hear, O mistress, that after many days Malik Muhammad wondered whether or not Giti Afroz also missed him in the same manner he longed for her. He drank a few cups of wine in quick succession so that intoxication might dispel thoughts of her from his mind. But from drinking wine his longing to see her only increased. He smashed the cup against the ground, started sighing loudly, and headed restively for the hills.

He arrived at Giti Afroz's palace and called out: "Open the gates!" A voice enquired: "Who is it?" He answered: "It's me, Malik Muhammad the Faithful!" Upon hearing Malik Muhammad's name, the parizads opened the portals forthwith.

When he went inside, he saw his beloved, beautiful as the full moon, seated on her throne and scores of paris and parizads standing respectfully beside her.

The moment Giti Afroz beheld him, she smiled and said: "O Malik Muhammad, you underwent much suffering. If you had considered the consequences and not kissed my hand, you would have saved yourself much hardship. Now I grant you permission to kiss my hands and feet. But do not yearn for more, lest you should come to regret it."

Malik Muhammad felt very happy upon hearing this, and offered thanks to God that he now had leave to kiss the hands and feet of the one he longed even to see from a distance. At night, Giti Afroz had her bed placed next to Malik Muhammad's, and said to him: "O Malik Muhammad, beware, lest you should find yourself culpable of another transgression." He answered: "My life, you have granted me leave to kiss your hands and feet. I shall not transgress these limits." Inebriated with wine, they lay in their beds. But sleep was far from Malik Muhammad's eyes. Every now and then he would kiss Giti Afroz's hands and feet, and long to kiss her mouth, but dared not do it for fear of turning into an animal.

Malik Muhammad pretended to be unconscious, and brought his mouth closer to hers. She woke up from the warmth of his breath on her face, and said to him laughing: "O fool, remain steadfast to your word or you will turn into an animal in no time, and then you won't be able to see me." Malik Muhammad felt embarrassed and returned to his bed and fell asleep.

The two lovers woke up at the time of morning prayers, and spent the whole day in joyful and pleasuresome pursuits.

At night-time, as before, the two beds were laid beside the pool. When Giti Afroz had fallen asleep, Malik Muhammad rose, lifted her hand and pressed it to his eyes, and recited this couplet as he regarded her mouth:

God knows what will become of us
For I am impatient and she is obstinate

Much did he try to restrain himself, but his heart prevailed; he lost all control and kissed Giti Afroz's lips. She woke up and with her brows knitted in anger, said: "O wretched waterfowl, what have you done!" At these words Malik Muhammad immediately rolled on the floor and turned into a waterfowl.'

. . .

When Saman Rukh heard these words from Dana Dil, she said: 'That poor man had returned to human form after such hardship. And his pitiless beloved turned him into a waterfowl again! One can only imagine the troubles that await him.'

Azar Shah expressed his great indebtedness to Sheikh Sanaan and his two disciples, upon witnessing Saman Rukh becoming conscious to the extent of commenting on the story.

. . .

Dana Dil continued: 'In short, after turning into a waterfowl, Malik Muhammad spent the whole night in the pool. In the morning, Giti Afroz looked at him, and said: "O impatient man, had you listened to me, you would not have suffered like this. Now go to your uncle. Perhaps he will be able to cure you." Malik Muhammad realized that even if he were to languish there for a hundred years, that pitiless creature would not show him mercy. Helpless, he flew off towards the city.

As luck would have it, the king was out on a chase, and was hunting by the pond. Seeing a waterfowl fly past, he released a hawk. The waterfowl tried to evade the hawk but could not find a way of escaping his talons, and finally dove into the pond. Despite giving chase, the hawk was not successful in catching him. The waterfowl told himself that as long as the king remained by the pond, he must not come out of it.

Hear, O Queen, that when the hawk failed to catch the fowl, the king turned back towards the city. Along the way he saw the master of the hunt bringing a royal falcon with him. The king was irritated with him and said with annoyance: "Why did you not bring the royal falcon at the time of the hunt? There is a waterfowl in the lake. Go and hunt him down with this falcon or you will be severely punished." As per the king's orders, the master of the hunt arrived by the pond.

Meanwhile, the waterfowl, witnessing the king's conveyance move away, flew out of the pond and towards the city. The master of the hunt, who was ready, released the royal falcon after him. The waterfowl tried to escape, but the falcon caught him in his clutches. However, some days yet remained to his life so that the waterfowl fell out of the falcon's clutches and into the pond, thus escaping capture again.

After the master of the hunt returned to the city dejected, the waterfowl—that is, Malik Muhammad—came out of the pond and headed to Danishmand's house. There he saw hunters present the animals they had caught. They expressed their regret that a waterfowl had escaped the royal falcon. Malik Muhammad listened to the whole account himself, and gave thanks to the Almighty. Then, wounded and bloodied as he was, he climbed into his uncle's lap.

Those present wondered after the bird entering a human assembly.

Noticing the fowl's wounds and broken wings, Danishmand reckoned that it must be Malik Muhammad who had been attacked by the royal falcon. He called out: "Is it you, Malik Muhammad?" Malik Muhammad shook his wings in assent. His uncle upbraided him, and said: "O unlucky fellow, I had forbidden you from ever setting foot there again, but you did not listen to me. Now I will only restore you to human form after you have sworn that you will not go there again." Malik Muhammad moved his head, forswearing ever going there.

Danishmand sent for the same medicine jar and administered Malik Muhammad a little lincture. By the power of wondrous God, Malik Muhammad returned to human form immediately, upon licking the medicine.

Danishmand sent for Malik Muhammad's clothes, and after giving him many injunctions, said: "Now I have no lincture left. If you go back there, you will be on your own; do not expect me to cure you." Malik Muhammad took his leave and returned home.

His servants recognised him from afar, and came to greet him, and by way of advice, said to him: "O master, what frenzy has possessed you? One of these days you will lose your life in its pursuit. This time your uncle has forsworn that even should his nephew die, he will never cure him."

Malik Muhammad said: "I have made a pledge, too, never to return to the hills." Thus replying, he entered the women's quarters and helped himself to whatever there was to eat, and then rested. He spent the next few days living in comfort and luxury at home, and visited his uncle daily.'

SIXTH TALE

Of Malik Muhammad visiting Giti Afroz; Of the arrival of King Unsar's vizier Felsuf to reason with Giti Afroz, and she not consenting to part ways with Malik Muhammad; Of Malik Muhammad and Giti Afroz visiting King Farkhanda Shah's garden and spending the night there; Of the king learning about it and inviting Giti Afroz for a feast; Of Giti Afroz insisting the king visit first as her guest, and King Farkhanda Shah accepting the invitation

Dana Dil said: 'Listen, O Saman Rukh! One day, in the middle of the night, Malik Muhammad was home when a commotion was heard in the sky. When he looked up, he saw Giti Afroz flying like the wind on her golden throne, with thousands of paris in her entourage. Malik Muhammad lost all restraint at the sight of his beloved, and said to himself: "Verily, I am a fool to be languishing here, away from such a wondrous assembly." He left his home that instant and headed for the hills, and told the servants he was going to visit his uncle.

When he arrived at the palace, he called out to be admitted and the paris opened the portals for him. When he went inside, he saw his beloved sitting on a crystalline throne dressed in red in great array. Seeing Malik Muhammad, she called out: "Come! What an opportune time you chose to visit, as I was occupied with thoughts of you." She seated him beside her and asked him to recount all that had transpired with him. Malik Muhammad drew a sigh from the depths of his heart and recited this couplet:

See what a frenzy your love engendered
I lost all honour, and earned disrepute besides

Giti Afroz was delighted to hear this. She threw her arm around Malik Muhammad's neck and conversed with him for a long time, allowing him to kiss her lips when he wished. Malik Muhammd was delighted to have his wish granted.

Of a sudden, noises were heard in the sky. Messengers brought tidings that Felsuf, vizier to Giti Afroz's father King Unsar, was approaching. Even as they conveyed the news, Vizier Felsuf arrived and after making an obeisance, presented King Unsar Shah's letter. After reading it Giti Afroz lowered her head. Then Vizier Felsuf addressed Giti Afroz thus: "What is this course you have adopted, that you have dropped all regard for your repute and honour, and made friends with a human being? What business do paris have with humans? Your mother and father are wroth with you for this reason. It is now incumbent upon you to banish all thought of him from your heart, and return home to Paristan[17] where your parents, siblings, and other family long to see you."

Giti Afroz raised her head after a long time, turned her face to Felsuf, and said: "All your injunctions are true, but this human has undergone troubles and hardships for me that cannot be described. Indeed, a number of times I turned him into an animal, causing him ignominy and disgrace, but even then, he did not give up my companionship. I feel so indebted to him for his fortitude and generosity that should he even bestow me upon another, I will make no protest." Thus speaking, she put her arm around Malik Muhammad's neck, kissed his lips, and said: "O Vizier, let alone my parents, even if the whole world should become aggrieved with me, I will not turn from this human's friendship, but remain steadfast to my word.

Whether I live or die, I shall not waver in my resolve
I shall not betray him, let the whole world turn away from me

Indeed, it is I who am wroth with my mother and father, and renounce all links with them. Tell them as well to banish my love from their hearts."

The vizier marvelled upon witnessing this, and said: "May we be cursed by God if we should ever look at your face!" She answered: "You snatched the words out of my mouth. I am loath to see your face!" Vizier Felsuf then left, and along with his entourage returned to Paristan.

Upon arriving before Unsar Shah, he narrated all that had passed with Giti Afroz. Unsar Shah was devastated upon hearing his daughter's decision. Giti Afroz's brother, who was present, said: "Should you order me, I will persuade Giti Afroz to return home." The king said: "Very well! And make sure to kill that human at the first opportunity."

. . .

Malik Muhammad was overjoyed when Giti Afroz turned away her father's vizier, and reckoned that she too loved him, or else she would not have spoken thus harshly to her father's vizier in his defence. Giti Afroz said: "O Malik Muhammad, did you witness how I sent off my father's

17. Paristan: The land of paris in Mount Qaf.

vizier unceremoniously for your sake?" Then she beckoned Rooh Afza, who brought a flagon of strong wine that dispossessed one of the senses, and the two of them had a cup each. They exchanged words of love and affection until it was late, and then went to sleep by the pool.

Giti Afroz said: "Beware, O Malik Muhammad, lest you should imagine in your conceit that since I have turned away Vizier Felsuf, it gives you the freedom to act with impropriety!" Malik Muhammad replied: "My love, you have allowed me to kiss your lips. I shall not transgress those bounds."

But when is a lover's heart ever restful and tranquil? After Giti Afroz had fallen asleep, he got up and regarded that her face was wet with perspiration, which dripped onto her bed. Malik Muhammad restively recited the couplet:

Is it perspiration or rose water that drips from your face
A marvel that dew should drip from visage's flame

He kissed her mouth, and placed his hand on her body with desire. She immediately woke up at his touch, and said with knitted brows: "O shameless man, despite my reasoning with you, you did not desist from mischief. Do you wish to get caught in another calamity?" Mortified at these words, Malik Muhammad returned to his bed.

In the morning, when the moon hid itself and the sun's rays broke, Giti Afroz got up and, taking Malik Muhammad along, headed for the garden where the two promenaded along the flowerbeds. Then she sent for the jewel-studded golden throne and the two lovers flew on it to hunt in the forest. Having reached the forest, at first, they hunted lions, tigers, stags, deer, male buffalo-calves, and bovines. Then they hunted pigeons, partridges, quails, painted quails, waterfowls, jays, geese, ruddy-geese, demoiselle cranes, and coolen cranes.

A short distance from there lay King Farkhanda Shah's beautiful garden. They set up camp there to roast the game, and after having their meal, busied themselves watching dance recitals. At nightfall, they had the garden lit up and golden carpets of silk and brocade were laid out. From night until daybreak everyone in the garden remained occupied with singing and dancing. A few hours before sunset, they rose and returned to Giti Afroz's palace.

The royal garden-keepers and watchmen had never seen such a spectacle. They gave King Farkhanda Shah a detailed account of the night's festivities, and told him of Malik Muhammad's presence in the paris' assembly. Upon hearing this King Farkhanda Shah also felt a desire to see Giti Afroz.

He forthwith sent for Danishmand, and asked him: "Where is Malik Muhammad?" He replied: "These days that wretch has fallen in love with the pari Giti Afroz. Twice he came to see me, after he was turned into an animal, and your slave administered him a lincture and restored him to human form, and counselled and forbade him from continuing in his ways. I exhausted myself giving him injunctions against this folly, but he does not desist from her company. Powerless before his actions, I have cut all ties of affection with him. God only knows what passes with him now." The king said: "Should he visit you again, do bring him before us, as we have some business with him."

. . .

One day, while inspecting the contents of her jewels chamber, Giti Afroz asked Malik Muhammad: "Do you possess any jewels?" Malik Muhammad answered: "I have two rubies that glow in the night. In the darkness, they light up the whole house like moonlight. If someone were to see them from afar, he would take them for two burning lamps." She said: "Do bring those jewels tomorrow, for I would like to see them."

At night the two of them rested beside the pool. At the time of morning prayers, when the moon set and the sun rose, Malik Muhammad took leave of his beloved and returned home to fetch the night-glowing rubies.

His servants and retainers had long been waiting for him. They greeted him when they saw him arrive on horseback, and merrily led him indoors. Malik Muhammad received their salutations and entered his quarters. Just as he had lain down to rest after his repast, Vizier Danishmand, having heard news of his nephew's return, arrived to convey him the king's summons. Malik Muhammad immediately headed with his uncle to answer them, and made an obeisance to the Refuge of the World, King Farkhanda Shah.

The king said: "O Malik Muhammad, if Giti Afroz would somehow accept our invitation to a feast, we would be able to behold her beauty and be indebted to you." Malik Muhammad carefully weighed his words and answered: "If this is Your Honour's wish, I shall find a way of making it happen." Then the king said: "Take my salutations to the princess of the paris, and tell her that if she would allow us to host her for a day, we will consider that a signal honour."

Malik Muhammad left the court and went home, and took the two night-glowing rubies and presented them to Giti Afroz as an offering, who had them transferred to her jewel collection. Then Malik Muhammad conveyed Farkhanda Shah's invitation to a feast in her honour. Upon hearing of it, Giti Afroz said: "If the king accepts my invitation to host him first, I will have no qualms in attending his feast thereafter. I have no interest otherwise in being hosted by any king of the humans."

When Malik Muhammad conveyed Giti Afroz's message, King Farkhanda Shah was delighted, and gladly accepted the invitation. Malik Muhammad then returned and informed Giti Afroz that the king had accepted her invitation.'

SEVENTH TALE

Of Giti Afroz ordering her servitors to arrange a feast; Of her sending for the houris Mehr Angez and Shor Angez from Paristan, and dispatching Malik Muhammad to escort Farkhanda Shah to her palace

Dana Dil said: 'Hear, O Mistress, that when Giti Afroz learned of Farkhanda Shah accepting her invitation, she summoned all her servitors and ordered them to make arrangements for the feast. She sent for the master of the kitchen, and said to him: "Prepare all kinds of delicacies and all manner of fine pulao for the king that you can make ready with excellence in time for the feast, and set about it." She deputed another attendant to provide for all the ingredients and necessities. Everyone got busy carrying out their assigned duties, as per her orders.

Then that beauty wrote the following missive, addressed to her father and older brother, and dispatched it to Parsitan with a messenger:

I plan to present myself before you in the coming days. If you were to send someone to escort me, I will leave for Paristan from here. King Farkhanda Shah, who is the lord of these lands, has expressed a wish to be hosted once by me, and I have made preparations for a feast in his honour. I am hopeful that you will send the houris Mehr Angez and Shor Angez along with many attendants to help with the feast for the king; they will return to your service once the feast is over.

When Giti Afroz's messenger brought the letter before King Unsar Shah, he tore it up in great anger after reading it, and said: "I shall not send that shameless wretch even a dog of mine, let alone send paris and attendants."

Giti Afroz's messenger was alarmed by the king's outburst. Dejected by the king's reaction, as the messenger made to depart, Giti Afroz's brother made a bow before the king and said: "Giti Afroz is indeed unworthy and manifestly in the wrong; but however the young may err, their elders must not deny them love. She is deserving of being pardoned. Farkhanda Shah has sought to be hosted by her on account of hearing your august name. If you were not to dispatch Mehr Angez and Shor Angez as requested by Giti Afroz, it will be your name that will be sullied."

Upon reflection, Unsar Shah realized that his son spoke the truth. At his son's advice he ordered Mehr Angez and Shor Angez to be bedecked in fine garments and gold jewellery studded with precious jewels. He sent them with Giti Afroz's messenger, along with many attendants, and said to him: "All of them I confer on that wretch. She need not send them back."

The messenger made an obeisance and departed, and brought the paris before Giti Afroz, and narrated before her all that had passed in Paristan. Giti Afroz was delighted at the arrival of the paris, and said to Malik Muhammad: "Go and let Farkhanda Shah know that he may visit my humble abode on the third day from today—along with all his nobles, courtiers, and his army—and grace it with his presence."

After obtaining her permission, Malik Muhammad forthwith went before Farkhanda Shah and made an obeisance. The king, who was awaiting him, asked: "O Malik Muhammad, what news have you brought?" He narrated the message sent by that damsel in her exact words. The king smiled in ecstasies of delight, and said: "Why did she inconvenience herself by arranging a feast for the whole army?"

In answer, Malik Muhammad said: "She considers Your Honour's arrival a signal honour; there is no inconvenience. However, she has conveyed that nobody else may accompany you in the hills except Vizier Danishmand, for the parizads loathe the company of humans. Your entourage should set up tents around the hills and camp there." The king accepted these conditions and was indebted to Malik Muhammad. He longed for the remaining two days to pass so that he could behold the beautiful pari.

In short, on the day of the feast, Malik Muhammad said to himself: Let me first go and check whether or not Giti Afroz has made preparations for the feast. He mounted a horse and went to the palace gate and announced himself. The paris immediately opened the portals. When he went indoors, he saw the walls of the garden covered with gold and jewels, and the roofs finished with such beautiful enamelwork that no praise could do it justice. A gold brocade carpet was spread in the courtyard, and wearing a regal dress, his beloved was sitting on a golden throne in such array that the tongue is powerless to describe it. At the sight of her, Malik Muhammad recited this couplet with great passion:

Some dote on Mani's work, some on Bihzad's
I adore the One who made her visage

Giti Afroz smiled, and said: "Come, I was just thinking of you. Did you ever long for me when away?" In reply, Malik Muhammad recited this couplet:

Without you my sleep was robbed and my heart ached
I kept restlessly turning from night till morn in bed

Giti Afroz was delighted to hear this. Both of them had a cup of wine each, and for some time remained occupied in love talk. Then Giti Afroz said: "My love, now go with dispatch and tell Farkhanda Shah to honour my humble abode today with a visit."'

EIGHTH TALE

Of King Farkhanda Shah going to attend Giti Afroz's feast and being enthralled by the feast and charmed by the palace

Dana Dil said to Saman Rukh: 'Malik Muhammad started from Giti Afroz's palace and upon arriving before the king, made an obeisance and conveyed Giti Afroz's message. The king immediately ordered his army to make preparations. The proclaimers forthwith made the announcement in the camp. Before long, the whole army gathered and kettledrums were beaten to announce their departure.

Farkhanda Shah sent for a fleet-footed bay horse, so swift the dust clouds raised in his wake were also far apart.

MASNAVI

How may I properly narrate his praises
The one who bests wind with his speed
The moment the king was in the saddle
He ran swifter than wind
To describe the grandeur of the entourage
Would tire and split the writing reed
In short, as the king set out with his whole host
multitudes of soldiers accompanied him
Flanked on left and right by mounted royal guards
Who moved in hordes and swarms
At regular intervals the proclaimers' cries
Addressed them constantly and repeatedly thus:
Do not let your mount break from the troop
O men! Be mindful of your chargers' paces!
Neither charging ahead, nor lagging; neither stepping early, nor late
Step for step, they should march in tandem

In short, when the king's entourage neared the hills, he granted his men permission to set up their tents and bivouac there, and taking Vizier Danishmand along, ascended the hills. As Malik Muhammad announced their arrival at the palace gates, Giti Afroz instructed Rooh Afza to go and let them in.

When Rooh Afza opened the door at Giti Afroz's orders, and made an obeisance to the king, Farkhanda Shah fell in love with her upon beholding her beauty. Turning to Malik Muhammad, he asked: "Is she the one called Giti Afroz?" He replied: "This is Giti Afroz's humble attendant, Rooh Afza, who serves as her cupbearer." The king said to himself: "If her humble attendant possesses such beauty, how great would be the beauty of Princess Giti Afroz herself?" He stood frozen like an image on the wall, unblinkingly staring at Rooh Afza's face.

After a long interval, Malik Muhammad said to him: "Your Honour may step inside to promenade in the garden and behold the sights in its grounds." The king drew a sigh and recited this couplet:

I stand engrossed in the vision of my beloved's face
In yearning for her, I stand unmoving like a wall

Speaking to Rooh Afza of his desire, when the king stepped into the garden, he found it peerless in its appearance. Even the garden of paradise could not match its beauty and bloom. A carpet of velvet and gold brocade covered the whole courtyard, and the golden walls displayed portraits made with such a delicate mosaic work of pearls, rubies, cornelians, emeralds, and other jewels that the artists of China would admit defeat and Mani and Bihzad would confess their inferiority.

In the four corners of the garden, row upon row of wine ewers made of rubies and emeralds and filled with colourful wines were laid out on crystalline slabs. Beside them, bowls made of cornelians and diamonds were placed on golden stools in a festive arrangement. In short, every bit of the garden was so beautifully festooned that the houris in the garden of heaven would long to see it. Paris stood so elegantly at every few steps bedecked in beautiful dresses, that it was a sight to behold. After regaling himself with the sights, Farkhanda Shah promenaded in the garden.

When I stepped into the garden, every nightingale was singing
Redolence of the blooming flowers surrounded one at every step

In an apartment made of sandalwood, Giti Afroz was sitting elegantly on a lapis lazuli throne and in such a charming manner that a lover would instantly forfeit his life as her sacrifice. She rose gracefully and offered salutations to the king. Upon beholding her beauty, the king very nearly fainted, but at a sign from Danishmand, he gathered his wits.

Giti Afroz descended from her throne and joined him in his promenade. They arrived in an apartment whose entire floor was made of crystal. When they entered, they found within a platform made of jewels, spread with a lovely carpet, the likes of which the king had never seen. They went and sat on the platform beside which there were many pools filled with rose water in which waterfowls, ducks and other aquatic birds made of jewels and controlled by magic swam with the motion of the wind.

The king turned towards Danishmand, and said: “We have never beheld such a marvel of a house and these wonders in all our life. You are older and have more experience of life; have you, perchance, ever seen such things?” He answered: “Nobody except the paris has access to such houses and wonders.”

At a sign from Giti Afroz a hundred attendants forthwith brought ewers of strong wine whose one sip would make a human lose all self-regard and turn into a savage. The princess said to Rooh Afza: "Be the king's cupbearer, while houri Zauq Angez will ply Danishmand with wine."

Rooh Afza said: "We filled up many cups for the king, but Danishmand has not touched a drop." The king realized that Danishmand did not drink alongside him from considerations of decorum. He said: "O Danishmand, drink the wine for there is no reason to refuse it."

This is no occasion to offer excuses, such as you do
In this assembly, anyone who is a mystic must imbibe wine

He answered: "I gave up drinking since entering old age." The king picked up a cup and said: "Have one, as I am now become your cupbearer!" Danishmand realized that the king was showing him great favour by the gesture, and if he did not partake of the drink, there was no knowing what calamity would befall him. Then Giti Afroz spoke up, and said: "O Danishmand, what greater favour could there be? Do recall what Sheikh Saadi wrote in the *Gulistan*, that one must be on guard from the fickle temper of kings who sometimes take offence at a person's salutation, and at other times bestow robes of honour upon hearing abuse."

Danishmand could do naught but take the cup from the king's hand and drink it. Then the houri Zauq Angez plied him with cup after cup of wine. At Giti Afroz's orders, fountains started sprinkling, and for some time they all watched the play of water. Then Giti Afroz ordered food to be served. A hundred paris immediately laid out the food and served many kinds of pulao on diamond and emerald plates, put out an array of delicacies and kebabs, and various kinds of sweetmeats and almond confections. They placed many rows of apple and quince preserves on turquoise platters, along with a range of pickles.

At every bite Farkhanda Shah proclaimed praises of the food. He turned to Danishmand and softly said to him: "We have never eaten such tasty food in our life!" Danishmand replied: "Only the paris have access to such delights."

In short, once the drinking and feasting was over, the king offered blessings in giving thanks to his hostess. Giti Afroz said: "All this was made possible on account of Your Honour's august presence. Your arrival at my humble abode raised my rank among my race, and indeed in the eyes of the whole world."

Then, comely paris who were beautiful as Venus and before whose vision the sun and the moon hid their face in shame, arrived garbed in dresses of gold cloth and silver cloth and a dance recital began. Giti Afroz's servitors plied the king's whole army to their heart's content with fine food such as they had not even seen in their dreams. All the beasts in the camp as well were served with grass, grains, and kibble.'

NINTH TALE

Of Farkhanda Shah spending the night at Giti Afroz's palace; Of Rooh Afza attending to the King and Zauq Angez to Vizier Danishmand; and of King Farkhanda Shah returning to his city on the second day

Dana Dil said: 'Hear, O Queen, that in the evening Danishmand whispered to the king that it would not be advisable to stay there any longer. After a while, Farkhanda Shah sought his leave from Giti Afroz. She said to him: "You have already shown me great kindness by granting me a visit; pray regale us by staying another night for my sake." The king himself wished the same, and said to Danishmand: "We hold the pleasure of Princess Giti Afroz dear; we shall spend the night here." Danishmand answered: "As you please!" Then they became engrossed watching the dance. Every now and then Rooh Afza passed a cup of wine to the king, and Zauq Angez passed one to Danishmand.

Giti Afroz said: "Rooh Afza, the cupbearer, shall attend Your Highness and you may take your pleasure of her as you desire." The king was delighted to hear this. At a late hour of the night Giti Afroz ordered a royal chamber to be furnished with a bed for the king, and a separate apartment for Danishmand. Giti Afroz beckoned Rooh Afza to attend to the king in his bedchamber, and bid Zauq Angez to please Danishmand with her company.

Then Giti Afroz took the king's arm, and with Vizier Danishmand and her lover Malik Muhammad accompanying them, she led him to the upper storey of the palace. They saw there a beautiful apartment made of jewels, whose beauty could not be described in words. A fourteen-year-old pari, beautiful as the moon, was sitting there on a jewel-studded gold chair with such grace that no human could behold the sight without his senses taking flight. Regarding her beauty, Farkhanda Shah asked with great wonder: "What is the name of this beauty?"

Giti Afroz answered: "She is the houri Mehr Angez, elder sister to Shor Angez. These sisters have only recently arrived from my land." The king asked: "Where is Shor Angez?" Giti Afroz turned to Mehr Angez, who replied: "She left a moment ago along with a few attendants to promenade in the moonlit garden." Giti Afroz sent an attendant to summon her and he forthwith brought Shor Angez.

When the king looked at her, he found Shor Angez to be her sister's spitting image. The king now beheld one sister, and now stared at the other one with rapt engrossment.

Now the king felt attracted to the first one's face
And now, captivated, looked at the other's visage

Giti Afroz noticed King Farkhanda Shah's passionate engrossment, and, afraid lest he should express a wish to have them, she led her guest to the palace roof where a jewel-studded throne lay, and on its four edges four peacocks filled with musk, ambergris, and saffron were thus installed that the whole garden was redolent with their perfume.

The king asked: "Why is this throne kept here?" Giti Afroz said: "This throne is my conveyance. Should I wish, I can ride it from the farthest reaches of the East to the farthest reaches of the West." Thus speaking, she hastened to the throne with the king, and seated Danishmand and Malik Muhammad in the compartment before her. For the pleasure of the king, she appointed the houris Mehr Angez and Shor Angez as their cupbearers, who served each of them a cup of wine with great coquetry and many blandishments. Giti Afroz ordered some paris to join the entourage, who forthwith busied themselves with the preparations. Thousands of paris and parizads, each as beautiful as the moon, presented themselves at that very moment. Torchbearers lit up countless torches, and at Giti Afroz's bidding, the throne-flier damsel bore it heavenwards.

Mehr Angez and Shor Angez kept serving cups of wine to the company and made them all intoxicated and forgetful of reserve, such that they spoke to each other without inhibition.

MASNAVI

In that assembly everyone was unrestrained
All shame and modesty were cast aside
The musician was engrossed in playing
And the beautiful beloveds displayed their airs

In short, they returned to the palace in the middle of the night after travelling all over the land. Giti Afroz said to Farkhanda Shah: "Today, you were inconvenienced by staying up late. Kindly rest now in your bedchamber."

When the king went to his bedchamber, he found the whole apartment decorated so beautifully that words fail any attempt to describe it. Perfumes wafted up from all four sides. Rooh Afza looked beautiful as the full moon sitting on a wreath of roses spread over a coral bed, and a captivating perfume rose from her body. She stood up gracefully at the sight of the king. He led her by hand to the bed and said:

O pari, you are beautifully bedecked, I swear
Your tight bodice displays to advantage your captivating form

Then he put his arms around her neck and kissed her lips and face, and the two of them bided their time in pleasure-seeking the whole night.

When Vizier Danishmand went to his bedchamber, he fell down in a swoon upon beholding Zauq Angez's beauty, despite his advanced years. She sprinkled rose water on his face at once and helped him to his feet, and then seated him on the bed and gave him a few cups of wine. Reckoning her company worth more than the world's empire, Danishmand spent the whole night making merry with her.

Malik Muhammad saw both the king and Vizier Danishmand deriving pleasure with their beloveds, and he went to Giti Afroz in the hope that God may finally allay his suffering, and his heartless beloved take pity on him and grant him his wish.

When Giti Afroz seated him on her bed, Malik Muhammad recited this couplet:

Where all make merry and seek pleasure with their beloveds
I alone have long nursed my anguish and pain

Upon hearing this, Giti Afroz felt pity for him, and said: "O Malik Muhammad, do not show impatience! Put your hope in God's court—where nothing is outside the realm of possibility—that your wish is granted. Well received is that which is belatedly received. Do not disgrace yourself or me by any unseemly actions before the king and Vizier Danishmand."

Then the two of them drank wine and lay down in the same bed to rest. Once Giti Afroz had fallen asleep, Malik Muhammad was overpowered by lust, and made to satisfy his desire. Giti Afroz woke up with a start, and said with a frown: "O stupid man, you will never attain your purpose in this manner. Why do you humiliate yourself thus?" Mortified, Malik Muhammad lay down again.

Early in the morning, upon getting up, Giti Afroz ordered: "All carpetry in the apartments should be refreshed. It is my order that it be done without delay." The stewards immediately arranged for new carpets, and speedily replaced them so that it looked that they were never moved.

The king rose weary from the night and after washing his face joined Giti Afroz. Danishmand, too, got up rubbing his eyes which were red with sleeplessness, and presented himself before the king, and made an obeisance. Rooh Afza and Zauq Angez changed into new clothes and became cupbearers, pouring each of them a cup which dispelled intoxication. When it was Danishmand's turn to be served, he recited this couplet:

O Cupbearer, do no pass me cup after cup
Allow me a while to see my intoxication build

King Farkhanda Shah then took his leave of Giti Afroz, after expressing much gratitude. She accompanied him to the gates of the palace as a token of respect. From there the king bid her adieu and mounted his elephant. Danishmand and Malik Muhammad on horseback flanked the king on the left and right. The kettledrums were beaten and the king with his army returned to the city.

When Malik Muhammad returned home on horseback, his servants and attendants, who had wondered what might have become of him, were very pleased to see him arrive, and exclaimed: "God be thanked that this time Malik Muhammad has returned home safe and sound."

Malik Muhammad dismounted and entered his house. As he had not slept through the night, he lay down and immediately fell asleep. He woke up late in the afternoon and had something to eat, changed, and then went to the court accompanied by his uncle.'

TENTH TALE

Of Giti Afroz going to Farkhanda Shah's feast and spending the night there; And of her turning Malik Muhammad into a bull

Dana-Dil said: 'Hear now, O Queen of the World, that Farkhanda Shah sent for Danishmand and said: "It is incumbent upon me to invite Giti Afroz as a guest." He answered: "Very well." Then the king summoned Malik Muhammad, and said to him: "If Giti Afroz is agreeable, we would like to invite her to attend a feast." He answered: "I am certain she will agree, but even if she were to have any reservations, I will ensure that she consents to the visit."

The king immediately gave orders to the royal stewards to convey to the master of the kitchen that the greater the number of delicacies, pulaos, and variety of kebabs and almond confections he could prepare with excellence and dispatch for Giti Afroz and all her grandees and other companions, the bigger the reward he could expect from the king. And he told them that the same order held for preparations in all other areas. Thus, everyone got busy in their respective preparations.

The king said to Malik Muhammad: "Go and convey my blessings to the pari princess and tell her that although we lack the many marvels God has granted her, yet we wish that she illuminates our humble abode today with her beauty."

Malik Muhammad set out, and arriving at Giti Afroz's palace gate, called out to the paris. Someone enquired from within: "Who is it?" He answered: "It is I, Malik Muhammad the Faithful." The female attendants immediately opened the gate upon hearing his name, and he went inside. Giti Afroz seated him beside her on the throne, and asked him the news of Farkhanda Shah.

Malik Muhammad said: "The king has sent his prayers and the message that if you could illuminate his humble abode with your presence for even a little time, he would consider it a great honour." Giti Afroz answered: "There is no harm in it if it pleases you. We will visit at the hour you give us." Malik Muhammad said: "He awaits your presence." Upon hearing this, Giti Afroz said: "All the paris and parizads should present themselves." She got ready herself, wearing a fine dress and bedecking herself cap-a-pie with rare jewellery. She also ordered the houris Mehr Angez and Shor Angez, and Rooh Afza and Zauq Angez to dress themselves in fine vestments and jewellery.

Then she turned to Malik Muhammad and asked: "Should I travel there on the flying throne or on horseback?" He answered: "You may choose as you please." She said: "It is against decorum to visit kings seated on thrones." She then sent for and mounted a horse more fleet-footed than the wind, and made ready to leave, flanked by Mehr Angez and Shor Angez on two horses richly caparisoned with jewels. Malik Muhammad also accompanied her on his horse. Nearly a hundred thousand paris and parizads, trimmed out in beautiful dresses and bedecked with adornments, surrounded Giti Afroz as stars do the moon.

In short, when they approached the walls of the city in this majestic array, Malik Muhammad went ahead and informed the king. He looked towards the sky but did not hear any commotion, and said to Malik Muhammad: "It seems that she is still some distance away." He replied: "She has come on horseback and is at the gates of the city. She did not come on her flying throne out of respect for you."

Upon hearing this, the king went on foot to the gates of the city to welcome Giti Afroz, who dismounted, and taking along Mehr Angez and Shor Angez and Rooh Afza and Zauq Angez accompanied the king inside the city.

Farkhanda's Shah's men began pestering the paris, and upon noticing this, Giti Afroz rose and addressing the king, said: "You know well that the paris avoid humans at all costs, and we only came here out of an obligation to you. It would be well if you commanded the men badgering the paris to stop, otherwise they will turn to animals in an instant." The king furiously commanded his men to desist, and gave orders that none may look at the paris and parizads with ill intent.

Then, holding Giti Afroz's hand, he turned to the garden. She was delighted to see the garden's trim and bloom. In the nave of the garden was a summerhouse with gold and jewel adornments, furnished with a velvet and brocade carpet of immaculate smoothness. The gold-cloth canopies reflected the sunlight and bedazzled the eyes with their lustre. They sat down in the summerhouse, and becomingly adorned female attendants, beautiful as the rose and redolent like jasmine, started plying the wine, as the qawwals and melodious singers began their strains.

MASNAVI

Everywhere the zephyr made flower buds bloom
Everywhere one looked, roses swayed in the breeze

The roseate wine performed its magic
And the passion of nightingales was expressed in their song
The musician was engrossed in playing
And the beautiful beloveds displayed their airs
On one side the cypress stood defiant
On the other the straight-statured one took hearts captive
From all sides voices rang out for the cupbearer and wine
Everyone present longed for a sip
The beloveds were engrossed in drinking
From intoxication all were unconscious
So lost in inebriation were they
They were lost to both faith and the world

Meanwhile, the superintendent of the kitchen arrived, and said: "The repast is ready." The king said: "Serve it!" At his orders, the royal attendants put a food-cloth of white satin, and attendants beautiful as Venus laid out all manner of food in gold dishes. Musk, aloeswood, and ambergris burning in gold censers perfumed the air.

Whatever food Giti Afroz tasted, she found it tastier than the food she had served. After everyone had eaten and washed their hands, female attendants brought perfume boxes, betel-boxes, and spice-boxes. The king rubbed perfume on Rooh Afza's clothes himself. Giti Afroz rubbed perfume on the houris Mehr Angez and Shor Angez. Then she looked at Malik Muhammad, and said to him: "If you desire, you may rub perfume on my clothes." With great delight Malik Muhammad rubbed her clothes with perfume before the king and Vizier Danishmand.

The king addressed Giti Afroz, and said: "The wonders and jewels you possess are not available to us. Although this feast's arrangement was not commensurate with your dignity, you did us a great honour by setting foot in our house."

She replied: "Your Honour, rubies and cornelians are mere stones, and worthless to us; we only seek to be in your good graces." Thus speaking, she rose to promenade in the garden. Making polite conversation together, they remained in the garden until evening. Then she returned to the summerhouse and rosy-cheeked cupbearers began serving rounds of wine. Intoxicated from imbibing the wine, everyone in the assembly lost their reserve and began talking drivel.

The king signalled the attendants to lay a bed for Giti Afroz in her apartment. Then he and Giti Afroz occupied themselves with enjoying the moonlight. After revelling in the moonlight for some time, Giti Afroz took the king's leave and retired to her bedchamber. When she arrived there, she saw a canopy made of roses, and a layer of jasmine flowers spread on a golden bed, and she went to sit in it.

Meanwhile, Danishmand also took his leave and went home, and Farkhanda Shah returned to his palace. Malik Muhammad headed for Giti Afroz's bedchamber. Upon sight of him, Giti Afroz said: "Come my beloved, for I was sad and inconsolable without you." She held his hand and made him sit beside her. She spoke to him for a short while, then lay down to sleep.

Malik Muhammad was so overpowered by lust and inebriation that he became mindless of all considerations; and regardless of the consequences decided to take his pleasure of Giti Afroz. She started at his touch when he tried to have his way with her, and irritably said, "O mindless bull, I advised you many a time against this, and gave you countless injunctions, but what am I to do when you knowingly invite shame upon yourself?"

Immediately upon her speaking these words, Malik Muhammad rolled on the ground and turned into a bull. At a sign from her, the attendants put a silk rope around his neck, and tied him to a tree so that he would not trample the king's garden. Giti Afroz looked at the bull and smiled and said: "Hang the night-glowing ruby around his neck."

Malik Muhammad now repented, realizing that just a short while ago he lay beside his beloved, and that, had he not sought more, he would not have invited trouble upon himself. That he mistakenly believed Giti Afroz had shown him favour, and would not turn him into an animal. It is true that:

Infidel is the one who relies on a beloved's friendship
They are heartless, and instantly destroy whom they wish

He said to himself: "One must be mindful of the beloved's heartlessness; after throwing me into this calamity, she is sleeping comfortably, and without a care."

Had my heart not become besotted
It would have found peace and comfort

In short, all night long Malik Muhammad remained engrossed in these thoughts. At the time of the morning prayers, Farkhanda Shah emerged from his private chamber and sat on the throne, and Giti Afroz, too, rose from her bed. Yawning and stretching herself to dispel her inebriation from the previous night, she stood a while before the bull, then went and sat beside the king, and after drinking a few cups of wine that dispelled intoxication, took her leave of him.'

ELEVENTH TALE

Of Giti Afroz returning to her hills after taking King Farkhanda Shah's leave; And of the king having Malik Muhammad changed from the bull to human form, and sending him for news of Giti Afroz

Dana-Dil said: 'Hear O, Saman Rukh! At the time of Giti Afroz's departure, Farkhanda Shah placed many kinds of gifts as offerings before the princess, but she only picked up a few pearls to please the king, and after taking her leave, departed towards her hills.

The king was delivering encomiums of Giti Afroz and speaking of her excellent conduct and demeanour when he noticed the bull. He wondered where it had come from. Then he thought of Malik Muhammad, whom he had not seen since morning. Those present there said, "We do not know where he is. Perhaps he departed with Giti Afroz." The king said, "Had he departed with her, he would have taken our leave. Go and look for him at his uncle's house." Danishmand, who was present at the court, offered his salutations, and said, "I do not know his whereabouts either." Then Danishmand sighted the bull that stood there caparisoned with jewellery, and he deduced that Giti Afroz had turned Malik Muhammad into a bull. He rose and respectfully submitted before the king: "Your Honour, Malik Muhammad is standing before you in fine array."

The king asked: "Where is he?" Danishmand answered: "Right before you, Your Honour! Giti Afroz has turned him into a bull to help cart water to the palace." The king replied: "It is a marvel! Just yesterday, during our gathering Malik Muhammad was kissing her mouth, and now the poor man stands before us in this state."

Danishmand approached the bull and harshly scolded him, saying: "O wanton creature, you show not the least shame before anyone. I forbade you the pari's companionship many times, but you did not give it up. Now even if you were to die carrying water, I will not take pity on your situation." Danishmand said to his servants: "Take him away from here. Make a large waterskin for him to carry the water needed for sprinkling the royal household."

They led Malik Muhammad away and tied him up with the other bulls in the cowshed. The servants made him carry heavy waterskins all day long, and at night gave him chopped straw mixed with grain. He lost all hope living in the cowshed, with Danishmand showing him no mercy.

Six months passed in this manner, and after that Malik Muhammad's luck changed for the better. One day when Farkhanda Shah was inebriated with wine, he thought of Giti Afroz, and said to himself: "Whom can I send, who will bring me news of her? What should I do now that Malik Muhammad, who was most suitable for these errands, she has turned into a bull."

While he wondered about it, he sent for Danishmand, and said to him: "If you can change Malik Muhammad from an animal to human, you must do so without delay." He replied: "I no longer have any lincture left that could turn him into human form." The king said: "Prepare some more of it." He answered: "The herb that is the lincture's main ingredient is only found in Serendip. If it could be fetched from there, the lincture can be made ready."

The king summoned two fleet-footed messengers who travelled a hundred kos in a day, and assigned them the mission of fetching the herb from Serendip. The messengers asked Danishmand the name and particulars of the herb, and left at once. Traversing the six-month distance in one month, they arrived at the mountain in Serendip. After procuring the herb, they rushed back like the wind, and presented themselves before Farkhanda Shah. The king lauded and praised them and conferred on them rewards and robes of honour. Then he summoned Danishmand and gave him the herb.

Danishmand added several other ingredients and made a large enough quantity of lincture to suffice for a hundred doses for Malik Muhammad. The king sent for the bull and had it brought close to his throne. Danishmand looked at the bull, and said: "O wretch, you are being returned to human form by the kindness of His Honour, otherwise, as God is my witness, I would never have cured you as long as I lived. I give you the lincture on condition that you will never again profess love for Giti Afroz."

Although Malik Muhammad felt reassured to see the full jar of lincture, he nodded his head reluctantly and hesitantly, to please Danishmand. When Danishmand witnessed that he had repented, he mixed a little lincture in water and poured it down his throat. Immediately, Malik Muhammad rolled on the ground and regained his human form. He said a benediction for the king and then fell at his uncle's feet. Then Malik Muhammad went for a bath, changed, and returned before the king.

Farkhanda Shah said: "O Malik Muhammad, I have received no news of Giti Afroz since she left. I would that you find out how she is faring." Malik Muhammad himself wished to learn news of her. He immediately took his leave and headed to the hills. When he arrived there, he found the palace gate open, and boldly went inside. Giti Afroz, clad in a green dress, was sitting on an emerald throne, reciting this couplet:

Many a day has passed and I have not beheld my lover
Perhaps it means he does not love me with the same passion

Upon hearing this, Malik Muhammad recalled these verses by Khvaja Mir Dard:[18]

Although she acts annoyed, yet she loves me
She acknowledges not her love, yet she loves me
Do not lose your heart to such a beloved, O Dard!
The one who is both affectionate and a coquette

When she saw Malik Muhammad, Giti Afroz called out: "Come, my beloved! Where have you been all this time? I thought you got annoyed with me and gave up on my companionship."

He answered:

"This heart would sooner renounce the pleasures of both worlds
Than agree to turn away from servitude in your love

No beloved would have inflicted such suffering on her lover as you have made me suffer.

What does that indifferent coquette care what passed with me
Only my heart knows, or my God knows"

18. Dard: The classical Urdu poet Khvaja Mir Dard (1720–1785).

Upon hearing this, Giti Afroz's heart filled with pity and she embraced Malik Muhammad, and Rooh Afza served them with wine.'

TWELFTH TALE

Of the arrival of Giti Afroz's brother and his returning to Paristan taking along Giti Afroz and Malik Muhammad; Of Giti Afroz meeting her parents and busying herself in her brother's wedding preparations; And of Malik Muhammad becoming inconsolable at separation from her

Dana-Dil said to Saman Rukh: 'Hear, O Queen of the World, that Malik Muhammad and Giti Afroz were drunkenly exchanging words of love and affection when a commotion was heard in the sky. When Giti Afroz looked up she saw her brother's conveyance approaching. When it drew near, she rose in his honour and saluted him. She seated him on her throne beside her and for a long time enquired after everyone in the family and their health and well-being.

Seeing Malik Muhammad sitting near her, Giti Afroz's brother asked: "O Sister, is he the human whom you have befriended?" She replied: "Yes." Then he asked: "What is his name?" She replied: "Malik Muhammad the Faithful." He asked: "How has he been faithful to you?" She answered: "He has undergone such dreadful trials and hardships on my account that I have not the words to describe them. In fact, a number of times I even turned him into an animal, and yet he did not give up on my friendship."

Malik Muhammad was listening to the conversation with apprehension, wondering what might be its outcome. Seeing the colour drain from his face, Giti Afroz said to him with great affection and encouragement: "My beloved, you have business only with me. Do not feel the least uneasy." Malik Muhammad was buoyed up by her heartening words.

Giti Afroz's brother said: "O Sister, on the fifteenth day from today your older brother's nuptials will be held. I have told our parents that I shall be responsible for bringing you to Paristan. Lest you humiliate me by refusing to come along on some excuse, let me tell you this: I have sworn by God, and pledged in Suleiman's[19] name that if you

19. Suleiman: King Solomon.

refuse to accompany me, I will also not return home, and shall never show my face again to our parents."

Giti Afroz carefully considered before answering: "I swear on your head that I had no intention of returning to Paristan ever. But now that you have taken the responsibility and pledged to bring me along, your boastfulness will discredit you if I did not accompany you. I cannot help but go with you, provided I bring Malik Muhammad the Faithful with me, and nobody harms him there." Her brother answered: "Come as it pleases you. Nobody shall do anything against your wishes."

Giti Afroz left behind all her servants and masters of the household, and seated Malik Muhammad on the throne beside her and set out. In due time she entered the frontiers of her father's land. Upon hearing of her arrival, Unsar Shah sent a delegation of his nobles and viziers, along with his elder son to usher her before him.

After Giti Afroz reached Paristan, and presented herself before her father, he enquired for a long time about her welfare with kindness and indulgence. Then he asked: "Where is the human you have befriended?" Giti Afroz did not answer out of modesty; however, at a sign from her, Malik Muhammad came forward to throw himself at Unsar Shah's feet. The king raised his head with his hands and embraced him.'

Dana Dil said: 'O Queen, although outwardly Unsar Shah spoke to Malik Muhammad with an open countenance, he grieved inwardly. Malik Muhammad perceived that King Unsar Shah found his presence irksome, and there was no knowing if he would allow him to live.

All trouble that visits me on my beloved's account is bliss
It would be my signal honour even if she should kill me

Then he said:

What I had in my heart remained in it, we did not talk
There was no occasion even for a single meeting
We exchanged glances from afar
What was in my heart did not come to pass

From there, Giti Afroz took her lover to see her mother. She embraced her daughter the moment she saw her, and after giving her words of advice, said: "If your heart is set on this human, may the union be auspicious! We are not disinclined to give you our blessings. But your leaving home and setting up in a foreign land, while we long to see you, is not appropriate. It is our wish that you stay here now, and keep this human also with you. The one to whom you were engaged to be married keeps sending missives to enquire about the wedding day, and the whole world reproaches us. This is how you have brought us disrepute."

Giti Afroz replied: "I am not willing to get married. I am happy with this man's companionship. Do let me live here in peace for a few days if you can, otherwise I will leave and find some quarters where neither shall you receive news of me, nor will I hear what passes with you."

Her mother realized that she had become so besotted with her human companion that she wished to have nothing to do with another; that if she spoke further, Giti Afroz might leave. She told herself that her daughter had just arrived, and after some days she would begin to see reason; that it would not be advisable to nettle Giti Afroz. Her mother placated her, saw to her comfort, and arranged separate quarters for her residence.

Giti Afroz retired to the palace with Malik Muhammad, and said to him: "You know it for a fact that everyone here is thirsty for your blood. Beware! Do not do anything that humiliates me and causes you to lose your life." He answered: "I am not such an idiot that I will put my life at risk knowingly."

The day came to an end while they were conversing together. In the evening, Giti Afroz changed her clothes and was sitting with her lover making love prattle when some paris dressed in beautiful clothes sent by Unsar Shah arrived to attend upon them, and reverently saluted them.

Giti Afroz kept talking with Malik Muhammad for some time before she was overcome by sleep. Malik Muhammad said to himself: "I will surely not escape with my life at the hands of the Paristan folk. It is therefore prudent to fulfill my desire, so that there is no regret left in my heart." Thus decided, he wished to touch her, when she opened her eyes and said: "O fool, I have counselled you against it, and expressly forbidden you, but you are not afraid to risk your life. If you wish to remain whole, do not dare think of it for as long as we are here!" A dejected Malik Muhammad went to sleep.

Giti Afroz got up before sunrise, and when the morning hour sounded, she dressed and went before Unsar Shah to make her salutations and then got busy with her brother's wedding preparations.

With the king's permission his stewards had decorated the alleys and bazaars of the city so beautifully for the occasion that it was a sight to behold. For seven days Giti Afroz did not have time even to visit her lover. Malik Muhammad was inconsolable at separation from her, and longed for her, like a fish out of water longs for it.'

MASNAVI

How may I state what passed with him
He was left with no occupation but crying
One moment he threw dust on his head
Another moment he tore up his tunic
He made plaints like one wounded
He writhed like one slaughtered
He neither slept nor ate
Nor did he for a moment rest
If Qais[20] *had seen his state*
He would have found his own sorrows light to bear

THIRTEENTH TALE

Of Giti Afroz visiting Malik Muhammad and taking him along in her brother's wedding procession, and of her brother's nuptials taking place; Of Saman Rukh speaking, and Sheikh Sanaan signalling his second devotee to narrate what he had heard and witnessed

Dana Dil said: 'Hear, O Saman Rukh, that while in Paristan one day Malik Muhammad stepped out of the palace with a heavy heart. Arriving under Unsar Shah's palace, he saw Giti Afroz dressed in red vestments standing on the roof, forlorn and by herself. Malik Muhammad addressed this quatrain to her:

What is this ritual, of coming together to separate?
To rob one's heart and then be inconstant
O love! If love was not agreeable
Wherefore must one begin a friendship?

20. Qais: Popularly known as Majnun. A legendary lover and protagonist of the tale of Laila and Majnun.

She looked at him and recited:

I too yearn badly to be with you
But I have no power, am helpless
Do not imagine that I am happy without you
I hide my face from the world and shed copious tears

"Return to the palace and wait. God willing, I will, howsoever, find some way to be with you tonight." Malik Muhammad was somewhat consoled upon hearing this, and returned to his quarters, praying to God that it become dark soon.

In the evening, Giti Afroz flew into the palace on her throne as promised, and sat beside Malik Muhammad in bed. She beckoned to a pari who became their cupbearer and liberally plied them with wine. The lover and the beloved both became intoxicated, and for a long time uninhibitedly made love talk with each other, until they both fell asleep and lost all consciousness. They got up in the morning and washed their hands and faces. Giti Afroz said: "O Malik Muhammad, my brother's nuptials will be held today. If you desire to witness the sights of the wedding procession, you may come along with me." He answered: "Very well!"

Giti Afroz seated him beside her on her throne, and took him to the place where the wedding procession was to start.

Hear, O Queen, that the king's stewards had made a double-rowed passage in the bazaar for the wedding procession to pass, and gold cloth canopies extended from shops on both sides to provide shade. From early in the evening the whole bazaar was lit up so brightly, the moon's luminance was reduced to a yellow smudge.

When the first part of the night was over, at an auspicious hour the bridegroom was led with great fanfare on horseback to his father-in-law's doorsteps. The bride's relations greeted the procession and ushered them to the many residences where they were to be housed, and led the bridegroom into the female quarters, where the nuptials were held according to the bride's traditions and customs. The bride's relations housed the wedding procession for five days, and performed all the duties of hosting them in the finest traditions. The guests were looked after in every regard, and nothing was left to chance in their care and indulgence. In the end, the bride's father gave in dowry numerous gifts from many lands and countless appurtenances and accessories. Then he clasped his hands together humbly, and said: "Today, my honour and prestige has risen among my tribe." He gifted robes of honour to Unsar Shah's commanders and officers according to their station, and sent his daughter off with the wedding procession.

With joy and happiness Unsar Shah set out from there along with the wedding procession, and returned home. In his joy he spent the whole day giving alms. In the evening, after seeing off all the guests, he retired to his palace.

Accompanied by Malik Muhammad, Giti Afroz, too, headed for her palace, and the two of them sat on the bed and drank two cups of wine each. After Giti Afroz had become drunk and laughed merrily and talked uninhibitedly with him, Malik Muhammad said: "O inconstant beloved, I have long avowed my love for you, yet your heart shows no constancy. Will there ever be a time when you will take pity on my condition?"

How long will my humility hold before your pride?
There is a limit and end to everything

Giti Afroz was moved by what Malik Muhammad said, and replied: "O kindly friend, and O tender bliss of my soul, indeed you alone could have borne the terrible calamities you suffered on my account. Only my heart knows how indebted I am to your loyalty. But in this place the fulfillment of your wish is beyond the realm of possibility. Have patience for the few days that we are here; in the end you will attain your desire."

Malik Muhammad heaved a sigh, and said: "O breaker of promises, earlier too you made many such promises, but never fulfilled them. I firmly believe that you distract me with false hope. Even now, I do not think it is in your heart to ever grant me my wish. Perhaps:

You will wish to meet me only then, if ever
When a sliver of breath, if any, remains in me"

Giti Afroz made no answer but poured him a brimful cup of wine, with her own hands to comfort him, and drank a little herself. They spoke happily to each other for some time and then Giti Afroz fell asleep.

Malik Muhammad said to himself: "She will never give me her consent on her own. Come what may I must now fulfill my desire!" When Giti Afroz fell into a deep sleep, he tried to couple with her, but she awoke with a start the moment he touched her, and smilingly said: "My love, what is this madness that has come over you? I consider you the very flavour of my life and you are bent upon scattering away your life and earning me ignominy! In the past days too, you have committed unseemly actions, but I did not punish you for your trespasses because if anyone learned about them, your life will become forfeit in this foreign land. The time for the fulfilment of my promise approaches. Heed my advice and show some fortitude for a few days more, or I swear by God that you will pine even to glimpse me."

In reply, Malik Muhammad only heaved a sigh and recited this couplet:

> *"A thousand times I dove in vain, to find pearls for my ornament*
> *Why blame the sea, when my fortune is to blame?"*

. . .

When the narration reached this juncture, Saman Rukh turned in bed and said: 'O youth, Dana-Dil! Pray tell whether that poor fellow who suffered such troubles and calamities attained his desire, or died with his desires unfulfilled?'

Sheikh Sanaan smiled, and said: 'It will be revealed upon further narration.' Azar Shah fell at Sheikh Sanaan's feet in gratitude at Saman Rukh's articulated speech, and expressed his gratefulness to Dana Dil as well, saying: 'I know it is your auspicious narration that has rekindled speech in Saman Rukh, for it is well-nigh impossible for qissas and tales of magic to restore someone's faculties.'

Dana Dil answered: 'Truth be told, your first wife had cast such a powerful spell on her that even if a hundred thousand qissas were narrated to her, it would have had no effect. It is all the doing of our master, whose tending to her with all his heart has brought about this improvement.'

They were conversing together thus when Saman Rukh became restive and said: 'O Dana Dil, keep this conversation for another time! Now give me the account of Giti Afroz and Malik Muhammad, as my heart is distressed on account of that poor lover.'

When Sheikh Sanaan noticed that Saman Rukh yearned to hear Malik Muhammad's tale, he beckoned to his other disciple, Roshan Zameer, and asked him to narrate what he had seen and heard.

FOURTEENTH TALE

The tale told by Roshan Zameer; Of his narrating before Saman Rukh the account of his departure for Egypt with a caravan; Of a huge snake encircling the caravan along the way, of all members of the caravan safely escaping the monster and Roshan Zameer alone remaining captive

It is said that when Roshan Zameer received sanction from his master, he addressed Saman Rukh and said: 'O Queen, now lend me your ears and pay heed, and hear that once in my youth I was travelling to Egypt with a caravan. One day the caravan set up camp under a hill. As was the custom, all day long the people remained busy in cooking and making food. At night everyone lay in their beds.

In the middle of the night, I felt my stomach churning. I got up and, carrying the water ewer in my hand, headed out of the caravan to void my bowels. As I came out, I saw a high wall surrounding the caravan. I wondered how it had materialised, since it was not there when we set up camp. When I touched it, its surface felt soft and warm. I explored its surface for some time, and realized that it was a huge snake which had encircled the caravan. I felt certain that all of us would be killed by the monster, and God had sent us on this path to provide him a day's sustenance.

I was lost in these thoughts when suddenly there was an uproar in the caravan upon the sighting of the snake, and everyone began crying. One said: "Alas, my children will become destitute!" Another said: "O Friends, the pity is not that we will die, but that the news of our death will not reach our homes." Someone else said: "Had we known, we would not have left our family behind to go with this caravan." Yet another said: "Had we known that it was the snake's domicile, we would not have camped here at night." Another proclaimed: "A thousand pities that we will die in a place where neither will we hear from our loved ones, nor will they ever learn of our fate." Another fellow said: "It was an evil hour when we set out on the journey, to be engulfed by untimely death."

I said to them: "Friends, as the proverb goes, 'To the dead the world is dead.' Why lament over the death of our children when we ourselves will not be alive? If all of us are to be killed by the monster, then so be it. It is proverbial that many condemned to die together makes for a festive occasion. Do not lament, for what good has ever come from making lamentations?"

We continued in this vein until dawn broke, and in the morning light we beheld the giant snake encircling the caravan, holding his tail in his mouth. Every now and then he made a loud hissing sound which travelled for many kos. He showed no inclination to attack, but neither gave us way. Everyone was desperate to find a solution, and while the monster lay unmoving as before, they prayed to God that they escape any harm from it.

Of a sudden it occurred to me that I should shoot arrows at the snake. If he were killed it would save thousands of lives of God's creatures, for surely he meant us harm. I nocked an arrow, and drawing the bowstring to my ear, targeted his head, so that the arrow would shoot through it. Upon seeing this, the snake moved his head away by a distance of two arrows' flight. As I tried to break free from his cordon at the opportunity, he caught his tail in his mouth as before. In short, I drew the bowstring five times, but each time the snake moved his head away, and closed the cordon afterwards.

Then I said to myself: The snake has not yet harmed anyone, but if I shoot arrows at him, he will forthwith swallow everyone in the caravan. I went before the head of the caravan and said: "The snake has not blocked our path without reason, but there is no knowing what he wants. If he had wished to kill us, by now none of us would be alive. It occurs to me that all the old and wise people in the caravan must hold council together, and we should follow whatever is decided as the best solution."

The leader of the caravan summoned all the old and wise men, and said: "There must be some reason for the monster to have blocked our path." They were yet to answer him when an old man from among them spoke: "Hear, O friends! If the snake had any intention of killing us, he would not have allowed us to live until now. He has some other objective in his heart, but is unable to state it, as he cannot speak. If someone were to approach him and ask what his intention is, he would reply with a sign." At this, everyone looked towards me, and said: "None but Roshan Zameer has the courage to approach the snake."

Thus, I sought God's refuge and headed towards the monster, and upon approaching his head, said: "O Speechless Creature, why are you intent upon making so many of God's creatures suffer? Everyone here is travelling on their business, but you bar their way and do not let them proceed onwards. If there is a reason why you do so, share it with me so that I can find a resolution." Upon these words the snake raised his head to the height of three lances.

I returned to the leader of the caravan and reported on how the snake had acted.

The old man who had suggested that I communicate with the snake, said: "Have no fear. The snake has agreed to give way. Follow me, and I will lead you out of the cordon." Everyone in the caravan gathered their sacks and bundles and followed him. But none had the courage to go past the snake. Then the old man rode out bravely past the snake. Seeing this, the others also slowly began to leave. But when it was my turn, the snake again closed the cordon by holding his tail in his mouth.

I told myself that the snake was cross with me because I had drawn the arrow to kill him. When I stepped back, the snake gave way to the others, and they began to file out. After a while I again tried to leave with a group of people, and the snake once again barred my way, letting the others pass after I had retreated a few steps. The few others who remained within the cordon also made their exit, and presently I alone was left inside. I reasoned with myself that if the snake wanted to kill people, he would not have let the others pass. He must have some business with me, or else he would have accosted others, too.

Then the leader of the caravan called out: "O Roshan Zameer, you know well that we have no power over the snake. We are powerless before him and depart now, leaving you in God's care. If you have some days of life remaining, you should have no fear of the snake; there is no contesting the decree of fate, otherwise."

I answered: "My good fellow, what you say is true. If this snake is the instrument of my death, nobody can save me from him, but it is against all considerations of humanity that all of you go away, leaving me alone at his mercy. God alone knows whether my life is over, or, like in the case of the seventy men who expelled one from a temple and were all killed, it is your death which is ordained, and I am to live like the one expelled." The leader of the caravan said: "O Roshan Zameer, narrate in detail what passed with those seventy men and why they expelled one from among them, and how they died?"'

FIFTEENTH TALE

Of Roshan Zameer narrating the tale of the seventy men before the leader of the caravan, and the latter making a pact with Roshan Zameer to await his return for eight days

Roshan Zameer said to Saman Rukh: 'I told the leader of the caravan thus: It is said that a long time ago seventy men from a city set out to travel in a group. They had reached a wilderness when it started to rain. The forest had no shelter where they could take refuge and keep themselves dry. They espied a dome, little more than a kos away, and all of them rushed towards it and stood inside. After they had taken refuge, a billowing cloud hid the sky, and the whole land darkened. The earth shook from the sound of thunder; lightning flashed menacingly above them, threatening to strike any moment; and the ensuing downpour was so heavy the whole land became flooded within a short time.

So heavily did the rain fall
It came near to drowning the trees
It thundered so mightily
That the earth and the heavens shook
How to describe the bolt of lightning
In the blink of an eye it flashed a hundred times

Upon noticing this they said amongst each other: That lightning reaching continuously for the dome is not without cause. One may say that there is always lightning when it rains, and it would be true, but it occurs infrequently in different places over a wide area; it does not flash continuously above one place. One of them said: "I reckon that one of us is destined to die, and lightning converges on us every instant to strike him, but holds back on account of the others inside. Eventually, it will strike, and for no reason others will die for the sake of one person. I suggest all of us go individually and touch the date palm tree across from the entrance to the right. The one destined to die will be struck and the rest of us will be spared." Everyone liked the suggestion and they went in their turn and returned after touching the date palm tree, until sixty-nine people had gone and returned, and only one man remained. The lightning flashed ever closer with every passing moment, and everyone was convinced that it sought that man for its mark. They insisted that he too must go and touch the tree. He realized that each of his companions had already gone and touched the tree, and if one of them were destined to die, he would have been felled by lightning; that, indeed, he was the one fated to die from it.

He pleaded before them, and humbly said: "My friends, I too know in my heart that every instant the lightning reaches down for me. But if you would allow me to sit here in a corner, my life will be saved because of you." They answered: "O Fool, do you not regard that the dome barely escapes being struck by lightning? If we were to let you remain here, all of us will die untimely deaths because of you."

In short, much though he cried and made plaints, they showed him no mercy, and forcibly grabbed him by the arm and pushed him out. Reconciled to his death, he had taken only a few steps when lightning flashed with a deafening thunder and struck the dome. All his companions were killed, and he alone reached home in safety. Had they taken pity at his pleading, all of them would have survived, and he would have been forever indebted to them. But why indeed should they have shown him pity, when they were fated to die thus?

In like manner you callously depart, leaving me alone to face the monster, believing the snake will kill me, when the end is known only to God. Who knows if I will die, or survive like that man, while you are killed. Even though you are unsure if I will live, it is proverbial that hope only departs with the last breath. I have faith in God that I will remain safe from this monster.

What I said made no impression on the leader of the caravan. But he made a pledge and said: "O Roshan Zameer, two kos from here lies a garden, where we will await your return for eight days. If you are released from the power of the snake during that time, and return, you will find us there. On the ninth day, we will be obliged to continue on our journey." I said to them: "Very well, but do leave behind a bowl of water that may be of sustenance to me." They left me a bowl of water and departed.'

SIXTEENTH TALE

Of the snake taking Roshan Zameer to his abode; Of Roshan Zameer killing the scorpion that was the snake's mortal enemy, and meeting a pious old man; And of the snake conducting Roshan Zameer back to the caravan

Saman Rukh said: 'O youth, Roshan Zameer, narrate how you escaped the monster's clutches, and what the reason was for his taking you captive.' Sheikh Sanaan answered: 'It will all be duly revealed in the narration.'

Azar Shah again expressed his boundless gratitude to Sheikh Sanaan.

Roshan Zameer said: 'O Queen, after the caravan had departed and was lost to sight, the snake, sitting curled up until now, took out his tail from his mouth and stretched to the length of three and a half kos, and raised his head to look in the direction the caravan had taken. Terrified for my life, I found it a good opportunity to make my escape. But the snake coiled his tail around me and pulled me towards him, and made a sign to climb onto his back. When I did not climb up from fear, he caught me in his mouth and pulled me onto his back, and headed to the right. As his back was very slippery, I slid down from it. He then pulled me up and put me on his neck. There was a cavity in his neck in which I put my hand and took a firm grip. Helpless as I was, I resigned myself to my fate, and wherever the snake might take me. When he noticed that I was sitting securely with a good grip, he picked up speed.

After some time, he arrived at a large cave at the foot of a hill where he set me down, and beckoned me to go inside. I recited "In the Name of God!" and went into the cave but saw nothing inside. When I came out, I saw the snake making a sign to me to go back inside. I reckoned that there must be some beast inside the cave more powerful than the snake, fear of whom prevented him from entering. Once again, I went into the cave and saw nothing. I came out of the cave and said to the beast: "I went in and looked all around but saw nothing." Upon hearing this he let out a powerful roar that shook the ground, as if an earthquake had struck. I reckoned that he was angry because I had come out empty-handed from the cave, and it was just a matter of time before the creature swallowed me. Seeing my face drain of blood, he made a sign as if to say that I should have no worries; I was not in danger.

Some time after the snake roared, a scorpion that was about a cubit in length came out of that cave. At the sight of him, the snake, despite his great size, retreated hastily in terror. When he had gone farther than a kos, he rose and made a sign to me, saying: "This scorpion is my mortal enemy. Kill him if you can, or else I will kill you." I nocked an arrow and barred the scorpion's path. It now advanced on me. I drew the bowstring to my ear and shot the arrow, which cut him in two, killing him instantly. When I tried to collect my arrow, I marvelled upon discovering that the scorpion's poison had burnt it to ashes.

The snake rushed towards me jubilantly, and prostrated his head at my feet. Those were the times when if a person showed kindness even to a beast, it felt indebted to him. In present times, even if one were to give one's life for someone, he would not be grateful in the least. In short, that snake put me on his neck and took me inside the cave. After a time, we arrived in a place where it was so dark that a person's hand could not find its pair. The snake went onwards, and presently we arrived at a beautiful house more luminous than sunlight itself, where night-glowing rubies, each worth the price of a kingdom, were piled up in heaps. It was the light from these jewels which illuminated the house.

The snake made a sign to me to pick up as many of those jewels as I could carry. I said to myself: If I were to take these rubies, the snake will deem it my compensation. It would be better to have helped this creature without recompense, in God's name, saving his life from his mortal enemy. Thus decided, I said to him: "I do not desire them. If your purpose has been fulfilled, pray take me out of here, so that I may depart on my business." He made a sign that until I had picked up some jewels, he would not let me go. Helpless, I picked up two jewels and tied them around my arm.

The snake put me on his neck and brought me out, where I found a green-clad old man with a flowing white beard holding a staff. Upon seeing the venerable old man, I offered him salutations. He returned them, and said: "O Roshan Zameer, that scorpion was the snake's enemy, and tormented him daily. You arrived at an auspicious moment to kill him. May God recompense you for this kindness."

Surprised, I said to him: "O Venerable Sir, how did you learn my name, as even your face is unfamiliar to me?" He answered: "By the grace of God!" Then he said: "The scorpion has a female, who killed the snake's female a long time ago. At present she is nursing her eggs and will leave them after six months. Therefore, you must return then. Make sure that you do so without fail; and be warned, that if you do not come back, this snake will find and kill you, wherever you might be. This snake has two young ones, whom he gave unto my care for fear of the scorpion. I have hidden them in a secret place and will show them to you upon your return. The snake daily begged me to kill the scorpion but I said that the scorpion is not fated to die at my hands; that destiny will bring a youth named Roshan Zameer here, and the scorpion will be slain by him. Accordingly, you killed the male scorpion today. The scorpion's female has some more days of life allotted to her. You will kill her too, and perform other feats besides, as you are destined to."

Thus speaking, he said: "I would that you join me in eating whatever food I have to offer at my humble abode, and stay the night." I answered: "Although it is a sin for a follower of the True Faith to refuse an invitation, you must be aware that everyone in the caravan awaits me in that garden. I therefore cannot stay. Pray do let me know your kind name."

Upon hearing this, the old man said: "O Roshan Zameer, you may now depart. I will give you my name when you return. Do not forget your word, and make sure to return."

The snake waited while I conversed with the old man. After I took my leave, he put me on his neck as before and headed towards the caravan.

After some time, I saw the caravan's tents in the distance, the sight of which gladdened my heart. When I approached closer, the people in the caravan panicked at the sight of the snake and said amongst each other: "The snake has come again to surround us! Had we known this might happen, we would not have waited here for Roshan Zameer." I called out to them, and said: "O Friends, have not the least anxiety in your heart. He will not harm anyone." After some distance, the snake set me down and turned and left for his home.

I entered the caravan and went to the caravan leader's tent. People were surprised to see me return, and said: "O Friend, what magic did you perform that not only did you escape whole from that maneater's clutches, he even brought you here on his back!" I narrated all that had passed from beginning to end. Everyone in the caravan lauded and praised me for my courage. The caravan leader said: "O Roshan Zameer, may God recompense you with blessings! Your manliness is akin to the valour and loyalty shown by Zarivand." I asked: "O kind friend, do give me Zarivand's details, and tell me about his deeds of valour and loyalty."'

SEVENTEENTH TALE

Of the caravan leader narrating Zarivand's tale to Roshan Zameer; Of Zarivand's arrival in Rum after his parents' deaths; Of the King of Rum taking umbrage at his daughter's speech and giving her away to Zarivand, and of his going away with the princess

Roshan Zameer said: 'O Queen, the caravan leader said to me: O youth, it has come down from narrators that there lived in Hamadan a very wealthy man who lacked for nothing. He bided his time in happiness, and his days passed in joy and merriment without the least apprehension or fear. He had a son, Zarivand of name. Ever since he had attained consciousness, he had been so taken with the pursuits of archery, marksmanship, spearmanship, and swordsmanship, that he showed no disposition for anything besides. Finally, he attained such command over these arts that if he shot his arrow even at an ant in the moonlight, his mark never faltered. He could cut an adamantine mortar in two with a clean blow from his sword and none would see the cut.

After many years his parents departed from the mortal world to the future state, that is to say, they passed away, for such is the fate apportioned to all of us.

O Friends, it is only a matter of when, one must
Depart from the abode of existence without fail

After the death of his parents, Zarivand showed no forethought, and scattered away their wealth, not understanding that:

The garden of life is only pleasant
When one has gold like the flower does pollen

Those who had lavished praise and plaudits at his every word when he was rich, turned their backs on him when they found him in penury. Neither a friend nor neighbour showed him any kindness. Indeed, they taunted him, saying: "A girl is preferable over an unworthy son. He wasted his life being cosseted and pampered by his parents, and being made much of. Had he learned something useful he would not have come to this end." Zarivand smarted inwardly at these comments, and would say to himself: It is indeed true what someone has said:

Indigence robs all things of their shine
Even calls into question a man's worth

He realized that continuing to live there would only prolong his humiliation. It is proverbial that in one's own land one is reduced to thieving to keep up appearances, but in a foreign land one may make a living even as a beggar, without shame. He decided that he would seek his fortune abroad, and put his trust in Providence. Thus resolved in his heart, he sold off the remaining belongings in his house to provide for the journey, and headed for the land of Rum astride his horse.

Traversing the stages of the journey he arrived before the King of Rum as he was setting out with his entourage. Noticing that he was a foreigner, the king asked him: "O young man, what is your name? Whence have you come, and what brings you here?"

He made an obeisance and answered: "I am from Hamadan, and my name is Zarivand. Putting store in your beneficent indulgence, I set out from Hamadan for your court, and it is my desire to remain in Your Honour's service for the rest of my life. Your Honour may entrust me with the most challenging of tasks." The king asked: "What will you take for wages?" He answered: "I will take a thousand gold pieces, for I cannot subsist on less."

The king made no answer at that time but said to himself: The man is given to making tall claims. I will keep him for a month on the wages he has demanded; if he proves himself in the office, well and good, otherwise I will expel him from service.

At night, in the palace's female quarters, the king mentioned the arrival of the youth and his demand to be paid a thousand gold pieces. The queen had not yet spoken when the princess spoke up, saying: "One who demands such a large sum for his services must indeed be brave. It would be proper to accept him into your service." The princess's comments rankled in the king's heart, and, seething inwardly, he replied: "O shameless girl, what business do you have with these matters? Do you wish his companionship that you entreat on his behalf? If I were to take him into my service now, the whole world will say that the young man was hired because the princess showed preference for him. Even in faraway lands the mention of my name will invite odium."

The princess answered: "God forbid that I should nurse such thoughts in my heart, being the daughter of an august king like yourself. To date no strange man has even glimpsed my shadow, nor have I seen the face of a strange man. I will not protest even if it should please you to give me away to a beggar."

The princess's words only displeased the king further, and he said harshly to her: "I give you to the same young man from Hamadan." She answered, "Very well! If you wish to expel me with such humiliation, so be it. My fortune shall accompany me where I go. I pray that God may never separate me from his mercy."

The king signalled to a eunuch to take her hand and put it in the hand of the young man from Hamadan, and tell him that the king had conferred her upon him.

The princess's eyes filled with tears. She looked at her father, and said: "O Father, you have treated me ill; let us now see what God has in store for me." The queen wished to say something to intercede for her daughter, but the king looked at her with knitted brow and said: "Hear O Wretch! If you utter a word in this matter, I will have you as well thrown out of the city this very instant." Then he turned an angry glance at the eunuch, who led the princess away by her arm and handed her to the young man saying unto him: "Take her! God has shown you favour in the king conferring his daughter on you. Give thanks to God and leave the city without loss of time."

Bewildered by the turn of events, both Zarivand and the princess left the city, and set out together in one direction.'

EIGHTEENTH TALE

Of Zarivand killing a lion and two elephants along the way; Of his arrival in Khurshidabad and entering into the service of its king; And of his marrying the princess of Rum

Upon hearing this account, Saman Rukh said: 'O Roshan Zameer, was the King of Rum possessed by madness that he thus shamefully expelled his innocent daughter? He feared inviting gossip for his daughter admiring the youth from Hamadan, but did not feel any shame leading his daughter by her arm and himself conferring her upon the same youth? God's curse upon such reasoning! If she was blameworthy, he should have killed her, but not given her away to the youth from Hamadan.'

Roshan Zameer answered: 'O Queen, did you ever hear the Hindustani proverb which says that when something is preordained, one's thoughts align to bring it about? Who can avert the decree of fate? When something must materialise in a particular fashion, one's mind accordingly wills it. It was fated for the princess to leave thus with Zarivand. The actions of the king who did not heed any considerations, provided the circumstances.

'Hear O Saman Rukh, the two of them left Rum and on the fourth day they came upon a forked path where they stood a while wondering where the two paths led. A large stone lay there which had an inscription that read:

> *The path that goes left is full of perils and hardships, and the path that goes right is safe and free of all danger. The one who takes the path that goes left will never arrive at his destination. It is incumbent on the traveller to pay heed to this injunction, and take the path that goes right so that he may reach his destination without encountering any hazard.*

Upon reading the inscription, Zarivand looked at the princess and said to her: "O damsel, I have repeatedly asked your name of you, but you make no answer. What is the reason for this? And which path do you suggest we take: the one that goes rightwards or leftwards?"

The princess's eyes welled up with tears as she answered: "O youth, what purpose will it serve to give my name? The evil that I was to see, and the ignominy that was my fate, have come before me. If you must insist on knowing my name, then know that my parents gave this inauspicious creature the name of Mubark-ul-Nisa,[21] but the inverse came to pass. You may give me any name you please. And why do you ask of me whether to take the leftwards or the rightwards path? Take a measure of your valour and bravery and if you find the courage in you, take the path that goes left; otherwise take the path that goes right. Regardless of your choice, I will follow you."

Upon hearing her reply Zarivand turned his thoughts to God, then set out on the path that went leftwards. For three days the two of them continued on the path, and encountered no mischance. On the fourth day they arrived in a wilderness where neither any creature of earth nor air could be seen. They looked in all directions but not even the sign of a tree was visible to the farthest reach of their vision. Winds hotter than the simoom engulfed them from all sides.

The princess asked: "O youth, what is this dreadful place where one cannot even see a bird or beast?"

While they were having this conversation, they beheld a great lion coming towards them. Seeing him advance upon them, Zarivand asked; "O Mubarak-ul-Nisa, what is your counsel?" She replied:

> *"A man holding the bow and arrow in his hands*
> *Does not fear the lion or the rutting elephant*

21. Mubark-ul-Nisa: A name that means 'Auspicious among women'.

It is clear that he is headed here to kill us. He will make short work of us if you falter." Meanwhile, the lion drew near, growling at them. Zarivand drew the bowstring to his ear and shot an arrow at the lion's head, which sank to the notch into the lion's skull. With a mighty roar the lion fell down dead. Zarivand beheaded the lion with his sword, severed his feet, and kept his claws for himself. Then he went forth.

Conversing together, they went onwards for seven days without encountering any threat or danger. On the eighth day they reached another wilderness more terrible than the first in which they had encountered the lion. The princess said: "O youth, beware, for danger lurks in this wilderness too."

She had not finished speaking when they saw two rutting elephants advancing on them from the right. Zarivand was not the least afraid and, drawing the bow, first blinded them from afar, then riddled them with arrows. Every arrow sank to the notch into their bodies. Finally, the two elephants turned back and ran with what life remained in them, and Zarivand pursued them on horseback. After running for the distance of a kos, both injured elephants collapsed. Drawing his sword, Zarivand severed their trunks and killed them.

Mubarak-ul-Nisa greatly admired Zarivand's bravery and skill with the bow. The elephants had a mark the size of a human palm on their foreheads. Noticing it, Mubarak-ul-Nisa said to Zarivand: "O youth, such marks are not seen on elephants' foreheads. Do cut them open to see what lies underneath."

Zarivand cut open the elephants' foreheads with a knife and found, embedded in each elephant's forehead, a luminous pearl whose glow rivalled the sun's brightness. He and the princess offered gratitude to God for finding the pearls, and continued on their journey.

After many days they arrived in the city called Khurshidabad. After lodging themselves at an inn, where he left the princess, Zarivand headed for the bazaar, asking a man there: "Who is the king of this land?" He answered: "The name of the king is Khurshid-Chehar and it was he who founded this city."

Meanwhile the vizier's entourage went past in great estate. Zarivand asked the man: "Who is he?" The man answered: "That is King Khurshid-Chehar's vizier, on his way to the court." Zarivand went before the vizier and made salutations. Seeing a stranger before him, the vizier asked:

"Who are you, O youth, and whence have you come?" He answered: "I am from Hamadan but I have come here from Rum." The vizier asked: "How did you arrive in safety on that path?" He replied: "I did so by the grace of God."

The vizier was perplexed and asked him: "Did you meet any misadventures along the way?" Zarivand replied: "Along the way I met a lion and two elephants. By the grace of God, I killed all three of those beasts." The vizier said: "O youth, why tell such blatant lies? Those beasts were not such easy prey as could be overcome by ordinary mortals. Numerous times the king dispatched his army to kill them and it always failed in the mission. Why should I believe that you killed them? If your claim is true, show me some proof." Zarivand answered: "Each elephant had a pearl embedded in its forehead. Those pearls and the lion's feet are kept at my lodging." The vizier said: "I will believe you if you were to produce them before me."

Zarivand forthwith went to the inn, and fetched the giant pearls and the lion's feet and put them before the vizier.

Seeing the pearls and the lion's feet, the vizier said: "Bravo, young man! By God's grace it was only given to you to accomplish this feat. For a long time, the lion and the elephants obstructed this path, and from their terror all travel along it had ceased."

Then the vizier took Zarivand along to the emperor's court. Zarivand saluted the king reverently. The king asked the vizier: "Who is this man?" The vizier answered: "He is from Hamadan, but he has come from Rum. On his way he killed the lion and the two elephants at whose hands no traveller journeying on the road heretofore survived, and extracted these pearls from the elephants' foreheads." He then placed the two pearls and the lion's feet before the king.

The king conferred those objects on Zarivand, and asked: "O youth, did you have any companion on the journey?" He answered: "My only companion was the daughter of the King of Rum. There was no other." The king asked: "What is the princess's business with you?" Zarivand narrated to him all that had passed from beginning to the end.

Upon hearing his account, King Khurshid-Chehar reviled the King of Rum's reasoning, and said to Zarivand: "From this day you should enter my companionship." He replied: "It is also my wish to spend the rest of my life in your service." The king asked: "What wages would you like to receive?" Zarivand answered: "I will take a thousand gold pieces." The king accepted it and admitted him into his service at a monthly salary of a thousand gold pieces.

Zarivand then said to the king: "To date I have not touched the Princess of Rum. I considered it a sin to do so until I had married her." As per the august king's orders, the court officials arranged for the princess to be married to Zarivand according to the religious law.

The king's favours on Zarivand continuously increased from one day to another on account of the excellence of his service.'

NINETEENTH TALE

Of a son being born to Zarivand and of Khurshid-Chehar setting out for chase and of Zarivand killing a lion

Roshan Zameer said to Saman Rukh thus: 'The leader of the caravan narrated that one day the king said: "O Zarivand, tell the princess of Rum to enter into the service of the Queen of the World."[22] He answered: "Very well." But when he went home and communicated the king's wishes to the princess, she refused, and said: "There is no call for me to enter into anyone's service." Zarivand tried to reason with her, but to no avail; she remained adamant in her refusal. The next day Zarivand communicated to the king the princess's refusal to enter into the queen's service. Upon hearing this the king was convinced that Zarivand's wife was indeed a king's daughter.

It so happened one day that the Queen of the World herself honoured the princess with a visit to her house. The princess received her with royal decorum, seated her on the throne with great honour, and remained in attendance on her throughout her visit. Charmed by her excellent social graces, at night the queen praised her highly before the king.

The following day the king said to Zarivand: "O Zarivand, you are free to do as you please during the daytime, but at night I would that you guard the royal bedchamber." Thus, Zarivand remained present in the king's service night and day.

After many days a boy was born to Zarivand. Upon hearing the news Khurshid-Chehar showed him many favours. In short, Zarivand

22. Queen of the World: An honorific. Refers alternately to King Khurshid-Chehar's wife and Saman Rukh in the story.

so pleased the king with his devotion that he took him along wherever he went.

One day Khurshid-Chehar set out for a hunt. In the forest he chased a deer for a few kos and was separated from his entourage. Zarivand, however, remained by his side. The king lost sight of the deer, and a lion emerged from the woods on their left. The king hesitated a little upon sighting the lion. Zarivand said: "O Lord of the Land, should you command, I shall forthwith behead this monster." The king said: "Do so without delay! Kill the monster before it can do any harm." Upon receiving his master's order, Zarivand challenged the lion who roared and leapt at him. Zarivand quickly drew his sword from the scabbard, advanced, and dealt the lion a powerful blow which beheaded him.

The king was very pleased to see Zarivand's courage, and said: 'O youth, bravo and well done!' Then they returned to their camp.

Upon returning to his palace, the king showed Zarivand even greater favour by conferring on him a seven-piece robe of honour with headgear surmounted with a gold ornament, a pearl necklace, a bejewelled armour for his mount and an elephant and horse; and with every passing day he raised him in honour.

Zarivand attended on King Khurshid-Chehar night and day, but despite the king's continued favour, Zarivand considered serving the king alike to feeding a snake, and did not let pride in his valour make him become conceited.'

TWENTIETH TALE

Of a woman's cry reaching King Khurshid-Chehar's ear; Of the king sending Zarivand to discover its source and following him clandestinely; Of Zarivand arriving at a dome and finding the old woman who made the cry; Of Zarivand preparing himself to kill his son to save the king's life, and of the king appointing Zarivand his vizier

Roshan Zameer said: 'Hear, O Queen of the Heavens![23] The leader of the caravan thus narrated: During the rainy season, one day King Khurshid-Chehar was resting in his palace as usual, when a dust storm began to blow, and the violence of the wind disturbed his sleep. After some time, when the dust storm had subsided and the air cleared, the

23. Queen of the Heavens: An honorific used for Saman Rukh.

king heard a woman sighing and crying: "I depart! Is there such a person who could make me stay?"

From his bed the king heard the woman make this lament a few times. He went to the roof to find the source of the voice. When he came out, he saw Zarivand standing guard at the back of the palace, armed with a bow and arrow. It was raining and it was so dark from the rain that a person's hand could not find its pair. Beholding the silhouette of the king, Zarivand drew his bow and asked: "Who stands at the royal bedchamber in the middle of the night?" Khursheed-Chehr perversely stayed quiet. When Zarivand did not receive an answer, he was convinced that it was a thief. As he pulled the bowstring to his ear to shoot, King Khurshid-Chehar spoke up and said: "Hold your hand, Zarivand! It is I, Khurshid-Chehar. I heard a woman sighing and crying and came out to investigate. Did you also hear her plaints?"

Zarivand answered: "My master, it's been eight days that I have heard the same cry from the middle of the night until dawn. God alone knows what is this mystery, and who it is who makes the cry. I stand at my post and dare not leave it to investigate the matter without express orders from you. If you were to order me so, I will investigate and find the truth."

The king answered: "Indeed, find out all the details of who it is who makes the plaint and what is behind it."

Zarivand forthwith set out in the direction from which the voice came. Khurshid-Chehar took a short sword, climbed down from the palace and stealthily followed Zarivand at a distance so that he would not learn of his presence. Zarivand came out of the city's fortifications and discovered that the source of the voice was inside a dome. He went towards it and entered the dome, while the king hid outside.

Upon entering, Zarivand saw an old woman sharpening a knife. Every now and then she sighed and cried out: "I depart! Is there such a person who could make me stay?" A lamp which had a little oil left flickered beside her. Seeing Zarivand, the old woman asked: "Who are you? And what brings you to my house at this hour?" He said: "I am a fellow human, and have come to enquire about your well-being. Why do you sigh continuously and to what purpose, and to where do you depart?"

She replied: "O human, I am King Khurshid-Chehar's life, and I now depart as he stands at death's door. I called out for the last many days, so that someone may show mercy on him. There is oil in this lamp to last the night. The king will remain alive until then. The lamp will be extinguished by the time of the morning prayers, and with it the king's life will leave his body."

Zarivand asked: "O wretch, is there nothing that can forestall it?"

She answered: "There is a man named Zarivand Hamadani in the king's employ. If he were to cut his son's throat with this knife, and bathe me with the infant's blood, the king will live. Besides that, there is no remedy."

The king was observing the scene through a hole from without the dome, and heard the whole exchange. Zarivand was stunned at the old woman's words. He considered that if he favoured his son's life over the king's, his master would lose his life; and if he saved the king's life his son would die. He reflected on it a while, and finally his duty to the king prevailed, and he reckoned that should he live, he could always have another son, but he would never find another master like the king. That it was for this day that Khurshid-Chehar paid him a thousand gold pieces and treated him with such honour.

Having resolved on this in his heart, he said to the old woman: "Wait a little while, and I will return shortly." Then he came out of the dome and headed back to the city.

MASNAVI

He came out and hastily stepped homewards
With the king stealthily following
So rent with anguish was Zarivand's heart
That his senses were entirely consumed
Upon arriving home, when he looked
He found his beloved asleep in bed
The lamp was extinguished, but her bright face
Had lit up the whole room like a lamp
He stood respectfully beside her
As he did not wish to awaken her
Standing there, he cried and tears issued from his eyes, rivulet-like
They fell on her face and she awoke
And said to him: 'O my faithful lover,
Tell me truthfully, what is the matter?
Give me the details of what has come to pass
For your crying like this wrenches my poor heart.'
Upon hearing her words, he cried again
And narrated what ill-luck had befallen him

Mubarak-ul-Nisa cried bitterly at this calamity, and said: "Is it hearsay what you tell me, or is it the truth? I swear by God I will not be able to live even for a moment without this child. Tell me how you will be able to put the knife to his throat with your own hand!"

Zarivand said: "My beloved, grieve not. For if our son is destined to die in this manner, he will not be saved by our ploys. When King Khurshid-Chehar hears about it, he will have him killed to save his own life. It is preferable that I, with my own hands, bathe that blood-thirsty creature with our son's blood, so that we earn lifetime renown in the world for our devotion in paying the king's dues."

Finally, his wife, too, gave herself into the hands of fate. But when Zarivand took their son from Mubarak-ul-Nisa's arms, she took off her head covering, pulled her hair and, shouting her son's name, followed him, crying bitterly and reciting these verses:

MASNAVI

Leaving me alone to mourn you
You leave me, severing love's bonds
I knew not that sudden death
Would carry you away, my life, thus
What hand has cruel heaven dealt me
It has taken your life, leaving me your mourning
I will find no rest or peace without you
I will cry ceaselessly night and day
Now I shall not return home
In a day or two I will die from pining

. . .

O Mehr, she would stop to catch her breath
Then recite again the opening couplet of Soz:[24]
If such are the rewards of life
It is preferable then to embrace death

In short, Zarivand carried his son into the dome, with Mubarak-ul-Nisa following. The king stood listening in his hiding place.

That accursed woman awaited Zarivand indoors. The moment she saw him, she asked: "Did you bring the boy?" He replied: "Yes, I have brought this innocent creature. Now do as you please." She answered:

24. Soz: The takhallus (nom de plume) of Mir Soz. A classical Urdu poet.

"I have no business with your son. If you wish the king to live, however, you should cut his throat and bathe me in his blood."

Zarivand steeled his heart and taking the knife from the old woman's hand, made to cut his son's throat. Upon that the old woman stayed his hand, and said: "Do not waste the boy. I wished to test your devotion and fidelity, and have been satisfied. A thousand bravos to you and plaudits to your parents who gave you birth. None could do what you were ready to do, sacrificing your son to save your master, without wavering in the least. Go now, for Khurshid-Chehar's life has been extended by your deed. He was destined to die today come fajr time."

After hearing this the king returned to the palace, and stood waiting at the spot from where he had dispatched Zarivand to investigate the source of the voice. Zarivand, too, returned to the city from the dome, and after conducting Mubarak-ul-Nisa home, presented himself before the king.

Upon seeing Zarivand, the king said: "O youth, you took a long time to return. Now tell me who it was who made the cries and for what reason." Zarivand replied: "O Master, it was a woman who had quarreled with her husband and left her home; I reasoned with her and reconciled her with her husband. She has now returned to her house."

The morning light appeared while they conversed. The king said: "O youth, I followed you when you set out, and saw and heard everything that transpired. Bravo, that you did not show the least hesitancy in sacrificing your child for my sake. Nobody in the world could have done the favour you did me."

Then Khurshid-Chehar conferred a royal robe of honour on Zarivand, and appointed him his vizier. And for the rest of his life Zarivand lived in great comfort and luxury.'

TWENTY-FIRST TALE

Of the caravan progressing and arriving in Egypt, and of Roshan Zameer going into the city of one-legged men; Of the snake arriving there, and Roshan Zameer killing the female scorpion; Of his entering a building at the old man's bidding, and killing a dev, and rescuing the imprisoned daughter of the King of Damascus

Roshan Zameer said: 'Hear, O Saman Rukh! After the leader of the caravan had narrated Zarivand's tale to me, the caravan headed onwards. After many days the caravan arrived in Egypt. From there everyone went onwards on their business. I stayed there in a mosque for six months. When the seventh month started, I told myself that the holy man had asked me to return in six months, and that if I did not return the snake would find and kill me. I told myself that if I travelled to some place a month's journey from my location, the snake would not be able to follow and track me to such a distant place. I set out on my journey with this plan in mind.

After fifteen days, I arrived in a city and saw that all who lived there were one-legged. While I marvelled at the sight, they wondered at mine. They laughed and made fun of me, and said amongst each other: "How is this man able to walk on two legs?" A crowd of them caught and led me before their king. I saw the king sitting on the throne and others standing around him on one leg. I made my salutations and stood in a corner.

The king looked at me and said: "O man of marvellous form, whence have you come? Is everyone in your land of the same form as you?" I answered: "You marvel at the sight of me, and I marvel at how you are able to walk with one leg."

Meanwhile, cries and an uproar went up that a great snake was rushing towards the city. The whole city was thrown into upheaval from terror, and people began to scatter and run for their lives. I realized that the snake had come searching for me, and even if I were able to hide for the moment, he would not stop pursuing me. That on account of me everyone suffered at his hands for no reason. I abandoned all hopes for my life and went towards the snake. He rose to his full height when he saw me, and when I approached, he put me on his back and we headed back to Egypt.

When we arrived in Egypt, I communicated to him by making signs that I was famished and overcome by thirst. Upon learning this he set me down. I went into the city, and returned after satisfying my hunger and thirst. He put me on his neck and set out again, and after twenty days we arrived at his dwelling, and he brought me to the same cave.

What did I find there but the female of the scorpion I had killed, coming towards me with the intention of killing me. I immediately shot an arrow at her, but it did not fatally wound her. I shot a second arrow and that too only grazed her. The third time I turned my thoughts to God Almighty as I stretched the bow to my ear and shot another arrow. The female scorpion was fated to die, and the arrow hit its mark, piercing through her body and breaking it apart. I shot another arrow at her for good measure, and she thrashed about and died within moments. Searching for the arrows I had shot, I found they were corroded by her poison. The snake was very pleased at the death of his enemy and placed his head on my feet to express his gratitude.

In the meantime, the green-clad old man arrived there holding his staff. I said to him: "Peace be upon you, O Venerable Sir!" He answered: "Peace be upon you too!" Then he held me by my hand and led me atop the hill and showed me the snake's two babies.

A tall building stood there, and I asked him: "O Venerable Sir, what is inside this building?" He replied: "It is a dev's house. He, too, is destined to die at your hands." Then he gave me an inscribed tablet, and said: "Go near the building. Recite *In the name of God!* thrice before setting foot indoors. And have no fear! There is no danger to you. However, you must bring low the vile dev using kicks and blows, but no weapons." I went to the entrance of the building, carrying the inscribed tablet, and after reciting *In the name of God* three times, stepped inside.

Within, I found such a beautiful house that even the houris of heaven would long to set eyes on such a place. I saw a beautiful girl of fifteen or sixteen sitting on a throne inside a three-doored chamber. Upon beholding me, she said: "My good fellow, how did you find your way here, as no one can gain entrance to this place? Do you not value your life that on your own accord you have set foot in your grave? I feel pity for your youth. Depart forthwith whence you have come, or you will be killed momentarily."

I answered: "O beauty, whatever has been apportioned my lot from the beginning of time is irrevocable. Do tell me how you, with your delicacy and elegance, were caught in the clutches of the dev?" Upon hearing this, her eyes welled up, but she held back her tears.

The eye welled up, the tears repressed
Like the narcissus holds aloft in its bowl the dewdrops

She remained silent for a long time, then sighed and spoke thus: "O youth, how should I begin my tale! I am the daughter of the King of

Damascus. In the heat of summer I was sleeping on the rooftop with my hair loose when perchance, this villain and malefactor happened to pass there, and became enamoured of me. From that day he would daily arrive in the middle of the night and sit before me until dawn. He forbade me from telling anyone about his visits, upon threat of carrying me away. My secret was a case where:

Should it remain in the heart, the heart would burn, may my mouth burn should I utter it
Like a speechless one having a nightmare, he may cry but cannot describe it

"The misery of my situation made me corrode away, and my skin turned pale. When my parents noticed my condition, they asked me the reason for my debility and weakness. But for fear of the dev I did not tell them a thing. Slowly and gradually, I reached a state where all flesh dissolved away from my body, and my rib-cage and bones became plainly visible.

"One day my mother took me into seclusion, and said: 'My dear daughter, what has happened to you that you wilt away with every passing day? If you are suffering from some malady, reveal it to me so that one can find a cure for it. Or are you in love with someone, and it is longing that eats you from within?'

"O youth, upon hearing these words from my mother, I found myself in a quandary. If I were to reveal the truth I feared the dev's retribution, and if I didn't do it, I was afraid my mother would become convinced that I had fallen in love. For a long time I remained in perplexity whether or not to speak. Finally, after much consideration, I said to her: 'O kind mother, I do not as yet know whether love is something to eat or drink, or a thing to wear. As to the word itself, I have heard it in the name of the flower called ishq-e pechan.[25] Perhaps it is that which you call love? If I had some ailment, I would have revealed it to you myself. What is to be gained from concealing it? But do not ask me why I dissolve away, for it is something unspeakable.'

"Upon hearing this my mother became so curious to learn the truth that she ceaselessly demanded it of me. I said to her: 'O kind

25. Ishq-e pechan: A species of ivy that bears red flowers.

mother, do not insist in this matter. If I opened my mouth I shall be taken away, and then you will long to even see my face.' Upon this she became even more eager to learn the truth. A hundred times she insisted upon knowing it, saying: 'It would not do to conceal the truth. Reveal the issue so that we may act to bring about a resolution.'

"When I realized that she was eager for me to divulge it, and I would not have peace until I had confessed, I could do naught else but narrate everything to her about the dev, from beginning to end. I told her that he had forbidden me from telling anyone, and that the day I told anyone he would carry me away. I told her I was certain that he would take me away that very day.

"The moment she heard my account, my mother rushed from my side and forthwith informed my father. He immediately sent for all the soothsayers in the city and had them prepare amulets and charms and put them around my neck. Come evening, my bed was flanked by my father's bed on one side, and my mother's bed on the other side. Charms were burnt in the taper-holders and an expert necromancer sat outside the purdah to exorcise the dev with his art when he showed himself.

"The monster arrived in the middle of the night. Killing with just one blow of his hand the man waiting to exorcise him, he carried me away with my bed and brought me here. Every day he tries to broach the matter of his desire with me, but I forestall him on the pretext of illness. From the day I was brought here I have longed to see a human face. Today, upon your arrival, I saw one after four years."

Hear, O Saman Rukh, that after she had given me her account, the girl asked me: "O youth, now tell me, why have you arrived here of your own accord to squander away your life?"

Then I narrated my account from beginning to end, and said: "I have come at the behest of a pious man to kill this giant dev. Upon hearing this, she smiled and said: "To kill him is not an easy proposition. If you value your life, drive this idle thought from your mind, and depart from the same path from which you have come. Why do you wish to throw away your life?" I replied: "Let what is destined come to pass. I shall not turn back without killing the dev or being killed in the attempt." She said: "If that be your decision, so be it, as you are your own master. But it is well-nigh impossible to kill him. It is not within your power to do so." After stating this, she said: "Now it is time for the monster to arrive. Let me hide you in a nook." She secreted me away in a place where the dev could not find me.

After some time that blackguard, tall as a hill, came walking, sat down beside her, and tried to touch her. She said with knitted brow: "O wretch, I am dying of my illness. Do not touch me yet. Wait some days. When I am well you may do with me as you please."

I glanced at the paper tablet in my hand, and it said: "O Roshan Zameer, come out and hold this tablet before the dev. Kill him using only blows from your hands and feet, and do not use any weapons."

After reading the tablet I came out. The dev charged towards me in anger. I held up the paper tablet before him, and the moment he saw it he became all limp. I grabbed him by the neck and threw him to the ground, and with powerful kicks brought him to death's door. But forgetting the old man's injunction in the struggle, I drew my sword from the scabbard and beheaded him. The moment his blood fell on the ground a thousand devs cropped up, and surrounded me. When I looked at the tablet in panic, it instructed that I must command the devs, in the name of Prophet Suleiman, to burn themselves. Thus, from the command I gave in the name of Suleiman, their bodies caught fire, and they burnt to a cinder by themselves. I offered thanks to God, and taking the girl by the hand, came out of the building.'

TWENTY-SECOND TALE

Of the green-clad man meeting Roshan Zameer, and the latter departing with the damsel and arriving in a dominion of the kingdom of Damascus; Of his departing from there with an army and bivouacking in a garden, and of the devs arriving there and taking Roshan Zameer prisoner; Of the green-clad man securing his release, and of the princess arriving in Damascus and reuniting with her parents

It is narrated that Roshan Zameer said to Saman Rukh: 'Hear, O Lady of Lofty Honour! When I came out of the building with the damsel, the same old man met me at the entrance. I bowed to him and made my salutations. He returned my greetings, and said: "O Roshan Zameer, bravo, for you showed great manliness."

He led us to a nearby hut where he served us plentiful food, and said: "Go now, I give you into God's care! But I have another task for you to carry out before you do: take along this girl and return her to her land. And beware that the devs will try to kill you, and you must be alert during the journey."

I said: "Very well. But do please let me know your good name, and what is the reason that you live in this bleak desolation?" He answered: "My good fellow, I am from the line of Prophet Suleiman, and my name is Khalifa. Considering the world and all its associations a dream, and my borrowed existence like a bubble, I spend my life in this barrenness in devotions to the Almighty."

After he had spoken these words, I took my leave and set out with the girl. We travelled during daytime and rested when we reached a habitation at the end of the day. We would spend the night there and set out again when the morning gong sounded.

On the afternoon of the thirteenth day, we arrived in a land that was a dominion of the Kingdom of Damascus. The damsel offered thanks to God upon arriving in her father's dominions, and turned a happy face towards me, saying: "O young man, it is the height of impertinence, indeed, it is most discourteous to make demands on you, for it was on account of you that I received a new lease on life; without you it was impossible to be released from that monster's clutches. If every single fibre on my body acquires a thousand tongues and each tongue offers your praises a hundred thousand times, I shall not be able to recompense you in the least for all the favours you did me. Indeed, it would be befitting to call myself your slave girl, and take pride in that.

If every hair on my body acquires a thousand tongues
And I offer your praise from every tongue a hundred thousand times
It would not even measure up to a mote
Of all the kindnesses you have done me

"Since there is none other to whom I can express my need, I find no recourse, and each time in my helplessness I make demands on you. Pray forgive my trespasses. My request to you is this: Visit the ruler of the city and give him news that his king's daughter, kidnapped by the dev, has now returned."

O Queen, when I brought the news to the ruler of the city, he rushed on foot to pay his respects to the princess. Then he sent many a palanquin resplendent with gold and worked with jewels, and many an elephant with lustrous brocade howdahs arrived for her conveyance. The damsel sat on one elephant and put me on another, and we started out with great pomp and ceremony. The ruler of the city offered alms in gratitude at her return, sent scores of beautiful female attendants to wait upon her, and made offerings of an array of clothes and costly jewellery to her.

The following day the princess said to me: "My good fellow, let us rest some more today, and tomorrow we will leave for Damascus." I said to her: "You have now reached your land. Pray give me leave to depart so I may attend to my affairs."

She replied: "O youth, how can I let you go away now? Kindly stay at your humble servant's abode and spend a few days there. Thereafter, wherever you decide to go, you may take along the royal army and reach there with the greatest of ease." I made excuses but she did not pay the least heed. She placed me under many pledges, forcing me to stay.

Early the next day, before the sun had risen, she arranged a royal entourage. She provided a swift paced charger for me, covered in gold and bejewelled accoutrements, and herself sat with great magnificence in a jewel-enchased howdah dressed in a yellow dress and twined doshala, and we started for Damascus. The ruler of the city ran on foot accompanying the entourage, and the proclaimers marshalled the troops, calling out: "Keep advancing, O Lions and Bravehearts!"

I glanced at her face, and her fair visage framed by the twined doshala looked like a moon shining through dark clouds.

I imagined when I saw her face in the black doshala
The sun shining through dark clouds, or the moon in its halo

To this day that vision of her beauty is impressed upon my heart.

After we had travelled for some four kos, we came upon a garden. The princess dismounted and went into the garden. Holding my hand, she promenaded in the garden for some time. There was an octagonal chamber made of marble in the garden. She ordered a velvet carpet and food-cloth to be laid there. The attendants laid out the cloth and served food. After some time, the princess returned from her promenade, and ate breakfast with me sitting beside her. After we had eaten, the food spread was removed. Tired from the journey, I lay down and my eyes closed in sleep.

When I awoke, I reckoned I was in need of a ritual bath.[26] There was a brick-lined pool in the garden. I went there, and unfastening the paper tablet from my arm that the old man had given me, put it on the ledge, to lower myself in the pool.

The devs had lain in pursuit, awaiting an opportunity. They took the paper tablet, securely tied me up, and destroyed the army. Those who were not fated to die escaped with their lives. The devs wished to defile the princess but one of them took pity at her beauty and said: "Friends, we must not defile such a fine damsel. We should instead make her our cupbearer." In short, that assembly of revelry became one of mourning.

At night the devs tied me to a tree. In that devastated state, despairing for my life, I thought of the old man. Immediately upon thinking of him, he stood before me. He secured the paper tablet from the devs and gave it into my hands, saying: "O unwary person, be alert and beware! Do not give this tablet to anyone except me." Then he unfastened me with his own hands, and said to me: "Invoke the name of Suleiman that all of the devs are torn to pieces." After making that proclamation he disappeared.'

. . .

When Roshan Zameer reached this point in the story, Saman Rukh said: 'O young man, I want to ask, how was a decrepit old man able to secure the paper from the devs, who had destroyed a whole army in an instant?'

Roshan Zameer answered: 'It is indeed reasonable to ask this, but have you not heard:

These Sheikhs, although they are friends of God are themselves not God
But from God's will they are not separated even for an instant

If someone enters into a person's service for a few days, he too treats him kindly. Those who spend their whole lives in devotion to God are given the power to make things happen with their will.

'Hear, O Saman Rukh, that when that old man disappeared, I called out to the devs and invoked Prophet Suleiman's name that they be torn

26. Ritual bath: Bath taken after intercourse or seminal discharge to become ritually pure in order to perform prayers.

to pieces. Immediately upon my command, their bodies and heads fell apart, and they were left in pieces.

When the men from our army, who had escaped, beheld this scene, they marvelled greatly, and happily returned and camped in the garden for the night. Some time before the break of dawn, we continued onwards.

When we arrived near Damascus the delighted king joyfully sent his vizier to greet us. Upon arriving in Damascus the princess kissed her father's feet, and he seated her with honour and asked about her welfare. She narrated all that had happened from beginning to end, and then gestured towards me, and said: "This young man freed me from that monster's clutches and brought me back, otherwise it was impossible for me to be freed. Along the journey he saved me from many calamities that he alone could have overcome."

Her companions then related the details of the devs attacking us in the garden. The king sent for me and said with great kindness: "Dear fellow, it is thanks to you that after five years I see the face of my daughter. It is impossible for me to recompense you for the favour."

The king provided me with a house and appointed fifty men to attend upon me. After a week I sought leave of the king. He said: "O youth, what is the hurry to depart? Stay here for some ten, twenty days more, so that you may recover from the fatigue of your journey. Thereafter, wherever you wish to go, I will send my army with you so that you may arrive there in comfort."

When the king went to his daughter and told her about the arrangement, she said: "O father, do not let this man go." Through hints and suggestion, she conveyed to her father that if he had no objections, he should give her hand in marriage to me.

O Queen, when I heard of these plans, I pretended to be mad and started talking nonsense. I tore up my clothes and rushed out of the city. If I saw anyone along the way, I threw stones and bricks at them. In this manner I released myself from their power.

I had gone some one kos when the same old man appeared before me. I stopped and greeted him. He answered my greetings then said: "O young man, return me the paper tablet as I have further use for it." I untied it from my arm and gave it back to him. He took it from my hands and disappeared and I headed onward.'

• • •

Saman Rukh praised Roshan Zameer upon hearing his account. As Saman Rukh regained the exercise of her senses, Azar Shah was continuously more grateful to the Sheikh and his disciples.

Sheikh Sanaan asked: 'O Saman Rukh, how do you feel now?' She answered: 'Thanks to your ministrations, I am fully well, but I am desirous to know the remaining story of Malik Muhammad, to learn what passed with him, and whether or not he attained his desire.'

Sheikh Sanaan smiled and said to Dana-Dil: 'My son, pray now narrate what remains of Malik Muhammad's story.'

TWENTY-THIRD TALE

Of Dana Dil narrating the remaining story of Malik Muhammad; Of Giti Afroz returning from Paristan after her father's death, and her turning Malik Muhammad into a dog; Of Malik Muhammad going to his uncle, and Danishmand handing him to the kennel-keepers

It is said that upon receiving his master's permission, Dana Dil began thus: 'Hear, O Saman Rukh, the narrators have related that after Giti Afroz's brother was betrothed, she sought leave of her father to return. His eyes welled up with tears, and he said: "O daughter, I know well the reason why you will not live here any longer. But now that you are here, stay a few more days for my pleasure."

At her father's request Giti Afroz perforce prolonged her stay. After some days, Unsar Shah became ill and passed away from the illness. His wife, family and the officers of the state beat their heads and lamented but it was all to no avail, and they saw no recourse but to reconcile themselves with the decree of fate. Indeed, everyone must take that path of departure from life. One only sheds tears in the memory of the departed who was the cause of the comfort one has received in the world. For no one is revived from others crying over him. Would that it were so:

Everyone would have cried all their lives, made plaints and grieved
Had crying resurrected the dead, none would have died ever

In short, after performing Unsar Shah's last rites, the officers of the kingdom enthroned his eldest son.

After some days, Giti Afroz's brother said to her: "O Sister, formalities aside, if you wish to stay here you must give up your friendship with this human, as humans have no business amongst us." Giti Afroz answered:

All your sermons and injunctions are right, O Adviser!
But what should I say to my heart that will not be checked?

"O brother, although it is improper to say it before you, forgive my saying that the lover's heart finds no rest. These verses which have risen from my heart speak of its situation:

The one fatally pierced by the arrow of love
Finds his life in this world a burden
The one who tastes the restiveness of love
Finds no rest ever in the world
Love does not release its hold until death
On one who finds his true beloved

"For as long as I breathe, it is impossible for me to renounce the love of my faithful lover. In fact, I will leave all of you for him.

May God ever save me from committing wrong
God forbid that I ever betray my lover
Love is a fierce monster, may God never
Deliver into its clutches even an enemy"

Thus speaking, she sent for her flying throne.

When the parizads saw that she was ready to leave, everyone counselled her, and said: "O Giti Afroz, why do you take offence at what we say? Truthfully tell us, why must our race make friends with humans? And to be the daughter of a mighty king like Unsar Shah and guilty of such a lowly deed! Have a thought for your family's repute and name! Do not roll your parents's honour in the dust. Your actions should be such that nobody belittles them and people do not castigate them. Your name will earn disrepute in the whole world. Why do you wish to become the proverbial example of a misdemeanour?"

After hearing all that they had to say, Giti Afroz replied:

"O Counsellors, whom do you counsel, for I have no power over my heart
Have you lost your senses, why do you torment me with your words?

"Understand that when I did not pay heed to my parents, or to my older brother who is like a father to me, why would your injunctions make the least impression on my heart! Except for my lover, I care neither for esteem and reputation, nor my parents' good name."

Herein lies my peace, my consciousness, my life
Herein lies my faith and my belief

She held Malik Muhammad's hand and, mounting her throne, departed from Paristan for the hills with her whole army. She arrived there after some time, and graced her old home with her auspicious presence.

Malik Muhammad offered thanks to God for arriving there in safety. Giti Afroz made a sign to Rooh Afza. She brought a flagon of wine and liberally poured it for both of them, and dance recitals continued the whole day.

Come evening, Giti Afroz retired to the bedchamber with her lover. Intoxicated on the wine, they remained busy in kissing and embracing for some time. When Giti Afroz lost herself to slumber, that is to say when she fell asleep, Malik Muhammad said in his heart:

She has neither fondness, nor attachment, nor love, nor affection
I have neither patience, nor strength, nor am able to sleep or rest

Come what may, today I will achieve my heart's purpose. He rose and approaching Giti Afroz tried to fulfill his heart's desire. The moment he touched her, Giti Afroz opened her eyes and with her brow knitted in anger, said: "O wretched dog, you long to do that very thing from which I expressly forbid you. I had hoped that you would not get caught in some trouble. But you purposely seek trouble for yourself."

O Queen, at the utterance of these words that poor man forthwith rolled on the ground and turned into a dog. Giti Afroz's servants beat and drove him from the palace. Helpless and repentant, he headed for the city, reciting this couplet in his heart:

I bore much oppression and tyranny, such was my fate
And my heart's desire yet remained unmet, such was my lot

Arriving in the city, he saw Danishmand riding towards the river. He rushed towards him and leapt up to kiss his uncle's feet. Danishmand discerned that it was Malik Muhammad. He said: "O wretch! Many times you made pledges and repented. But you did not renounce Giti Afroz's friendship, and chose the fellowship of the paris. From a man of faith, you became faithless. I swear by God that now even if you were to die in this state, I would have no pity on you!" After addressing these words to Malik Muhammad, Danishmand gave permission to his servants to hand him to the keepers of the kennel, and to house him with the rest of the dogs.

Malik Muhammad said in his heart: "Giti Afroz left her parents and renounced her whole family for me. How can I now give up her love at Danishmand's bidding!"

Let alone my faith and heart, even should I lose my life
It is yet impossible for my heart to be emptied of her memory

In short, for three months Malik Muhammad was kept with the other dogs by the kennel keepers.'

TWENTY-FOURTH TALE

Of Farkhanda Shah departing to meet Giti Afroz; Of Rooh Afza turning him into a cat at Giti Afroz's behest, and Danishmand returning him to human form; And of Giti Afroz returning Malik Muhammad to human form and carrying him away

The recounter has narrated this story in this wise that Dana Dil said to Saman Rukh: 'Hear, O Queen of the World, that one day King Farkhanda Shah recalled that he had sent Malik Muhammad to bring news of Giti Afroz, and he had not returned. He considered that he may have become occupied with festivities and revelries when he went to meet his beloved. He decided that he should himself go to get news of Giti Afroz, and also find out what had detained Malik Muhammad.

Farkhanda Shah mounted his horse and headed for the hills, taking along a small detachment of ten or twenty soldiers. When he arrived at the gate of Giti Afroz's palace, he went in by himself. From afar, Giti Afroz saw Farkhanda Shah arriving and greeted him and escorted him inside, seating him on the throne with great honour. At a sign from her mistress, Rooh Afza brought a flagon of strong wine and became the cupbearer.

In the evening, after they had finished the meal, Giti Afroz sent for Rooh Afza and said to her: "If you could somehow turn the king into an animal today, he would learn what trials Malik Muhammad has faced. As Sheikh Sa'adi has written in the *Gulistan*:

The value of safety is truly appreciated by the one in peril"

She answered: "Very well! I have nursed the same desire in my heart." Then Rooh Afza took leave of the princess, and brought the king into her bedchamber. She plied him so liberally with wine that Farkhanda Shah lost all control of his person, and involuntarily fell down at his beloved's feet reciting this couplet:

Beholding you, O pari-faced, I have become engrossed, and have lost
All command of my body and being, soul, senses, and all faculties

Then, after kissing and embracing her, he tried to take pleasure of her. Angered by his advances, Rooh Afza said with vexation: "O cat, do not exceed your bounds!" The moment these words were uttered by her, the king rolled on the ground and turned into a cat.'

. . .

When Saman Rukh heard of the king turning into a cat, she turned in bed, and asked: 'O Dana Dil, it is a marvel that a human should turn into an animal or beast at a word from the paris.'

He answered: 'O Queen of Heavens, it is nothing to marvel at, as the utterances of paris still have the same power.'

. . .

Then Dana Dil continued: 'In short, when Farkhanda Shah turned into a cat, Rooh Afza drove him out of the bedchamber. All night long Farkhanda Shah cried and recited these lines by Mirza Rafi Sauda:[27]

What a fate that my heart became enamoured of that coquette
What a fate that I came into the power of that tormenter
What a fate that I invited a calamity on my head
What a fate that my heart was trapped without a bait
What a fate to possess a crazy heart that acts thus

He regretted that he did not know that such a thing might happen, or he would not have come there to be thus disgraced. He wondered how he would return to the city in his current form.

27. Mirza Rafi Sauda: The classical Urdu poet Mirza Muhammad Rafi Sauda (1713–1781).

Early the next day, before the sun had risen, he came out of Giti Afroz's palace and headed for the city. Arriving near his palace, he hid himself in a nook and awaited Vizier Danishmand.

When the king had slunk out from Giti Afroz's palace in cat's form, the princess had deputed two spies to follow him, and said to them: "Remain hidden and observe all that passes with him, and bring me a report." As ordered, they had followed the cat.

The few men who had accompanied the king to Giti Afroz's palace, asked about him at her palace gate after waiting for the king, but received no news of him, and returned to the city without him.

When King Farkhanda Shah did not return to the palace at night, everyone believed that His Honour had spent the night at the palace of the paris. Danishmand kept awake all night, wondering what passed with His Honour, and hoping that he would return to the palace safely. He wondered if perchance the paris' magic had turned him into some animal from the good fortune of the king's enemies, or if he had fallen into trouble on account of the paris' sorcery and mischief-making.

When the morning gong was struck, he set out alone from his house on foot, to obtain news of his beneficent master. When he approached the king's palace, Farkhanda Shah, who was in the shape of a cat and looking his way, rushed towards him. Danishmand discerned that it was the king, and in astonishment caught his finger between his teeth at the ill treatment the paris had shown him. Farkhanda Shah meowed and moved his tail royally. Danishmand picked him up, and hiding him in his doshala so that none may witness the scene, gave him a little amount of the lincture. Upon having it Farkhanda Shah rolled on the ground, and was immediately restored to human form. Danishmand dressed him in royal vestments and led him into the palace, mounted on a horse.

May God never inflict such humiliation on a person, as the mortification felt by the king at the incident. He peevishly said to Danishmand: "We are human and do not have power over the parizads, but it is my ardent desire to kill Malik Muhammad who is Giti Afroz's beloved, so that she may grieve till the end of her days."

O Queen, even though Malik Muhammad was wicked and unworthy in Danishmand's eyes, he could not countenance the thought of his nephew being killed. He interceded on his behalf, saying: "Your

Honour, he is after all your own subject! But you may act as per your auspicious discernment."

The king said: "Where is Malik Muhammad? Produce him before us and order the executioners to cut open his belly." Danishmand answered: "That poor fellow is living in the form of a dog with other canines in the kennel keepers' custody." Upon hearing this the king dispatched executioners to fetch him.

O Queen of the Heavens, Giti Afroz's spies witnessed these events and brought her news that Malik Muhammad had been condemned to die in this manner on account of his friendship with her. Sighing with grief, Giti Afroz mounted her throne, and rushed to the city with some parizads.

A hundred executioners led Malik Muhammad away for execution, inflicting on him all manner of torture and suffering. He told himself that there must be a reason why they were torturing him thus, and wondered what trespass he had committed for which he was being punished. He told himself that if he was being taken to be executed, losing his life would be no tragedy; but he yearned for his beloved from whom he would die separated.

Let us see whether I behold her before my last breath
Or whether my soul leaves me with my last laments

He was occupied with these thoughts when Giti Afroz arrived there and called out: "O Malik Muhammad, faithful as you are, why do you not sit beside me on the throne?" At these words, Malik Muhammad rolled on the ground and returned to human form, and broke out from the pack of dogs and sat beside Giti Afroz on her throne. She returned to her palace with her dearly beloved, and when the news reached Farkhanda Shah, he lamented Malik Muhammad's escape.

Upon reaching the palace Giti Afroz said to Malik Muhammad: "My love, do you know at all what I just did?" Malik Muhammad had no inkling of what had transpired. He answered: "I have no knowledge of it." Then Giti Afroz narrated from the beginning all that had happened, and upon hearing about it, Malik Muhammad was very pleased and joyously recited this couplet:

You are my soul-searing grief, and also my balm
I reckon you as the very soul of my universe

Giti Afroz embraced him. Then Rooh Afza plied them liberally with wine and at a sign from the princess, dancing began. The lover and the beloved sat together merrily watching the dance. Intoxicated on wine, now Malik Muhammad would touch her breasts, and now Giti Afroz would boldly kiss his face in a drunken stupor. In this manner, in the tradition of the lover and the beloved, the one transported by the fervour of love and the other from coquetry, they became oblivious to all worries, and derived happiness and pleasure from their intimacy, and received each other's love in a happy and unbridled manner.'

TWENTY-FIFTH TALE

Of the arrival of the vizier of the king to whom Giti Afroz was affianced, of Malik Muhammad attaining his heart's desire and the vizier returning empty-handed; Of Saman Rukh making a full recovery and a son being born to Azar Shah; and of Sheikh Sanaan departing and the book coming to an end

The narrators have recounted this engrossing tale thus: Dana Dil said to Saman Rukh: 'O Queen of the World, Giti Afroz and Malik Muhammad were kissing and embracing in the throes of pleasure when they heard the voices of parizads in the sky. When Giti Afroz looked up, she saw that the vizier of the king to whom she had been affianced was arriving.

In the meanwhile, the vizier approached and bowed and made his salutation. Giti Afroz looked at him and said: "O vizier, it appears that your master has sent you. Tell me what message he sends."

The vizier made his salutations in the manner of decorous plenipotentiaries, and conveyed this message from his master:

After the death of King Unsar Shah, we sent a messenger to your brother to communicate our desire for our nuptials with you to be held. But he and your mother gave answer that they had no say in the matter, and that Giti Afroz was sovereign in her affairs. Indeed, they made other remarks too, which is beyond me to utter.

The vizier said: "It is for this reason that my master has dispatched me to you. With great yearning and desire, and with much longing, he pleads with great hope thus:

'I remain engrossed in thoughts of you night and day.

Infidel is the one who desires one other than you
I would that God never show me another's face

But none of this affection is returned by you. I now put my hope in your kindness that you will indulge the passion of this longing heart and illuminate my eyes with the vision of your beauty, for this life passes night and day like flowing water, and there is no chance of it returning. As Sauda has said:

The seeker finds all that he seeks in the world
Except the life spent; it is nowhere to be found

And if you think little of me, and are loath to associate yourself with me, you must give a clear answer, for waiting is akin to dying, and I must not idly wait.'"

Upon hearing this message from the vizier, Giti Afroz replied: "Wait a while, and you will leave with an answer to his message."'

. . .

Saman Rukh said: 'O youth, you must first tell me whether or not poor Malik Muhammad, having borne such hardships, and undergone all those trials, will now attain his heart's desire, or be caught in some new calamity. I feel great pity at his situation.'

Dana Dil laughed and replied: 'Indeed, it is a situation to be pitied. Now just a little of the story remains, and you will learn what transpired.'

. . .

He continued: 'O Queen, having spoken to the vizier, Giti Afroz held Malik Muhammad by the wrist, and took him into seclusion. There, the lover and the beloved began imbibing wine. Drunk on wine, Malik Muhammad recited this couplet in the hope that she may yet take pity on his burning desire:

What a fate I was apportioned to live in her love
The lamp has no inkling of how the moth burns

Upon hearing this, Giti Afroz replied:

O lover, you know not the being of love
Itself the lamp burns before the moth

"A lover is not given even a tenth of the ardour and tenderness that lies in the beloved's heart, as the former unburdens himself with crying, but the latter must sear within. As someone has said:

The moth has not the wherewithal, like the taper to burn
Trembling, beheaded,[28] *silently crying, and consumed whole*

"My lover, the hardships and afflictions that you bore in my love are imprinted on my heart like an engraving on stone. But do you also regard my devotion to you that for your sake:

I left my home and loved ones, departed my city and land
In order to become your lover, I renounced one and all"

Having spoken thus, she bashfully and demurely lay down with great coquetry and silently drew a veil across her face. Malik Muhammad had suffered great hardships in the hopes of union with her, and the desire for intimacy with her had made him undergo many trials and tribulations. Believing that her silence was the indicator of her consent, Malik Muhammad was as jubilant as a corpse become infused with life, or a beggar come upon the treasures of Qarun.[29] His pain was replaced with relief and his grief with joy. That is to say, he succeeded in fulfilling his craving, details of which are beyond the scope of this narrative, and what he had yearned for since ages was received in abundance. The bud of Giti Afroz's desire flowered from fulfilment and the tree of Malik Muhammad's yearning bloomed with flowers; that is to say, the union of bodies that is the fruit of life was attained by both lovers as they wished.

MASNAVI

The two lovers, their moon-like bodies united
There was neither the threat of law nor of rival
Enamoured of each other, the two sweethearts met
Both receiving together the pleasure of life
As their breasts were bursting with love
The two tightly embraced each other
Both their hearts were filled with this yearning:
O Lord, allow the bud of desire to flower!

28. Beheaded: Refers to the trimming of the wick.
29. Qarun: Korah of the *Book of Numbers* of the Old Testament.

When the beloved's glories were fully unveiled
The anxiety in the lover's heart was quelled
All the signs of pain and suffering departed
When their bodies and cheeks were together pressed
Their desires were together fulfilled
When their lips and mouths were joined
Their chins were together, their legs were entwined
The breasts of the two lovers were joined
When the drop of rain fell into the oyster
Within their possession was the pearl of desire
Who can offer the expositions of pleasure
Only he who possesses that wealth knows
Joy thus announced in heart's dominion:
All sorrows departed O Mehr, and bliss prevailed

The pleasure that Malik Muhammad derived from his union with the damsel cannot be described aright in words. The empire of seven climes was worthless to him in comparison. He joyously recited this couplet:

The beloved's doorstep is preferable to the throne of a kingdom
And the shade of the beloved's wall to the shadow of huma[30]

In short, having consummated his heart's yearning, Malik Muhammad's heart at once became unburdened of all the sorrow and anguish that had weighed it down. After Giti Afroz had tasted the fruit of life through union with her lover, she sent with an attendant the bedsheet to the vizier waiting for her response, with the message that he should take that as clear answer to his master.

The vizier marvelled at this astounding event. Having lost all hope, he returned dejected to his land. There he narrated before his master what he had seen of Giti Afroz. Anger blazed in his master's heart upon hearing what had transpired, and he declared: "Summon the advance camp so that we can attack and ravage that wretch."

His wise viziers, sagacious court officials, and counsellors said to him: "The lion does not eat a dog's leftovers. Now that foul wretch is unworthy of Your Excellency's companionship. It would be idle to

30. Shadow of huma: In Persian and Urdu classical texts, the shadow of the Huma bird or its alighting on a man's head or shoulder was taken to foretell that person's kingship.

launch a campaign against her. At present nobody has heard the news, but then it will become known in the whole world that Giti Afroz, who was affianced to such and such a king, soiled her repute by lying with a human."

Upon reflection on the advice the king was convinced of its wisdom, and maintained silence and gave up the thought of Giti Afroz's chastisement. And thus, the lover and the beloved lived in great joy and comfort in those hills.'

. . .

Saman Rukh was delighted to hear the account of Malik Muhammad fulfilling his desire, and said joyously:

MASNAVI

A thousand thanks that he received his reward
A thousand thanks that his heart was sated
A thousand thanks that after the plaints he made night and day
His beloved turned on him the eye of favour
A thousand thanks that after a long wait and much grief
He found delight in his beloved's embrace
A thousand thanks that after boundless suffering
His fortunes turned and the heavens sent help
A thousand thanks that he found comfort through union
A thousand thanks that his stars are in favorable mode
A thousand thanks that the days of hardship are past
A thousand thanks that his lips are joined with his beloved's lips
A thousand thanks the heavens hold no calamity in store
A thousand thanks that his beloved is now in his embrace
A thousand thanks that after suffering anxiety
He received joy in union with his beloved
All were dispelled: his grief, his pain, his restiveness
A thousand thanks that he attained his heart's desire
Joyous times that the beloved has met his lover
Joyous times that the seeker and the sought are together
Joyous times that Mahjoor[31] *meets his beloved*
Joyous times that the sorrowful receives joy
Joyous time the spring when the garden is in bloom
Joyous times that the beloved, the envy of the rose, is in one's embrace

31. Mahjoor: Muhammad Bakhsh Mahjoor. Author of the Urdu classic *Nauratan*.

Joyous times that in the garden the rose and the nightingale are together
Joyous times that the beloved, songstress, drinks and grape wine are gathered
Joyous times, O Mehr, that the friends meet and derive joy from the meeting
Joyous times that warmth, affection, and love among friends grows
Joyous times that there is seclusion without fear
And that in intimacy the lovers are happy together
Joyous times that there is neither the threat of law nor of rival
Joyous times such when one is united with the beloved
Joyous times that no grief or trouble of the world remains
Joyous times when lovers are gathered together
May that happy period prove a blessed time
When the lovers' desires come to fruition

By the grace of God, that lover saw his desire fulfilled after undergoing much suffering.

Happy is the day when after waiting
The hopeful has his hope fulfilled

Saman Rukh recited this couplet, then got up from her bed and kissed Sheikh Sanaan's feet, and expressed her gratitude to his disciples.

Sheikh Sanaan asked her: 'O Queen, how do you feel? And how are your spirits?' She folded her hands respectfully and said with great humility and submission: 'From your heart's focus on my condition, I have been fully healed. There are no signs left of torpidity.' King Azar Shah conducted Saman Rukh to the baths where she took a bath of recovery.

King Azar Shah was greatly indebted to the venerable Sheikh and said with humility: 'She came to her senses on account of your kind indulgence, for there is no possibility that a person under a spell should come out of it from listening to qissas and tales, and be restored to health.'

Then the king had the wily Zalala, his first wife, put to death with much ignominy and suffering, and ordered celebratory music to be played. He joyfully joined the Queen of the World in the palace, and busied himself in pleasure-seeking which is the fruit of life.

The following day, Sheikh Sanaan said to him: 'O Azar Shah, it does not behove religious mendicants like us, who live in our faraway nooks, to spend too much time in the companionship of kings. Furthermore, our task has been accomplished, and from His beneficence and grace God has restored Saman Rukh to health. Now give us leave to depart to our habitation.'

Upon hearing this, Azar Shah humbly submitted: 'Although you have neither desire for material things nor care to receive them from me, but for my own weal and prosperity I wish you to accept some land for the expenses of your servants and guests.'

The Sheikh smiled and answered: 'O king, what business do the religious mendicants have with property and estate? We have neither wife nor children for whom one should gather wealth. And there are no guarantees with life. One may or may not draw the next breath.

GHAZAL

A long time ago we came to the realization
There are no certainties in life
We do not put our store in this world
Or in anything, except the Creator
We have no desire for gold and riches
For we have acquired a taste for indigence
We have dyed ourselves in the colour of the Being
Before Whose hue all colours are dull
God is the one who provides everyone sustenance
Why must we worry about destitution
On whom should we rely, since ages past
This line has become our heart's refrain
The world is full of emperors and kings
But Mehr has chosen to beg in your alley

'So where is the need to make elaborate plans for a short existence! The Ultimate Nourisher provides us sustenance without pleading. If you desire your weal and prosperity through this, feed the mendicants and the destitute, and treat your subjects—who have been given to you in trust by God—with mercy, kindness and forbearance. Then regard what weal and prosperity you will discover.'

The king understood that the Sheikh would not accept the estate. He could do naught else but maintain silence. Then he put twenty purses of gold coins as offering before Dana Dil and Roshan Zameer, who also refused to accept them. Azar Shah then entreated and insisted that they take it, but they continued in their refusal, saying: 'We dervishes roam the world and the jungles, and possess neither home nor wife and children for whom we may need riches. God provides for us without our having to plead before his creatures.' In short, they took nothing, and departed.

King Azar Shah and Vizier Khajasta Rai accompanied them for a day's journey to see them off. The next day they bid them adieu on their onward journey, and returned to the city.

Azar Shah considered the companionship of Saman Rukh the asset of his life, and lived with her in great pleasure and comfort. The purpose for which he had made a second marriage was met that very year, that is, he was blessed with an illustrious son. He received in his last years and old age this great wealth which ensured the continuity of his name in the world, and he spent the rest of his life in great pleasure and luxury.

Thank God, I give Him thanks a hundred times, O Friends,
That the king successfully met his desire
After many years by the grace of God
The king's wish was fulfilled
Where there was at first grief, such joy arrived
That the whole house thrived and prospered
O friends, it is Mehr's prayer
That in like manner everyone should attain their wishes
Today, on a Saturday, in the evening
I, Mehr, finished the Nau Aaeen-e Hindi
For as long as the moon and the sun decorate the heavens
For as long as there are the revolving heavens
For as long as the garden of the world is in bloom
Although I will not be there, it will be my memorial

End

Qissa 5

The Victim of Malice

A first translation of *Qissa Maqtool-e Jafa*[1] from the Urdu as orally narrated by Hafiz Ghulam Nizamuddin Dehlvi to the compiler Hafiz Muhammad Amiruddin Maani

TRANSCRIBER'S PREFACE

Blessed is He Who made constellations in the skies, and placed therein a (burning) Lamp and a Moon giving light.[2]

Unbounded praise for the taintless God
Who from His power created the heavens
And populated them with constellations
Whose bounds cannot be reckoned
Who appointed for the sun and moon
Times of audience thereby creating day and nighttime

Aside from the heavens, He has created such rarities, whose intricacies of construction cannot be fathomed. In fact, if you turn your mind to it, there is nothing which is purposeless. What may be denigrated by all shows itself capable of such deeds that confound and overwhelm. Take the race of women, for instance, of whom everyone speaks ill, and which everyone thinks is impressionable, and believes can be easily prevailed upon; one prone to be fooled and trapped with just a few sweet words. By His lofty glory, such reserves of steadfastness are to be found within her, which many a man of indomitable nature can only

1. First published in 1870 as *Qissa Maqtool-e Jafa* by Naval Kishore Press, Lucknow. Translation from the fourth edition (1890) in the collection of the Raza Library, Rampur, India.

2. Quran (25:61).

dream of possessing. That is to say, whatever God Almighty has created is without equal. If you see with eyes that seek unity in what they behold, you see Him reflected in all His creation. As Mir Hasan[3] has said:

There is nothing that does not have His essence
He is not a thing, but exists in all things

But one must have seeing eyes in order to observe this. Our eyes are blind, and such lofty perceptions beyond us. It behoves a man not to offer idle comments when he is incapable of comprehending something, and, instead, observe silence.

REASON FOR TRANSCRIBING THE QISSA

The lowest of all slaves, error incarnate, sinner, reprobate, hopeful of pardon by the Pardoner, Hafiz Muhammad Ameeruddin, whose pen name is Maani, and who is the son of Hafiz Ghulam Nizamuddin Dehlvi, states that there lives in Delhi an estimable personage who has a bond of deep affection and closeness with my respected father. At a time long past, he heard my father narrate the story told in these folios. The good disposition, generosity, affability, kindness, and conferring of favours of the said personage are renowned from East to West; he comes from a noble family, trusted at the court for generations. He remained attached to the court with honour and dignity, receiving titles and robes of honour and retaining his influence until the end; even in present times, from the bounty of God. He has an excellent access to the ruler of the day, which nobody else enjoys. My memory fails to remember his royal title, but throughout Delhi, and in the length and breadth of other lands and dominions of the British, he is known as Nawab Nabi Bakhsh Khan Esquire. God be praised! He is an elegant, lofty-minded man, peerless in both liberality and bravery, of affable and wholesome nature, without equal in courage and dauntlessness, bestowed with the sum total of virtues, and in whom God Almighty has gathered the totality of fine qualities. May his value and stations be augmented by God's grace! In the month of Muharram,

3. Mir Hasan: The name of an eighteenth-century Urdu poet, author of the masnavi *Sihr al Bayan*.

1287 AH [April 1870 CE], he sent my father a missive with a message that read: In the past I heard you narrate a wondrous tale, and if you remember it still, I would that you have a copy made for me, for the great friendship we profess for each other.

Although my respected father had been unwell, with fever and other ailments for the past two months, on account of my dear uncle writing to him, who in addition to the bonds of brotherhood also had great affection for him, he indulged his request even in that state, considering the request a great boon, and asked this humble creature to sit by his bedside with inkwell and pen, to transcribe what he narrated. This abject man, on account of not having affinity for reading and writing, made many an excuse. At a loss to read or write, and denied this great blessing on account of my ill-luck, but taking cognizance, nevertheless, of my esteemed father's insistence, and considering that obedience to his command is warranted, I told myself that if I were to write as commanded by my father, this magical account would be remembered for a long time to come. With that in mind, on Sunday the second of Muharram, 1287 AH [1870 CE], I began transcribing as dictated by my esteemed father, and named it *Qissa Maqtool-e Jafa* (The Victim of Malice) and its chronogrammatic name[4] as *Fasana-e Gham Aamood* (Ruptures of Anguish).

I wish to submit before the wise and the seeing, my admittance before God regarding my ignorance and inability to write, and of having no discerning sense. But due to the grace of blessings, and the influence of the company of my esteemed preceptor, I have developed some familiarity with Urdu to the extent that I make do while struggling to write, and floundering with erroneous spelling and composition. Again, as some master has said, the human being is a compound of error and forgetfulness. In the name of God, if you find the idiom employed incorrectly, ignore my error, and do as Saadi has said:

VERSE

If you see some fault in my work
Indulge me as the Maker of the world would

and with the intent of improvement, do gracefully rectify.

4. Chronogram: A combination of words or verse the value of whose letters determine the year of a work's completion.

THE MARVELLOUS TALE OF A KING QUERYING HIS FOUR VIZIERS ON A MATTER; THREE VIZIERS DENYING AND THE FOURTH VIZIER CONFIRMING

The writer of the dastan gallops the steed of pen on the papery expanse of the page thus, that there was in the land of Hindustan a city both lofty and glorious, prosperous and paradisiacal, dotted with fine houses and elegant shops. It had a marketplace with crossing paths provided with every convenience, with level and clean roads, and a canal of water running across it, whose sprinkling fountains were a sight to please the eyes. Young and lively shopkeepers displayed the merchandise piled before them to its best advantage, selling their wares with charming ways and sweet speech. There was no commodity one could not find in that bazaar. All manner of fine things and choice items were available in abundance, wherever one looked. The populace was prosperous and fully content. Nobody had any cares, nor any wants or needs. Night and day, the people bided their time at home in great leisure. The city was a model of good administration. A man could walk in the dark of the night without fear of anyone stealing even a twig from his possessions. The doors of the houses were never locked at night. Thieves and brigands lamented their sorry fate, for they dared not even covet anyone's possessions. Nobody dared wrong or violate anyone; the lion and the goat drank water alongside, and everyone lived free of care.

The ruler of the land was King Sultan Bakht, of lofty station. Many monarchs paid him tribute, and many a mighty sovereign was under his writ. He was without equal in liberality and bravery, grandeur and majesty, equitability and justice, and charity and munificence. His treasury was plentiful, and, like the billowing waves of the sea, his armies were without count or number. His hours were devoted to the administration and financial care of his kingdom. He had four viziers of wise counsel who acquitted themselves with great distinction in carrying out their duties. They were known as the first vizier, second vizier, third vizier, and fourth vizier. The fourth vizier, named Masud Ali Khan, was wiser than the rest. His counsel was well reasoned and his answers to the purpose. Whatever he said was well considered and agreeable. The king often sought his advice over that of others', and followed his counsel, for which reason the other viziers were jealous of him, amongst whom the first vizier was foremost.

One day in the court, the king addressed the viziers with the question: 'Have you seen a woman who has these four qualities: Being without equal in beauty and charm; a past master of music who is peerless in her art; a religious scholar of surpassing ability, who may rightfully be called a master; and so modest that no one has ever glimpsed her shadow nor heard a word of her speech?'

Upon hearing this question, the first vizier joined his hands together in submission and said, 'O Refuge of the World, such a woman has neither been seen nor heard of. Let alone us, no one would have witnessed or heard of a single woman having these four qualities. Someone might have one quality, another two, and a third one three, while a fourth may have none of them. If one is a peerless beauty she might not know the art of music; and if she had those two talents, she might not be modest; and if one were highly modest, what business would she have singing and playing music? And which religious scholar has affinity for songs and musical instruments, for the religious law proscribes these entertainments. Your Honour, the four qualities that you have mentioned are the conjunction of opposites; their combination is impossible.'

The august king then asked the second vizier for his answer. He, too, like the first vizier offered the same answer before the king, substantiating it emphatically. Then the king, the Shadow of God, turned to the third vizier and said, 'Do speak if you have seen or heard of some such woman.' To which he replied, 'O Refuge of the World, what the first vizier and the second vizier have submitted before Your Highness is true and contains not the least falsehood. Let alone the present time, earlier generations, too, would not have seen or heard of such a woman.' In short, each of the three viziers seconded the other, and supported and corroborated their replies, offering many an example before the king to drive away the thought from his mind. But this was not to be.

After their speeches, the king turned to the fourth vizier and said, 'Speak what you have to say in this matter. Do not delay telling me if you have seen or heard of such a woman.' Upon this demand, the fourth vizier became silent and lowered his head, making no answer to the king. The king was grieved by his silence, and said, 'You give no answer to my question and grow mute. Quick, give me a proper reply.' Frightened by the king's displeasure, the fourth vizier kissed the foot of the throne, and after offering prayers and praise to the king, said, 'O Master of a Court Lofty as the Heavens, how may I tell you that my silence was on account of diffidence and reserve? I seek your forgiveness!'

The king said, 'You have explained yourself. Now make answer.'

The vizier replied, with hands folded respectfully at the waist, 'O My Master, hear then that God has indeed made certain persons superior to other persons; He can do as He pleases. It is not difficult for Him to gather these four qualities into one individual. Let alone a human, should He wish, He may even endow a mere beast with the sum total of all qualities.'

The king answered, 'God, exalted be His might, has verily such, and even greater power, as you describe. But do tell me if you have seen such a woman. When I ask you about one thing, do not divert me by mentioning something else.'

The fourth vizier submitted, 'Your Honour, pray do not ask me to answer at this moment. I shall give you my answer in private and tell you all without the least prevarication. Pray excuse me from speaking, as this is a public assembly.'

The king insisted, and said, 'We shall have your answer right now, and adjourn the court only after receiving your reply.'

The pertinacity of the woman, the child, and the king are proverbial; none may be passed over. The vizier sought reprieve from answering, but the king still insisted. When the vizier saw that he had no recourse but to answer, he submitted, 'Your Honour, it is not uncommon to find women invested with the qualities you enquired about. As it happens, the wife of this born slave of Your Majesty's is endowed by God with all these four attributes.' Thus speaking, the vizier fell quiet.

The king was not satisfied by his reply. He said, 'Answer in detail what you have described in brief, so that your assertion is held to be fully creditworthy, or else you will be deemed to have made an idle claim.'

The vizier was stupefied and said to himself: 'What I said will now be an idle claim. If I do not provide details, the king will not believe me; and it would be indecorous to offer further details.' Feeling powerless, and noticing the king's look of displeasure, the vizier's fear for his life made him speak as follows: 'O My Lord and Master, my wife, your born slave girl, is lovely, Venus-like in her charms, and endowed with such natural beauty that neither the race of man nor jinn can produce her equal; if the houris and paris see her, they would be stunned by her beauty and rendered speechless; dazed and overwhelmed, they would become engrossed in her visage. The bright orb of night hides its face from her in shame; be it the brightest star in the heavens, or the full moon, they both glow dimly before the refulgence of her face. Neither has my tongue the elegance, nor my speech the eloquence to do justice to even a particle of beauty of her face, or the virtues of that moon-like creature, radiant as light itself. Let alone a lowly human, even the heavens, which revolve night and day, sporting the spectacles of the sun and the moon, would not have seen such an enticing face. The pen, even though it has two tongues, has no power to describe even a mote of her beauty. The grace of her face and her qualities lie outside the realms of speech and the written word. As to her learning, let me offer a small glimpse of her ascendancy: the greatest scholars and learned men of our time do not dare debate her in any discipline; with just a single question she confounds them into silence. She knows all books of logic and etymology and syntax, et cetera by heart, and beyond these subjects, she has command over medicine, astrology, arithmetic, and the Holy Quran and the seven modes of its recitation; in short, she is a master in every branch of knowledge. Her continence and chastity is such that she was betrothed to me in childhood, and from that day she has not visited her parents' home. She did not come out of the veil even before her real brothers when they visited us, and did not show them her face; in all things she seeks only my will and pleasure. And how to describe her mastery of music! Suffice it to say that had Tansen[5] himself listened to her singing, he would have forgotten his strains and sworn never to sing again; and if Baiju Bawra[6] had heard the sound of her singing and playing, he would have lost his mind and never uttered another musical note. To what extremes can I praise her, for she possesses every quality, and is indeed a master in every art. Especially in the four qualities Your Honour mentioned, she is unrivalled.' Thus speaking, the fourth vizier of wise counsel became quiet. The king, too, having received an adequate and acceptable answer, was satisfied.

But the first vizier, who was extremely jealous of the fourth vizier, and nursed a deep-seated animosity and grudge against him on

5. Tansen: Name of a legendary sixteenth-century Indian musician.
6. Baiju Bawra: Name of a legendary musician from medieval India.

account of the latter's wisdom, was incensed by hearing his speech before the king. In high dudgeon, from a feeling of envy, he addressed the fourth vizier in his heart thus: 'Just wait and see how I avenge myself on you for this address. No matter, if you deprecated us before the king! God willing, you shall pay for it!' Thus resolving, he maintained his silence, and bided his time.

THE ACCOUNT OF THE FIRST VIZIER ENTICING THE KING DURING A HUNTING EXPEDITION TO ALLOW HIM TO CORRUPT THE FOURTH VIZIER'S WIFE, AND TAKING A SIX-MONTH LEAVE FROM THE KING FOR THE PURPOSE, AND DEPARTING FOR HER HOMETOWN

Authors of doleful tales and narrators who tell of torments relate the story thus: Perchance it so happened that once, when the king went for the chase, the other three viziers were occupied in looking after the administrative and financial affairs of the kingdom, and only the first vizier accompanied the monarch.

Sitting alone in the howdah behind the king, when that envious fellow saw the field all to himself, he laid the trap in this wise: along the way he gradually brought the conversation to bear on the fourth vizier and then broached the question the king had put to the viziers. When he found the king attentive, he said, 'O Beneficent Master, the exaggerated praise of his wife sung by the fourth vizier rings utterly false. To this day none of us has witnessed any woman who is so devotedly faithful, nor have we heard mention of such a one. On account of the encomium offered by him regarding her chastity, yours truly reckons that she is a strumpet and harlot of monstrous appetites. She has fed him owl's flesh[7] to strike him dumb; caught in her net of deceit, he is no longer his own person. Or else, he resorted to prevarication in order to humiliate us before Your Honour, as three of us denied the possibility, and stated that no one would have seen or heard of such a woman. He offered such adulation for his woman that our senses took

7. Owl's flesh: According to folk belief if someone is fed owl's tongue in food that person loses the ability to speak and protest.

flight. His speech made it clear as day to yours truly that his wife is a harridan, and he, a liar. If Your Honour should give me, your humble servant, a few days' leave, I would travel to her hometown, and get to the bottom of the matter so that it is settled, once and for all. In fact, there is a good likelihood that your humble slave will be successful in corrupting his wife, and then publicly show the fourth vizier to be a teller of untruths. For lying, God forbid, is a heinous sin, and worse than all other transgressions. And mendacity before a king, especially, is a great crime.'

After the king had heard the first vizier's wicked speech, he said, 'The fourth vizier is not a liar. It would be a small wonder if his wife turned out to be as he described.'

The malicious-natured first vizier then said, 'What Your Honour suggests is a wonder. From the earliest times, no one has come across such a woman. Many people have tried womenfolk, and never found any of their kind free of guile. Some master has said, and Your Honour may have heard it mentioned, that: Who has ever seen a horse, a woman, or a sword which was loyal?

The king replied, 'Another master has stated the opposite.' The vizier said, 'Pray share it.'

The king said, 'That every woman is unlike other women, and every man unlike other men; for God has not made the five fingers alike.' Upon hearing this saying from the king, the vizier said, 'Your Honour, what you related, and what I submitted, are both sayings by men. But God Himself denounces women in the Quran in these words: Behold! It is a snare of you women. Truly, mighty is your snare.'[8] After reciting these words, the first vizier said, 'Your Honour, such is the race of women. May God save everyone from their deceit.'

The king remained quiet after his speech, but that wretch was not deterred, and kept fulminating against her. Finally, the king asked, 'And what should be your punishment if you are unable to corrupt the fourth vizier's wife?'

He answered, 'Your Honour should give your humble servant six months' leave. If during that time I am successful in corrupting his wife, whose chastity he speaks so highly of, and present proof positive before you, then that liar and falsifier should be beheaded. And in the

8. Quran (12:28).

event that yours truly is unable to corrupt his wife, and present the proof before you, this born servant of yours should be buried up to his waist in the ground and riddled with arrows.'

The king asked, 'Do you make a firm compact or speak idly?'

He answered, 'Your Honour may have yours truly at once submit a warranty attested by his signet, and only then grant him leave and opportunity.'

The king said, 'Very well, we shall see.'

• • •

Several days had passed after the king's return from the chase, when the first vizier again found a private moment with the king, and submitted, 'Your Honour, have me pen a warranty attested by my signet before witnesses, and allow me six months' leave to carry out the proposed mission.'

In order to put an end to the matter, the king said, 'Remember then, that if you are unable to bring proof that you corrupted her, you shall be instantly beheaded.' He answered, 'Very well! And what will be the course if the proof is presented to you?' The king said, 'In that case, the fourth vizier will meet that fate instead.'

The first vizier said humbly, 'I accept!' He immediately wrote a pledge detailing these terms, took his signet ring off his finger and attested the pledge with it. He then made four of his relatives witness the document. Then, obtaining six months' leave, he prepared his belongings for the journey, and taking with him a large purse of money, left clandestinely for the hometown of the fourth vizier, with some excuse circulated for his absence from the court.

THE FIRST VIZIER ARRIVING IN THE FOURTH VIZIER'S HOMETOWN, AND RECRUITING A KUTNI'S HELP TO CORRUPT THE VIZIER'S WIFE

The first vizier, feeling pleased with himself but also somewhat anxious, supplicated tearfully before God, thus: 'O Lord, my honour is in your hands; keep me from disgrace before the king and the entire court. I set out from the house, relying on your aid.' Praying to God, and distributing alms to the destitute, he steadily traversed the stages and stops along the journey. God of Lofty Station Who is all oblivious, Whose retribution for good and evil is deferred until Judgment Day, and Who in this world confers upon everyone from His bounty what they seek, accepted his tearful supplication in His court from the giving of alms, and his prayers were answered in a small way.

The first vizier entered the fourth vizier's hometown after a twenty-day journey and acquired on rent a fine mansion fit for nobility in Chandni Chowk. Having furnished it with carpets and glass lights, and recruited a few nobles to serve him, he would go out morning and evening in great pomp, to take the air.

After he had been living there for a number of days, he searched for kutnis[9] and sent for them. Whenever one presented herself, he would ask about her best talent. One told him that she could cleave the earth and disappear inside and reappear. Another claimed that she could bring him the stars from the night sky. Yet another claimed that she could bring him a pari from Mount Qaf in the flash of an eye. In like manner, every day countless such women would arrive and relate their skills, but none found favour with him.

One day an old kutni presented herself before the vizier. She was the very aunt of the devil (may God blacken his face), and the preceptor of all kutnis. She was one who could leave the greatest disguisers and artists in the dust. She was a past master in all kinds of trickeries, and well versed in reading and writing. She was a brazen creature; a great deceiver and beguiler, from whom the devil himself sought refuge. She was so adept in portraiture that she need only to look at someone once in order to draw that person's perfect likeness, and make it so lifelike that the only thing that distinguished between the original and the portrait would be the power of speech. She was a woman so accomplished in the art of disguise that she could at once take on the appearance of another person, with the effect so remarkable that it would call into doubt the original. All the disguisers who ever lived were her disciples in the art; she outperformed all in trickery. She could even pierce the sky and bring news from there. May God save us all from her guile!

When she presented herself, the vizier, as was his wont, asked her too about her best talent. In reply, she made such outlandish claims

9. Kutni: A devious woman who performs the office of messenger between lovers and also carries out deceitful acts on payment.

and exaggerated talk that the vizier was amazed and delighted to have found her, and told himself that with her help he would of a certain be able to attain his heart's desire.

He said to the kutni, 'There's a task I need done, and if you are successful in carrying it out I shall pay you so well that it will suffice not only for your lifetime but also your seven generations to come.' She replied, 'May my life become your sacrifice! Tell me what it is you need done.'

He answered, 'Arrange a private meeting for me with the wife of Vizier Masud Ali Khan, who lives here and belongs to this town's nobles. It is only the desire to meet her that has brought me here, and I am mired in it up to my eyes, and have lost all perception and sense. Have no worries about money: expense is no consideration as long as my desire is met, which is that she warms my side and spends the night with me.'

Upon hearing this, the kutni said, 'Have you seen a portrait of her, or heard her praise from someone, that you have become thus besotted with her person and come here? Give me a complete account, as you know it.'

The vizier said to that harridan, 'What business do you have with it? Take the money you require and carry out the task I have assigned you.'

She answered, 'My good man, one cannot properly strive in a mission without comprehending the essence of the matter. If you have made a wager, just a token from this woman would be sufficient for your purpose. And if you wish to see her face, one could strive accordingly to bring that about. Now you should narrate the whole matter, so that I can carry out your wishes to the best of my abilities.'

The vizier replied, 'Her husband and I serve as viziers to the same king. One day, her husband praised his wife's beauty, virtues, chastity and modesty so highly that the desire to see her gripped my heart, and it keeps me restive. Moreover, unbeknown to the vizier, I claimed before the king that I would return after corrupting her, and should I fail in my endeavour, he should have me beheaded. Now you understand that if she meets me, and I keep her with me for the course of the night and bed her, I will continue to enjoy life; otherwise I will lose it for nothing. Take now whatever money you require, and get busy, and strive to bring that Venus-like beauty to me for an intimate meeting.'

That kutni was beside herself with joy when she heard the request and the promise of receiving untold riches. She said to herself: 'After a long time and prolonged wait I have caught in my net of cunning an idiot who is a slave to his devilish desire.' She said to him, 'May I take all your burdens upon myself! Have not the least anxiety. It is no such difficult task that you despaired over it. Give thanks, for you are in luck that you've met a singularly accomplished and many-talented woman such as myself. Now bring solace and cheer to your despondent heart. It is no momentous task to arrange your meeting with the vizier's wife. The woman you speak of is, after all, from this world; I could even bring you Venus and Jupiter in an instant. Regard now my cunning and masterful actions in your service. Just make sure that the money you have promised is not lacking.'

The vizier answered, 'Have not the least worry about it. I guarantee it with my life. Take the payment in advance, then begin with the task, but do make haste to unite me with this woman. My life depends upon her meeting me, as I have taken six months' leave from the king and have furnished him with a written guarantee.'

She said, 'Very well. Pay me something now.' The vizier gave her a purse containing a thousand gold pieces and after saying many words of flattery and praise to her, said, 'Take this! And go with dispatch!'

The harridan then departed and went home, and safely put away the purse of gold pieces.

THE KUTNI MAKING A FIRST ATTEMPT AT GAINING ACCESS TO THE FOURTH VIZIER'S WIFE AND BEING FOILED IN HER PLANS

The kutni set out from her house after the morning prayers and arrived at Vizier Masud Ali Khan's house. She beheld a magnificent mansion, built like a fortified castle, with walls so high that even a bird could not fly above them. There was such excellent organization in place that even the wind did not have free passage and had to seek admittance. The house was guarded on every side by troopers and foot soldiers, deployed at a short distance from each other, all of whom stood alert and sentry in their positions. The building was ringed by seven antechambers, the doors of which remained shut. The kutni enquired from those who lived nearby why the doors of the house remained closed. They told her that, as a rule, while the master of the house, Vizier Masud Ali Khan was present, the doors remained wide open. However, when he returned to his duty at the court, the doors were closed shut as she had witnessed. She asked if they opened at any time during the eight watches of the day, or always remained closed. They told her to be gone and mind her own business, and demanded to know what business she had making these enquiries. The kutni made a sorrowful face, and said, 'I only asked because I wondered how the food was supplied indoors if the doors remained shut all eight watches of the day.' They answered, 'There is an old maidservant, most honest and loyal, who enjoys the family's utmost trust. She comes out of the house once a day and sends for whatever rations are needed through the errand-boy, then returns to the household, closing all the doors behind her.'

The kutni was stunned and wonderstruck upon hearing of these stringent arrangements. She left in exasperation and went straight to the first vizier. After giving him the whole account, she said, 'My good man, we are in a pickle. Where even a bird cannot gain access, how will a person find admittance?'

The vizier again flattered the harridan, tempted her with money, and said to her, 'No matter how you do it, just find some way to carry out the task.'

The kutni, already tempted by the prospect of money, demanded another purse for her expenses. The vizier forthwith handed her another thousand gold pieces, and said, 'Take this and depart, and quickly think of some way to carry out the mission.'

She carried the money home, put it away safely and then busied herself in thinking of some new artifice. After some contemplation, she wove a new, marvellous net of deceit.

She bought five rupees' worth of sweets and a basket of flowers, and went to the entrance of the vizier's home, and said to the guards, 'Some twelve years ago my son ran away from home. I underwent much hardship in separation from him and, with dust in my hair, went from door to door searching for him. I pledged offerings for his return, cast lots endlessly for his whereabouts, sought recourse to threads, amulets, and the jinn, but could not learn where he had disappeared. Finally, exhausted and hopeless, I gave up the search, and gave myself up to crying night and day. One night, I fell asleep while thinking of him. In my dream I saw a pious and virtuous old man, who said to me: 'What good did it do you, your wasting away your life in separation from your son, and searching for him in futility? Listen to me now and do as I tell you. God willing, you shall soon meet your son. Here is what I have to tell you: The wife of Masud Ali Khan, who is a noble of this city, is very pious, virtuous, devout, and reverent, and the like of a living saint. Make a pledge in her name, and after you are united with your son, you must take her sweets and flowers as offerings.' Thus speaking, he held my hand, raised me, and disappeared. At that moment I made a pledge, saying: "O God Almighty, as a sacrifice of that pious woman, reunite me with my lost son, so that as per the instructions of the holy man of my dream, I can make offerings to that living saint." May my life become the Lord's sacrifice, and I scatter my existence at His grace; He reunited this sorrowful woman with her son, missing for twelve years, upon the intercession of that devout woman. He returned home yesterday in safety and well-being. I was beside myself with joy at the sight of him, and all grief was cast away from my soul. At last, my deprived self found fulfillment. The separation was removed and my wish was granted. God be praised! What to say! My lady is indeed a living saint. The holy man in my dream had given me truthful annunciations. I have now come to make the offering, bearing sweets and flowers. I shall do so for three consecutive days. There is little possibility of my meeting the lady, but I shall distribute the offerings among you, and leave the basket of flowers at the doorstep.'

She put the flower basket in front of the antechamber, distributed the sweets among the guards, and went away.

The following day the door of the house opened as per routine, and the old maidservant who was a sharp woman came out. When she saw the flowers scattered outside the door, she asked, 'Tell me at once why these flowers are lying outside the door today.'

The guards narrated the whole story the kutni had told them, and said, 'That woman will come again tomorrow.'

That maidservant cursed and abused the guards, and angrily said to them, 'Beware! If you value your lives, you must arrest that wicked kutni the moment she arrives, and then inform me. Most certainly she is a kutni. What business could that ill-born woman have, darkening our door with her shadow? If you fail to arrest her, I will have your bellies cut open and stuffed with hay to make an example of you.'

All the guards were frightened and said with hands folded at the waist, 'We will arrest her without the least delay. Upon her arrival she will be forthwith taken into custody and put in strict imprisonment. Do you imagine that we would waver in the least in obeying your orders, and bring trouble on our heads? Have not the least worry on that account.'

The maidservant reiterated her instructions and went back into the house, closing the doors behind her. That day was followed by the night and soon it was day again. At the time of the morning prayers, the maidservant came out and asked the guards about the kutni. They answered, 'She has not arrived yet, but should be here soon.' The maidservant went back into the house upon hearing this.

After some time, that harridan, Satan's own mother, appeared with the flowers and the sweets. Misfortune lay in wait for her. The guards set upon her, raining blows and kicks. They tied her arms behind her back, put shackles on her hands and feet, and an iron ball and chain around her neck. Then they dragged her away and locked her in a dark chamber. She cried out and pleaded with them and shed copious tears. She begged in the name of all things holy and cried, 'At least tell me my crime! What sin have I committed? What wrong have I done, for which you punish me thus?' But no one paid any attention to her. For one day and one night she was kept without food and water in the dark chamber, under heavy imprisonment.

The following day, when that pious, angelic old woman came out, as per usual after unlocking the doors, she sent for food and victuals with the errand boy, and sat guarding the door herself. The guards presented the captive harridan in chains before that woman of pure disposition, and all of them said with one voice: 'We arrested her as you had ordered, and did not listen to her protestations. Now she is before you. Pray give us your orders regarding her.'

After hearing them, the old maidservant regarded the harridan carefully, and after rebuking the wretch severely, said to her, 'I am sparing you this once. But beware, never think of coming this way again. If you come in this direction again and I find out, I swear by God that I will have your skull cracked by mallets. Mind that you never again show your face here, or even look in this direction.' In short, after much censure and chastisement, she released the kutni, and returned indoors, shutting the doors behind her.

Upon her release from imprisonment, the kutni headed straight to see the first vizier and narrated to him all that had passed with her, saying, 'My good man, whatever praise you had heard of that woman, she is four times as chaste. There seems to be no chance of you seeing or meeting her. The most I can do is bring you a picture and token from her with my craftiness and cunning, but this will not be an inexpensive undertaking.'

The vizier dejectedly replied, 'I so very much wished I could have an intimate meeting with her, and that that beloved would spend the night here so that I could fulfil all my heart's desires.'

She answered, 'Let alone you, even an angel could not dare see her shadow. When I offer to bring you her picture and a token, do not imagine that this will at all be a simple thing to accomplish. It is going to be back-breaking work and require much ingeniousness, hard work and labour. If my plan works, at least your life will be spared and you will not be humiliated before the king. If I am successful you shall have countless thanks to give for escaping with your life.'

The vizier thought to himself, 'She speaks the truth. It would be enough, indeed, if I could provide even a small something to the king for face-saving.' He said to her, 'Fine! Hurry and do what you suggest.'

The kutni answered, 'Very well, but do furnish me with some more money.' The vizier gave her another purse of a thousand gold pieces and sent her away. That harridan put away the money safely at home.

THE KUTNI IS SUCCESSFUL IN GAINING ACCESS TO THE VIZIER'S HOME UPON A SECOND ATTEMPT

The kutni went into the neighbourhood and made enquiries about the vizier's wife's hometown, and where her parents lived. She was told that her parents lived in a city named Sialkot in Punjab, from where she had come after her marriage. Once the kutni had learned all the details, she gathered all her apparatus of trickery, some travel money, and headed for Sialkot.

She arrived there after a few days and lodged herself in a serai, and made enquiries about the house where the family lived. Once she had discovered their house, she presented herself to them as a destitute woman, and begged the mother of the vizier's wife to take her into her service. When she looked at the innocent face the kutni presented, she hired her as a servitrix.

The kutni lived there for a month and learned all she could about the family. She acquainted herself with all their circumstances, and observed well the mother's looks, disposition, features, height and posture, manner of walking, pace, and speech, memorising them well.

Finally, one day she said to the lady of the house, 'I feel anxious and must return to my family.' The family tried to dissuade her from leaving, advising her to stay longer, as she had been there merely a month. They advised her to take leave once she had worked there some six or seven months, and come back after spending time with her family.

The kutni cooked up a falsehood, and said, 'My good woman, my grandson is very attached to me. I miss him terribly. He must be inconsolable without me and crying his heart out. In truth, I am not so poor and destitute as to need employment. It was on account of a quarrel with my daughter-in-law that I felt unhappy and left home. Now I am miserable, not having seen my grandson, and the separation from him is killing me.' After giving them this excuse, she obtained her salary for the month and left.

When the city to which she was returning lay six days journey away, she lodged herself, provided herself with a palanquin, and hired a number of men as servants and attendants. Already a past master in the art of disguise and appearance, she made herself into an exact likeness of her recent employer, the vizier's wife's mother, so that not the least difference remained between her and that woman in height and posture, features, appearance and disposition, pace, speech, and etiquette. In short, the kutni disappeared entirely into the guise of the vizier's mother-in-law. She dressed herself in the same kind of dress and jewels as that woman did. Using her excellent writing and reading skills, she penned a letter to the vizier's wife, handed it to one of her newly recruited servants, and bid him deliver it to the address she had provided.

The letter read: O light of my eyes, the strength of my heart and liver, and the solace of my soul! The shock of separation from you has kept me restive. My heart is content on all accounts but disunion from you has tormented me, not letting me have a moment's peace. I made your father and brothers write you many a letter, requesting you to visit and show your face, but you did not come. Since the day of your betrothal, I have longed to see your face and my eyes have searched for you. I have now lost control of my heart and decided to visit you myself. I am sending you my present location and have sent this letter to alert you. God willing, I shall arrive in due time and see you.

When the servant arrived with the letter at the vizier's house, he said, 'I have brought the letter of the vizier's mother-in-law. Pray tell me where he can be found.' The vizier's men and attendants told him that the vizier was not at home and that his letter would be sent into the house the following day, as it was not possible to do so then. They told him to relax, order some food from the grocer and eat something. They said to him, 'Once your arrival is announced, and the letter is asked for, it will be sent inside.' The servant could do naught else but wait.

The following day, when the maidservant emerged from the house at the appointed time, she learned that a man had arrived with a letter from the vizier's in-laws the day before. She went and announced to her mistress that a letter had come from her family, and if she so ordered, it would be produced before her. Her mistress told her to go and quickly fetch it. The maidservant brought her the letter. When the vizier's wife read it, she learned that her mother was due to arrive. She felt anxious about what to do, as the vizier was not home. If she were to admit her mother and meet her, she would be doing so without her husband's prior permission. How could she see her without his leave, she wondered. But she also considered that if she were not to admit her own mother into her home, it would displease God and his prophet because the duty to one's parents, and obedience to them, pleased Him. While she wavered in her decision, she started receiving news at regular intervals as her false mother approached near, traversing the stations of the journey. One day, at the time of morning prayers, a man came running with the news that her mother had arrived near the riverbank. In her anxiety, the vizier's wife sent the maidservant to call her foster son, whom the vizier had adopted and raised, and who lived in a separate house in great comfort and luxury. She had the maidservant narrate to him the complete account of her mother's arrival at the riverbank. Then she said to her adopted son, 'Take some high-ranking people with you to greet my mother and bring her with you.'

The boy said, 'Very well!' He mounted a horse and, taking some nobles with him, met the false mother of the vizier's wife, brought her to the house with honour, and conducted her into the vizier's house.

THE KUTNI SUCCEEDING IN DECEIVING THE VIZIER'S WIFE INTO BELIEVING AND CONFIDING IN HER

The false mother cried many fake tears when embracing her daughter, and did not loosen her embrace for a long time. After some time, they sat together and exchanged personal news. The false mother asked about the vizier. The daughter answered, 'My mother, he returned not too long ago to his work at the court.'

In short, that day and night were spent in the serving and partaking of food and drink. The following day, the false mother said to the daughter, 'May my life become your sacrifice. Why do you wear such a slovenly look and garb? You look like one of the poor people in rags. You are neither wearing proper jewellery, nor an appropriate dress. What is this perversity that you neither care for your house's appearance nor your own person?! What has happened to your senses?! What grief, God forfend, eats away at your heart that you look so doleful?'

The vizier's wife answered, 'Mother, God forfend that I suffer a reverse. Praise God, He has bestowed everything on my humble self from His bounty and munificence. I do not want for anything. A thousand thanks for all His favours! It is a principle with me that when my husband is home I wear jewellery, and put on fine dresses and bedeck myself. I decorate the house too, as is appropriate. When he is home, in God's protection, everything is displayed suitably because a woman's dress and jewels are best displayed only before her husband. But when my husband—may God keep him in safety—is not home, nothing at all matters.' Thus speaking, she led her mother by the hand to the jewel room, the wardrobe, and all other stores of the house, and after offering thanks to the Almighty, said, 'You can see that I lack for nothing.'

The kutni was astonished and amazed at the sight of all these rarities. She gestured to take the daughter's troubles upon herself by cracking her fingers, and said, 'Your mother sacrifices herself for you. You were married while you were a minor. I have not seen you dressed up as an adult. If you could have a bath and dress and bedeck yourself I would see you in finery and it would gladden my heart. What I really wished was to see both you and your husband together, joyous and happy, but it can't be helped as he is not home. For now, just seeing you all made up will bring bliss to my eyes and comfort to my soul.'

The vizier's wife made many excuses and kept busy showing the false mother her possessions. It was evening by the time she was done showing her the glass lights and arms and armour in the house. They whiled away the night talking of this and that.

At the time of the morning prayers the false mother again insisted on seeing her dressed up. Unable to refuse her mother's wish, the faithful daughter ordered the bathwater to be warmed. Meanwhile, she conversed with her mother. She said, 'You should know, Mother, that there are two objects which belong to your son-in-law which comfort me greatly during his absence. One is the ring that he wears. Before leaving he takes off his ring and gives it to me and takes mine. Once he is gone, I keep that ring with me, and do not part with it even for a moment. The other object is a dagger that the king had given as part of the robe of honour he bestowed upon him. The vizier holds it dear and, after he leaves, I keep it beside me at night. Only then am I able to sleep.'

While they were having this conversation, a female attendant presented herself, and said, 'Mistress, the bathwater is ready. Please come and take your bath.'

THE KUTNI PREPARING A PORTRAIT OF THE VIZIER'S WIFE AND OBTAINING HER PERSONAL TOKENS

The vizier's wife rose to have her bath in seclusion, as was her wont. But her false mother did not let her step into the bath by herself. She accompanied her inside and asked her to take off her clothes so that she could have a chance, after a long time, to bathe and rub her body.

The vizier's wife said, 'Mother, to this day, not even a bird, let alone a person, has glimpsed my body. My attendants all leave me when I enter my bath. Kindly sit outside; I shall finish and join you presently.'

Upon hearing this, the false mother said, 'Are you saying that you will take purdah from me now?! My daughter, you did not take purdah from me nor showed any such considerations for the nine months that you remained inside my womb, and when I gave birth to you and saw you in the clothes nature gave you, or when I nursed you on my milk and raised you! Now that you have grown up, by God's grace, you hide yourself from your own mother?! How wonderful! Have some sense, my daughter, and hurry and take off your clothes.'

The vizier's wife dewed from shame, but she could not offer a suitable reply, and was obliged to take off her clothes.

While rubbing down her body, the kutni observed every inch of the vizier's wife's body and made a note of everything down to the smallest mole. After washing and bathing her she said, 'Now go, my child, and take out a new dress from your wardrobe, and put on all your jewels from the jewellery box. Dry your hair, oil and plait it, and line your eyes with antimony and tinge your teeth with missi; then sit in the golden seat. I shall join you soon, after washing myself.'

The vizier's innocent wife knew no subterfuge. She did as her false mother told her and sent for her dress and jewels. A female attendant arrived with her beauty box to braid her hair.

Meanwhile, the kutni found an opportunity to go to the rooftop with all her paraphernalia of trickery, cunning and portraiture, and in no time prepared a portrait of the vizier's wife in the nude which was her perfect representation; there wasn't the slightest dissimilarity between her body and the portrait. After completing the portrait she hid it in her belongings. Then she hurried to where the vizier's wife was sitting dolefuly, beautifying herself. That trickster woman quickly dressed her up in a resplendent dress and jewel-studded adornments, and seated her on a golden chair. She warded off the troubles from the vizier's wife's head, offered herself as her sacrifice, embraced and kissed her, and gave away alms as offerings to avert adversity.

Thus passed one day and one night, during which time the kutni did not let the vizier's wife take off her clothes and jewellery. It was only on the following day that she finally changed her clothes and took off the jewels. The kutni retired to the rooftop again and drew another portrait of the vizier's wife, this time fully adorned, and so captivating that if the angels were to set eyes on it they, too, would become besotted with her, like the angels Harut and Marut,[10] who were subsequently punished. The portrait she painted of that Venus-like beauty was so magnificent that human tongue would become dumb and the tongue of the reed pen, incapacitated. The kutni now had these two portraits of the vizier's wife: one in which she was shown naked, and in the other, fully adorned.

10. Angels Harut and Marut: According to Islamic belief, two angels who gave in to temptation when they fell in love with a woman named Zohra and were punished by God with captivity in a well in Babylon.

Some days after she had completed them, the kutni made an excuse to the vizier's wife, saying, 'Now I cannot stay any longer. Your nephew is very attached to me; he did not leave my side even for a moment and must be disconsolate at my absence. I missed you so badly that I did not even think about him when leaving and arrived here in my anxiety, with my senses all in disarray. By the grace of God I see you content and happy, and it brings me cheer, returning the light to my eyes, and comfort to my heart.

'One of my ardent desires, however, remains unfulfilled, for I arrived here at an inopportune time, when your husband was not present. Poor me! How could I have known that he would be away, otherwise I would not have visited at this time, but rather when he was at home. I wished very much to see my son-in-law but, alas, I cannot stay longer on account of my grandson. When your husband returns, tell him that I take his troubles upon my head. Enquire of his well-being on my behalf and visit many blessings upon him.'

Upon hearing this, the vizier's wife, who believed the kutni to be her mother, became tearful and said, 'Dear Mother, do not speak of leaving. You have only just arrived. Please stay a while longer. There is nothing much for you to do at your home. We have seen each other after years and it is unfair of you to be planning to leave already. My poor heart has not been filled with the sight of you, nor have you met your son-in-law. When he returns, and hears of your visit, he will be very cross with me, and reproach me and ask why I let you depart and not make you stay until his return. Then I will have no answer for him. Please do not leave just now.'

The vizier's wife pleaded with her in this vein, but she was unable to persuade the false mother to change her plans. The kutni had accomplished her mission and had no reason to stay longer. The poor heart-broken daughter kept beseeching and imploring her, but the kutni kept offering all kinds of excuses, and completed all her preparations to depart. When the daughter saw that she would not desist, she gave up, and sent for some money to make an offering to her mother. When she humbly made her offering, the kutni said, 'My daughter, what will I do with money? As you know well, God in His kindness has bestowed much wealth upon me. But I would not mind it if you were to give me some jewellery or weapon to take; as it would please your brother and his wife to see that you have sent them keepsakes. If you wish to do so, and give away some such thing, it would redound well on you, and make me happy, as there is no want of money in my household, God be thanked.'

Upon hearing this, as the poor woman pondered over what she could send for her family, the kutni spoke up, saying, 'My child, allow me a suggestion. If you so wish, send the chandan-haar necklace you are wearing for your sister-in-law, and the dagger that you sleep with for your brother. I am certain that they will be delighted upon receiving these gifts. Do give me this silver ring that you wear on your hand so that I can keep it with me as a memento of you and your husband. As to your younger sister, if you wish you may send her something, or not. She will be made happy by whatever you send her, and if you don't send anything, she will soon forget all about it, as she is just a child. In fact, she is so innocent that just the pair of nauratan armbands that you are wearing would fully satisfy her.'

The vizier's wife fell quiet upon hearing what her false mother had to say, and thought to herself, 'All of these four objects are priceless. How can I give them away without my husband's permission? Another consideration is that only two of them belong to me, and giving them away would not matter too much. The ring and the dagger, however, are not mine. How can I possibly give them away? Moreover, the possession of the latter two objects gives me reason to live. If I were to part with them, it would cause me untold distress; but, again, if I don't, it would make my mother unhappy, and she would think that after she asked them of me in so many words, I still refused her.' She took off her necklace and the armbands and put them before her mother but hesitated about the other two items.

That trickster woman, however, was not to be turned away from her purpose. She guessed the daughter's conflict from her face, and said, 'My child, you seem to be very fond of your sister-in-law and your little sister, in that you did not hesitate in taking off and giving away the gifts for them. But you do not seem all too fond of your only brother—born after much prayer and supplications—for you send nothing for him. Wouldn't it sadden him to learn that his sister did not send him anything? As for me, what great treasure did I demand of you that you are in two minds about it?'

The vizier's wife felt powerless before this deceitful address, and immediately gave the dagger, and the ring from her finger, to the kutni.

She decided on an auspicious day for her false mother's journey, and on the day had kulchas cooked for her breakfast, gave her some money for the journey, and had her conveyed to the other side of the river, in great state. Then the vizier's wife returned to her daily routines.

Here ends the account of the proceedings at the vizier's house.

THE FIRST VIZIER SUBMITTING THE PORTRAIT AND PERSONAL TOKENS OF THE FOURTH VIZIER'S WIFE BEFORE THE KING

Now hear of that harridan's doings, and what mischief she stoked after taking away those four tokens and the two portraits of the vizier's wife, for it is a tale worth hearing. Once she had crossed the river, she released her attendants from her service after giving them suitable rewards for their work.

Happy and satisfied, she then went to the first vizier, gave him the two portraits and the four tokens, and said to him, 'My good man, with much effort and guile, I was able to obtain these portraits and these four objects. Know that the fourth vizier's wife is four times as chaste as the reputation you had heard of her. I had never seen nor received word of a woman who had all her qualities. If you did not have a cunning and devious woman like me to serve you, your life would have been forfeit. Now take these portraits and tokens and leave. When you see the king you can tell him that you were able to corrupt her; that for two months she spent every night with you, and at the time of your leaving you sent for the portraitist and had a portrait made of her unclothed, and one in which she was fully adorned, both of which you have as proof for the king to see with his own eyes. Give him this ring, which belongs to the fourth vizier, which he had left as his memento with his wife. And here is the dagger that the king had bestowed upon the vizier, with a robe of honour. This is a chandan-haar necklace that belongs to the fourth vizier's wife, and this pair of nauratan armlets are hers too. Once you have given him these tokens with the portraits, the king and the fourth vizier will have to believe you. Take all these objects and spare a thought for all the effort I made in carrying out your mission, and confer on me the reward you promised.'

When the vizier saw the objects and the portraits, he was beside himself with joy. He gave the kutni a thousand gold pieces, a robe of honour, and other things in reward, and she took her leave, happy and satisfied with her recompense.

After the kutni had left, the vizier had a good look at the portraits, and from beholding the woman's beauty such a powerful swoon came upon him that he was very nearly carried away from the world. When he recovered, he packed his belongings and headed back home. Traversing stages and stops of the journey, he arrived after twenty days in the seat of the kingdom and his ministerial office. He bathed and rested after reaching home, and early the next morning presented himself in the king's service. After kissing the king's feet, he resumed his duties.

Later, when the first vizier had a private audience with the king, he gave him the account as follows: 'O Munificent King, everything transpired as yours truly had submitted in your illustrious presence. The wife of the fourth vizier is a harlot and strumpet without equal. Now consider the falsehoods the fourth vizier uttered about her chastity and other qualities. Your Honour may now send for him and deliver the punishment.'

The king said, 'Give me all the details, and produce the proof you promised.'

The first vizier presented to him the two portraits, ring, dagger, chandan-haar necklace, and the pair of nauratan armlets, and said, 'Your Honour, every night for two months that bawd warmed yours truly's bed. When leaving, I asked her for a portrait. She sent for a portraitist with one of her servants, and then unclothed herself to have her portrait made; then got another done all dressed up and fully adorned. Here are the portraits, and you may examine them. When I asked her for a memento when leaving, she immediately took off this necklace and armlets to give me. When I told her I could not always keep on my person the things she had given me, and that she should give me something I do not have to part with, and may keep near me throughout the day to comfort my heart, she took off and gave me this ring and dagger, and said they belonged to her husband, the fourth vizier. I was delighted to receive these tokens. Along with the dagger, I kept all of them as keepsakes, and took my leave.'

After narrating this story, the vizier said, 'Your Honour may now decide whether such a liar and henpecked man is worthy of the rank of vizier, or deserving of beheading. Moreover, to make up lies before a mighty potentate such as yourself (I seek God's protection from the devil) is doubly reprehensible.'

Upon hearing his account, and seeing the portraits, the king was convinced, and grew enraged. He forthwith sent for the fourth vizier. When that innocent man presented himself, the already indignant king became infuriated upon seeing his face, and said, 'Tell me, is your wife chaste and pure?'

The vizier humbly submitted, 'Yes, Your Honour, your humble servant does not have words to describe her continence and chastity. In truth, she is a paragon of these virtues.'

These words further enraged the king. With bloodshot eyes, and trembling with ecstasies of anger and rage, he said: 'You are a great liar and a cuckolded idiot. Regard whose portraits these are, and to whom this ring and this dagger belong! Regard the dagger well, and tell me if it is not the one I had conferred upon you with the robe of honour. Tell me, as well, if this chandan-haar necklace and the nauratan armlets do not belong to that harlot of a wife of yours. Showing him the portraits and those objects, the king narrated the whole account of how the first vizier had gone and taken his pleasure of her for two months.

The fourth vizier became pale with mortification upon hearing this account, and upon regarding the objects which indeed he recognised as his own. His head lowered in shame, perspiring with embarrassment and unable to lift his eyes from chagrin, he did not have an opportunity to kill himself at that moment, or he would have gladly done so. Ashamed and humiliated, he kept sitting mute with his head bowed in embarrassment.

The king sent for the executioners, who soon presented themselves at his command. Upon their arrival, the king gave orders regarding the fourth vizier, saying 'Speedily behead him!' At the king's word, the innocent vizier's arms were tied behind his back, and he was led outside the city to be executed.

Upon reaching the execution grounds, the executioners awaited further orders from the king, as it was ancient custom that until the king had sent three orders to the execution grounds, the executioners did not behead the person. Following the tradition, the executioners awaited the three orders.

After some time, the first order was received. A while later, a second order was received, confirming that the vizier should be speedily beheaded. Upon receiving the second order, the executioners said to the vizier, 'Good man, eat or drink what you wish, and if you want to meet someone, send for him or her; for only the third order is awaited.'

The vizier said to the executioners, 'Take me before the king so that I can submit something before His Honour. I shall be eternally grateful if he grants me an audience.'

The executioners sent his request to the court and the king called him into his presence and said to him, 'Speak then, and tell us what you have to say!'

The fourth vizier kissed the ground before the king, and said, 'O Refuge of the World, I hope to receive from your lordship the permission to cast my eyes on that slattern and bawd one last time. Then you may order my execution.'

The king granted him his request, and said, 'You will be taken as a prisoner, with your legs in chains, and guards and troopers accompanying you. Be warned, that you must not kill her.'

The vizier accepted these conditions, and said, 'Your Honour may send me as he desires.'

Then the king dispatched him in shackles in bullock-cart, and deputed foot soldiers and troopers to guard him. After giving instructions to the soldiers not to let the vizier kill his wife, the king sent them off. Thus the ill-fated vizier started for his hometown as a prisoner.

The world is the abode of admonition. For that reason, O dear friend, listen to these words of advice: Never do anything that may bring ignominy, and no gain except shame. Dispel ego from your heart. Make yourself proof against vanity and arrogance. Avoid conceit, and do not be boastful. Lower your head before the True Lord in humility and meekness. Do not make tall claims before anyone, lest you, too, should be humiliated and degraded before the True King—like the fourth vizier—and find no refuge. Had he not boasted about his wife's chastity before the king, he would not have seen such humiliation and disgrace. The world is not a place where one should vaunt. One must, at all times, fear God, and not have any need or want from another.

THE FOURTH VIZIER RETURNING TO HIS HOMETOWN A PRISONER AND DIVORCING HIS WIFE, AND SHE LEARNING OF THE CAUSE AND HEADING TO THE KING'S COURT IN A SONGSTRESS'S GUISE

The narrator resumes this unhappy history from here. The fourth vizier, the victim of heaven's barbs and an unforeseen calamity, sighed and lamented his fate all through the journey, and after several days reached his home. Immediately upon his arrival, accompanied by guards, he went within and, after announcing an irrevocable divorce upon his innocent wife, turned back and stationed himself at a distance of two kos from the town.

Now hear of his wife. When the vizier showed up at their home a prisoner, and left after divorcing her, without saying anything, or bothering to hear anything she had to say, she was bewildered, cried bitterly, and decided on killing herself from the twin shocks of the vizier showing up in that state, and divorcing her without cause. She wondered what had caused these events and sought recourse to putting an end to her life with a dagger. A woman present there stayed her hand, and said to her, 'One could always kill oneself; at least first find out the cause of what has transpired. Afterwards, you are free to take your own life.'

Upon hearing this advice, the vizier's wife sent her maidservant to call her foster son, who lived in a separate house. When he arrived, and saw her state, he panicked and asked her to tell him what had happened. When she hesitated in telling him, he said, 'For God's sake, hurry, and tell me what has happened, and from what grief you cry and shed tears so profusely.' Between tears, that poor woman told him the circumstances in which the vizier had arrived, and how he turned back after divorcing her without giving any reason.

She said to him, 'My son, go now and discover, however you can, the cause of your father's imprisonment; and hear from his own mouth the reason he divorced me, so that I may learn the details as well.'

Upon hearing this, her son left on foot in his anxiety. He headed out of the town, asking everyone en route for some trace of the vizier. He had gone some two kos outside the town when he beheld some troopers and foot soldiers gathered under a tree. He asked them if they could tell him where he might find his father, who had come as a prisoner and was the vizier of the king. They answered, 'There he is, sitting beside the bullock-cart.'

The foster son turned towards him with tearful eyes. The vizier asked permission of his guards to let him approach. He embraced and kissed his son and cried bitterly at his state of affairs. After a while, the guards said, 'Enough of these tears! Now speak together, hear what each of you has to say to the other, and then send the boy away.'

The vizier narrated to his foster son the whole story from start to finish, and said, 'The first vizier visited here secretly, and bedded your mother for two months. He took away two portraits of her, in one of which she is shown naked, and another in which she appears with all her clothes and jewellery. He also took as keepsakes my ring, dagger, chandan-haar necklace, and a pair of nauratan armlets, and presented them before the king. Then, to denigrate and humiliate me, he narrated to the king the entire account of her wanton ways. The reason I was imprisoned and condemned to death is this: One day in the court, the king asked if anyone had seen a woman who possessed unheard of beauty, masterful command in musical arts, pre-eminence in knowledge, and the highest degree of modesty. While the other viziers replied that there was no such woman in the world, I invited trouble on my head by praising your mother, and telling the king, the Refuge of the World, that all those four qualities he had enquired about, were gathered in my wife. I maintained my silence after saying that, and don't know what happened thereafter. I have no knowledge how the first vizier arrived here. I only found out about it once he returned from here, with proof contrary to my assertion, and redeemed his estimation in the king's eyes. The king sent for me, humiliated and disgraced me in the extreme, and ordered my beheading.

'Upon receiving the second order of execution, I requested that I be allowed a chance to behold that cursed and damned woman. It was my intention to go home as a prisoner and kill her. God willed that the king accepted my request but imposed a condition that I not kill her. Because of the constraint placed by the king, I did not kill her when I saw her, and merely announced an irrevocable divorce and came away. I am certain that upon my return, I will be beheaded forthwith.' After narrating all this, the fourth vizier cried copiously, and said goodbye to his son.

After taking his leave of the vizier, the son returned to his mother tearfully, and gave her the complete account, as received from the vizier.

When that poor woman heard it, she realized that this must all be the doing of the kutni who had visited her as her mother. She told herself that whatever happened was God's will; the kutni was merely an instrument of fate, and no purpose would be served by blaming her; that it was her destiny to be thus defamed and calumniated, and have her household destroyed.

She speedily manumitted all her slaves and attendants, gave away half of all her possessions and properties and wealth in the path of God, and conferred her effects, money and gold on her foster son. She then took along with her two or three faithful attendants, who were intelligent and beautiful, and knew how to play the tabla and the dholak. Wearing a rich dress and jewellery, and travelling in a horse-drawn carriage with her attendants, she left for the seat of the kingdom where her husband was formerly a vizier, and travelled night and day without breaking her journey.

She completed what was a ten-day journey in just five days, lodged herself in a house in a serai, and advertised her talent in music and singing. She became so renowned that her fame also reached the king's ears, who heard that a beautiful woman, whose allure even the eyes of heaven would not have seen, had lodged herself in the serai. That in addition to her beauty, she was excellent in her manners. That she possessed a heavenly voice, and when singing she enraptured all; humans and jinn, and walls and doors alike fell into a trance by the power of her voice. That the whole world had become her devotee and hundreds of thousands worshipped her singing. Thousands remained in attendance at her door, just to catch a sight of her, and from morning until evening, and from evening till morning, the populace crowded her habitation. She had been endowed with such beauty that God Himself marvelled at His work; words did not exist to describe her fairy-like beauty; the cap-a-pie[11] description given here offers just a glimpse of her grace; and the splendour of that houri-like creature far exceeds this description that His Honour might wish to hear:

. . .

11. Cap-a-pie: Head to foot.

Cap-a-Pie Description

I shall now pen her head-to-foot description, augmenting the honour of speech in her service.

The stature of that peerless tree of the Garden of Beauty would delight even the heavenly tree of Tuba.[12] In comparison with that heart-ravishing cypress of elegance the pine-tree would cut a sorry figure.[13] She is the past master of coquetry and charm and knows full well all of a beloved's blandishments. Reflected in her proud glance is the modesty that is its wherewithal. Fidelity receives lessons from her existence. Judgment Day would salute her for the destruction she causes with her captivating gait. If the box tree were to compete with her, its straightness would be found imperfect. The perfect proportions of her limbs are incomparable; they are the marvel of the True Maker's art. Her head is the model of elegance and beauty, like the orb of the sun. Before the darkness of her hair, the Land of Darkness seems made of light; and her parting is like a stream of the Water of Life. Everyone who beholds this galaxy exclaims wonderstruck how it shines through dark clouds. Her dark locks are a marvel; a trap for tender-hearted prey. Her forehead shines like a tablet of light sprinkled with glitter, the likes of which none has heard of or seen before. Her eyebrows are like a perfectly shaped bow, and the arrow of death itself among its ardent admirers. Whoever sees her intoxicating eyes and glances becomes spellbound. The bewitching pupil of her eyes dances like a pari kept captive inside a glass flagon. Her sharply pointed eyelashes are a marvel, and sanctiond to spear the world. How else could I write praise of her ears except to say they are the two doors that open from a house of elegance. I am unable to speak of the beauty of her nose, as it is the apogee of the house of beauty itself. Whoever takes a glance at her cheeks will shed the sun and moon as tears. Spells and magic will be rendered ineffective if they witness the magical hue of her ruby lips. The sight of her lips is ravishing; they resemble the Yemenite agate. The pen is unequal to the task when called to praise the gem receptacle that is her mouth. Its aperture is so narrow that

12. Tree of Tuba: A tree in heaven mentioned in the Quran (13:29).

13. Cypress of elegance the pine-tree: The cypress is considered the model for a good stature.

speech barely makes way through it. Foul and idle speech could never find purchase on her well-formed, shining and bright teeth. In the praise of the dimple of her chin I will swear upon my faith that had Yusuf found this well in his path, he would have happily fallen into it. If the sun were to see her refulgent face, he would be shamed and find himself at a disadvantage. That coquette's neck is so exquisitely delicate that upon holding it the hand receives the same pleasure as it does clutching a wine flagon's neck. Do not ask me about the glory of her shoulders, for they are the port of tranquility for grieving hearts. Her delicate arms, full of allure, are superior in brightness to lightning. The one who discovers her hand in his, will have no peace until he has grasped her by the wrist. Her fingers could easily shame the moon's rays. Who could speak of her dazzling existence? Her bosom is transparent and crystalline. Her breasts are wondrously full of light; fondling them is a distant prospect. Her abdomen is softer than velvet, its perfection coveted night and day by the moon. Her navel was the nave of the sea of beauty, the lover's heart was lost in its eddies. Her waist is more slender than a hair; it would be more proper to call it the line of the gaze. The brightness of her thighs and their power of reflection puts to shame the mirror. If lightning were to see a glimpse of her leg, it would drown itself in a sea of shame. Her painted feet tramples underneath the hearts of lovers.

At the end of this cap-a-pie description, I pray that I draw my last breath in my faith. In this world, O God, safeguard humble Maani's honour, in the name of the Holy Prophet (PBUH) and his exalted progeny.

. . .

When the king heard such praise of her beauty and was made aware of her excellence in singing, he ardently desired to see her, and forthwith dispatched his private mace bearer to the serai, to bring her into his presence with all haste.

When the mace-bearer went to the serai and told her to accompany him speedily, as the king awaited her, she answered, 'Kindly submit before His Honour from this humble slave girl, after conveying my greetings and salutations, that I have come here only from the desire to kiss His Illustrious Highness's feet, but the long journey has exhausted me, and to allow me a few days' reprieve in order to dispel the tiredness of the journey. Then this devotee of His Majesty will present herself at the court, without the need of summonses, and kiss His Honour's doorstep.'

She used this ruse because she had arrived early, completing two and three days' journey in single days, and now awaited the vizier's arrival so that she could narrate to him the account of her chaste conduct, and tell him about the vilification and denigration suffered by her at the hands of the first vizier. It was an excuse to await the arrival of her condemned husband, the former vizier.

In short, the mace bearer returned to the court and conveyed her reply to the king, who granted her request.

THE FOURTH VIZIER'S WIFE REQUESTING TO HAVE THE WHOLE COURT ASSEMBLED FOR HER PERFORMANCE

After five days, when the fourth vizier also arrived in the city as a prisoner, and his wife got wind that he had entered the city and would be executed that very day, paroxysms of grief and anxiety overtook her. She quickly dressed and beautified herself, and secreted away a dagger in her dress. Carrying musical instruments, and with her ensemble of female musicians alongside, she started in her horse-drawn carriage for the king's palace. When she reached the palace, she announced her arrival at the court through the usher.

The king who eagerly awaited news of her, sent for her forthwith. When she approached the carpet of the private hall of audience, she stood at the saluting station and duly made her obeisance, surprising the court nobles with her etiquette. The moment the king's eyes beheld her beauty, it enraptured and stunned him into silence. All those present in the court also became restive, and began reciting the benediction. After a brief silence, the king gathered his wits, and asked her to approach. Upon receiving his permission, she again made an obeisance and further salutations, before taking a step forward.

As she was a vizier's daughter and vizier's wife, she knew courtly etiquette full well, and she stepped forward with such remarkable grace and regard for the royal audience that all those present were enthralled. As she approached the throne, the king gestured for her to sit down.

She replied, with hands folded at the waist, 'This slave girl would not dare to commit such offence.'

The king then proclaimed with his auspicious mouth, 'We give you permission to seat yourself.'

She offered praises and prayers for the king, kissed the foot of the throne, and after thrice making an offering of her life for the throne, with more salutes and obeisance, she sat down with her companions to the left of the throne, and submitted, 'Your Honour may command what is his pleasure, and this slave girl will carry it out.'

The king was so engrossed by her beauty that he did not hear her words. When she made the same submission again, the king said, 'The renown of your singing has spread throughout the city. We are also desirous of hearing it. Do sing a little for us.'

She lowered her head in acquiescence, and said, 'Very well! What this slave girl remembers, she will recite. But do kindly invite all the nobles and viziers and officials of the court. Since Your Honour's slave chanced to be present here, it would be generous not to deny anyone participation in this assembly, as audience.'

The king sent the mace bearers in all directions to gather the court. When they arrived, and she saw that everyone was present, and only the ill-fated vizier who was her husband was not there, she said, 'Your Honour, your devotee has learned that His Highness is vexed with one of his viziers, who is being held prisoner. I beg Your Honour to show me indulgence from his boundless charity and summon him here as well, for a short while.'

After a moment's consideration, for her sake, the king sent for the fourth vizier too. When that ill-starred fellow, flanked by his guards and jailers, and with his hands and feet restrained with chains, arrived and stood apart from the court, the king said, 'Now everyone is gathered here; nobody is missing. If you wish, you may sing something.'

As per the king's wishes, she and her entourage of musicians harmonised their instruments, and she began to sing in such a mode that even inanimate objects went into raptures. All those present in the court were stunned and became stock-still and spellbound. The king was thrown into such ecstasy that he could neither remove his gaze from her, nor utter a word. Some among her audience sighed in passion, others lauded her with praise.

How can one describe the scene that unfolded in the hall when she began singing! Suffice it to say that everyone forfeited possession of their senses.

When the king regained the possession of his senses somewhat, he uttered, 'Ask what you may desire. You shall receive whatever you demand!'

She answered, 'By Your Honour's bounty, this humble servant has all she needs.'

Then she resumed singing. She now sang so dolefully that all those present rolled on the floor like fluttering, slaughtered birds.

The king again said, 'Ask what you wish for. Whatever you ask, I shall fulfill your wish. If you were to demand my throne, I shall surrender it to you this instant, abdicate, and go into seclusion.'

She folded her hands at the waist, and said, 'O Refuge of the World, may God make possession of the throne auspicious for you. Thanks to Your Majesty, I have more than I need. This slave girl of yours only came here to kiss your feet and present herself in Your Honour's service, not to seek gold and riches.'

After making her reply, she sang with such heartfelt passion that Venus and Jupiter became restive in the heavens.[14] How to describe the humans, the seraphs, along with all the jinn and paris, and beasts of the land and air, who swooned from the strains of her singing, and lay unconscious at their stations! The entire court along with the king had lost sense perception and self-possession. Everyone was affected in a unique manner. Some made lamentations, some sighed; some sat unmoving with the lock of silence on their lips and still like images painted on a wall. In short, everyone at the court, including the august king, was affected by her singing. When she witnessed that everyone present had been deeply moved by her singing, she fell silent.

The king and the nobles recovered their senses somewhat after a full hour, but their souls did not yet stir, and they were alive only in name.

The king smiled in his state of bedazzlement, and said to her, 'Whatever you ask I shall confer upon you immediately, and without a moment's thought. Even should you ask me to give my life, I shall not

14. Jupiter and Venus: The planets Jupiter and Venus are said to influence music.

hold back. Ask me without delay. You shall receive not the measure of your request, but well over and above it.'

THE FOURTH VIZIER'S WIFE SEEKING REDRESS FROM THE KING FOR HER CALUMNIATION

After the king had made the offer a third time, the fourth vizier's wife realised that it was time to disclose her heart's desire without delay. She stood up with great decorum, prostrated herself to kiss the ground at the king's feet, and after folding her hands at the waist, spoke thus: 'May God keep Your Honour in all your majesty and grandeur till the end of time. Your slave girl is not greedy for, or in need of, gold and riches, wealth or property. The bountiful God has conferred a lot upon her by your grace. However, this slave girl now presents herself before you as a plaintiff. Your devotee has been the victim of maliciousness and injustice, which is why you see her anguished face before Your Honour.'

When he heard these words, the king said, 'What is this you tell me? Who subjected you to cruelty and malevolence? Tell me quickly, so that you may find justice this very instant. Speak without delay!'

She said humbly, 'Your Honour's first vizier bedded this poor slave girl of yours for two months and did not pay me any recompense. A sum of two hundred gold dinars per diem was agreed between us but throughout the two months he kept delaying the issue until he left for the court. I have come to seek justice so that you may have the payment for two months restituted to me, at the agreed rate as decided.'

Upon hearing this, the king regarded the first vizier furiously, and said, 'Not only did you commit a sin, but also demonstrated viciousness. If you wish to be spared, pay her the amount immediately and bring me the receipt of settlement, or else I shall have your stomach cut open and stuffed with hay.'

The first vizier paled with terror upon hearing the king's words, and said, 'My Lord and Master, your humble slave never even saw the face of this woman before today, let alone touched her. Your Honour may wish to have her claim be proven, before ordering the receipt of settlement to be produced. I do not know who she is, and whence she has come.'

The king now turned to the woman, and said, 'Did you hear what the first vizier said?'

She replied, 'Your Honour, the vizier is a liar and your slave girl speaks the truth.'

In short, for a long time the two of them held on to their respective claims. Finally, the woman said, 'Your Honour, the matter will not be settled if he keeps refuting the claim I make against him. You may ask him to suggest and write down his own punishment, if I, your humble servant, were to produce satisfactory evidence for my claim.'

The first vizier interjected even before the king could speak, and said, 'Your Honour, she has proposed an excellent solution. Let me give you in writing, right now, that if it is proven that I have even sighted this woman before today, let alone touched or bedded her, I may be tied to a cannon's mouth and blown up.'

The king asked him to present a written undertaking to that effect. Once this agreement was drawn up, the woman said to the king: 'Your Honour, he has submitted the written undertaking. Now you may send for and study the portraits of the fourth vizier's wife that this cursed man had brought, as proof of his claim before you that he had corrupted her.'

Upon hearing these words, the first vizier hung his head in mortification. The king sent for the two portraits to be produced before him at once. The king looked at the portraits, and compared them with the woman before him and noticed not even the least difference between her face, and the face depicted in the two portraits. Indeed, there could have been no disparity, since they were her true portraits.

Now the king became certain that the woman was the fourth vizier's wife. He said to the first vizier, 'Explain why you now claim never to have seen her in your life, when you brought us these portraits and declared before us to have corrupted her. Either stick to your earlier claim, or refute it.'

The first vizier was now trapped in the deception of his own weaving. If he persisted with his earlier claim, he would die from the power of the written pledge he had submitted to the king. And if he were to take back his claim, he would die by the pledge he had made about corrupting the fourth vizier's wife, and for which he had taken a six-month leave. In other words, he was damned if he opened his mouth, and damned if he did not.

Finally, the first vizier chose to refute seeing the woman until that day.

The king asked him, 'If you never saw this woman before today, what are these portraits? How did they come into your possession? Tell me truthfully.'

Upon this, the woman submitted respectfully, 'It may please Your Honour to command this humble servant to narrate this story.'

When the king gave her permission, she narrated the whole story of how a kutni arrived in the guise of her mother; how she insisted upon bathing her and later begged her to dress up and wear her jewellery; how, at the time of leaving, she asked directly for the necklace, armlets, the ring and dagger; how she gave them to the kutni with much reluctance, provided her money for the journey, and saw her off. Then she said, 'I took her for my own mother, as there was no difference in her features, nor her manners. But now I am certain that it was a kutni who entered my home in the guise of my mother, and with her deeds brought me to the pass that I had to present myself before Your Honour. She unclothed me with the excuse of bathing me, so that she could draw my body unclothed, and later dressed me up so that she could draw me fully adorned. The proof of her deception is the two portraits brought to you by this ill-begotten man. Now your devotee is certain that my necklace, armlets, and the ring and dagger were also given to him by that wretched woman, his true aunt, and he brought them here with the portraits.' After narrating the story, she said, 'Your Honour may consider how sordidly this wretch slandered my good name, smearing my reputation needlessly, and maligning me without cause. Your devotee will not be satisfied until this wretched, habitually vindictive man is hacked to pieces and fed to the crows and kites. Only then would I consider the wrong done to me redressed, as this iniquitous, wicked man wantonly destroyed my family, and chagrined me before the eyes of God and men.'

THE KING PUNISHING THE FIRST VIZIER AND RESTORING TO HONOUR THE FOURTH VIZIER

Upon hearing this account, the king, and all present at the court, cursed and execrated the first vizier. The king forthwith ordered that the first vizier's arms be tied behind his back, and that he be hacked to pieces and fed to the kites. He also ordered that the fourth vizier be produced into his presence with honour, after removing his chains. The moment they heard the king's orders, the officers and members of the court who were castigating the first vizier thus far, immediately collared him, and dragged him out of the court. His face was blackened, he was put on a donkey and led to the execution grounds, where he was hacked to pieces and fed to dogs and crows.

While this event was taking place, the king ordered that all of the first vizier's belongings and properties be confiscated and made over to the royal treasury.

When that woman had the first vizier killed, because of whom she had been humiliated and discredited, and after her husband had been released and restored to honour in the court, she said to the king, 'May God preserve you with your justice and equity. This humble servant received full justice for her complaint.' Thus speaking, she pulled out from the scabbard the dagger she carried on her person, plunged it into her stomach, and submitted her life to God.

While the king and the courtiers were wringing their hands at her death and bemoaning her loss, her husband, who had heard her entire story with his own ears, and now witnessed her tragic death, could hold back no longer. He rushed towards her corpse like an infatuated lover, and with the same bloodied dagger which had taken that moon-like beauty's life, put an end to his own by scattering his pearl of life on that martyr of chastity. Then, putting his arm around her neck, that true lover embraced his faithful beloved, and fell dead.

Upon witnessing this twofold tragedy, the king and the entire court were shocked and left aghast. For a long time, the king and everyone at the court cried over their deaths. At this great tragedy, the court rang with exclamations of grief like Judgment Day. Finally, the king and the courtiers realised that, what had happened could not be reversed. Resigning to it as the will of God, they recited the Quranic verse: Verily we belong to Allah, and verily to Him do we return,[15] and maintained their silence.

The nobles of the court who were present tried to separate the couple's corpses but found they were joined together and could not be pulled asunder. They attempted to force the bodies apart, trying many

15. Quran (2:156).

ways, none of which proved successful. Unsuccessful in their attempts, they made the decision to put both of them in the same winding sheet and bury them together in one grave. The couple's corpses were wrapped in a winding sheet and put into a casket. Everyone garbed themselves in black, in mourning. A cloth covered the casket, and it was carried forward with great dignity, surrounded by a crowd of mourners crying and wailing.

When the funeral procession reached the bazaar, the shopkeepers and craftsmen closed down their shops and, weeping, accompanied it. The crowd became so dense that let alone someone getting a chance to put their shoulder to the casket, it was difficult even to touch it. The procession slowly moved out of the city and headed towards a beautiful garden owned by the fourth vizier, which lay beside Moti Lake. The two of them were buried there, as counselled by the royal advisers. After closing their grave and saying benedictions, everyone left, nursing grief at their deaths. The couple's tragic story circulated in the city. Wherever one went, one heard their tale being told, and friends and strangers alike mourned them.

On the third day, when they finished with the prayers for the soyem,[16] the courtiers removed their mourning clothes and presented themselves at the court. The same day the king ordered one of his trusted officials to go to the hometown of the fourth vizier and bring with respect and honour whomever he could find among his heirs, be it his son or one of his nephews. After these orders, he furnished him with conveyance and money for the journey, and sent him off. Thereafter, he sent for the ensemble of women musicians who had accompanied the fourth vizier's wife and gave them employment at court. He asked them about the details of what had passed with their mistress. They told the king about the chastity of the vizier's wife, how that kutni had arrived at their mistress's house and all that had subsequently passed, in such a heartfelt manner that the king and the courtiers were greatly pained, and rued that the deceased had died for nothing, and made a thousand laments that it so happened.

The following day the king ordered that a mausoleum be constructed on the site of the couple's grave. The construction began immediately.

16. Soyem: The third day of a person's death when prayers are held for his absolution.

Meanwhile, the king's official arrived in the hometown of the fourth vizier. When he searched for the vizier's heirs he found the fourth vizier's foster son. He first asked the king's official to give him a complete account of what had happened with his parents.

After narrating the happenings at the court, the first vizier's execution, the fourth vizier and his wife dying by their own hands, and the king feeling sad at their deaths, the official said to him, 'The king has sent for you by a conveyance that awaits you. Kindly prepare quickly and come with me.'

When the boy heard of his foster parents' deaths he was greatly saddened, and said to the official, 'My dear fellow, kindly wait for a few days. I wish to arrange benedictions for the two deceased, and until that is over, I will not go anywhere.'

The official stayed there for two days and the foster son arranged for benedictions to be said and food to be prepared in large quantities and distributed widely in the community and the city. Then he made preparations to leave for the court. The foster son was very competent and had been trained by the vizier. He took along many salvers of gold and jewels as offerings for the king, and set out with the official. On the way he continuously enquired about and learned the ways of the king and the courtiers.

After some days, he entered the seat of the kingdom with the official, presented himself in court at the time of the king's audience, and waited at the station of salutations. When the king turned his eyes towards him, he made his salutations and obeisance, and then stood humbly before him. The king asked who the stranger was and why he had presented himself.

The court official who had brought him saluted the king and answered, 'Your Honour, this boy is the foster son of the deceased fourth vizier. Your humble servant has brought him from his hometown at your orders.'

Upon hearing this, the king said warmly, 'O noble boy, come forward!'

The boy again saluted and made obeisance and kissed the ground before the king's feet, and made offerings of the gold and jewel salvers he had brought.

The king was much impressed by his propriety and accepted his offerings with all his heart. The king offered him many a word of commiseration and consolation, and placed his hand of affection on the boy's head. Then he asked him with great indulgence, 'O blessed boy, what was your relationship with vizier Masud Ali Khan?'

He respectfully submitted, 'Your Highness, your born slave was adopted and raised by the deceased as his son. I was his brother's son whom he adopted and raised as his own.'

Upon hearing this, the king was most pleased and in the open court conferred the fourth vizier's robe of honour on his adopted son, vouchsafed to him the responsibility of his official correspondence, and made him his senior vizier. The boy again saluted him and made an offering. The king accepted his offering and conferred on him the first vizier's entire possessions, including elephants, horses, garden and properties that had been confiscated. He also gave him a large and majestic house in the centre of the city, for his accommodation. The boy was delighted and resided in the house after taking charge of the vizier's office. The women musicians who had accompanied his mother moved to his house, with the king's permission.

He arrived at the court at the time of morning prayers and performed the duties of his office with such excellent competency that it delighted the king. In due time, the other viziers lost their worth in the king's eyes, and all courtly matters were assigned to him, and he was given the charge of both financial and administrative affairs.

Meanwhile, a stately sepulchre rose where the fourth vizier and his wife were buried. The couple's death anniversary was commemorated with great fanfare, and a large crowd gathered, before which Procession of the Florists[17] seemed like a small affair. The king, the viziers, and the whole city were present to offer their respects. After the recitation of the Quran, sweets and food were distributed. The event was celebrated in the same manner the following year, and in future years, which is to state that the names of the two lovers are sure to remain in people's memory until Judgment Day. Indeed, those who leave this world steadfast in their faith are sure to earn distinction, regardless of the manner of their death.

17. Procession of the Florists (Phool walon ki sair): A three-day annual celebration held in the Mehrauli region by the flower-sellers of Delhi.

EPILOGUE

This tale is now ended but something remains yet to be said. It appears insignificant on the surface, but if you consider it carefully, it embodies an important truth and is pregnant with meaning. If one considers it, the world is a domain of care; there is the anxiety of inquisition in the afterlife. If one were to remain alert and anxious at all hours of the day, and have no connection with world's affairs, there is a likelihood it could save him, otherwise harm is certain. Everyone must die; death stalks us at every step. One must live as if one has embraced death in life, and has passed away before the day of passing. As some master has said:

Live thus that after you're dead and gone
Your life's oft celebrated by the living

Indeed, all on Earth perish, and eternal God alone abides, majestic and splendid.[18]

Anxiety for its writing kept me on tenterhooks
By God's grace this tale came to completion

END

18. Quran (55:26–27).

Qissa 6

A Girl Named King Agar

A First Translation of Saadat Khan Nasir's *Qissa Agar o Gul*

CHARACTERS (IN ALPHABETICAL ORDER)

Aflatun: Agar's maternal uncle. Also the name of Agar's maternal cousin

Agar: Vizier Khush-haal's daughter. Mahmood's twin sister

Ajooba Pari: Vizier Jawahar's beloved

Aqil: Vizier to King Mansoor

Bahram: Vizier to King Gul

Basant: Vizier to King Gul

Bhabhut Rani: Jogi's first wife

Buqalamun: Jogi's vizier

Dil Aaram: Man who knew the path to Raja Basik's land

Fox: An artful creature who brought King Agar the offering of a miraculous flower

Gul: Son of Quraish and Lal Dev

Gul Andaam: Agar's fmale attendant and his maternal cousin Aflatun's beloved

Gulnar: Lal Dev's daughter and Mahmood's beloved

Hameed Dev: Dev cured of leprosy by King Agar's miracle

Horse: Flying horse given in the dowry of Ajooba Pari

Humayun: Jogi's vizier

Jawahar: Vizier to King Gul

Jogi: Occult master. Mentor of Agar

Kamil: Vizier to King Mansoor
Khush-haal: Vizier to King Mansoor
King Mansoor: King of Khashkhaash
Laal: King Mansoor's son
Lal Dev: Dev who kidnapped Prince Laal
Mah-e Taaban: Jogi's fourth wife
Mahmood: Vizier Khush-haal's son. Agar's twin brother
Mah-Parwar Pari: Pari in love with Prince Laal
Mahtab Pari: Jogi's third wife
Manuchehr: Vizier to King Gul
Moti Rani: Raja Basik's daughter
Mushtri: Attendant of Mah-e Taaban
Parizad: Father of Ajooba Pari
Princess Khurshid: Jogi's second wife
Qabil: Vizier to King Mansoor
Quraish: Wife of Lal Dev
Raja Basik: Father of Princess Moti Rani
Roshan Rai Pari: The pari ruler of a far-off land, pursued by Agar
Royal falcon: Falcon who lived in the land beyond the seven seas
Sarv-Aasa: Vizier Basant's beloved
Shahryar: Vizier to King Gul. Lover of Moti Rani, daughter of Raja Basik
Simurgh: Bird who cured jogi's headache and informed Agar about the falcon
Zahra: Attendant of Mah-e Taaban
Zulaikha: Agar's maternal aunt

NARRATOR'S PREFACE

PRAISE OF GOD

The verdancy of the garden of speech sings the praises of the Gardener of Nature. If the rose had not rent its tunic in His love, it would have appeared a thorn in the nightingale's eye.

VERSES

The songster of the phrase 'Let there be!'
The Gardener of World's Nursery
Whose fragrance lies in every bud and flower
Whose name the nightingale constantly recites
He is the hue, the flower and the thorn's point
He is the Maker of the Spring's Carriage
The nourisher of beasts, birds and humans
The Creator of the Two Worlds, the Almighty God
Of whom all are subjects, He their Master
He is the one Praiseworthy, and the Praised

PRAISE OF PROPHET MUHAMMAD

And the spring of the garden of narrative is the praise addressed to the cypress of the nursery of prophethood. Had the cypress not witnessed with its index finger the sign of his prophethood, it would have been reduced to gallows in the ring-dove's eye.

VERSES

Muhammad, the reason for all creation, the favorite of God
Whose doorkeeper is Isa[1] the denizen of the fourth heaven[2]
The lamp of the niche of heavens, the moon of the skies of Medina and Makkah
Whose miracles are witnessed by the Quran itself
How can philosophy, mathematics or imagination
Ever fathom his station and stature
When on the night of Miraj[3] his wind-paced charger Buraq[4]

1. Isa: Jesus Christ.
2. Denizen of the fourth heaven: According to Islamic belief, Jesus Christ rose to the fourth heaven after Ascension.
3. Miraj: According to Islamic belief, the ascension of the Prophet Muhammad into heaven.
4. Buraq: According to Islamic belief, the winged creature who carried Prophet Muhammad into heaven.

Flew beyond both the material and spiritual worlds
O Aasi,[5] *he is God's light incarnate, the Lord of Absolute Zenith*
You have no wherewithal to lay claim to his praise or sing his glory

. . .

Thereafter, the avis of the pen offers profuse praise of Ali son of Abu Talib,[6] the Victorious Lion of God, whose lofty station lies beyond reach even of the Archangel Jibrail,[7] who has not the wherewithal to fly there should he aspire to it.

VERSES

Ali, the evidence of benevolent God,
Upon whom lie prayers and benedictions
Ali is the essence and hue of the garden of piety
Ali is the friend who dispels the terrors of the grave
Ali's friendship is the recompense of heaven
God's determination is manifested in Ali's will
The prophet's heir, the lion of God
The intrepid swordsman, the one who divides heaven and hell
At a station where there is no companion
My hand firmly holds the corner of his robe

And all praise and glory to the immaculate progeny of the Prophet, submission to whom is akin to submission to the Almighty. As my master has said:

VERSE

O Havas,[8] *we are the slaves of the Twelve Imams*[9]
For us all Twelve Imams are equally holy

Now, this humble fellow and insignificant mote, presents before the sagacious audience and connoisseurs of subtle speech, the colourful tale and delightful yarn called *Qissa Agar Gul*, transformed into Urdu from the Persian language at the request of friends.

5. Aasi: Poet's nom de plume.
6. Ali son of Abu Talib: Prophet Muhammad's cousin and the fourth caliph of Islam.
7. Jibrail: Gabriel.
8. Havas: Poet's nom de plume.
9. Twelve Imams: The Twelve Imams are the spiritual and political successors to Prophet Muhammad in the Twelver branch of Shia Islam.

THE BEGINNING OF THE STORY

Among the ancient cities was one called Khashkhaash, whose people were affluent and prosperous. The master of the throne of that heaven-like abode, the victorious and clement King Mansoor, was the guardian of his subjects, a just and benevolent ruler, one of venerable God's favored creatures, master of land and wealth, inheritor of army and ensign, and possessor of might and magnificence. He had four viziers, the like of four elements, who were his companions and counselors.

VERSES

Aqil was the chief vizier, and Khush-haal the second
Qabil was the third of whom there was no equal
Kamil was the name of the fourth vizier
Renowned in the inhabited world for his excellence

But like a fluttering leaf on an autumn-struck tree dried of sap, the king's heart was assailed by cold winds of grief from the thought that the benevolence of the Gardener of Life had not nourished and made verdant his tree of life and garden of kingship, which manifests the flower and fruit of yearning in the bloom of progeny.

One day, a merchant sought admission into his august and superior presence, and after presenting some salvers of priceless jewels, submitted: 'May the Refuge of the World prosper! The Grantor of Petitions has conferred on your slave a night-glowing jewel to light the house of his repute, to wit, blessed him with a worthy son. I am hopeful that Your Excellency will confer a name upon him with his Messiah-like tongue, so that from its blessing he may attain his natural age.'

The king declared that the boy should be named Mohabbat Bahadur.[10]

VERSE

Give him the name, Mohabbat Bahadur
So that his love may forever fill your heart

The merchant made his salutations and returned happy and joyous from the king's court. But the king was overcome again by grief at his state of childlessness, and, rising from the throne, did not emerge from his quarters for many days.

10. Mohabbat Bahadur: Love Worthy.

One day he summoned Vizier Khush-haal, who was also childless like the king, and said to him: 'I am unable to devote myself to the affairs of the state, as I have no heir to inherit my house and kingdom. It would be preferable if I should abdicate my throne, and go into seclusion and spend what remains of my borrowed life in devotion to God.'

Khush-haal submitted respectfully: 'By all means do so, but your slave has heard that the prayers of true men of God have great power, and their pleas are favourably received in the court of heavens. We must at first make our best efforts to find a way; it is said that it is for man to strive in seeking, and for the Almighty God to grant what he seeks. Let the Master of Fate decide what He will. If Your Honour be so inclined, this slave of yours will accompany you like your shadow.'

In short, deciding on this course, the two of them set out for the deserts and forests, leaving the control of the kingdom in the hands of the three accomplished viziers, Aqil, Qabil, and Kamil.

After many days, they arrived in a desert, where they beheld a prayerful, pious, chaste, and devout dervish; a desert-dweller, given to seclusion. He was a remedier of anxiety, succour of those in need, and of illuminated conscience on account of his piety and saintliness. His overgrown eyelashes covered his face, and he was busy in his devotions to the Almighty. Both of them bowed and stood before him, their hands respectfully folded at their waists.

That dervish of illuminated conscience first addressed the king, and said: 'O King, how did you find your way into this desolation? This is where abject beings like us have their domicile, and the homeless exiles their refuge.' Then he turned to the vizier, and said: 'O Khush-haal, you did well to follow your lord of beneficence.'

Both Khush-haal and the king replied: 'Lost in the desert of despair, the two of us have arrived before you from our auspicious fortune.'

VERSE

Help, O Khizr of the Desert,[11] *we have lost the way*
Help, O Knower of the Divine, for we are sinful

'Our purpose and quest is not hidden from your venerable self, either.'

11. Khizr of the Desert: According to Islamic belief, the holy Khizr guides the lost on their path and leads them to safety.

That divine-knowing mystic said: 'It is the Bestower of Desires who grants wishes. Were I able to have my prayers answered, I would not be consigned to this desolation.'

Dejected to hear this, the king and the vizier rose and left his presence. Thereupon, the dervish called them back, and turning his thoughts to God Almighty, said to them: 'O King, divine aid arrives when a man firmly sets his mind upon something. Take this staff, which is my crutch, and go into the garden. You will receive the fruit destined for you from the apple tree.'

The king carried the dervish's staff, which was in essence his hand of supplication, into the garden of hope. Upon approaching the tree, he regarded the tree laden with fruit and bare of leaves. He recited 'In the name of God!' and struck the apple tree with the staff, whereupon a fresh fruit fell down from atop a branch. The king picked it up from the ground and carefully cradled it as if it were his son. The king then gave the staff to his vizier, and said to him: 'You must also try your luck.' The vizier too hit the tree of yearning with the staff, and from the power of providence, received fruit as well: a pearl-like apple fell down on the ground, and the vizier filled up his skirts of desire with it.

The king and the vizier returned from the garden into the dervish's presence, and narrated what had transpired.

The dervish said: 'O King, may this fruit prove auspicious for you; the tree of your desire bore fruit.'

The king asked: 'If God grants me a son from your blessing, what name should I give him?' The dervish answered: 'My son, what would be a more auspicious name for that ruby than to call him Laal?'[12] Then he said to the vizier: 'Yours is a twin apple. By the grace of God, you will be blessed with twins: a boy and a girl. Name the boy Mahmood, and call your daughter Agar, and be mindful that they remain safe from life's calamities, for not only humans, but parizads,[13] too, will scatter themselves like moths upon the flame of their beauty. The king must not let the prince leave the safety of the dungeon until the twelfth year of his life, and keep that priceless pearl in the oyster of safety. You will rue it if you show the least negligence in this matter.'

12. Laal: Ruby.

13. Parizad: Creatures born of paris, who are fairy-like beings of Persian and Indo-Pak folklore.

At last, the king and his vizier took their leave of the dervish and returned to their kingdom.

OF PRINCE LAAL BEING BORN TO KING MANSOOR FROM THE POWER OF THE APPLE, AND OF MAHMOOD AND AGAR BEING BORN TO VIZIER KHUSH-HAAL

It is related that when King Mansoor and Vizier Khush-haal took their leave of the dervish of illuminated conscience, and returned to the city of Khashkhaash, the three viziers were greatly relieved, and the royal subjects and the soldiery were overjoyed.

At nightfall, the king retired to rest in his palace, fed the dervish's gift to his wife, and made his bedchamber the envy of the garden of heaven. By the grace of almighty God, that very night, his oyster of longing was filled with the pearl of desire, and in anticipation of the child's birth, celebrations were made for a full nine months, with days festive like the day of Eid, and nights like the night of Shab-e Baraat.[14]

After the appointed time, at an auspicious hour in the first half of the night, a world illuminating, worthy son was born in the king's palace, who was like a piece of the moon in beauty, the star of the sky of excellence, and the light of his eyes.

VERSES

He was a marvelous, luminous moon
With whom the full moon became enamoured
In this he differed from the Moon of Kanaan[15]
That he was manifest, while the other was hidden

Celebrations were made throughout the land. Slave girls, attendants, nannies, nursemaids, all gathered together and brought the auspicious news of his birth to the king. Some of them received bracelets, some anklets, some purses of gold, some robes, some gold coins, and others received gift salvers. The midwife received an open palanquin for cut-

14. Shab-e Barat: A religious festival celebrated on the 15th night of the Islamic month of Sha'ban.

15. Moon of Kanaan: An allusion to Joseph.

ting the umbilical cord. The servants received a year's wages in reward. Many a foot soldier was promoted to trooper, and the troopers promoted in their turn and made elephant-mounted warriors. The king had received such a luminous jewel from God's grace, that he scattered away the equal of Qarun's[16] treasure in celebrations.

VERSE

When naming him Prince Laal
He gave away diamonds and rubies as his sacrifice

In the king's palace, the first part of the night was festive as the Eid morning. Then cries of celebrations and felicitations rose from Vizier Khush-haal's palace. The last part of the night became like the first, with female attendants and servants delighting in the happy news, and the retainers and domestics being invested with rich rewards. Beholding the beauty of their son and daughter, which was like the conjunction of the Moon and Jupiter, the mother was beside herself with joy, and the father was euphoric. They named that worthy son Mahmood, and gave the daughter of happy fortune the name of Agar.

VERSES

An auspicious Mahmood, whose slaves were mighty emperors[17]
Who was liberally bestowed from the store of beauty
He was not a luminous star, but a lustrous moon
It embarrassed the full moon to show him its face

And the beauty of that daughter of happy fortune, on whom the paris and houris stood in attendance, was the destroyer of one's faith. Her delicacy was like the exquisiteness of the sandalwood powder meant for a Brahmin's forehead. That silver-bodied beauty was dainty like a freshly-bloomed flower, and her silvern body had the redolence of aloes. The vizier prostrated himself before the Almighty to offer his thanks, and showed such munificence and liberality that from fear of capture the pearl hid itself in the sea, and the ruby concealed itself in flintstone.

Vizier Khush-haal took this pair of pearls found from the jewel house of Nature, and put them at the king's feet. The king picked up

16. Qarun: A fabulously rich man, Korah, of the Bible.

17. An auspicious Mahmood, whose slaves were mighty emperors: Allusion to King Mahmood of Ghazna's devotion to his slave Ayaz.

those pearls in the oyster of his embrace, pressed them to his breast, and invested the vizier with a robe of honour. The celebrations continued for many days. Thereafter, King Mansoor had an elegant and captivating garden constructed.

VERSE

It was such a rare, soul refreshing garden
That you may call it an image of paradise

Lined with trees and numerous fountains, the garden's rose bushes were like veritable rosariums, where every verdant plain was a parterre, and every pond like a sea; it was a place whose expanse was like the expanse of a forest, which abounded in nightingales, and rang with the singing of doves who warbled and sang this song apposite to their circumstances:

VERSE

There is breeze, clouds, the cup-bearer and garden's red wine
Felicitations to the doves, the cypress of beautiful gait[18] *approaches*

Constructing a cellar in that garden, hidden like the heart's chamber, the king consigned the prince into that stony house, like a ruby.

But there is no escaping the vicissitudes of destiny. One day, as fate had predestined, that precious pearl was sighted by a dev named Lal Dev. The arrowhead of love for the prince pierced the dev's heart, but did not become manifest to others.

VERSES

There is none aware of its secrets
The mysteries of love are visible only to lovers
Where there is rose, there must be thorn
With the taper burns, there is the moth

In short, when the period of twelve years was over, and the luminance of that Moon of Nakhshab's[19] visage shone like the emanations of the full moon, the day came for the prince and the vizier's son to emerge from the cellar. All the paraphernalia of the entourage was organized in great splendour on both sides of his path, from the gates of the garden to the royal courtyard.

18. Cypress of beautiful gait: Metaphor for the beloved.

19. Moon of Nakhshab: An artificial moon created by the eighth-century occultist al-Muqanna, who claimed to be a prophet.

OF PRINCE LAAL GOING ON A HUNTING EXPEDITION IN A HAZARDOUS VALLEY AND BEING TAKEN CAPTIVE BY THE TYRANNICAL DEV

The prince emerged from the garden like the brilliant sun from the sky of majesty, holding the vizier's son's hand. They made pleasantries together, their hearts brimming with the ardour of friendship. The vizier offered salvers of jewels as their sacrifice, seated them in a golden-canopied elephant litter, and recited the verse:

VERSE

Offer thanks to God, O Heart, that with propitious fortune
We received what we fervently desired

For a period of time, they regaled themselves with the sights of the environs. Then they returned to the garden which the pari-like songstresses and singing girls turned into the court of Raja Indar.[20] Venus,[21] the songstress of the heavens, admitted her inferiority upon hearing their strains, and Tansen[22] realised his mediocrity upon listening to their sublime beat. These festivities continued for three days and three nights, after which the hosting and entertainment abated.

The prince and the vizier's son often passed their time in the pleasures of the chase. One day, mounted on his horse which was fleet as the wind, the prince headed to the forest in search of prey, when suddenly rows and clusters of gazelles emerged from the forest's expanse, and with their frolicking and beauty roused the prince's passion for the hunt. The prince gave chase, pursuing the fleeing deer closely, with the vizier's son following right behind, like the dust he churned in his wake. Finally, the gazelle disappeared from sight, and they came to a stop, looking frantically around for their prey.

Then, a flock of gazelles slowly appeared and blocked their vision as if they were a magical wall, and they saw a garden manifest itself. The prince dismounted and entered it. Finding it to be a paradisiacal garden, he became engrossed in its beauty like a love-struck nightingale.

20. Raja Indar: The king of the gods in Indian mythology, the regent of the visible heavens (Platts).

21. Venus: Venus was considered the presiding deity of music and dance.

22. Tansen: A legendary Indian musician.

The vizier's son said: 'O Master of the World, regard that some parts of the ground are made of gold, and the flower-beds are made of pure silver. Behold that every tree is a marvel and a wonder: The branches are made of diamonds, the leaves of emerald, the fruit made of Yemenite agate, and doves and nightingales made of gold and silver warble on the tree branches. This appears to be a magical garden. We must not explore it further or promenade here even a moment longer.'

The prince made no reply to him. He went forth and entered an apartment in the garden. He saw a jewel-encrusted bed laid within, and varieties of wine and roasted viands lying in dishes. But there was no sign of any human; it seemed that some parizad or human had left, upon hearing the sound of their footsteps.

The prince was tired and lay down to rest in the bed while the vizier's son Mahmood massaged his head. Before long, the armies of slumber toppled the throne of the prince's senses. The vizier's son went out to answer the call of nature, and when he returned, he did not find the prince where he had lain sleeping. He was beside himself with anxiety, and rushed around like a crazed creature, inhaling the perfume of every plant and tree, and striking his head in anguish like the wind. He cried like the cloud of spring quarter, made plaints like the nightingale, and circulated like a rivulet in the garden. At times he would remonstrate against fate for his loneliness, and sometimes heaved cold sighs at his friend's wandering away.

Meanwhile, Vizier Aqil, who was deputed to keep them in his protection and care, arrived there in search of them with an army. He became unnerved upon hearing Mahmood's account, and conveyed the calamitous news to King Mansoor's lofty hearing. When this unsettling news was conveyed to the king, he clutched his heart, and the queen struck her chest with a stone.

Vizier Khush-haal rushed to Mahmood in great anxiety, and inquired of him about the incident. He narrated all that had happened, and pleaded and begged him in God's name not to remove him from that garden, as he could not imagine a life separated from his friend. Mahmood said: 'How can I show my cursed face to others, and bear the humiliation of their reproachful words! But should you still take me away, imprison me in a cellar, so that nobody ever sees my inauspicious face again.'

In the end, Vizier Khush-haal brought him back and housed him in a cellar. Mahmood cried and recited this verse in separation from his friend:

VERSE

To not see you in the world in all your glory
Is the same as not beholding a thing

OF PRINCE LAAL LEARNING THAT HE WAS LAL DEV'S CAPTIVE, AND OF HIS DISTRESS

Now hear of what happened when Prince Laal half-opened his sleep-laden eyes, and found himself all alone, and did not see Mahmood by his bedside. Unnerved, like a caged captive, he tried to break free like a newly caught bird. He involuntarily called out Mahmood's name and recited this verse:

VERSE

There's neither the dove and the cypress, nor the nightingale and the rose, nor a companion like you
What became of the garden, who is the trapper whose house this is?

Then Lal Dev presented himself and said: 'Mahmood is not here, but your slave of old, this Ayaz,[23] is present.' The prince answered: 'My fellow, I have never set eyes on you. You do not appear to me old-serving, but a calamity newly-arrived.' The dev answered: 'O Prince, for many a year I have remained lovesick, with my heart pining away for love of you.

VERSE

I am the one who loved you since the earliest days
I was held captive by your locks, from the time you had none

Before finding you, a precious jewel, for years I searched and quested for you in the forests, with thorns of anxiety wounding my soles.

The prince realised that he had no recourse except to show fortitude. Turning his heart to the True God to petition for His mercies, he

23. Ayaz: An allusion to Malik Ayaz, who rose from a slave to the rank of general in the army of King Mahmood of Ghazna, and is remembered for his loyalty to the king.

asked the dev for a ewer and prayer mat. Lal Dev brought him both items. After making his ablutions, the prince offered his prayers with great devotion. Once he finished saying his prayers, the dev made an offering of salvers full of jewels, and presented him with tasty fruits and fine beverages. The prince partook a little of the food.

To divert the prince's mind, the dev organized a musical assembly, but the prince remained engrossed in his grief and suffering, and the very sound of singing was a source of affliction for him. Finally, he stopped everyone from singing and playing music, and left the assembly for his bedchamber, where he cried himself to sleep, thinking of Mahmood.

OF PRINCE LAAL FALLING IN LOVE WITH MAH-PARWAR PARI UPON HEARING A PIGEON'S ACCOUNT OF HER BEAUTY

When the gold-winged peacock, the world-illuminating sun, set out from its house in the West towards the East, Prince Laal emerged from his bedchamber and arrived at his seat in the garden. The whole garden was illuminated and became loftier in status than the ethereal sphere from the rays of his beauty. Lal Dev also arrived there as was his wont, and offered his salutations; and thereafter busied himself with his affairs.

The prince was sitting by himself when a pair of beautiful, high-flying roller pigeons landed on the ledge of the nearby pond. The female pigeon said to the male: 'Regard what a calamity has befallen the prince. Where is the comparison between our prince and that tyrannical dev!'

VERSE

Regard his beauty and then behold the other's dreadful face
That ill-starred monster is like the darkening eclipse of this moon

'Come, let us take this marvelous news to Mah-Parwar Pari, and narrate to her the amazing tale of our finding a human in the tilisms of Lal Dev; one who is superior to paris and lovelier than houris. She will likely be most delighted to receive the news, and be grateful to us.'

The prince said: 'That a bird without power of speech should converse, is more wondrous than what passed with me. The animals of my land do not have such power.' The pigeons replied: 'O Prince, this is a manufactory of tilism. Let alone living beings, even the ground has the power of speech.' The prince asked: 'How far is the world of humans from here?' The pigeon answered: 'The world of humans lies some twelve years' journey from here.' Thus speaking, the pair of pigeons disappeared and the prince writhed like a slaughtered bird in ecstasies of love for Mah-Parwar Pari.

The pigeons gave Mah-Parwar Pari an account of the prince and of Lal Dev's tyranny. Immediately upon hearing it, the pari was overpowered by yearning for the prince, and felt the awakening of desire.

VERSE

The beloved's news is akin to the beloved's sight
Desire is no less pleasuresome than union itself

Meanwhile, Lal Dev dressed the prince in a royal golden robe and a jewel-studded crown, and brought him to a festive gathering. He summoned paris, and arranged a musical assembly. While all this was in progress, Mah-Parwar Pari, donning a splendid dress, arrived in that garden aboard her golden throne, and concealed herself in a corner to observe the proceedings. Engrossed in the sight of the rosy-cheeked beloved, and marked by the flame of love like a moth, whenever she beheld the prince, she involuntarily recited these verses:

VERSES

Neither moon nor Jupiter can approach your beauty
The sun's visage too cannot claim brightness like yours
The houris and pages in heaven have not a like claim on beauty
Your lovely face is the envy of Azar's[24] *sculpted works*
No matter how highly I eulogize it, your beauty is beyond all praise

Mah-Parwar Pari, a lovely damsel possessing enchanting grace, who was the beloved of the world, and a great seductress of her time, was so wholly enraptured by love for the prince that it made her frenzied like a mad person, and she was struck silent like a portrait. Lal Dev, too, had fallen unconscious from the vision of the prince's beauty. Indeed, such is human beauty that devs and paris alike are attracted to it, and yearn for it with all their heart; its flame equally melts both iron and stone.

24. Azar: A sculptor. Father of Prophet Abraham.

Although the prince was listening to the singing, he was also partly engrossed by the thought of Mah-Parwar Pari. Finally, the prince's eyes fell upon the place where she lay concealed. He made an excuse and rose from his place to investigate. Lal Dev wished to accompany that cypress-statured beauty like a shadow, but Prince Laal angrily forbade him. Going onwards, he saw the wonders of beauty on display: A beloved as delicate and lovely as the rose was sitting Bilqis-like[25] with great pomp on a golden throne. He swooned upon beholding her, and fell down unconscious from the vision of her beauty. That beloved put the head of the Suleiman[26] of the land of beauty in her lap, sprinkled the rose water of her tears on his face, and fanned him with the skirts of her dress, offering a more potent restorative for his mind than any aromatic ungent.

She brought to senses the one who had forfeited them, and said: 'O Human-born, what use all this rapture and fainting, and to what purpose this writhing and dizziness? What is the use of it, since you show such perverseness to the one who holds you in his power? How will you be able to make me happy? If you desire and wish union with me, gratify Lal Dev, and please him with your sweet words.

VERSE

You should follow the example of the nightingale
For the rose's sake she contends with a thousand thorns

'Now go, lest this secret should become known to another.' Thus speaking, she rose and mounted her throne, and the wind bore it away.

The prince returned to the assembly, and sat there for a long time. He offered everyone a reward by his own hand. Then he rested on his canopied bed. He said to Lal Dev: 'O my consoler, friend and faithful companion, I wish you to lie beside me tonight, and warm my side like a father's warm hold.' The dev replied: 'I seek God's protection from the thought! I am a creature unworthier than a pebble under your foot. I dare not lie beside you.' The prince said: 'That tells me that you have no love for me, and your heart is full of rancour, and you nurse some enmity towards me.'

From fear of displeasing the prince, Lal Dev lay down beside him, but worried lest the prince should receive the least injury from him, as

25. Bilqis-like: Like Bilqis, Queen of Sheba.
26. Suleiman: King Solomon.

the dev's limbs were like mountains, and the prince's body softer than a freshly bloomed flower's petal. From that consideration, Lal Dev kept his distance from the prince, but the prince embraced his neck, and to a distant eye it appeared that a jasper amulet inscribed with Naad-e Ali[27] was clasped around the dev's neck.

Noticing the prince's show of affection towards him, Lal Dev asked: 'I wonder why you show me such kindness, all of a sudden. What has occasioned it? Pray tell me what you wish, and order your slave to carry it out.'

The prince said: 'I consider you my benefactor. I will only tell you if you do not deny me my wish.' The dev replied: 'Pray speak! If what you desire is something within my power, your slave shall not fail you, and make his best efforts to carry out your wishes.' The prince said: 'Carry a missive from me to Mah-Parwar Pari.' The dev asked: 'How do you know Mah-Parwar Pari? Who told you this secret, and gave you her name?' The prince answered: 'I heard her name from someone.' The dev wrecked his mind trying to get to the bottom of the mystery but failed. In the end, he agreed to take the prince's missive to the pari, and bring back her reply.

OF LAL DEV TURNING INTO A PEACOCK TO TAKE PRINCE LAAL'S MESSAGE AND MISSIVE TO MAH-PARWAR PARI

When the sun's peacock in the sky spread its golden wings of light, and went preening from East to West, Prince Laal smilingly rose from his bed. He picked up a roll of paper and wrote out this missive to Mah-Parwar Pari.

VERSES

O comfort of the souls of the restive
O pupil of weeping eyes
My heart is agitated, yearning for your beauty
Engrossed in thoughts of you, I lie sleepless
I deeply grieve your leaving me
Without you, my life is like dust

27. Naad-e Ali: A prayer for safety in the name of Ali.

I long for our union
I await an opportunity
When I can hold you in my arms
And our bodies and lips are joined

When the missive was ready, Lal Dev turned himself into a golden peacock, and the prince made the letter into an amulet, and tied it around his neck. In no time, Lal Dev arrived in Mah-Parwar' Pari's garden. The parizad was swinging in the garden with other paris. The peacock approached her, and communicated this from the prince:

VERSE

Lovers are strung from the knot of separation's grief
While my rivals in my beloved's garden swing

Understanding the substance of the speech from the peacock's words, Mah-Parwar ordered an attendant pari to bring pearls in a golden basin, and put it before the peacock. The attendant did as she was told, but the peacock did not pick up a single pearl, and flew away to sit in another part of the garden. After Mah-Parwar was done with her recreation, she ordered privacy, and said to the peacock: 'O Bird, I bid you in the name of your God, approach!' The peacock flew into her lap. The pari carried the peacock to her bed and drew the curtains in the courtyard.

The peacock said to her: 'O Mah-Parwar, where did Prince Laal see you that he sent me here as messenger?' Upon hearing this, Mah-Parwar threw him off her lap, and said: 'O Wretch, ill-starred creature, may you be cursed by God! May your face become black, and your hands and feet turn blue! Who is Prince Laal, and when did he see me? How dare you slander and revile me! Just you wait! I will crush your head with a stone!'

The peacock said: 'O Flying She-serpent, do not spew venom, and go on prattling, but untie the missive from my neck. I have no fear, as there is no threat to messengers. Master your anger, and do not challenge me.'

Mah-Parwar's anger was subsided by the dev's cajolery. She untied the missive and read it, whose ending words said:

VERSES

You had promised that you will send for me
Or you will yourself return, to visit

But neither did you send for me
Nor have I received your messenger
I am burdened by the grief of separation
What use will be your visit, if you visit my grave

Mah-Parwar was delighted to read the letter. She wrote out her reply, and tying it from the peacock's neck, sent him off.

OF PRINCE LAAL ENTERING LAL DEV'S PRIVATE CHAMBERS AND MEETING HIS SON GUL AND WIFE QURAISH

Now hear of what passed with Prince Laal. Before leaving, Lal Dev had left the keys to his house with the prince, with the injunction that should he feel lonely, he may divert himself by opening its apartments and regaling himself with their sights. He granted him permission to visit three sides of the house, but not the fourth, and proscribed him from setting foot there.

VERSE

For that is indeed a place full of peril
You must refrain from setting foot there

After Prince Laal had visited three sides of the house, he went towards the fourth. He found a locked door, barred with an iron padlock. He opened it and went inside and arrived at another door of pure silver set in an alabaster edifice. Prince Laal unlocked it, too. He found a beautiful carpet spread inside, and a third door within, which was of great height and made of gold; which he opened as well.

Upon the door opening, he encountered a wise woman, adept and adroit in all matters. From an excess of pity and affection, she cried upon seeing the one bent upon scattering his life. By way of stopping the prince from that course, she said to him: 'O one enclosed in grief and anguish, this is the house of the sanguinary one who is a flower in appearance, but a thorn in his essence.' The prince said: 'I am far from my land. I wish to remain within the refuge of your kindness! O Dear Mother, I wander around, separated from my parents, and my heart in a hundred pieces. Turn upon me the glance of mercy, and introduce me to the flower whom you likened to a thorn.' She answered: 'O Dear Child, my name is Quraish and he is none other than my son, Gul. I stopped you from entering this place because he will arrive shortly, tear you to pieces, and feed you to the devs. I have explained the whole situation to you, and the decision is up to you.' Prince Laal fell at her feet to plead with her, and Quraish felt pity for him and hid him inside her robe.

Meanwhile, King Gul arrived and made a bow to his mother and offered salutations. She gave him her blessings. King Gul said: 'Today, a fine smell is rising from your robe.' She answered, 'You are the flower raised in my lap. Why wouldn't the redolence reach you?' Then Gul sat beside his mother. As was the custom, a large plate of sheer-baranj[28] was served him. Gul said: 'Today the servings are large. Pray have some yourself, too.'

Quraish nudged Prince Laal, and he too ate a few morsels where he was hiding. Then that luminous moon, Prince Laal, came out from behind the cover of clouds. Exclaiming, 'O Brother!' Prince Laal embraced King Gul.

Gul was vexed at his brazenness and presumptuousness. But on account of having shared the same milk,[29] and at his mother's intercession, he, too, called Prince Laal his brother. Both of them had the sheer-baranj together.

After some time, King Gul's vizier, Jawahar, arrived with the register of daily accounts, and sought leave to present it. King Gul said: 'O Vizier, if you were to wager a rich sum as offering, I will display before you something so rare that it will ravish your senses.' The vizier said: 'I am willing.' King Gul showed the vizier his guest. Upon beholding him, Jawahar fainted from the power of Prince Laal's beauty. When he came to, he presented to Prince Laal a night-glowing jewel the size of a bird's egg whose refulgence made Jawahar's hand glow like Musa's hand.[30]

The prince said: 'What will I do with the jewel, and where will I keep it?' King Gul said: 'Dear brother, accept it and do not let your

28. Sheer baranj: A confection of milk and rice.

29. The story suggests that Laal and Gul have become foster brothers since they shared the same milk confection.

30. Musa's hand: A miracle given to Moses that made his hand glow. Mentioned in the Quran (28:32).

heart be clouded by anxiety and sorrow. You shall see what happens.' Upon that the prince accepted Jawahar's offering.

The prince was still there when Lal Dev returned with Mah-Parwar Pari's reply, and found the prince missing from the house. Anxiously searching for him, he arrived on the scene. Quraish tried to conceal the prince, but King Gul said: 'Let him go. In the evening, I will go and bring him along.'

At the sight of Lal Dev, the prince rose from his place. The dev held the prince's hand and pressed it against his chest. To admonish him, he scolded and reproved Prince Laal, saying: 'Beware! Do not visit there again, for Quraish is my enemy.' The prince answered: 'But she was like a mother to me, and King Gul like my brother.' Lal Dev answered: 'It's been twelve years since Gul's mother has been estranged from me. I fear lest she should harm you in her anger towards me.' Thus speaking, Lal Dev who was tired, fell asleep.

The prince lay in his bedchamber, rolling restlessly in bed, occupied by thoughts of Mah-Parwar Pari, when King Gul arrived and carried him away, without Lal Dev finding out. All night long the two of them played chess. At times, Prince Laal's castle trampled King Gul's pawns, and at other times King Gul defended his position.

OF THE PRINCE PERUSING MAH-PARWAR PARI'S MISSIVE, THEN WRITING OUT A REPLY, AND OF THE MEETING BETWEEN PRINCE LAAL AND VIZIER'S SON MAHMOOD

When the chess-master of the heavens rolled up stars' pieces in twilight's chequered spread, and the sun king checkmated the king of stars, the prince stopped the play, and rode haste's horse to his bedchamber and fell asleep.

When Lal Dev rose, he woke up Prince Laal by kissing his foot, and gave him Mah-Parwar Pari's missive. In his ecstasy, the lover would put the beloved's letter now to his tearful eyes, and now on his head, until he finally opened and read it. The perfumed letter with its elegant language, the honeyed words whose every dot was more beautiful than the pupil of the eye, and the graceful writing revealed the passion of a pure-hearted one.

VERSES

It was written therein that your letter reached me
Which brought consolation to my heart
It is the source of comfort and joy to me
In fact it is the very recipe of blessedness
Did you touch the letter against your locks
That it is redolent with the perfume of musk
The desire for union that you wrote of
Understand well, it is but a fancy and dream
When did a human ever have union with a pari
And not end up burnt like a moth
The human heart is empty of love
Of wile and deceit are humans made
They have not the least perfume of fidelity
Their love is as fickle as their professions of love

When Prince Laal read her letter, he realised that she, too, longed for him, and the verses depicting her indifference were only meant to further ignite his passion by thwarting it. He immediately wrote a reply to the purpose:

THE LOVER'S REPLY TO HIS BELOVED'S MISSIVE

May you prosper, O bliss of my heart!
May you prosper, O my living soul,
After expressing my desire to see you
My glance darts around, revolving like a planet
Every night, it is fixed on the door
And every morning arrives like Doomsday
Peace was stolen from my heart
By your going away, O rose-like beloved!
Should the sword of death fall and bring me solace
My last words will be: You stole my heart! You ravished my heart!
Ah, what was that distressing message you sent me!
That I should give up my desire of union with you
You wrote I am a mere handful of dust and you are a pari
From all base passions of desire and longing you are free
I feel like a veritable Suleiman from pride
That I gave myself to you in slavery thus
There are no worthier creatures than humans
Both love and fidelity begin and end with us

He gave the letter to Lal Dev, and sent him off to the land of Mah-Parwar Pari. She had gone to promenade in the garden with her parents, and the magic peacock paced about, waiting for her.

Prince Laal, meanwhile, was enjoying himself in the company of King Gul when the king asked his vizier Jawahar to bring him the betel-box. When Jawahar brought it, King Gul served a paan[31] to Prince Laal, and had one himself. At that moment, the prince remembered vizier's son Mahmood of a sudden, and his heart was gripped by sorrow.

VERSE

The eyes welled up, but the tears did not fall
But gathered, dew-like, in narcissus's bowl

King Gul asked: 'O Brother, what happened just now to make you downcast?' Although he pressed his query, Prince Laal did not make a reply. The sagacious Vizier Jawahar made his deductions, and submitted: 'Perhaps at this moment the Prince of the Heavens has remembered the vizier's son, and become sad from the thought of separation from him.' Prince Laal highly lauded and praised the vizier's acuity and sagaciousness. Then King Gul heard the whole account of the vizier's son Mahmood.

King Gul expressed much remorse at Prince Laal's grief, and immediately rode his throne to the land of Khashkhaash. After questing and searching for the vizier's son, he brought him out from the cellar where he lay like a corpse, revived him with the promise of uniting him with Prince Laal, and in the flash of an eye seated him beside the prince.

VERSES

The two lovers met in this manner
As two rivers together merge
They narrated their woes of separation
And showed each other their hearts' wounds

The prince began his tale of wretchedness, and Mahmood narrated his hardships. Quraish said: 'O Prince, it breaks my heart to see you cry. Do dry your tears and give thanks, that today God reunited you with the one separated from you.' Then she gave Mahmood a lincture to strengthen his heart, which reinvigorated him.

31. Paan: Betel-leaf.

. . .

Now hear what happened in the other place: When Mah-Parwar returned after filling up her vision with the sights of the garden, the peacock preening his feathers approached that envy of the spring quarter, and displayed the amulet tied from his neck. Mah-Parwar opened it and began reading.

VERSES

At times that pari would merrily laugh
At times she would coquettishly shake her head
At times she would press it to her eyes with great joy
At times she read it holding it away

She opened and read it a number of times. Then she wrote a reply and tied it from the peacock's neck. When Lal Dev returned home, carrying that letter, he did not find Prince Laal and reckoned that he must be with his wife and son. He said to himself: 'The two of them wish to turn him, too, against me.' He went into Quraish's palace and turned an angry eye on Prince Laal. The prince rose, pleaded with Lal Dev and embraced him. Lal Dev said: ' Speak! What do you wish to say?' The prince said: 'My brother did me a great kindness by reuniting me with vizier's son Mahmood. In recompense, I wish you to forgive mother and embrace my brother.'

Lal Dev was very pleased to hear this, and said: 'Very well! Do ask her to be rid of her jogi-like appearance. She has been in that garb for a very long time.' Prince Laal now went to Quraish and pleaded with her and touched her feet. She raised and embraced him and agreed to do as asked. In the manner of a she-serpent, she shed the garb like dead skin that had given her the appearance of a ninety-year-old woman, and became as youthful as a twelve-year-old. That is to say, the dark night became the night of the full moon.

Vizier's son Mahmood also met Lal Dev. Then Lal Dev took Prince Laal into privacy and placed Mah-Parwar Pari's letter before him.

THE PARI'S RESPONSE TO PRINCE LAAL'S LETTER

O dearly beloved and eternal companion! Hear from the one burning in the fire of separation, and one pierced by the arrow of desire, that I read your letter word by word and letter by letter. The restiveness and agitation that you speak of is but a mere particle of the anxiety I feel, and all your tear-shedding a mere droplet in comparison to my weeping.

VERSES

Alas, my condition is indescribable
Which one of my many troubles should I first report to you
Every day is fierce as doomsday in separation from you
From my crying the world finds no sleep

When my heart is overcome with grief, I visit your garden in my imagination, but return from there more anguished and uneasy.

Upon perusing the missive that was full of tenderness the prince cried copiously, and drenched every word of the letter with his tears. He wrote a reply on the tablet of the heart with the pen of his eye-lashes.

THE REPLY SENT BY PRINCE LAAL

O newly sprouted bud in the garden of excellence, and the rare fruit of the garden of love, may God augment your beauty! Accept my all-encompassing desire and assemblages of longing, and know that I am in receipt of your bouquet of love and friendship, which redoubled the fervour of this weeping nightingale, and brought him boundless joy.

VERSES

Your love for me is mere words
My love does not follow the path yours does
You enjoy the bloom of Spring in the garden
In my heart the wound blooms afresh
Your feet follow the water courses
Like a mere bubble life exists in me
Your feet move across the meadow
The lancet of thorn pierces through my heart
You stand under the tendrils of vine
Here life's entire day comes to an end
That is to say I am restless for the sight of you
Each day passes with me like doomsday
Every night I cry with tears and laments
How are you able to have an unbroken sleep
Nothing that anyone says pleases me
I am not the least companionable
Although I am deserving of your abuse
Show mercy, as I am one of God's creatures

Lal Dev took this letter to Mah-Parwar Pari. She read the letter and replied by expressing a fervent desire for a meeting, and sought his indulgence by offering many an excuse.

THE PARI'S REPLY TO PRINCE LAAL'S LETTER

Your missive that was redolent with love, and full of remonstrances, was received. God knows that my promenading in the garden is not for recreation: its purpose is to regard your face in the rose, and behold your locks in the spikenard. I see your lovely stature in the cypress and the pine tree, and in the jonquill I see your eyes which cast spells. I promenade in the garden for a vision of you. If I did not wish to behold you, I would have no business with the garden.

VERSE

Your beautiful face thus resides in my heart
Wherever I look, it is you alone I see

Although I am a pari, I find myself helpless. The only difference between us is that your captor is your slave, whereas I am powerless before you.

VERSE

The hidden secret I do not even commit to my heart
How may I trust it to the pen?

After writing the letter, she gave it to Lal Dev so that Prince Laal may learn about her anxiety-ridden state. Lal Dev brought the letter to Prince Laal, and gave him an account of Mah-Parwar's distress. The prince was deeply grieved to learn of her grief and anguish. All colour drained from his face as he became engrossed in thoughts of her.

OF KING MANSOOR LEARNING OF MAHMOOD DISAPPEARING AS WELL, AND ENTHRONING VIZIER'S DAUGHTER AGAR

King Mansoor had been struck such a blow in the loss of Prince Laal that he went blind, like Yaqub[32] grieving for his Yusuf.[33] He stopped taking food and drink. Vizier Khush-haal sometimes prevailed upon him to have a few morsels. When Khush-haal communicated to King

32. Yaqub: Jacob.
33. Yusuf: Joseph.

Mansoor that Mahmood had also disappeared, the awful news further devastated the king. He said to the vizier: 'I can see no solution except to put an end to my existence.'

VERSE

The heart and the breast have filled up with regrets
Enough, O billowing grief, my heart has given up

'I had thought that Mahmood would become the master of the throne and signet after me, and would bring some consolation to my grief-filled heart. But nothing turned out according to my plans, and no stratagem has worked.

VERSE

My seeds of hope become grains of gunpowder
They do not sprout until kindled by thunder

In the end, King Mansoor declared the vizier's daughter Agar as his son and heir. The news was blazoned abroad that the prince, whom even the eye of sun had not seen, had ascended the throne of kingship. Upon hearing this vivifying news, the whole populace went to behold the heir. They saw a twelve-year-old whose beauty was the envy of the rose and the tulip, and who was both handsome and pretty, with dark ringlets, the curls exuding the fragrance of musk, and a charming beloved, like the full moon. Everyone who regarded him derived wholesome bliss from the sight, and the world received great joy, and the earth prosperity from his presence. He issued his judgment in many cases, judiciously resolving them. He became known in all his dominions for his justice, and young and old alike were convinced of his wisdom. He came to be known as a Yusuf in looks, Naushervan[34] in justice, Hatim[35] in liberality, and Rustam in courage. Strife and sedition, and discord and discontent disappeared in his reign of felicity.

King Mansoor felt inspirited and joyous. Vizier Khush-haal was gratified. King Agar made his residence beside the entrance to the city. He commissioned for his instruction the learned and people of merit. In a short while, he duly acquired the knowledge, and then turned his brilliant mind to the pursuit of mathematical sciences.

34. Naushervan: A king of the Persian Sassanid dynasty renowned for his justice.
35. Hatim: An Arab chieftain renowned for his liberality.

OF AGAR LEARNING ABOUT A JOGI'S POWERS THROUGH ASTROLOGY, AND REAPING BENEFIT FROM THEIR MEETING

By the guidance of destiny, Agar learned well the sciences of astrology and jafar and ramal, and surpassed all his learnings with the capacity of his mind. He learned from astrological divination that a jogi who is peerless in astrology would arrive in those parts at an appointed time. If a lavish house were kept ready, supplied with food and beverages, and suchlike things that are the part and parcel of hosting, one day the jogi would arrive to stay there and offer Agar his leftovers. From the power of that food he would learn the secrets of futurity and the occult, and receive many unforeseen gifts besides. Furthermore, forty august kings would profess vassalage to him and pay him tribute. Once he had learned this through the calculations of astrology and ramal, King Agar constructed a palatial palace, and every night circulated like fragrance in search of the jogi.

After some days, the jogi passed that way. King Agar showed him the utmost respect, and with great honor and esteem conducted him to the palace. The jogi turned his attention towards her and said: 'A hundred congratulations on your wisdom and sagacity. A thousand sons may be sacrificed for a daughter such as you.' Agar said: 'Venerated sir, I am not a girl. You must have been mistaken because of my plain appearance.' The jogi laughed, and said: 'I swear by God that you are far preferable to a son.'

In short, the jogi ate a little from the feast served, and gave Agar his leftovers to eat. Then he said: 'O Son, forty kings will become your vassals, and secrets of the unknown and speech of animals will become known to you.' After imparting several occult arts, he sought his leave. King Agar kissed his feet and said: 'I consider you like my father. Pray do not withdraw your hand of guidance from me, and do visit me from time to time.'

The jogi granted the request with pleasure, and departed. King Agar returned to his palace. After saying the morning prayers he gave audience on the royal throne. Then intelligencers brought news that several kings have banded together and descended to invade his lands.

King Mansoor said: 'I deem this land a sacrifice for King Agar. Whoever wishes to possess this land may take it, but they must not torment Agar.'

King Agar answered: 'If my venerable lord had such plans, why did you make me the heir to the kingdom?' King Agar then attacked the invaders in a manly, intrepid manner, striking their harvest of life like a lightning bolt. The foe could not withstand the assault and carnage. His advancing ranks covered the battlefield. Torsos and bodies fell at their advance and the dead lay in heaps. King Agar's armies besieged the forty kings, and the ganjifa-playing[36] heavens conferred such a disadvantage upon them that all kings were captured by Agar.

Then King Agar, envy of the resplendent sun, constructed forty majestic houses, and separately housed a king in each of them. The world rang with the news of his great victory, and besides humans, the tidings instilled Agar's fear even in the hearts of the jinn and paris.

King Mansoor ordered festive music to be played, and had all the captured enemy's goods and riches given away as King Agar's sacrifice.

Thereafter, King Agar spent his days looking after the affairs of the kingdom, and attending to the jogi at night, in the finest traditions of service and hospitality. He so pleased the jogi with his devotion that the jogi gave him a splendid garden for habitation in his land, and divulged to him thirty powerful names from the book *Maaden al-Badaya*,[37] taught him a hundred spells for changing shape, and instructed him in all the secrets of the arts of trickery and sorcery.

It was King Agar's wont to spend his time promenading in the garden. One day, he met the jogi's deputy, who was his principal agent. He asked Agar: 'Who are you?' Agar answered: 'I am the jogi's son.' He said: 'The jogi is a recluse. How did he beget a son? When did this fruit grow in his garden?' Agar replied: 'He found a son after twelve-year-long devotions.'

Then the jogi's deputy rose and made salutations. King Agar showed him many kindnesses and favours and the deputy became increasingly attached to him. The deputy had a tunnel dug from that garden to Agar's palace, and said: 'You inconvenience yourself with the travel. Now you may come and go by this path.'

When the jogi learned of it, he conferred on Agar the ring from his hand, which controlled all knowledge and excellence. It was set with a night-glowing jewel whose light lit up the tunnel. In the morning,

36. Ganjifa: A game of chance.

37. *Maaden al-Badaya*: Name of an occult book.

King Agar would attend to his kingly duties, and the forty kings came and made salutations to him. It continued thus for a long time.

One day Agar said to the jogi: 'Should you wish, I could survey your land and its environs. I shall deliver justice to those who have been wronged, because on the day of judgment, dispensing justice to the subjects is held to be the duty of a king.'

VERSE

If the Creator has granted you prosperity
It is incumbent upon you to make His creatures prosper

The jogi said: 'Very well. Attend to caring for the subjects and dispensing justice to them.'

THE TALE OF VIZIER SHAHRYAR WHO WAS ENAMOURED OF RAJA BASIK'S DAUGHTER, AND OF KING AGAR'S GREAT FEAT OF UNITING THE LOVERS

On most nights, King Agar occupied himself with surveilling his dominion like the full moon. One day, he saw a humble fellow call out to someone named Dil-Aaram in his house. At his call, someone angrily answered from within: 'O Ill-starred Wretch, why do you interrupt my peace and comfort at this hour? Begone, or I shall slaughter you like a cockerel which crows at the wrong hour.' The poor person was struck silent at the harsh words. Dil-Aaram's wife said to him: 'Do not show such indifference and harshness to those calling you in need. Do give him whatever is apportioned for him.' Then Dil-Aaram gave him a few leaves of paan. The man returned whence he had come.

King Agar followed him and arrived in a garden where King Gul's four viziers, Manuchehr, Jawahar, Basant, and Bahram were gathered like the four elements. The fellow Agar had followed there was Shahryar, the fifth vizier, who was enamoured of Raja Basik's daughter. He joined the company of his comrades, like the five elements coming together.

VERSES

Stung by the snake of the beloved's ringlets
His clothes were in tatters, from his collar to his robe's skirts

His face looked wan and the eye shed blood
In manifest signs of love

King Agar, too, joined them like an uninvited guest, to partake of their companionship. Although irked by his presence, they took delight in his beauty and his sweet speech. Vizier Shahryar asked him: 'Tell us who you are, and what brought you here.' King Agar replied: 'I am the son of such and such a man, and often roam in wastelands and deserts.' After they had been introduced to him, King Agar said: 'O Shahryar, the signs of love are manifest on your face. Why are you denied union with your beloved?' He answered: 'The conditions set by my beloved lie beyond the remit of possibility. I must first race as a dragon, then jump in a cauldron of boiling oil, and finally bathe in a hammam heated for twelve years.' King Agar answered: 'To the moth, combusting himself in the flame is the very Water of Life, and the thought of the beloved's curls a dragon incarnate. What is so difficult that you cannot do it, except you do not possess true devotion and perfect love?' Shahryar replied: 'O Young fellow, the sting of love is not known to you, nor are you the moth of someone's luminous visage. What do you know of love?! All this bluster, these heart-breaking comments do not become you.' King Agar answered: 'O Shahryar, hand me your sword so that I may show you my mettle.' In short, that selfish man handed Agar his sword, and said: 'If you can fulfill this mission, I will forever be your slave.'

Then King Agar left, and, arriving at Dil Aaram's doorstep, called out his name. Dil Aaram said: 'My dear fellow, have you gone mad that you call out my name every few moments?! Begone, O Wretch!' King Agar replied: 'I am not the one whom you sent off after giving him paan. I am the son of the jogi of whom you are a subject, and I am in love with Raja Basik's daughter. You must guide me and direct me on that path.'

Frightened to hear these words, Dil Aaram came out of his house, and after visiting many prayers on King Agar, recited these verses:

RUBAI

It is better to avoid that path
That is to say, a path of safety it is not
The one who sets out on the path of death
Departs with longing in the heart

King Agar replied: 'Perhaps you imagine that I will follow your cowardly ways, which is why you are reluctant to guide me to the path.' Much though Dil-Aaram made excuses, King Agar prevailed, and Dil Aaram could do aught but give him all the information and clues and send him off. Then Dil Aaram rushed to the jogi and narrated to him all that had passed.

The jogi felt anxious upon receiving the news, and went and accosted King Agar at Raja Basik's gate, and said to him: 'Dear son, this task is far beyond your power and ability. You risk losing your life in it. Let alone a human, even a dev and a jinn would be unable to fulfill these conditions.'

King Agar said: 'I have given my word. I will not flinch in carrying it out, even if I should die. Come what may, I shall not be deterred. Now I am desirous that you do not stop me from this undertaking.' Upon hearing this, the jogi gave him a flower, which had the property that if one smelled its petals, he became a dragon; and if one smelled its root, he returned to human form. He also gave King Agar a ring which had the property to cool the flames of fire. Then he bid him adieu.

When Raja Basik heard the news of Agar's arrival, he summoned Agar before him. Engrossed by his beauty, the raja asked: 'Will you fulfill the conditions of your beloved, and give your life for her?' King Agar answered: 'God willing, I shall!'

VERSE

I have scattered away my life in her love
At the moment, I have given up entirely on life

Raja Basik said: 'The first condition is that you race with me in the form of a dragon.' King Agar recited: 'In the name of Allah!' smelled the flower, and turning into a dragon, followed that snake for many miles, burning sticks and straws in the path with his flaming tail, and did not lose him anywhere during the journey. After he had met the condition to Raja Basik's satisfaction, the raja said: 'O True Lover, now you must jump into the cauldron of boiling oil.' King Agar recited: 'In the name of Allah!' and jumped into the cauldron, and from the power of the ring emerged from it unscathed and unharmed, as if he were stepping out of the sea. The third condition was that Agar bathe with boiling water, and King Agar fulfilled that as well.

When Agar, with his courage, satisfied all the conditions, Raja Basik prepared for the wedding of his daughter Moti Rani.

King Agar asked Raja Basik to betroth Moti Rani to the sword. With Moti Rani wedded to the sword, he set out with the bride for his garden with much fanfare.

Agar went before Vizier Shahryar, and said to him: 'There, my friend! May holding Moti Rani's hand prove auspicious to you.' Shahryar was astounded upon hearing that felicitous news. He pledged himself many times as King Agar's sacrifice, and offered him his blessings and thanks. In short, the whole world rang with the news of King Agar's courage and fortitude.

• • •

One day, Agar was giving audience on King Mansoor's throne, occupied with the affairs of the empire and the administration of the state, when a dragon arrived as plaintiff before him, rolling in dust, striking his head on the ground, shedding tears of blood from his eyes, and spewing flames with his sighs, and said: 'O Equitable King, I had once travelled to King Gul's kingdom and fallen in love with a she-serpent. For this transgression King Gul expelled me from his kingdom, and put that she-serpent under the captivity of monkeys and bears. I have come seeking justice and fairness, so that through you I may become reunited with my pair.'

King Agar served milk to the dragon, and said to him: 'Present yourself in the evening.'

The dragon left, and in the evening, he returned before King Agar who awaited him in his private chamber. Then King Agar turned into a fierce dragon himself upon smelling the flower given him by the jogi. He climbed on to the dragon who had come to him with his plaint, and set out for King Gul's land. When they arrived where the she-serpent was imprisoned, the bears and monkeys ran away, and the she-serpent said: 'O King, a thousand plaudits and commendations on your courage, and reproaches and rebukes on that thorny Gul, who separated me from my pair for no reason.' After some time, the two dragons returned safely from there.

Upon hearing this news King Gul punished the guards. They said to him: 'We thought that it was Your Majesty, come in a dragon's form.' In the end, King Gul expelled the she-serpent's parents from the kingdom and, after plundering and despoiling their house, goods and chattels, he imprisoned the she-serpent beyond the seven seas.

Upon hearing the news, the dragon again sought redress from King Agar. He offered the dragon much consolation, and said: 'Keep up your hopes.'

Troubled and concerned by the news, King Agar went into a bleak desert. There he began playing the reed-pipe. The birds and the beasts of the desert gathered to hear him. Except for the fox, who was a crafty, artful creature, all animals gathered around him.

Someone asked the fox: 'Why did you not go?' She replied: 'I will present myself when that lion-tempered creature comes himself to invite me, or send for me with honour and esteem.' Upon hearing this, King Agar said: 'The honorable creatures should go and bring the fox along.' In short, the fox arrived after much guileful back and forth, and brought along a flower as an offering.

VERSE

Was it a flower or a bouquet of deception and guile
That upon smelling it, a man became a woman; and a woman, man

King Agar took the flower from her, and said: 'Travel beyond the seven seas and bring back the she-serpent, who is this dragon's pair.' The fox left and landed on the other side like a wave, and in no time returned with the she-serpent. King Agar was very pleased at her acquitting herself laudably in the mission, and the dragon's joy knew no bounds.

When King Gul received the news, it marked him like a tulip and he made ready to attack King Agar. After some missives were exchanged between them, King Agar wrote to Gul:

You command the armies of devs and paris, and I command humans. You imagine yourself stronger on account of your power and might, and for that reason seek confrontation and war. But in truth we are superior to you, as King Suleiman had made devs and paris subservient to him. It would be preferable that the lives of God's creatures are not wasted. You and I should fight, and the one who prevails, should dictate to the other.

Shahryar, King Gul's minister who controlled the affairs of the state, and was indebted to King Agar, inveigled King Gul to forget hostilities, and was instrumental in peace being forged between the parties.

OF PRINCE LAAL'S BETROTHAL WITH MAH-PARWAR PARI ON ACCOUNT OF LAL DEV'S EFFORTS AND STRATAGEM

The gardeners of beauty and love's meadow thus adorn the bouquet that is the subject of lovers' union, that when Mah-Parwar's garden of beauty was made pale and disarrayed by the simoom[38] of separation, and the rosy cheeks of Price Laal wilted and turned wan by the thorn of disunion, her existence began to flicker like a taper nearing its end, and he became all scattered like the zephyr.

VERSES

Rose-like, his collar was torn
And she like the nightingale made plaints
She was unaware of her disheveled locks
But he was deeply conscious of his woes
If a single eyelash of hers became wet with tears
A river of tears surged in his eye

Prince Laal said to Lal Dev in a state of great unease and anxiety: 'Despite the affection you hold for me, I have not yet recovered from the malady of separation from my ill-fortune, and I long for the sherbet of union. My heart can no longer bear the violence of separation and withstand disunion. It is a matter of days before I am extinguished like the morning lamp.

VERSE

Tend O Friend, to your burning heart
Who knows when the morning lamp will snuff it out

Lal Dev said: 'I was not remiss in attending to your wishes, and performed all offices of a diligent messenger, but there is no countering one's fate.' Thus speaking, he submerged for a long time in the sea of anxiety, and upon finding the pearl of desire in the oyster's embrace, spoke: 'A solution occurs to me, if only it would work.'

Lal Dev then went before Mah-Parwar Pari, and conveyed to her Prince Laal's state of anxiety and restiveness. Mah-Parwar offered him much consolation and words of comfort.

38. Simoom: A hot wind from the desert.

VERSE

She lifted the veil that was between them
And revealed to him the suffering of her heart

Lal Dev asked her: 'How can this anxiety on both sides, and the agitation of the parties be put to rest? How can cheer be brought to your hearts?' The pari replied: 'How can I find a way?! The fear of my parents overwhelms me; I cannot act against their wishes. And I am not all alone in the world either, that I could accompany you at your bidding. My soul is afire, but I am helpless, and cannot think of a happy solution.' Lal Dev said: 'There is a solution: I can give you a physic that will make you vomit blood, and this stratagem will bring about an end to your misery.' The pari replied: 'Even poison is like a sovereign remedy if it will effect union.'

VERSE

I will not refuse poison, let alone physic
To break separation's fever that has me in its grip

In short, the dev administered her a physic which made her vomit blood. Her parents went into a panic and rushed about, trying to find some medicine or cure. The dev marked his forehead with sandalwood and minium and disguised himself as a Brahmin. Reciting the name of Bhagwan, and counting beads, he passed by there. Someone said to him: 'O Lord and Master, our princess has fallen under the power of some infernal being. Cast her horoscope and tell us the forecast.' The false Brahmin made the forecast, and said: 'Tomorrow a prince will pass this way with his wedding procession, whose boat will capsize in a storm and his wife will drown. If the pari is married to him, she will recover from her illness. According to the forecast, the prince will die, but her malady will leave her. Besides this, there is no other cure.'

The pari's parents replied: 'We accept. Pray keep a lookout for him, and when the boat arrives we should be informed at once.'

Then the false Brahmin rushed away and arrived in his garden. He dressed the prince like a bridegroom, advised and instructed him about the matter, and sent him off in a boat. When it was morning, Prince Laal rent his collar, and landed ashore, putting dust on his head.

VERSES

He cried, Alas and alack,
My whole household drowned in the sea
Why would a tempest not rise from my heart?
Calamities have made me their mark and destroyed me

He made these laments and cried loudly. The king was informed, and he became convinced that the Brahmin was right. He sent his viziers and commanders, after giving them injunctions, to inquire after the prince. One of them asked him: 'O Good Fellow, why do you cry and scatter away your life thus?' He replied: 'Ah! Indeed, why must I not cry and scatter away my life? Yesterday I had my nuptials, and today I find myself homeless. Like an oyster I thirsted for twelve years before I found myself an unpierced pearl. But the turbulent sea carried her away like a raindrop.'

The man said: 'One must submit before God's Will. If you agree to marry Princess Mah-Parwar, the daughter of the king of this land, we may intercede on your behalf with the king.' The prince said: 'God be praised! You see my state and suggest marriage?' In short, everyone tried to reason with the prince, and finally prevailed upon him to get remarried. The bridegroom said: 'Very well, but I shall marry her on the condition and agreement that I shall take her with me where I wish. I shall agree to your proposal if all the bride's relatives, her brothers, and parents put their signets to this agreement.'

The pari's relations were worried about the princess, and knew that the prince was going to die and become her sacrifice: that she would become well after his demise. Then young and old all swore oaths and put their signets on the agreement. Preparations for the wedding began, and Mah-Parwar was made into a bride.

VERSES

Where may I begin to describe her adornment
The parting of her hair spangled like the Milky Way
Those locks that held many a heart captive
The Night of Power[39] *was envious of them*

39. Night of Power: A night of religious celebration that falls within the final ten days of the Islamic month of Ramadan.

If one were to call her eyebrows a bow
Her eyelashes were entirely like a quiver full of arrows
Such eyes that the deer felt abashed before them
Her eyes were deer who grazed on lovers' hearts
She lined them captivatingly with kohl
As if the pupil itself was ground into kohl
Her ears were mines of beauty
Her nose showed her pretty face to advantage
Her lips were like grains of rock candy
Her mouth the pond of the Water of Life
The tinge of missi was there as an omen
Her lips turned blue from the mere thought of kissing
Her throat and neck were transparent
As if they were two crystalline decanters of pure wine
Her arm resembled a crystal branch
It was the image of the light that burnt at Tur
Her hand was an image of the radiant sun
Which engendered fondness and love
The lustre of pearl was envious of her bright breasts
They were like two bubbles on water's surface
There is no hiding them from the eyes
They were like the festive orbs of lac, full of colour
That flower's jewel-covered bodice
Was a much sought after object[40]
How to describe the thinness of her waist
One could only see it from one's good fortune
Her abdomen was bright like a mirror
And her navel was like the dimple in her chin
She had not yet flowered, she was still a bud
Whose thoughts made one full of anxious desire
More delicate than the veins of the rose petal was her secret passage
Concupiscence and lust could not find its way there
Her thighs offered no purchase to the glance
Whoever beheld them praised them aloud
If one could feel the weight of her feet on one's eyes
One could feel the weight of eyelashes on one's eyes
She was a veritable monster of beauty from head to foot
Her stature and bearing were a sight to behold.

40. This is a play on words, as the term *sonay ki chirya* is used for the tie that connects the cups of the bodice.

In short, that Venus came in a beneficent conjunction with that Moon. After the betrothal, the bridegroom was summoned indoors and seated beside the bride. The moment he saw her lovely face, Prince Laal swooned and fainted. The bride's family were very pleased, thinking that the Brahmin's prediction had come true. The bride sprinkled the rose water of her tears from which he was restored and blossomed like a rose. Those who wished him ill were humiliated, and scattered away discountenanced. The bridegroom put his arms around the bride's neck, and partook of the pistachio of her lips, the almonds of her eyes, and the pomegranates of her breasts. He embraced her, pressed her to his side, tickled and made her laugh, and made the bud flower and the oyster see rain. Then he rested, his passion sated.

OF THE BRIDE DEPARTING HER PARENTS' HOME AND THE PRINCE RETURNING TO LAL DEV'S GARDEN

When the bride of night hid her face from Emperor Sun in the veil of nonexistence, Prince Laal woke up. The bridegroom asked leave to depart with the bride. The family said: 'This is not possible. If you wish to stay here as our live-in son-in-law, well and good, otherwise you must go your own way.' The prince produced the agreement which they had written and witnessed. In the end, they could find no grounds to hold Mah-Parwar, and there was a great commotion as the bride's departure neared.

The thought of separation from Mah-Parwar oppressed everyone's heart. Young and old embraced her to say their goodbyes. The preparations for departure were made and the dowry was brought out (but providing the details of the dowry here will prolong the narrative).

Their hands humbly joined together, the family came before the bridegroom, and said: 'We send this slave girl to serve you.' Lal Dev said: 'Do not utter such words, for she is our honorable mistress.'

And thus, amidst the cries of the parents and the sound of festive drums, the bride left her home with great pomp and ceremony. Prince Laal returned joyously with his bride to the garden. Mahmood prostrated himself in offering thanks to God. King Gul made an offering of the night-glowing jewel. Quraish doted on Mah-Parwar with all her heart. All who came to see the bride, offered priceless jewels for the privilege and boon of seeing her face.

King Gul delayed presenting himself, and said: 'O Brother, modesty is part of faith.' The prince answered:

VERSE

'A sister does not take purdah from her brother

I bid you if you value my life, do present yourself.'

Then King Gul entered the house with his eyes lowered. Mah-Parwar refused to greet him, and said: 'We are their liege and they are our vassals.' But at Prince Laal's bidding she offered him her respects.

OF QURAISH AND GUL REENACTING PRINCE LAAL'S BETROTHAL, AND OF GUL'S LOVE FOR AGAR BECOMING MANIFEST

King Gul said to his mother: 'I wish for Prince Laal's betrothal to be performed again, so that we can also witness how our brother looks, dressed up as a bridegroom. You can make arrangements from the bride's side, and I will make preparations as the bridegroom's representative.' Quraish replied: 'May I become your sacrifice! What you said is after my own heart. I am also desirous of preparing Mah-Parwar as a bride. But do seek your father's opinion as well, in the matter.'

In short, after Lal Dev also agreed, they made preparations for the wedding. Invitations were sent out. A letter was also sent to the jogi, who was King Agar's guide and preceptor, which carried this convivial message:

> *'O Venerable Uncle! My brother is scheduled to be married to Mah-Parwar Pari on such and such a date. Along with your esteemed son, the freshly bloomed flower of your lineage, who has appeared after twelve years, you are requested to grace the event by attending it, and not hesitate in the least on account of the exchanges that took place between your son and me, owing to his youthful years.'*

The jogi decided not to attend the event for that very reason, since Agar had bested Gul at times, and breached decorum with his feistiness. He offered a number of excuses and sent a clear reply that on account of his health he was unable to attend the bustle of celebrations, and his son was not yet of age to attend by himself, and that he doubted that they would be able to come.

King Gul was angered by his artful speech. He said to Vizier Shahryar: 'Had I known that the jogi would not come, I would not have invited him in the first place. I am grieved at the jogi refusing to come, and at his guileful excuses.'

Meanwhile, the preparations for the wedding were made in a befitting manner and guests began arriving from all directions with great pomp and ceremony.

VERSES

The prince made such a handsome bridegroom
Glances could not find purchase on his face
A royal robe on his fair skin
Together they resembled the bloom of jasmines
A jewel-strung sehra covered his face
Its every string was a ray of sunshine
The henna, the missi, those garlands of gold lace
To this day that bloom is remembered
The days of youth, the prime of manhood
He was choice among the world's beautiful men
With locks that extended beyond his height
In short, he was a beautiful calamity from head to foot
His dark eyes were bashful and full of modesty
His glance took hearts captive
His eyelashes were like watered blades
Which cut lovers' hearts into a hundred pieces

Such a handsome bridegroom he made, that Old Man Heavens, in all his years, would not have seen the like. In the wedding procession he resembled a moon, and his companions like so many stars. In due time, he arrived at the bride's house. The fireworks started, and from the flower-shaped explosions every nook became a garden of light. Every heart was like a moth of the taper of illumination; the strains of the shehnai drove Tan-Sen into ecstasies. King Gul conducted the bridegroom to the throne, served him sherbet, garlanded him, and served him paan. As a burble of congratulations and felicitations rose, the music assembly started.

King Gul said to viziers Jawahar and Shahryar: 'I arranged this ceremony only to invite the jogi's son. It saddens me that he did not come. I would that the two of you ride the throne to his place and see if the jogi is in truth ill, or if it was all a ruse.'

In short, the two able viziers flew thence on the throne, and King Gul, too, clandestinely headed there. Unsuspecting and unwary that another was privy to their company, the viziers arrived in the jogi's land in the flash of an eye. They witnessed that the jogi had a headache and King Agar was devotedly attending to him. One moment he would be with the jogi, and the next he would be circulating without.

VERSE

No rest from his restiveness has he

Vizier Shahryar greeted him. King Agar asked: 'How did you happen by here? Wasn't there a wedding ceremony today?' The vizier answered: 'We left after making the excuse that we were going to attend the call of nature.' The king replied: 'How wonderful! Keep peeing in your master's mouth!' Those present burst out laughing, and the two viziers were deeply embarrassed.

King Gul, who was sitting on his throne, hovering above King Agar, heard these words and wondered about them. Then he surveyed King Agar from head to toe. He put the gold of Agar's beauty to the touchstone of intellect, and discerned that Agar was a woman. The arrow of love shot through his heart, and he became all unsettled and returned from Agar's house with great disquiet in his heart.

VERSE

King Gul, visiting there as an onlooker
Turned into a nightingale in Agar's love

The festive ceremony seemed to him like the night of lamentations; like a taper, his spirits were snuffed out. Prince Laal, who knew the sting of love, reckoned that someone had snared King Gul's heart, and it had fallen captive to someone's locks. A lover recognises a fellow lover's distress. All of them are enraptured by the pari of love, and are moths of the same taper.

VERSE

There is no hiding one's pain from a sympathiser
A wan appearance is a lover's telltale mark

Prince Laal became sad upon seeing King Gul downhearted. He participated in the ceremonies and rituals half-heartedly, then retired to the palace, but Gul's sorrow continued to weigh on his heart.

OF THE JOGI SUFFERING FROM A HEADACHE AND KING AGAR WANDERING IN SEARCH OF A CURE

On account of the jogi's illness, King Agar wandered in the wilderness, languorous like his eyes and disheveled like his locks, to find some cure for his master's irremediable pain. One night by the seaside, upon seeing him tearful and heavy-hearted, a simurgh said to him: 'O Youth, what tragedy has struck you, and what oppresses your heart?' King Agar said: 'I am devoted to a jogi and his headache has been unending and severe.' The simurgh felt pity, and pulled out a feather from his wing, and gave it to him, saying: 'O huma[41] of the zenith of kingdom, grind this feather and then put a couple of drops of its essence into his ear and nose. His headache will disappear without a trace.'

Agar blessed the simurgh, took the feather, and after taking his leave of the simurgh, went before the jogi. He ground the feather with his miracle-working hands and dropped its essence into the jogi's nose, whereupon the jogi made a full recovery.

To cut a long story short, the jogi, who for a long time had not eaten or slept, and whose heart was numb with severe pain, finally found comfort and peace and lay down to rest.

OF KING AGAR ENTERING THE JOGI'S PRIVATE CHAMBERS AND MEETING HIS WIVES

King Agar saw some keys lying by the jogi's bedside. Finding it an opportune moment, he started opening all the locked doors with the keys.

Inside one house he beheld a beautiful jogan[42] named Queen Bhabhut holding a tanbura[43] in her hand, and singing. She was of excellent disposition, her forehead was smeared with ashes, and she wore an agate and crystal necklace. Upon seeing Agar, she asked him: 'Who are you, O youthful, pleasant boy, for I have never before seen you.' He

41. Huma: A propitious bird. It is believed that a huma alighting on a person is a sign of good fortune.

42. Jogan: A female jogi.

43. Tanbura: A stringed musical instrument.

answered: 'I am the jogi's son.' The jogan visited blessings on Agar and took his troubles upon her head. She stroked his back and seated him beside her. Bhabhut Rani offered Agar two biras[44] of paan, of which he ate one and hid away the other. Then he took his leave of Bhabhut Rani and arrived at the second house.

There he saw a princess, beautiful as a pari and luminous like the sun, sitting on a throne with great coquettery, resting against a pillow. She too was surprised to see Agar and asked his particulars. King Agar gave her the same reply. She too treated him as Bhabhut Rani had done.

From there Agar went to the third house. There he beheld a pari, fifteen years of age, who was a paragon of beauty, and the embodiment of youth. The pari said: 'O Rosy-cheeked Beloved, are you some king, or angel or the moon?' King Agar answered: 'I am the jogi's son and the light of your eyes.' She marveled upon hearing this, and said: 'Who has ever seen a cane tree bear fruit? When did a jewel like you come out of that stone?' King Agar answered: 'God Almighty is without want and has all kinds of powers.' The pari too gave him two biras of paan to eat. He ate one and concealed the other.

Then he entered the fourth house. He saw three women sitting on a throne. One of them was Mah-e Taaban, the other Zahra, and the third was Mushtri. They were conversing together, and saying: 'If someone could conduct us to such and such land of the parizads, we would put the control of that kingdom at his disposal.'

Mah-e Taaban said: 'If I could have laid my hands on just one flower from the garden of Shah Lala, I could have turned twelve years old from its power. Alas, there is nothing to be done, as the jogi has no son.'

Suddenly, one of them beheld King Agar, and, astonished and astounded to see him, asked: 'Who are you?' Agar said: 'I am the jogi's son.' Mah-e Taaban said: 'That is not true.' King Agar proved it to her and she was delighted, and gave him two biras of paan.

King Agar said to her: 'O dear mother, do tell me about Shah Lala's garden and where it is located.' She answered: 'It is a treacherous place and the land of fear and death, where no one has ever set foot. In that garden there is a pond whose mouth is closed by a heavy iron lid. A mere ten or twenty people cannot hope to open the gate to the garden. It would need thousands of devs joining their strength together to lift it.'

44. Bira: A preparation of betel-leaf.

While King Agar was having these conversations, the jogi woke up and asked: 'Where is King Agar?' Someone answered: 'He has gone into your private chambers.'

The jogi went into his private chambers and asked about him. He was told that he had left for the second house.

King Agar heard the jogi's approaching, and presented himself before him, and asked; 'How is your headache?' He answered: 'By the grace of God and your efforts, I am restored to health.' King Agar said to him: 'You should tell me the names of your wives.' The jogi said: 'The name of the jogan is Bhabhut Rani, the princess is named Khurshid, and the parizad is called Mahtab, and the fourth one is called Mah-e Taaban.'

Then King Agar took his leave of the jogi and retired to his bed-chamber, and rested. In the middle of the night he went before the jogi. After saying the morning prayers, he took along Zahra and Mushtri, and headed for Shah Lala's garden.

OF KING AGAR GOING INTO SHAH LALA'S GARDEN AND BRINGING AJOOBA PARI, VIZIER JAWAHAR'S BELOVED, AND OBTAINING FROM SHAH LALA'S GARDEN THE FLOWER, HAMEED DEV THE FAITHFUL, AND A FLEET-FOOTED HORSE

It is said that King Agar, taking Zahra and Mushtri, the attendants of Mah-e Taaban, and travelling speedily like a dove, arrived in the land where Shah Lala's garden was situated. He asked the gardener to pluck a flower for him. The gardener went before Ajooba Pari and said: 'King Agar has come and asks for a flower.' Ajooba Pari said: 'A few soldiers should go and drag him here by his locks.'

Upon hearing the troopers approach, Zahra and Mushtri spread their legs as a supplicant does his hand of prayer. Those troopers, who considered themselves amongst the finest of their kind, disappeared, with their mounts, between their legs.

VERSE

It was a cellar like a deep sea
They drowned within, along with their mounts

Furious, the parizad sent another twenty troopers. They too were never heard from again. Armies of troopers and waves of foot soldiers assaulted them, and the two of them imprisoned them in their magic cellar. In short, the whole army disappeared between their legs. The two women, Zahra and Mushtri, defeated thousands.

King Agar said: 'O Zahra, I am overcome by thirst. It would be little wonder if my gall turns to water.' She answered: 'It is not advised to drink water from this land; let us head onwards, and we will find orchards and also water to drink.' Agar went onwards and beheld a finely trimmed garden with a colourful enclosure, hung with sweet fruit. He saw running fountains, trees swaying in the breeze, and birds singing. King Agar was delighted and overjoyed at the sight of the garden. As he cupped his hand to drink some water, he heard a parrot and a mynah call out from a cage hanging in the garden: 'O God's creature, it is not warranted to drink water from this stream.'

King Agar withdrew his hand and, addressing the birds, asked of their well-being. The mynah answered: 'O King, the master of this garden has not touched food or drink for three days. It is incumbent upon a guest to not partake of food or drink without the host.' King Agar said: 'Give me the name and particulars of the master of the garden, and tell me about him. Who is he? Why has he stopped eating and drinking? Is he sick, or imprisoned, or in love with someone?' The parrot answered: 'Hear then that this name is Jawahar, and he is the vizier of King Gul, and he is become dispirited in the love of Ajooba Pari, and the hardship of separation has made him immobile like a portrait.'

King Agar said:

VERSES

For some time I have known the fellow
And, God knows, I am sorry to hear of his suffering
Tell me at once where I can find him
I shall depart for that place without delay

The parrot gave him the directions to his house, and Agar headed in that direction. King Agar found Vizier Jawahar's father crying in the hall of audience, and asked him about Jawahar's state. He answered: 'There is nothing to tell; for three days he has enclosed himself within. He touches neither food nor drink, and cares not a whit about our name and honour.' King Agar called out to the lover mourning in his house. Jawahar felt a wave of hope building, and opened the door, and King Agar shed tears on beholding his state.

Then Jawahar narrated what had passed with him, from beginning to end. King Agar consoled him and returned to the parrot and mynah. They said to him: 'If you are leaving on the mission, do take us along; and put your faith in the handful of feathers that is our existence.' That huma of the pinnacle of prestige took along the parrot and the mynah, and departed in search of Ajooba Pari.

When they arrived at the parizad's house, they heard a commotion. They asked the reason for it and someone said: 'For a long time a parizad has had a persistent headache and his face has turned pale. He strikes his head night and day to allay the pain and is neither able to die, nor is fully alive.' The mynah said to King Agar: 'In Shah Lala's garden, which is in the possession of the other parizad, towards the East there is a garden patch, where a flower grows which holds the cure to this condition, and people are unaware of its properties. If it is fetched, his headache will disappear.'

King Agar said: 'I see no one whom I can send, besides myself. I shall go.' The parrot said: 'O King, a dev named Hameed Dev, who has suffered from leprosy for many years, has divined from astrology that, by the guidance of fortune, one King Agar whom the sun itself worships, will one day arrive in this garden. In the hope of that day, the dev lives in such and such tower in this garden. If you were to wash your hands and feet and splash some water on him, he will become well, and then he will bring you that flower.'

King Agar went there, and after saying prayers in gratitude, splashed the water left over from the ablution on Hameed Dev. Immediately, all signs of the disease left him.

After Hameed Dev's body was restored to health, he prostrated himself in gratitude at King Agar's feet and said: 'I shall remain your slave forever for this favour, and not leave your service.' King Agar said to him: 'Go to such and such garden and bring me a flower from there.' Hameed Dev answered: 'Very well. Your slave's life will become your sacrifice.' King Agar said: 'Do not go alone. We will accompany you. Then King Agar, Hameed Dev, the parrot and mynah, along with Zahra and Mushtri set out together.

The parrot said: 'O King Agar, when you pluck the flower, avert your eyes from the sight of the garden. Do not look at it afterwards, and heed not the hue and cry and commotion that follows.'

VERSE

Or else we will turn to stone
Forever we will be remorseful

In short, when they arrived at the gate of Shah Lala's garden, Hameed Dev quickly plucked the flower. Immediately upon plucking the flower, shouts of *Capture!* and *Seize!* and *Be alert!* arose. Thousands of devs came out, and Zahra and Mushtri imprisoned them in their prison cellar.

Upon receiving the news, the parizad was incensed and sent a message to Agar that, God willing, he would exact such retribution for the excesses that Agar would remember it for the rest of his living days. King Agar answered: 'Pray dispel all acrimony from your heart at my taking the flower, and bring me cheer by accepting me as your son-in-law. The young may err, but the old should not hold back favours.' The parizad was further incensed to hear this, and said: 'You now add insult to injury!'

After much back and forth, the parizad said: 'Very well, even though I am angry at your transgression, I shall grant your request, upon two conditions: The first is that I should recover from my headache; and the second is that my wife, who is sick, is healed as well.'

King Agar said: 'I am bound to help allay your suffering. As to the rest, God is the Creator of Causes.' Thus speaking, he entered the parizad's palace, accompanied by Hameed Dev.

He made the parizad smell the flower, which completely cured him of his headache. As the parizad had gone without food and sleep for many days, he slept for a long time until his body had fully recovered from the fatigue. He opened his eyes after some time, and realised that all vestiges of the headache had left him, and his body was no longer burdened by the oppressive headache. He prostrated himself to offer thanks, and conducted King Agar and the others into his private chamber. He showed them his deranged wife, who killed and ate a human daily, and looked agitated and sick.

Hameed Dev diagnosed her malady, from his wisdom and sagacity, and placed a cauldron full of milk by her bedside. Then he put a snake's skull in fire. From the burning smell, a huge black dragon emerged, hissing, from his lair inside her. The woman regained consciousness. She said: 'Who are these strangers?' The parizad replied: 'Thank God that you can now distinguish between family and strangers. Even though they are strangers, they safeguarded my name and honour.'

In short, the parizad was greatly indebted to Agar, and busied himself in making preparations for the wedding. He seated King Agar on the seat of son-in-law with great honor and esteem. King Agar gave his name as Jawahar. And thus a nightingale was betrothed to a nightingale, a flower bud to another. The dowry included pearls and rubies, gold pieces, silver pieces, slaves and slave girls. In the dowry was also included a horse, whose speed and charge are described in this manner:

VERSE

At times you could see him, at times he was invisible
At times that black horse was like a firefly's flash

Hameed Dev said: 'O King, it is a priceless horse, and will be of great service to you. It is from rare good luck that a slave like Hameed Dev, and a well-paced steed such as this are found. Even the wind's charger cannot catch this steed, and imagination's horse will stumble in pursuing it.' The horse laughed at Hameed Dev's words.

King Agar felt unhappy at the horse laughing indecorously. To bring cheer to King Agar's heart, the horse addressed Hameed Dev as follows: 'From the day the Creator of humans and the jinn made me, no one has ridden me. It is my ardent desire that King Agar should mount me.' King Agar was pleased at his speech and promised to ride him.

In short, Ajooba Pari's parents sent her off with Agar. They were accompanied by the singing parrot and mynah, and Zahra and Mushtri went chortling alongside. King Agar said to Hameed Dev: 'Go and deliver Jawahar the happy tidings.

VERSE

O Messenger, do not promptly give him the message of union
Lest the happy news should send him into the shock of death

Hameed Dev arrived there and after congratulating Jawahar, said to him: 'Rise and sit up and laugh and speak. The one whose face is luminous like a taper, and to whom you are devoted like a moth, has been secured by the auspices of King Agar to be the light of your assembly.' Jawahar lit up with joy like a flame. After decorating his house and making it the envy of heaven, he proceeded to greet King Agar.

King Agar gave Ajooba Pari into the oyster-like longing embrace of Jawahar. Carrying the flower from Shah Lala's garden, Agar rode the horse to see the jogi. He said to Agar: 'My good fellow, you risk your life in others' service for no reason. I, your father, am still alive! You should have presented Ajooba Pari to me.' Agar replied: 'Very well. Next time I will present them for Your Honor's pleasure.' Then, laughing, he went into the female quarters and gave Mah-e Taaban the flower from Shah Lala's garden.

From the power of this gift she turned twelve. From there, Agar returned to his court. He restored the crowns of the forty kings who had been forced into his vassalage, and sent all of them back to their lands.

OF KING AGAR ACCOMPANYING THE JOGI AND HIS WIVES ON A PROMENADE, ALONG WITH MOTI RANI AND AJOOBA PARI; OF HIS MEETING THE SIMURGH AND LEARNING ABOUT THE ROYAL FALCON, AND WANDERING IN SEARCH OF THE BIRD

When the gold-feathered simurgh of the West sported his gold crown and headed East, King Agar sent Hameed Dev to summon Moti Rani, Shahryar, Ajooba Pari and Jawahar. When all of them arrived at his summons, Agar said to the jogi: 'Today I wish to promenade in the garden as the stirrup fellow of Your Honor's four wives, and divert myself there for some time.' The jogi said: 'My child, I will accompany you, too.' He answered, 'Very well!'

Then King Agar rode out with the jogi, Shahryar and Jawahar, with Hameed Dev and the women accompanying them, and they arrived at the gates of a garden. Using his finger as a key, King Agar opened the gate to enter the garden. The others were astounded at the spectacle. Someone said: 'We witnessed this miracle, but do you also have the power to change form, and transfer your soul into another body?' Agar answered: 'Indeed, I can change into a hundred forms.' Thus speaking, that pari-like creature turned into a horrid dev with mouth spewing flames. It was such a terrifying spectacle that Moti Rani and Ajooba Pari were unnerved.

Perchance, King Gul was passing there on his throne. Upon seeing this spectacle he felt jealous and envious, and said:

VERSE

What art is there which she has not mastered
Sometimes she appears as a dev, sometimes as a pari
The form of a fire-spewing dragon she is
What regard has she of the lover's searing sigh

While King Gul was having this conversation with himself, the jogi caught sight of him. He was displeased with Agar and loudly remonstrated with him. At that, King Agar returned to his original form. The uproar of the praise showered at him rose to the heavens. King Gul was astonished and said:

VERSE

Is she a flame, or lightning, or wind
Whatever she is, remains unproven

Even though allured by Agar's gestures, and his heart racing at Agar's every manifestation, King Gul could do aught but return to his land.

. . .

King Agar organized Nowruz festivities in his garden. The musicians were sent for, and a music and dance assembly got underway. When the simurgh heard the news, he too arrived in the garden, and blessed Agar, and said: 'By the grace of God, my eyes received bliss again from the sight of you. I hear that when Your Honor smiles, your bud-like mouth showers flowers, and fills the skirts of vision with flowers.' That flowering bud of the garden of love laughed at his wish, and the simurgh's vision was filled with flowers.

Viziers Shahryar and Jawahar said to themselves: 'Had King Gul seen this shower of flowers, he would have offered himself a thousand times as Agar's sacrifice.'

The simurgh offered Agar a gold crown, which sat becomingly on his forehead. Then the simurgh said: 'O King, God's munificence is with you, and you possess all essentials of kingship. But the royal falcon does not grace your blessed hand. That falcon, worthy of a beloved such as yourself, has the property of the rara avis: It is impossible to find him, none has the wherewithal to travel beyond the seven seas and search for him, and it is well nigh impossible to capture him. The land where he is to be found is surrounded by billowing seas on two sides, and raging fires on the other two. If one fell into the sea, he would be destroyed instantly, and if one fell into the fire, he would at once turn to smoke. And if one were to safely cross that perilous path, the moment he calls out to the royal falcon and the instant the words are uttered, he would fall to the ground, a heap of clay. Let alone a human, even a parizad cannot capture him, and neither a dev nor beast can get there.' King Agar said: 'God willing, we shall go, and bring him with the sanction of God.'

The simurgh said: 'Beware! You must never head in that direction, and not set foot there even by mistake.' But Agar did not relent. Agar asked Hameed Dev and the horse for their opinion. They rejoined together that the journey would be entirely hazardous, and life-imperilling, and under no circumstances should one go there; that to give credence to the words of a dumb animal was far from wisdom and sagacity.

King Agar refused to listen to any arguments and prepared to leave. Helpless, Hameed Dev finally said: 'I have heard that the falcon does not answer to men. It would be best if you went in female attire.' King Agar put on the female attire that was sewn to his body measurements, mounted the horse, took Hameed Dev along, and in a manly fashion set out astride his horse, which traversed the heavens. By the grace of God, Agar traversed the dangerous paths and the seven seas and arrived at the shores of hope. He called out to the falcon, saying: 'O venturesome friend, I have come to you at great peril to my life. I bid you in the name of the One Who is oblivious to all, to come to me.' Upon hearing this, the falcon flew down and, with great coquetry, came and perched on the hand of the one whose forehead shone bright as venus.

VERSE

What pleasure they found in captivity, who can tell
The birds of the garden make a queue for the net

King Agar was released from his distress and said: 'I even caught the rara avis in love's net.'

He promenaded in the garden and saw many varieties of fruit hanging from trees. He wished to partake of it but resisted the temptation, lest eating them should bring about some new calamity. The horse said: 'Have no anxiety and enjoy the fruit.' Agar had a few grains of pomegranate and plucked some juicy fruit and stored it in the saddle bags. Then they started their return journey.

The high-flying horse showed him the sights of the heavens. In short, they journeyed through that land and arrived in their kingdom. While they were flying, the jogi caught sight of them in the sky. He imagined that it was some dev flying. The jogi, who was a great archer, had nocked the arrow in his bow, when the vizier called out: 'Wait! Do not make any blunder! King Agar is also fond of hunting and chase.' Upon that, the jogi put down the bow and arrow.

Meanwhile, they saw King Agar, the falcon perched on his hand, riding his steed which was the wind's charger, and Hameed Dev as his outrider, descend from the sky.

The jogi praised the vizier, chided Hameed Dev, rebuked the horse, and said these words: 'It is you who carry him all over God's wide world. I was about to make him the mark of my arrow, and myself the mark of regret. The vizier kept me from it and I am indebted to him.

VERSE

It would have been a calamity had I made him my mark
I would have killed myself with my own hands

Then the jogi said to King Agar: 'Drive away these wretches from your side.' King Agar said: 'Very well!'

Then the jogi celebrated King Agar's bringing back the falcon, and scattered riches as Agar's sacrifice. The auspicious news reached all kings, and messengers arrived from all lands to congratulate him, bearing offerings as sacrifice. King Agar served fruit from Shah Lala's garden to the jogi and also sent a few salvers to King Mansoor. The king and his vizier both became merry. The simurgh also came to offer felicitations, and recited:

VERSE

The royal falcon of your courage, made the rara avis its captive
This is true subduing; this is true prestige

Then King Agar sent a message to King Gul that said: 'You must have received the news of our journeying and bringing back the royal falcon, after overcoming great challenges. Your disquietude is apparent, as you did not have the courtesy to send the offering of oil and maash.[45] It appears that my triumph did not sit well with you.'

King Gul sent a message in reply which said: 'I did not send an offering, as I plan to make myself one by sacrificing myself for you. Our representative shall soon arrive, and explain the relations that exist between us and the jogi. Have no worries.'

The following day, Lal Dev sent Vizier Jawahar to the jogi. He conveyed Lal Dev's felicitations and congratulations on the return of King Agar, and on his securing the royal falcon. He also conveyed King Agar the greetings from Prince Laal and vizier's son Mahmood.

King Agar laughed and said: 'Your king is so miserly and cheap.' Vizier Jawahar answered: 'You may say as you please, but he is devoted to you with his life, and all that he possesses.'

In short, Jawahar departed and arrived before King Gul and said to him: 'The humans have a tradition that when someone returns safely from a journey, or triumphant from a mission, his friends and relatives, close relations and distant acquaintances, and friends and companions send something as his sacrifice.' King Gul said: 'What great battle has the jogi's son won?' Vizier Jawahar answered: 'I beg your pardon for saying so, but you must know in your heart.' King Gul laughed and said: 'You will, of course, say so, since you are indebted to him.'

In short, King Gul sent Vizier Jawahar to Agar with a royal offering as sacrifice.

Then Jawahar went before Agar and made salutations. King Agar said: 'It seems that the dev's child sent an offering with great misgivings. It seems his pecuniary circumstances have been further compromised. It seems that your master cannot bear to part even with a cowrie shell.[46] I would like to offer a sacrifice for him.'

Jawahar looked up and saw King Gul hovering above on his throne, and offering himself as Agar's sacrifice. Jawahar offered hints to King Agar to alert him of his master's presence. Agar and Gul teased each other in this manner, and would clandestinely watch each other.

45. Offering of oil and maash: When someone convalesces or returns from a journey he is shown his reflection in a cup of oil embedded in maash pulses as a ritual.

46. Cowry shell: Cowry shells were used as the smallest unit of currency.

Finally, King Agar adjourned the court and, returning to the jogi's house through the tunnel, sat on his throne and busied himself in the financial and administrative affairs of the state.

It so happened, once, that Vizier Jawahar arrived at the jogi's house before King Agar, when the latter was in company. Agar said: 'O Jawahar, you seem to live in a dire state these days. Your master does not even have a betel-box to furnish you with a paan?' He answered: 'What to say! Never mind paan, my master has not touched food or drink for many days. How can I have a paan?' King Agar said: 'If I were to persuade your master to have food, what offering would you make me?' Vizier Jawahar answered: 'My life and riches are ready to be sacrificed, but he will not touch food. Both Quraish and Lal Dev tried to prevail upon him, but he refused to touch food.

VERSE

Now it is no use, remedying with union
The poison of separation's grief has spread

King Agar said: 'Make a wager on it.' Jawahar said: 'Very well. What do you suggest should be wagered?' The king said: 'If I make him have food, I will strike you seven times with a shoe, and if I lose, I will give you the royal falcon.' He replied: 'I agree!' After making this wager he departed and alerted King Gul.

OF KING AGAR GOING TO KING GUL'S HOUSE OUT OF LOVE, AND FEEDING HIM

When the bread of sun came out piping hot from the West's oven, and the Ultimate Nourisher issued orders for the feast to begin, King Agar set out with great resplendence and brilliance to satiate the one longing for sight of him.

King Gul's heart alerted him that his beloved guest with his countless sweet blandishments was about to arrive in his house of mourning. That lovesick creature involuntarily raised his head to look, and recited this verse:

VERSE

I have received tidings that my beloved shall arrive tonight
My head is a sacrifice in the path on which he will come riding

Vizier Jawahar brought the news of his imminent approach. That infirm and frail creature sat up despite himself, and began cleaning his house. He made the arrangements and recited this verse before Vizier Jawahar:

VERSE

O friend, when auspicious days come
My beloved will come to me without bidding

As he awaited Agar with eagerness, that expert rider of the field of coquetry, the peacock of the garden of dalliance, appeared astride the wind-paced charger, sporting the golden crown and with the royal falcon perched on his hand. King Gul rose from his bed of grief, and his tongue involuntarily uttered:

VERSE

The one whom I awaited, today that beloved is here
My fortune has favored me that he is my guest

Stepping gingerly, with great blandishments and coquetry, King Agar arrived at the house, now making him rejoice with an indulgent look, now devastating him with a frown, and the sun of his visage lit up that dark house. The master of the house went to greet him and conducted him indoors. King Agar held King Gul's hand and seated him alongside. Beside himself with joy, King Gul lowered his head from gratitude. King Agar said: 'This quiet and silence reveals that you are loath to see us.' King Gul offered himself as a sacrifice many times and recited these verses.

VERSES

I find no occasion to disclose to you my heart's grief
And I do not find you by yourself, when I find such an occasion
And when I find both occasion, and you by yourself
I lose all sense of myself in my rapture

Thereafter, finding a new lease on life, that half-alive lover poured a concoction of perfumes in his palms and began rubbing it on Agar's body so that he may discover in it some further proof of his sex. But before coming to see Gul, King Agar had smelled the flower given him by the fox, whose perfume turned a woman to man. Not finding any signs of womanhood in Agar's body, King Gul was stupefied and felt much embarrassed.

King Agar said to him, 'O distrustful person, dispel false suspicion from your heart!' He answered, 'This humble being knows your disguise very well.' Agar said: 'Stop making prattle and send for food and spread the food cloth.'

Gul said: 'I have eaten. Please do help yourself to the food.' He replied, 'I am not used to eating by myself. This will not do.' There was much insistence and refusal on the two sides. King Gul said he had sworn not to eat, but he could not refuse Agar's request. He broke his oath, ate a morsel and then stopped and recited:

VERSE

Serve me a glass of your leftover water
It will taste like wine to my palate

King Agar said: 'Stop these blandishments that you make every so often, and have the food.'

He replied, 'Serve me with your own hand.' Agar said: 'One must not burden an acquaintanceship.' Gul had a few bites to please Agar, then stopped again. Agar also stopped eating. King Gul said: 'I swear by the Ultimate Nourisher, my heart became sated from the delicacy that is your vision.' Agar answered, 'It is not easy to digest this delicacy.'

In short, the two of them enjoyed their sweet talk, and ate their fill. When the food cloth was removed, King Gul said: 'Do visit my private chamber, and honour it by setting foot there.'

King Agar sent for Jawahar and said to him, 'Did you hear?'

He asks me to accompany him to his house
Regard his invitation, an expression of his desire

'Dear fellow, I had agreed to this unpleasant proposition only to win this wager. Otherwise:

VERSE

There's no parity between us, such assemblies are a dream'

Upon hearing this, Jawahar disappeared. Agar mounted his horse and left King Gul inconsolable with grief at their separation.

King Agar sent for Jawahar many times, but he did not present himself, out of embarrassment. Someone asked him, 'Why don't you go before King Agar?' He answered, 'I am embarrassed at losing the wager.

He calls me before him so that he can ridicule me before others.' In short, the wager was remembered in jest by both parties for a long time.

OF KING AGAR CONSTRUCTING A HOUSE WHICH WAS A COPY OF KING GUL'S HOUSE, IN EFFECT CREATING A DUPLICATE[47]

It is said that when King Agar returned to his palace, he said to the jogi, 'I wish to construct a house for you, which will be a copy of King Gul's house. Indeed, I wish to make the copy better than the original.' The jogi said: 'My child, he is a king while I am a mere beggar. But very well, begin in God's name, as you have the authority.'

Thereupon King Agar busied himself in the construction of the house.

VERSES

Such a finely designed building it was
Any who beheld it, their hearts bloomed like a flower
A fine garden was made therein
A garden the like of a thornless rose

Using the same combination of colours, the same kind of mosaic work, a number of marvelous tilisms were created in the house and fine paintings made for it, which enraptured and engrossed the onlooker.

After the garden had been made, Agar took the jogi there. He offered much praise for the garden and called it Bagh-e Benazir. King Agar arranged celebrations in the garden and invited many guests, and spent a few days playing chogan.[48]

Upon hearing of these proceedings, King Gul sent the jogi a missive which read:

One hears that your dear son has constructed a garden without equal. He took this hardship and inconvenience upon himself for no reason, as my garden was available, and I would have readily installed it in your land.

47. A play on words in the Urdu original means Agar moving into Gul's house.
48. Chogan: A horse riding game accompanied by music and storytelling.

Agar answered, 'Praise the Lord! He sent his niggardly sacrifice offering after much hesitancy, and you tell me he will lift his garden in the skies and install it here?'

The jogi smiled and maintained his silence.

Then King Gul's messenger said: 'My master sends many felicitations on the completion of the garden and mentions that since King Agar often plays chogan in his garden, it is his wish to come here bouncing like a ball.'

The jogi said: 'He is a king's son and Agar is a jogi's child. What association does a king have with a jogi? Tell him that he should consider this humble abode as his own house; he may freely visit here, but not with that intention.'

When King Gul was disappointed in this hope, he mounted his throne and clandestinely entered the garden to secretly watch Agar playing chogan. Whenever Agar's stick struck the ball, King Gul felt the blow in his heart.

Agar sat happy and joyous in his garden. When a noble presented himself, he conferred a reward and a robe of honour upon him. For as long as that true lover hovered in the air, Agar also gave audience. When he flew away, Agar also rose. Hameed Dev accompanied him.

Agar sauntered towards the horse. The horse reckoned that Agar was unhappy. To bring cheer to him, the horse said: 'O King, if you wish to distract yourself with sights and spectacles, climb into the saddle.'

Agar mounted the horse, who rose so high into the sky that the Earth seemed like a bubble. The horse said: 'Line your eyes with the foam from my mouth, and the earth will appear to you magnified, and what is far, you will see near.' Agar lined his eyes as told, and the horse gestured that he should look towards such and such house. Agar looked there and saw a female 315 sitting there. Agar said: 'I get the scent of familiarity from her.'

From her face I get an indication
This stranger is familiar to me

The horse said: 'This pari is the sister of King Gul, and she is destined to be married to Vizier's son, Mahmood.'

OF KING AGAR BEHOLDING THE MARVELOUS VISION OF SARV-AASA'S PROCESSION ON THE RIVER, AND ASKING VIZIER BASANT ABOUT IT

One night the luminance of the moon lit up the dark night and made Zulmat,[49] the abode of darkness bright as the abode of light, the Valley of Aiman.[50] The cluster of stars was the blinding flash which dispelled the darkest darkness. The water of the sea shone like a pearl from the reflection of the moon. The floor of the forest was like a sheet of light. The ruddy goose looked like a white bird, and the bat the envy of the sun in brightness.

VERSES

The earth was made of light, the sky too
There was a spectacle of light wherever one looked
There was radiant moonlight and surpassing glow
The moon offered its light as sacrifice
The full moon's presence was fully manifest in its brightness
There was no differentiation between night and day

Agar's heart became excited by the moonlight. He asked Shahryar, Jawahar, and Manuchehr, who were present: 'Why didn't Vizier Basant accompany you today?' Someone said: 'He is a little unwell.' Agar said: 'Let us head to the sea and enjoy the moonlight.' They all replied: 'In the name of God!' and accompanied him like so many stars accompanying the full moon.

When they arrived at the sea, a dark dust-storm rose, billowing with great strength, and the luminous night became pitch dark. They could not make out each other in the darkness; even a hand could not find its pair. The trees shook powerfully from the violence of the wind, and the mountains collided with each other from the upheaval.

Witnessing this dreadful scene, Hameed Dev and the horse said to Agar: 'Your Honour, you must leave. Regard the powerful wind, which has snuffed out the taper of the heavens. Who knows what calamity it portends, and what cataclysm is in the offing. For the sake of God and his messenger (Peace be upon him), get into the saddle.'

49. Zulmat: The land of darkness.
50. Allusion to the valley of Mount Sinai.

Agar said: 'If this storm frightens you, by all means, go! I shall enjoy this dust storm like I enjoyed the moonlight.

VERSE

Do not feel anxiety at what is yet unknown, take heart
The Water of Life is found in the darkest Zulmat

Thus they all stayed there. When King Gul received the news of this gathering, he immediately rode his flying throne there, and arrived above that sea of beauty like a wave. He found the beautiful Agar, radiant as the moon, sitting by himself in the darkness, concealed from the eyes of both friends and strangers. King Gul enjoyed proximity to his beloved. He could not restrain himself, and embraced Agar passionately, quickly kissed her a few times, and rubbed his eyes on the soles of her feet.

King Agar thought it was some ghost. He sought God's refuge from the devil, and recited and blew the verses of of *Surah-e Noor*[51] on himself. In short, when that violence of the wind began to subside, King Gul went away, reciting the verse:

VERSE

The dust storm and tempest made me forget the pain of separation, I am grateful
My heart derived a hundred pleasures from my beloved without imploring

Agar recognized Gul's voice and said in his heart: 'A wretched ghost he was! He took great liberties with me in the darkness.'

Suddenly, what did Agar see but a boat in the water, moving like an arrow shot from a bow, laden with forty caparisoned trees, with a beautiful pari-like damsel sitting decked out on each tree branch. Another boat followed, once that boat had passed. This, too, had as many trees and sweet-mannered damsels, as the earlier one. After it had passed, Agar saw a third boat laden with golden trees, on whose branches beautiful young girls were playing and chortling.

Afterwards, a splendid pleasure-boat manifested itself, staffed with attendants moving a fly-whisk made of huma's feathers. A sow was riding in it, and an old man, whose white beard reached down to his chest, was sitting beside her.

Agar said: 'I seek God's refuge from the devil! Why have this royal protocol for a filthy creature?'

51. Surah-e Noor: Chapter 24 of the Quran.

He wished to throw something at the sow or call out to the old man. Hameed Dev said: 'For what reason?'

VERSE

The sea of the world is a passageway
What one sees here, he sees not again

King Agar returned to his house, but he was consumed with the desire to learn the truth about the sight he had seen, and all night long he kept twisting and turning in bed.

The following day Vizier Basant presented himself before King Agar. King Agar related to him his moonlight excursion, and the strange sight he had witnessed. Upon that, Vizier Basant began crying like a cloud of spring quarter and writhed restlessly like lightning. King Agar said: 'O faithful, why do you cry?' He answered:

This hidden secret is not for telling
How may I reveal my ill fortune?

King Agar insisted, and put him under a pledge to tell him the truth. Then Basant said: 'It is a parizad in the form of a sow whose name is Sarv-Aasa. She has been in love with me for a long time, and longs for me with every breath. That old man is the father of that beauty. He is averse and ill-disposed towards me. He tells her: 'I will never marry you to Basant.' For this reason the pari has turned herself into a sow, so that people loathe the sight of her and nobody thinks of marrying her.'

Upon hearing this, King Agar remained silent, and saw off Basant. From the jogi's house he headed to his court. He dispensed justice to those who had sought redress, and made his mother and father rejoice from pride. In the evening, as was his wont, he arrived in the jogi's company and derived comfort and blessedness from his transformative companionship.

OF KING AGAR GOING INTO SARV-AASA'S COUNTRY AND CONVINCING HER TO MARRY HIM AT THEIR FIRST MEETING

When it was morning, King Agar went to the horse and stroked his legs. The horse asked him: 'O King! Have you news of Basant and what transpired from his fate? The jogi has got some inkling and orders have been issued to gatekeepers that none may come and go without his permission, and anyone who tempts King Agar away will be anathematized and declared accursed.'

King Agar said: 'He is the master, but I will go to Sarv-Aasa's land nolens volens, and wander in search of her. Our friend is wasting away in separation from her!' The horse replied, 'In the name of God! Climb into the saddle, take Hameed Dev along, and I will gallop skywards, and none will be any the wiser.' Agar did as he was told, and the horse flew him to Sarv-Aasa's land.

VERSE

His hooves never touch the ground
For this reason he is named the Sky-Voyager

Upon arriving there, King Agar beheld Sarv-Aasa sitting in sow's form, and her father, with drawn sword, set upon killing her, and saying to her: 'O wretch, come out of this guise or I shall kill you.'

Sarv-Aasa said: 'In God's name, proceed! This is indeed what I wish, as death will give me release from this dreadful life!' Upon hearing this, her father made to strike a blow, but King Agar rushed forward and stayed his hand, saying, 'Good Sir, stop! It is a marvel that a father should kill his daughter without cause.' He replied, 'This blight on my family's honour is deserving of beheading.'

King Agar said: 'This is true, but her heart is pierced by love's arrow and she believes death a better prospect than life, and being killed a happier proposition.

VERSE

Why would he not forthwith submit his neck
For whom the beloved's eyebrow's curvature is the sword

O venerated, honorable elder, love's path is unique and none has power over it. Regard the nightingale and see the moth." And in like manner, Agar mentioned countless other tales of love besides.

VERSE

While love remains imperfect, regard for propriety and decorum
burdens one
But those perfect in love are not constrained by fear of infamy

'It will end badly. On account of this unwarranted killing, you will be held to be a sinner and earn disrepute; in fact you will be discredited before all, high and low.' Upon hearing this the old man desisted from killing her, and asked: 'Who are you? From where have you come?' King Agar answered: 'I have come from the land of Khashkhaash. I am the son of the master of the land, King Mansoor. My name is Agar and I happened upon this place during my perambulations.' He asked: 'Would you like to be betrothed to one who is the envy of the roses?' The prince replied: 'There is no harm in that! I am willing!' The old man was mightily pleased that King Agar had agreed to the match. He sent word to Sarv-Aasa, saying: 'O wretch, a king from the human race, who is handsome, graceful, elegant and bewitching is agreeable to enter into marriage with you.'

VERSES

There is none better among humans
This human is a pari among mankind
We have seen many a man
But never a man of his like
Whether a pari, an angel, or a houri
Whatever he is, he is agreeable to the heart

After reflecting much, Sarv-Aasa answered that, except for Basant, nobody held any charm for her.

VERSE

I have no desire for him, even should he be an angel
I seek him not even if he is beautiful like a houri

'I shall not take off this guise. God willing, I shall surrender my life in it.'

Agar praised and lauded her fidelity, and said to the father: 'O venerated Sir, do not feel anguished by her reply. Allow me leave to persuade this pari myself, and bring her round.' He replied: 'I would like nothing better.'

Agar went into her private chamber and took her aside and said: 'O Sarv-Aasa, I am a man only in appearance, but am in reality a woman like you. Basant regards me as a close friend, and seeing him disconsolate for you, I came here to take you to him. Get rid of this guise, change and come along with me. I forbid you in the name of Suleiman from revealing the truth about me.' Sarv-Aasa was delighted to hear this auspicious news, and said to her parents: 'I seek your forgiveness for making you unhappy all these years. Kindly forgive me. You may betroth me to anyone of your choice; you have full authority.' Her parents were beside themselves with joy at her agreeable reply.

That very day they pledged her troth to Agar. The curtains were drawn and the two were sent into a private chamber.

VERSES

Such company we have seldom seen
Where a nightingale is gathered together with a nightingale
Where an oyster faces another oyster
And pleasure obtained from their stroking together
The pari was the turtle-dove and Agar the ring-dove
In the same manner they both together cooed

Sarv-Aasa was no less beautiful than Agar and in privacy together they appeared as if they were sisters born in succession. Agar narrated his story to Sarv-Aasa from beginning to end. She too narrated her love for Basant, her agony in the fever of separation, and the affliction of her jaundiced existence to the one who had brought solace to her soul.

Then Sarv-Aasa said to Agar: 'In my garden is a pond which has the property that if a man were to bathe in it he would become a woman, and if a woman were to bathe in it she would become a man. If you so desire, you may have a bath in it.'

King Agar answered: 'God has bestowed me with manly courage. By His grace I have accomplished many a task, and succeeded in numerous missions. This is how I captured the falcon; I helped King Gul's viziers marry their beloveds. It was all with the help and grace of God.'

As Agar spoke these words, a voice said: 'Praise the Lord! I see the rival happy, and the lover dejected. A vizier succeeds where a king fails!' Agar did not let Sarv-Aasa pay attention to the voice, and felt abashed that King Gul had heard all she had said.

To cut a long story short, Sarv-Aasa's father saw her off with much fanfare. King Agar said to Hameed Dev: 'You must proceed forth and bring Basant the happy news.' When that lover heard news of Sarv-Aasa's arrival, he flew to greet them like a dove cooing in love, and met them along the way. He offered himself as King Agar's sacrifice and recited this verse:

You have made me your slave forever
None could have accomplished the mission you did

Agar answered: 'My dear, I could not bear to behold your suffering. God Almighty gave me the power to help you. Now Sarv-Aasa is before you. May God make your union an auspicious one.'

Basant took Sarv-Aasa along and went his way, and Agar presented himself before the jogi. He said: 'O Agar, your actions cause me much anguish, and I suffer pangs of separation and dissociation on your account.' Agar said: 'I will be mindful of your wishes.' The jogi commanded his vizier, whose name was Buqalamun, and who was a veritable Plato in wisdom and sagacity, to write a narrative of Agar's adventures and display it on the gates of the fortress so that the news may be blazoned abroad. Buqalamun did as he was ordered.

OF KING GUL ARRIVING IN THE CITY OF KHASHKHAASH DISGUISED AS A MERCHANT AND PUTTING A NECKLACE AROUND KING AGAR'S NECK

While King Agar was busy with the affairs of the state, King Gul arrived at his lofty palace in the guise of an old, noble merchant with a flowing white beard, sporting a gown, turban and a heavy cummerbund. After he was announced, he was allowed leave to present himself. That merchant, who had come to sell his tear's diamond and his liver's agate, first evaluated closely his beloved's lips and mouth and the diamonds of his teeth, then produced a precious necklace from his chest whose diamonds shone with a rare refulgence, and proffered it. King Agar asked: 'Tell us its price.' The merchant replied: 'Your Honour may first adorn himself with it. If he finds it suitable and becoming, the price will be mentioned.' King Agar put it on after reciting "In the Name of God!" and found it to his liking. The merchant said: 'If Your Honour should so order, this slave will delicately transfer a pearl of speech to the oyster of your august ears.' With a movement of his brow King Agar beckoned him to approach. The merchant approached, saying prayers for the king, and said into his auspicious ears: 'When Your Highness revealed your secret to Sarv-Aasa, this humble slave heard all from behind the curtain. Although I had my suspicions even earlier, that your unpierced pearl was in need of a diamond needle, from that day I was confirmed in my belief. I hereby present this engagement necklace. Felicitations!'

The moment Agar heard this, his cheeks that were the colour of diamonds reddened from the flavour of speech. The merchant disappeared and Agar rose in anger. Seeing the necklace around Agar's neck, the jogi said: 'One must not wear whatever someone brings.'

Agar removed the necklace from around his neck.

VERSE

It is useless for me to send a necklace to that rose
She will wear another ornament, but not this one

OF VIZIER'S SON MAHMOOD FALLING IN LOVE WITH KING GUL'S SISTER, GULNAR PARI, AND PRINCE LAAL CONVINCING LAL DEV TO ALLOW THEIR NUPTIALS

Now hear the account of Vizier's son, Mahmood. One day Prince Laal took Mahmood along to the rooftop. While they were watching the sights, they espied a woman approaching like a strong wind, carrying a small salver on her head. She came to a halt at one spot, cautiously looked around, and lifting a plank set in the ground, disappeared inside. After some hours, she came out with an empty salver.

VERSES

From the coming and going it was revealed
That some secret was hidden there
That furtive arrival and departure was for a reason
Some mystery it surely did portend
Why did she look around upon arriving there
And why did she depart from there so soon

Prince Laal said:

VERSE

Let us go and investigate the matter
And discover what's hidden in the secret chamber

Mahmood said: 'Let it pass.' But the prince did not heed him. He went to the place where the woman had stopped, lifted the plank, and beheld that it covered a beautiful ornate door. He gained entry there with the key of his desire and found himself in a small elegant and pleasant house whose courtyard was smooth and level. In the courtyard, a beautiful pari, some twelve or thirteen years of age, whose image regaled the eyes and who was like the sun in beauty, was sitting leaning on the seat of coquetry of a gold enchased throne, reciting the Quran with the immaculate book of her visage open alongside. The moment he beheld her, the heart of vizier's son Mahmood was rent into a hundred pieces from love, and, reciting this verse by Nasikh, he fell down on his face:

VERSE

Your eyelashes are downcast, prostrating under eyebrows' niche
Your tablet of your visage inscribed with the ayat-e Sajda[52]

Out of regard for her repute, the parizad brought her face near Mahmood's and, reciting *Surah Al-Ikhlas*[53] on water, made him drink it. When he opened his eyes he found his head resting in Prince Laal's lap and the pari reciting prayers over him. He became delirious from ecstasies of joy. The pari said to the prince: 'In God's name, please take him away from my house, otherwise I will earn notoriety among high and low; indeed, I will earn universal opprobrium.'

VERSES

I am averse to the word love
For modesty is glass, and love a stone
I am neither capricious, nor play at love
Of all these intricacies I am unaware
Cleanse me from this contamination
Or else I shall put an end to my existence

Prince Laal called out Mahmood's name several times and finally he regained consciousness, and recited these verses:

52. Aayat-e sajda (Verse of prostration): One of several verses in the Quran upon whose recital the reader must offer prostration.

53. Surah Al-Ikhlas: Chapter 112 of the Quran.

VERSES

Do not raise me from this dust
My heart tells me I should not leave
My eyes are shut in thoughts of her
It is a happy dream, do not wake me
She sends me wafts of air from her visage
I must not turn away my face

Prince Laal could do aught else but carry Mahmood on his shoulders and bring him to his palace. When Lal Dev heard that the prince's minister was ill and on account of it Prince Laal was in despair, he visited him to comfort him, and found him in a wretched state. By conjecture and discernment, he realised that it was a pari's face and the vision of her locks that had set Mahmood's heart aflame and distraught. But he did not fathom that Mahmood was afflicted by the desire for his own daughter, Gulnar Pari. He recited thousands of spells and millions of enchantments but it did not improve Mahmood's frenzied state.

VERSE

When do I not seek a remedy for my pain?
But there is no prescription that cures it

When the one who was shy of his own shadow could not be persuaded by counsel, the prince said to Lal Dev: 'My dear friend is my life and soul. If, God forbid, anything happens to him, I will also put out my life.' Lal Dev said: 'My ploys had no success with him. Tell me what to do and I will carry it out.' The prince said: 'Pray admit him in your service as son-in-law. He has been consumed by love for Gulnar, and imprisoned in her locks.'

Upon hearing this, the dev fell into ecstasies of grief and suffered coils of anger but he dared not utter a word of refusal. Prince Laal reckoned that he had given his consent. He took his plea before Quraish, and used every method of pleading, cajoling, flattery and wheedling. Quraish was incensed and outraged, and expressed her anger and fury. She reprimanded and rebuked him and said: 'God be praised! Such a thing has neither ever come to pass, nor will it ever. I will do everything in my power to stop it. I will never give my daughter into a vizier's family, who is like a servant to the king. I would offer a thousand Mahmoods as the sacrifice of her shoe. You will provoke my ire if I ever hear this idea being discussed in this house.'

Upon hearing this firm reply Prince Laal broke into tears. King Gul said: 'Dear mother, I cannot bear the prince's sorrow; his grief weighs on my heart. He and Mahmood are like one soul in two bodies. Mahmood is the seeker and he the sought. Just like he loves Mahmood, I love him. If his grief consumes him, I too shall not survive. Besides, astrological calculations show that Mahmood and Gulnar are destined for union.'

After some reflection, Quraish said to Prince Laal: 'Very well! For your sake I am willing to agree to what is most disagreeable to me, out of regard for King Gul's delicate disposition.'

Prince Laal came out of the palace, holding King Gul's hand.

King Gul said to him: 'Your every wish is dear to me, but alas, you are not the least concerned about what passes with me, and care not a whit about my grief and sorrow. It is true that a stranger is after all a stranger, and a beloved is the beloved: there is no comparison between the two. You could not bear Mahmood's anguish even for a moment but never bothered to ask me how I fare.' Prince Laal said: 'Decorum did not allow me to inquire it of you, even though I knew that:

VERSES

You are become intoxicated in love
Someone's languorous eye has made you sick
You are entrapped by someone's black locks
You are the martyr of someone's glance

'Narrate your sorrow before me. I shall give my life for you, if needed.' King Gul broke into tears and said: 'Mahmood's sister has me tied up in her locks. I burn in Agar's love like aloeswood, and like the taper, remain aflame.' Prince Laal laughed and said: 'Once something is compensated, the complaint disappears. Take heart, God willing you will come into possession of her.' In short, Prince Laal brought everyone round, and gave Mahmood the happy tidings of his imminent union with Gulnar.

VERSE

That frenzied person came to his senses
When given the tidings of union

In short, the wedding preparations began.

VERSE

In giving an account of the paraphernalia of wedding
The pen in my hand frenzied becomes

At an auspicious hour, vizier's son Mahmood was made into a bridegroom and Gulnar into a bride, and they were married. That fellow of an auspicious future sated the fire of desire at the spring of their union. When the wedding ceremony was over, King Gul's viziers Jawahar and Manuchehr ennobled themselves with an audience with Agar, who asked them: 'Where were you all these days?' They answered, 'There was a wedding at the court. Vizier's son Mahmood has been betrothed to Gulnar, who is the daughter of Lal Dev, and sister of King Gul. We arrived here after attending the ceremony.' King Agar heard their account of the wedding ceremony with eager ears, and awarded the viziers with gifts and presents according to their station.

OF PRINCE LAAL AND VIZIER MAHMOOD MEETING KING MANSOOR AND VIZIER KHUSH-HAAL, AND OF KING GUL BECOMING AFFIANCED TO KING AGAR THROUGH THEIR STRATAGEM

The painter of love's picture galley has thus painted this tale of union on the page narrating the account of Prince Laal's meeting with King Mansoor, and Mahmood meeting with Khush-haal: When the acuteness of King Gul's desire and his pain of separation from Agar had made him wretched.

VERSE

A spark became a menacing flame
Conflagrated and was reduced to a dying morning lamp

Prince Laal said to Lal Dev: 'I can think of no better course than for you to take me and Mahmood along, and visit my revered father. He will find a new lease on life from beholding us, and willingly and happily carry out your wishes. And I myself promise that I will never remove the collar of your slavery as long as I am alive, and not inflict the pain of separation upon Your Honour.'

Willy nilly, Lal Dev was forced to make preparations to visit Prince Laal's land. He prepared a large procession, placed Mah-Parwar in a luxurious open litter, and placed Gulnar in a palanquin. Mahmood held Prince Laal's hand and they set out with great pomp and fanfare towards the land of Khashkhaash and speedily arrived there, filling up the whole city with crowds of jinns and paris.

King Mansoor was greatly perturbed at the sight and sent for Vizier Khush-haal. When the vizier presented himself, the king said: 'O Khush-haal, it is a marvel that the enemy entered our kingdom without the least fear or dread, and you never alerted us to their approach. What is the reason for this grave lapse of duty?' The vizier answered: 'Your Honor speaks the truth. But it seems that this host has not arrived here by way of our dominions. It is because the royal armies guard all the paths and highways and maintain order and arrangement. They would have clashed and fought, and hundreds would have died. It seems that this host is from the race of jinn, and none could foretell such a calamity, or have any advance intelligence.' The king and his vizier were having this conversation when a throne descended from the heavens, and both Prince Laal and the vizier's son Mahmood could be seen sitting on it. They dismounted and prostrated themselves at King Mansoor's feet. The king marvelled at the sight of them and said: 'Am I sentient or unconscious? Is this a dream or am I awake?'

VERSES

I did not expect from my fate and my destiny
For these marvelous events to materialise
Who could have guessed from my slumbering fortunes
That my blinded eyes would light up again
So auspicious did my fortunes become
That my dear held me in his embrace
He embraced his son and copiously cried
And said to his fortunes: Awake! You have long slumbered
Once his eyes beheld his son
His sightless eyes, found their sight
Ah, my dear son! Ah, my child!
He continuously made loving protestations

He embraced his son, and gave expression to the suffering his heart had undergone from their separation. Both were in paroxysms of grief, one restive, the other unquiet. Prince Laal's mother lost control of her senses when she heard of her son's arrival, and fell down as she rushed forward to greet him. She took Prince Laal in her embrace, and pacified her heart from their union. Her ceaseless and copious tears washed away the dust of the journey from the Prince's feet, and doused the fire in her heart. Everyone was overjoyed, and there were celebrations in both households. All the pledges they had made for their safe return were fulfilled, and the promised offerings made.

Vizier Khush-haal embraced Mahmood with great longing, and cried an ocean of tears. Everyone found a new lease on life at the return of their two sons, as their keenest wishes were granted. The cries of congratulations and felicitations arose from both households. Prince Laal's parents adored Mah-Parwar, and Mahmood's parents doted upon Gulnar. Nocturnal celebrations were made in the palaces, offerings were made in the name of Pir Didar,[54] Fatima,[55] Bibi Aasa,[56] Turat Phurat,[57] and Janab Mushkil Kusha.[58] Celebrations were planned everywhere.

At night, Prince Laal narrated to King Mansoor the story of the fateful hunt, and how Lal Dev treated him, and gave the account of Mah-Parwar and Gulnar. Then he sent for Lal Dev and introduced him to his parents. Praising before his father the kindnesses and love Lal Dev had shown him, he told him that on account of the fatherly care shown him by Lal Dev, he faced no hardship. King Masoor replied: 'You received relief because of him, he received solace from your presence, and I lost my sight from crying ceaselessly. Whatever was foreordained came to pass. I offer a thousand thanks that today God revived me.'

54. Offering for Pir Didar: A sweetmeat offering given in a clay bowl pledged in the name of the fictitious saint named Pir Didar, who is supposed to bring together those who are separated.

55. Fatima's salver: A sweetmeat offering made in a small salver in the name of Prophet Muhammad's daughter Fatima, which is partaken of by women who are pious, virtuous, and of holy ancestry.

56. Lady Aasa's bowl: An offering made in the name of a pious woman who is variously believed to be Prophet Muhammad's wife Ayesha, or his daughter Fatima Zahra.

57. Turat Phurat's Packets: A ritual in which women pledge an offering of sugar for the quick resolution of an issue and tie it up in a small packet. When the issue is resolved they make an offering of that sugar to women who are pious, virtuous, and of holy ancestry.

58. Mushkil Kusha's leaf bowl: A sweetmeat offering in a bowl made of leaf, which is pledged in the name of Prophet Muhammad's son-in-law Ali who is titled Mushkil Kusha (one who resolves difficulties).

In short, Lal Dev retired to his resting place and Prince Laal told King Mansoor about King Gul falling in love with Agar. In the course of the conversation, Prince Laal also mentioned that if the king wished him to stay, he should betroth the vizier's daughter Agar to King Gul, otherwise it would be impossible for him to stay and remain in his service; that if his father wished him to remain in attendance upon him, he must do as he asked. That there was no likelihood of his continuing to stay there without that condition being met. The king answered: 'She is renowned for her intrepidity. It is not agreeable to me to act against her wishes.' Prince Laal said: 'It seems that Your Highness is not agreeable to the matrimonial alliance.'

From there he went to Vizier Khush-haal's house. He narrated what had passed with Mahmood and gave a detailed account of King Gul, and then broached the subject he had come to discuss.

Vizier Khush-haal said: 'O Prince, my son Mahmood found solace because of Gul, and it would be fair, in recompense for my son, that King Gul also meets with success in his love. But there are many a hindrance and problem with this alliance: Firstly, she is not in our power. While you were away, she conquered many lands and is now loath to submit to anyone. Secondly, the jogi holds her dear and dotes upon her, and his consent is essential for this alliance to come to fruition. Thirdly, the jogi is highly accomplished in his arts, and has power over the race of paris and devs, and is not such a one over whom Lal Dev could exercise the least power. Fourthly, according to the religious law, Agar is discerning, mature, accomplished and her own master. Since it is your wish, when matrimonial alliances are discussed, if she seems agreeable, I will betroth her to King Gul.' The prince said: 'That would be most appropriate.'

The vizier sent for Lal Dev and King Gul, offered them a preparation of paan and tied on each one's arm a silver coin pledged to Imam Zamin.[59] Then he submitted: 'It is our desire that we hold Mahmood's wedding ceremony here again. Pray take Gulnar with you. On such and such a date we will arrive in a wedding procession with Mahmood as bridegroom.' Then Lal Dev departed with Gulnar.

59. Imam Zamin: The title of Imam Ali Raza, the eighth Imam of the Shia. A coin or precious object tied to the arm of a traveller or someone who is sick, in the Imam's name, to be given in offering to the poor upon recovery of health or safe return from the journey.

OF GULNAR AND MAHMOOD'S WEDDING BEING HELD AGAIN, AND OF KING MANSOOR, THE JOGI, AND KING AGAR PARTICIPATING IN THE WEDDING PROCESSION

When Lal Dev and King Gul arrived in their land, they started preparations for the wedding as the occasion merited. They sent out many an invitation, and guests began arriving with great pomp and ceremony. Lal Dev wrote a letter to the jogi that read:

O kind brother to this humble creature! Your nephew is due to be married and it is my desire that you, along with your son of lofty honour, and wives of chaste ways, should honour us by joining the wedding ceremony.

At first the jogi refused. King Agar said: 'Not participating in the procession would be inappropriate. Mahmood is my real brother. What would the world say?' The jogi said: 'In the name of God, do send out a reply you deem appropriate.' Agar wrote in reply:

It will be our utmost pleasure to come on the appointed date, God willing.

King Agar arranged for Mahmood's wedding to be held in the jogi's land, on account of its proximity. He ordered Vizier Buqalamun to spread a variegated carpet from there to the bride's house, and dot it with tents and pavilions which should be secure and guarded, and where all the paraphernalia of luxury and merriment should be provided and kept ready.

VERSE

In one place there must be baadla,[60] *mushajjar*[61] *in another place*
And the earth bedecked to compete with the beautiful heavens

He instructed him as follows: The scaffoldings for the lights should be planted in the ground, and the ground cleared of shrubbery and bushes. That the dark night should light up like a bright day, the deserts turn into blooming gardens, wilderness into the valley of Aiman.[62] The countless musicians, dancers and singers that accompanied the court,

60. Baadla: A kind of cloth.
61. Mushajjar: A kind of cloth.
62. Aiman: Valley of Mount Sinai.

the armed warriors, and the poor, the destitute, the impecunious, and the indigent should all receive largesse from the bounty of the king. Be warned and beware, to do everything in your power to make it happen. If the asking price of something is the coin of lowest denomination, purchase it for four times that price. Do not make anyone downhearted.

Then Prince Laal sent for his adopted sisters, and Shahryar, Jawahar and Basant sent off their wives with a large procession, with great splendour and pageantry. Guests from the land of Khashkhaash also gathered there. All apparatus of revelry was made ready. All the rituals were carried out with great majesty.

Finally, the day of the wedding procession arrived. At an auspicious hour, Mahmood was dressed as a bridegroom. King Mansoor put him in his lap. Khush-haal was there with all the viziers. King Agar sat on an elephant with the jogi, whose four wives were with him. Scattering jewels, the jogi accompanied the wedding procession. Upon hearing the news of their imminent arrival, Lal Dev, along with King Gul, came out with the parizads to receive them in accordance with the city's traditions, with great fanfare.

VERSE

Such throngs of the jinn and men were gathered
The desert's expanse could not hold all of them

King Gul was beside himself with joy upon meeting King Agar. Lal Dev was jubilant on the participation of King Mansoor and the jogi. In short, the wedding procession set out. The pitch dark night became bright as day from the illuminations set up along the way. Before the blast of fireworks, the clamor of Judgment Day would sound like a mere sputter. There were countless litters of dancers and musicians and thousands of singers and qawwals. In short, there's no end to describing the procession's grandeur.

The wedding procession finally arrived at the bride's doorstep, and everyone found relief at the end of the journey. The bridegroom dismounted the elephant and sat on the royal throne. Fistfuls of gold, strings of jewels and pearls were offered as sacrifices for the bridegroom. Young and old, kings and viziers, joined in the procession. Mahmood was seated on the seat of son-in-law, given sherbet to drink, and presented with garlands. The two fathers-in-law met, shook hands and embraced each other.

King Gul said to the jogi: 'Dear uncle, I am also a candidate.' The jogi replied: 'Come, child!' Agar realized that the crafty Gul had used that ploy to embrace him, and made himself scarce.

Gul hurriedly finished greeting the jogi and rushed after Agar. King Agar inclined her head while embracing and moved away. King Gul said: 'At least for once meet me without hostility.' Agar laughed. With great intrepidity, King Gul caught hold of Agar's hand and embraced her with desire, pressing the mirror of his heart to Agar's. Then he leaned forward and whispered: 'May you also see this day. Do drink up Gulnar's leftover water.'[63] Agar said: 'O Dev, give up these idle thoughts. It was Mahmood who accepted your sister. I would be loath to even spit on Quraish.' They thus conversed together in allusions and hints. Then Agar went and sat beside the bridegroom and a musical assembly started.

King Gul noticed that Agar looked sleepy. He said to the jogi: 'Agar is not comfortable. It would be better if he took some rest.' After some reflection, the jogi said: 'Very well!' He sent Agar to sleep in King Gul's bedchamber. King Gul beheld Agar's face. He would now rub his eyes on Agar's soles and now circle around his bed, offering his life as Agar's sacrifice, and reciting these verses:

VERSES

O my moon-like beloved, I was in transports of passion and I swear by your head
I saw you tonight in such a state of dalliance that you would not have believed
You were in stately repose when, unbeknown to my rival, I
Kissed your sole; of which the henna would have told you the story

Then something occurred to Gul, and he took King Agar's sword from his bedside. When Agar woke up he realised it could only be Gul's doing. He sent word to him to return the sword. King Gul came rushing, laughed and said: 'God be praised! You slept so soundly that you became forgetful even of your possessions. You became so incensed at my taking away your sword, and became so enraged. If I had taken possession of something else, you likely would have committed

63. Drinking a bride's leftover water is supposed to help an unmarried woman get married.

jauhar,[64] God forbid. And you claim to be a great warrior!' Agar said: 'I have no patience for all this teasing.'

In short, Agar returned to the wedding assembly. Mahmood's nuptials were read and the noise of congratulations and felicitations rose, and preparations were made for the bride's departure.

VERSE

The heavens manifested a new marvel
For it is peerless in creating marvels

The wedding procession had not yet started on the return journey, when spies arrived and announced to Agar that the enemy had attacked the land of his maternal uncle Aflatun, and was about to pillage and destroy it.

OF KING AGAR TRAVELLING TO HIS MATERNAL UNCLE'S LAND TO HIS AID, AND RETURNING VICTORIOUS IN BATTLE BY GOD'S GRACE

While the wedding party was making preparations for departure, King Agar mounted a horse without the jogi knowing, and in the flash of an eye arrived at his destination and met his maternal uncle Aflatun. He consoled and comforted him, saying that the war would be won in just one battle, God willing.

While he was speaking to his uncle, he saw a youth who was beautiful as the luminous moon. Upon inquiry he was told that the youth was his maternal uncle's son, and Agar embraced him. Thereafter, with great manliness and in a leonine manner, he fell upon the enemy. The sword of the foe was defeated by Agar's lightning-quick blade. By the stick of his majesty, he secured the ball of victory,[65] and put the enemy to flight. In the end, the hapless foe sought quarter, and received it from the crown-bestowing king. The enemy offered an apology for their contumely, and Agar saw to the foe's retreat.

64. Jauhar: In ancient India, the Rajput practice of mass self-immolation by women, or execution by their male family members, to avoid their capture by an invading army.

65. An allusion to the game of chogan.

While victory notes were being played, the wedding party Agar had left had turned into an assembly of lamentations upon his disappearance.

VERSES

That assembly of revelry became one of lamentations
Everyone present sat baffled and shocked
So distressed was Gul from grief
The insignias and flags seemed to him like the gallows
Whither wedding and what nuptials
Like a dark night, the bright day became
How may I narrate Gul's state
A mountain of calamities had fallen upon him

All of them were sitting dolorous, and had rent their collars in grief, when the august King Agar, the fortune and asset of lovers, returned. At the sight of him the lifeless bodies revived with the stirring of souls, like the fluttering of moths round the taper of the beloved's visage. The news of his return spread. Everyone asked about his welfare in their own manner. After briefly narrating the account of his journey and the battle, Agar handed a letter to Vizier Khush-haal. Khush-haal's brother-in-law had written:

Dear brother, may God preserve you! Praise be to God, that from King Agar's prestige, we were victorious over a doughty foe, and the kingdom, which was well nigh lost, was restored to us. May God preserve Agar of lofty stature. It would be idle to find suitable words to praise his great courage and manliness. End.

When the king heard the vizier read out the letter, he embraced Agar. But the jogi became irate and said to Agar: 'A thousand times I forbade you from undertaking these adventures without first informing me, but you do not pay my words the least heed.'

When Lal Dev heard the contents of the letter, he said to himself: 'Dear Almighty God! How would a girl, who takes such pride in her courage, ever agree to marry Gul!'

That night the wedding procession's departure was adjourned. After making a round of the city, the procession returned to the palace, conveyed the bride to her quarters, and an assembly of revelry was held as before.

As Agar rose from the assembly, Gul said to him: 'O Prince, there is a tilism in our garden, the likes of which you would never have seen. If you have qualms about my accompanying you there, you should visit it alone, and behold the sights.'

Agar did not make a reply then, but later, seeing Gul occupied elsewhere, headed for the garden. That devoted lover also surreptitiously followed him there and placed his head at Agar's feet and started crying. King Agar's heart melted, seeing his pitiful state. Agar unlocked the tilism of silence with his tongue and addressed words of cheer to Gul. He lifted Gul's head from his feet and spoke words of love and affection. Upon that, Gul's motionless body showed signs of life, and his avis of desire again fluttered with ambition. He said: 'Give me a kiss as a token of charity.' Agar said: 'You are such a recreant coward! I am loath to kiss your face.'

In the end, Gul rushed and embraced Agar. His embrace was a great oppression for Agar's delicate nature, and he broke out in perspiration and felt mortified from embarrassment. However, Agar extricated himself from that situation with his chastity intact, and returned to the wedding assembly. The jogi said: 'You look very disturbed.' Agar answered: It's the heat from all the lights which is making me sweat.' Meanwhile, Hameed Dev arrived, and said: 'Your maternal uncle is approaching with his family, but he is still some distance away.' Agar quickly rose and headed there. He met Aflatun and Zulaikha and conducted them into the assembly. Every now and then, Aflatun turned his glance towards Agar. Noticing this, Agar asked: 'What is the reason that you look towards me every so often?' He answered: 'Because I notice that your height has increased since the time I last saw you. What is the reason for that?' Agar laughed and removed his disguise. Witnessing his beauty, which was the envy of Yusuf, Zulaikha said: 'A thousand times, alas! The hawk is at hand but there's no bait!' Agar made a mental note of what she had said. He released the hawk of intelligence to investigate the allusion to the bait but it could not hunt down the prey it sought. The celebrations and festivities continued unabated for two days, and on the third day, the festivities of chauthi[66] began.

66. Chauthi: A ceremony observed on the day following a marriage in which the bride and bridegroom visit the bride's family, and the married pair, after feasting, make a show of beating each other with sticks covered with flowers and throwing fruits and vegetables at each other.

OF THE FESTIVITIES OF CHAUTHI AT THE BRIDE'S HOUSE, AND OF KING GUL SEPARATING FROM KING AGAR

Fruits and vegetables began arriving in jewel enchased salvers. There were throngs of paris and crowds of guests. The bridegroom was called into the palace to play chauthi, and was seated beside the bride. The gardener of the heavens brought the citron of moon, and sticks of moonbeams in a golden salver. Parizad damsels from all corners arrived to play chauthi. Flowers were hurled from all corners and the players struck each other with flower-covered sticks. Mahmood played with Prince Laal, Agar with Gul, and Quraish played with Mahmood's mother. If Gul threw even a rose at Agar, he tried to dodge it, and did not let the citron of his breasts be revealed. Gul tried hard to get an opportunity to touch Agar's breasts but was foiled. Thereupon, he recited these verses:

VERSE

Understand, and let me touch the citron of your breast
You will win in Faramosh,[67] *this is a new twin fruit*

Upon hearing this, Agar found a chance and hurled a citron at Gul's breast with such force that his face turned pale from the impact. He had not yet recovered from the shock, when Agar struck him with a stick and said: 'Take this! This welt[68] too shall stay with you for a long time!'

Upon beholding this scene, Lal Dev said to the bridegroom's father: 'Keep Agar from acting thus, lest his delicate nature is offended by someone getting grievously injured.'

At last, everyone finished playing chauthi, and preparations for departure began. At Gul's bidding, Lal Dev requested that the bridegroom's entourage stay a few days longer. But Agar refused to delay their departure, and ordered the vizier to send off the women in the wedding party.

King Gul's face showed great despair at the prospect of Agar's departure, and he pleaded and importuned thus: 'O Prince! Pray stay a

67. Faramosh: A game played by girls using twin fruits.

68. Welt: There is a play on the word *badhee* here, which means both a necklace and a welt.

few days longer to augment the honour of this humble abode with your auspicious presence. Your visiting here was fortuitous.'

VERSE

It was not in my stars that I host you
Such accidents of fate are God-ordained

King Agar said: 'To please you I stayed this long, otherwise such entertainments do not engross me.' King Gul was greatly flattered to hear this, and cheerily replied: 'In these few days you lost your disaffection towards me. I shall never forget these days spent together and your many kindnesses. I will sorely miss them.'

VERSE

I offer my life as a sacrifice for such accidents
I will die from delight remembering your kindnesses

'I am hopeful that you will revive me with a promise, so that I may longingly await your return.'

Agar answered: 'Earlier, reserve stopped me from visiting. Now there will be occasion to meet often.'

In short, leaving Gul on tenterhooks, Agar went to take leave of Lal Dev and Quraish. They embraced him and sought his forgiveness for anything that may have offended him, gave him into God's care and saw him off.

Agar said to Hameed Dev: 'Perhaps King Gul has gone to say farewell to the jogi.'

He answered:

VERSE

'The moth is where the taper is
The madman is with the pari'[69]

At Hameed Dev's words, Agar looked around and saw Gul there. Agar laughed and said: 'Farewell!' King Gul replied: 'I wish that you embrace me before parting.' Agar kept silent. King Gul put his arms around Agar's neck and said:

69. Pari: The influence or love of the paris was believed to bring on mental illness in humans.

VERSE

'My tormenter is inclined towards love and fidelity
Today my fortunes are favorable in every way'

Agar said: 'Do not make all these blandishments. I detest fawning and such shows of affection. Now depart! Farewell and be gone!' Gul said: 'I wish to communicate something; pray wait a short while.' Agar answered: 'You see that the jogi summons me by sending messenger after messenger. I cannot stay to hear it at this moment. I shall do so another day.' Thus speaking, King Agar departed, and left King Gul crying.

The hunter turned away from the slaughtered prey, leaving it in the throes of death, and returned safely to his land.

. . .

One day Agar's maternal aunt Zulaikha gave him a pair of pigeons, who conversed like humans. Agar, who was the envy of Yusuf, was greatly delighted by Zulaikha's gift. Seeing that he was happy and pleased, Zulikha once again said: 'It's a marvel that the hawk is at hand but there's no bait!' Agar said to himself: 'I do not yet understand what she means by that comment.'

VERSE

I must get to the bottom of her comment
That the hawk is at hand but there's no bait

He retired to his bedchamber but, try as he might, he could not unlock the mystery. Exasperated, he said to Hameed Dev: 'Bring me my horse.' Then he rode to Vizier Basant's house. When Hameed announced him to Basant, he asked: 'Is everything well, that His Highness King Agar has come? He must enter forthwith.'

Upon hearing of Agar's arrival, Sarv-Aasa came to greet him and Basant set up a seat for him. Speaking to Sarv-Aasa about the hospitality he had received, Agar said: 'Verily, Quraish and Mah-Parwar did not leave anything to chance in matters of hospitality.' Then he narrated his encounters with Gul, whole and entire, and said: 'He tricked me into visiting the tilism and wearied me with his embraces in private. That cursed man had no regard for anything else; the handle of the dagger he wore in his belt left two bruises on my breasts.'

Sarv-Aasa, out of respect and decorum, spoke in signs and allusions, and the two of them exchanged repartee. After some time Agar took his leave and arrived at the jogi's house, and rested there. Before the crack of dawn he went into his bedchamber, said the morning prayers, changed, and gave audience on the throne.

OF KING AGAR TRAVELLING TO KING GUL'S LAND AND ENJOYING ITS SIGHTS

When the world-measuring sun, girdled with the cummerbund of rays, retired into the guest chamber of the West, King Agar set out like the moon, all alone, for King Gul's house. He announced himself and Gul rushed out to receive him with great eagerness.

Agar said: 'I had promised you that I would come to visit you by myself, and I have fulfilled the promise.' King Gul said: 'You kept your word and revived me. Come, and give bliss to my eyes by pressing your soles against them.' Agar said: 'Your parents will recognise me.' He answered: 'They will not even get a whiff of your presence, and even their hamzads[70] will not see you.' Agar asked: 'And why do you wish to take me indoors?' Gul answered: 'So that you may rest awhile, enjoy the place, and revive my lifeless soul.' Thus speaking, he put a ring on Agar's finger, which had the property that it made Agar invisible to others, while he himself could see everything. In short, he brought Agar into his quarters and presented all manner of marvels to him.

VERSE

Sometimes he showed him his sea of tears
Sometimes the Badakhshan ruby of his liver

From there they went into Mahmood's bedchamber. They saw Mahmood and Gulnar lying in bed together with Mahmod's arms laced around Gulanr's neck. Mahmood said to Gulnar: 'Long May King Agar live, who opened up the door of pleasure for us, and because of whom our desire was fulfilled.' Gulnar answered: 'When the True Creator of Causes wishes to have something accomplished, he provides such instruments.'

70. Hamzad: A familiar spirit or a jinn.

Gul whispered in his beloved's ears: 'It is said that things receive influence from each other. For how long will you let me burn like aloeswood and ambergris in the fire of separation?'

VERSE

I await the day when my arms
Shall be truckled around your neck

Agar said: 'O shallow man, did the goblet of your ambition became brimful with just a drop of love, and you became addled with inebriation? Should the potter of revolving heavens make goblets a hundred times from your clay, the wine of my union shall not yet be poured into it. It is a pari who longs for a man's gaze. Here, I am least bothered, and oblivious to your fate. If you were a mirror, I would not see my reflection in it, and if you were a portrait, I would not have cared to look at the face.' Gul said: 'I am laughing at you. Since you are a man, it would be useless to desire all these things from you. Come, I will show you another spectacle.'

Then Gul brought Agar into the private chamber of Prince Laal and Mah-Parwar. The two of them were playing chausar. Both Agar and Gul concealed themselves. At that moment, Prince Laal said to Mah-Parwar: 'Tell me what you think of our traditions of hosting. Was anything remiss, and did any of King Agar's attendants go back dissatisfied with the arrangements?' Mah-Parwar answered: 'By the grace of God, everyone went back happy. But I wish to ask something of you. I insist that you pledge and swear upon my life to tell me, whether King Agar is the jogi's son or your vizier's daughter?' The prince said: 'This is a delicate secret, and you must also pledge and swear upon my life not to reveal it to anyone.'

VERSE

Even though she is the vizier's daughter
She is superior to a hundred thousand men
And now hear this marvel of an account
Gul with his life and soul is besotted with her

'He is smitten with her love, is willing to sacrifice himself in her name, and remains engrossed in thoughts of her night and day.' Mah-Parwar said: 'If Agar is a female, why do you not get her married to Gul?' Prince Laal answered: 'It cost me great effort to persuade Vizier Khush-haal in the matter of Mahmood. I am placing my trust in God that this matter, too, will be amicably resolved.'

Then Gul took Agar aside and said to him: 'Your Honor maintains that he is a man. But Prince Laal says otherwise. For God's sake have mercy on my pitiable condition. Give up this charade. You should know that I am engaged to you. I have a say in the matter and I am within my rights to press my case.' Agar answered: 'Indeed, I have heard that you have been engaged to the vizier's daughter. But as for me, I am merely a young jogi. A great deal of good it will do you to have any say or power in my affairs.' Thus speaking, Agar left the house and was very displeased with Gul and cursed him.

Gul recited this verse:

VERSE

Receiving scolding and censure is now a norm with me
The expletive received can be termed proper conversation

In short, with much effort and flattery, he was able to dispel Agar's anger. Finding Agar indulgent, Gul asked: 'Tell me now, who is superior: Prince Laal or Mah-Parwar? Is Mahmood more graceful or Gulnar?' Agar answered: 'There cannot be a debate about the beauty of the paris. The expression that such and such a person is beautiful as a pari is proverbial. Mah-Parwar is far superior to Laal, and by the same token, Gulnar surpases Mahmood.' Gul said: 'I would that you make such a comparison between us, too.'

Agar answered: 'Even my slippers will compare favourably with your face.' Upon hearing this, King Gul broke out laughing. In short, they amused themselves with such talk. Meanwhile, Lal Dev arrived looking for Gul. Agar said: 'How can I hide from this dev's eyes?' Gul said: 'Hide under the bed.'

Lal Dev went away after handing Gul a document of accounts. Then Agar sought his leave of Gul. Thereupon, that ardent lover was engulfed by the sorrow of separation. Gul said: 'At least embrace me before you leave.' Agar answered: 'Give up this hope.'

In short, Agar went his way, leaving Gul crying in a frenzy of love.

OF KING AGAR LEARNING OF KING GUL'S RESTIVENESS AND TAKING FOOD FOR HIM

One day, Agar was sitting down to have lunch with his companions, when some houseflies turned their attention to the meal. The servant drove them away with his kerchief.

VERSE

O Nasikh, thus uttered the humble bread:
Be not the fly of the wealthy's food cloth

The houseflies cursed and abused him in their language, and said: 'We have had this trouble for a week, since King Gul stopped having food and drink.' When King Agar heard the speech of the houseflies,

VERSE

Blood dripped from Majnun's veins when Laila cut open hers
There's power in love, if the heart lacks not in passion

Agar became agitated and restive, of a sudden, upon hearing of his lover's frenzy. He ordered some food to be put aside for the houseflies, and headed for King Gul's palace with a salver of food. The sky-voyager steed brought him there in no time, and Agar woke Gul from his sleep with his words. As a tearful Gul rushed towards him, he fell down from infirmity and lack of strength. King Agar said to him: 'Why such ecstasies of passion?' He answered: 'So that your delicate nature is not offended by my delay in presenting myself.' Agar laughed at his bombast, and flowers fell out of his mouth, which Gul gathered into the skirt of his robe. Holding Agar's hand, he sat on the throne. Then Gul said to Vizier Jawahar: 'I am overwhelmed by hunger.' The vizier answered: 'Your Honour has not touched food or drink for a week, since you felt put off by it, but I shall have it made ready presently.' Agar said: 'Send for Hameed.'

When Jawahar departed to call Hameed, Agar said to Gul: 'O King, do you wish to recover through starving what you spent on Gulnar's wedding?' Gul had not yet answered when Hameed came in carrying the salver of food. Agar commented: 'You will not commonly find a guest who will feed his host.' Gul answered: 'I am not dying for such favours.' Agar answered: 'Now stop all these blandishments and have the food.' He replied: 'You should have it instead.' Agar picked up a morsel in his hands and fed it to Gul, who ate it.

VERSE

If the beloved were to offer a wine goblet
Would the pious ever renounce it? Never!

Gul said to Agar: 'O Prince! Swear upon my life and tell me, how did you learn about my condition?' When Agar told him how he had learned about it, Gul said: 'God be praised! Even the insects have become aware of the dreadful tumult of my situation, while you remain completely oblivious!' Agar said: 'Wasn't it enough, all that I did for you today? What more do you want?' Thus speaking, Agar took his leave.

Upon her parting, Gul recited these verses by a master:

VERSES

I asked my beloved at the time of parting
To leave me some token of her love
My beloved replied: O arrant fool!
Is the stamp of my love on your heart a little thing?

OF KING AGAR BECOMING PERPLEXED WITH THE RIDDLE, *THE HAWK IS AT HAND BUT THERE'S NO BAIT!* AND INQUIRING ABOUT IT FROM ZULAIKHA

One day Agar spoke to his maternal uncle's wife Zulaikha, and said: 'You have often mentioned the phrase, *The hawk is at hand but there's no bait!* and I have been unable to solve this riddle.' Zulaikha answered: 'O beloved of the land of excellence, and O Yusuf for all lovers, I lament that someone like you exists, who is like a Yusuf without Zulaikha, and a Suleiman without the army of paris, but I see no one who could be a worthy match for you, with the exception of Roshan Rai Pari.

VERSE

She is Bilquis if you are Suleiman
She is Venus if you are the refulgent moon

'Beautiful and full of gracefulness, peerless in intellect and perception. Many a Khusrow[71] died like Farhad[72] in quest of that

71. Khusrow: A Persian king.

72. Farhad: The hero of *Khusrow o Shirin,* the famous tragic romance by the Persian poet Nizami Ganjavi.

Shirin-like[73] creature. Many a Wamiq[74] pined for that beauty, who is the envy of Azra.'[75] Agar said: 'And do tell us if you know of any sign, mark, address, or news of her.' Zulaikha said: 'I hear that there is a faraway castle called Naqsh-e Jahan-Ara, which is full of magical contraptions and tilisms. It is bounded by the raging Sea of Oman on two sides and blazing bright fires on the other two. Between these terrors the castle stands like a bubble or spark. Nobody can dock a ship there, and let alone humans, even devs and paris do not have the wherewithal to reach there.' King Agar consigned Zulaikha's speech in the oyster of his ear like a pearl, and yearned to visit the castle like a sea's waves long to reach a shore.

Agar commanded Hameed Dev to saddle his horse. As ordered, Hameed Dev made the sky-traversing steed ready. Agar rode the horse to King Gul's house, and knocked on the door a number of times but nobody answered it. Finally, he broke down the door and went inside. He saw King Gul lying on the sick bed, with a stone placed on his chest, with another serving him for a pillow, on which his head rested. Agar revived that frail and debilitated creature with the pistachio of his lips, the apple of his double-chin, the almond of his eyes, and a lincture of the ambergris of his locks. He made him get up and partake of food and drink. He spent a few hours with Gul, then took his leave, and recited these verses:

VERSES

Should I live, I shall sew up the skirts of our union
Torn asunder in our separation
And should I die, pray accept my regrets
For a great store of my desires have turned to dust

But that besotted creature did not understand the riddle.

Then Agar went to Sarv-Aasa's house and said: 'I will be effecting a meditative seclusion for forty days. If someone asks you for news of me, do not give them my whereabouts.' Then he whispered into her ears: 'Do not become unmindful of King Gul and take care of him. I now give you into God's care.'

73. Shirin: The heroine of *Khusrow o Shirin*, the famous tragic romance by the Persian poet Nizami Ganjavi.

74. Wamiq: Name of a legendary Arab lover.

75. Azra: Beloved of Wamiq.

In short, Agar took leave of all his friends and acquaintances. He took Hameed Dev and his steed into his confidence about the journey. Hameed said: 'O King! This journey is full of peril. If you permit, I will go and say farewell to my wife and son.' Agar said: 'Very well!' whereupon Hameed Dev went and said his goodbyes.

OF KING AGAR TRAVELLING TO THE LAND OF ROSHAN RAI PARI AND TURNING TO STONE

POEM

It is not love, but a terrible calamity
Every hope invents a new fear and dread
The roses in this garden are entirely like thorns
Its springs are like weeping eyes
It is unbearable to listen to this account
The ears become burdened listening to it
Zulaikha was distressed from the concern
That Yusuf had been lost to her

The traversers of the desert of tales of voyage and travelers on calamitous roads recount that King Agar gathered his belongings for the journey in a saddlebag, filled a water-skin and taking Hameed Dev along, he set out for his destination astride his steed. After traversing the stages of the journey and spanning the distance, he arrived at long last at the frontier of the Naqsh-e Jahan-Ara castle. He stopped to rest at a clean and pleasant place, and then headed onwards. Soon, he was upon the shores of the raging sea. The horse said: 'O Hameed, fill up a water-skin from the sea, as you will next arrive at the Dead Sea.'

Upon this, Hameed filled up the water-skin. By the grace of God the Almighty Skipper, he had forded the sea like a bubble's boat, when suddenly a dark and gloomy storm rose, which turned the day into night. Agar remained safe by the power of the Most Great Name, and he sped onwards and they passed above a mountain that was difficult to negotiate. The horse said to Hameed: 'O Hameed, sit atop me, otherwise you will be left behind like dust. And sprinkle on this mountain a drop of the water you had filled from the raging sea.'

Upon Hameed sprinkling a drop, the darkness was dispelled which had made it impossible even for a hand to find its pair, and that arduous stage of the journey also came to an end. The horse said: 'Now for some time you are free to rest and relax, and eat and drink.' Upon this, Agar dismounted and ate a little and rested. The horse said: 'O Prince, for a distance of twelve kos[76] the ground is made of gold and silver, but it is strewn with countless insects, snakes and scorpions. If someone calls out your name, make no answer and remain quiet. When you go farther, you will find roadside sellers and fruit vendors whose merchandise is mixed with drugs. They will call out to you and display their wares in the skirts of their robes. Beware not to approach them, and do not even make a reply to them or answer if they challenge you. Pluck a few narcissus flowers from here.' After saying this, the horse leapt up skywards like the wind, and traversed hundreds of kos in a flash.

When it was afternoon, they saw that for hundreds of kos, the desert burned from the sun's heat and the sand of the desert shone like a dragon. There was neither any tree in sight to offer shade, nor was there a lake, pond, tarn, or waterfall to be seen. Both Agar and Hameed Dev were so distressed by thirst that their tongues dried up and their palates felt as if they were sprouted with thorns. The horse's tongue was hanging out, and he winced with pain every few steps. In short, they went onwards in this manner for many miles and finally came upon some leafy mango trees.

VERSE

Every instant, the sun's glare draped the mangoes
As if they were filled with lightning

The horse said: 'There is no cause for fear in this place. Catch your breath and let me rest as well. Stay here awhile, then you may ride again.' Thus they stopped there for a while, rested and then resumed their journey. They came upon the caparisoned shops of fruit-sellers along the way, and beheld the vendors attired in colourful dresses. They cried: 'Drink and be merry!' They displayed many coloured ewers, and called out:

VERSE

Come, drink, for this wine is like the Water of Life

But Agar did not look in their direction, and did not offer a reply.

76. Kos: A unit of measurement equal to two miles.

After some distance, he came upon a group of women who were selling delightfully appetizing, freshly baked sher-maal and they too called out to him. Agar made no reply to them either. He passed safely from that stage of the journey as well, and arrived at a luxurious, verdant garden, filled with fruit trees. Its floridness and freshness fortified the heart and its luster and verdancy comforted and brightened the eyes. Hanging from a tree he saw a colourful cage of exquisite design in which there was a mynah, accomplished in the occult arts, and a storyteller par excellence, who chirped at the sight of Agar.

The horse said to Agar: 'O King, this mynah is a tilism. Recite, *In the name of Allah*, and shoot an arrow at it. If your arrow hits its mark, you will break the tilism, and if you miss, you will also become a prisoner of the tilism.'

Agar recited, *In the name of Allah*, and shot the arrow.

VERSE

Not only did it break the mynah's body
That arrow destroyed the entire tilism

Immediately upon the mynah's death, the whole garden blew away like a leaf and a bleak and barren desolation materialized in its place. Hameed lauded Agar's marksmanship.

Agar rested there for a few days, then rode onwards and came upon signs of human habitation. Seeing Agar, the dwellers of Naqsh-e Jahan-Ara castle lamented his imminent death at a young age, saying: 'Alas, this youth wants to put his life at stake in a perilous undertaking. Thousands of kings, glorious like Sikander, came here on their quests, and went away with their hearts stamped with failure and loss. What would he be able to accomplish all by himself?' Let alone make a reply, Agar completely disregarded them, and kept riding onwards with his head lowered. At last, he arrived at the gate of the castle, where he saw written: *It is proscribed to enter the castle. You will fail, until you have first killed the heron!*

When Agar looked up, he saw a heron flying overhead. With the fluttering of its wings, an admonitory voice exclaimed: *Many a great king came here seeking the pari but were turned into a heap of clay and stone. You imagine that you can carry away Roshan Rai Pari all by yourself? Until you have killed me, you will not be able to enter the castle!*

Agar took off the bow from his shoulders and nocked the arrow. Both Hameed and the horse said: 'Stop! Do not shoot the arrow! It will be folly, and completely unwarranted. He whose arrow misses the heron will rue the day he shot it. O King, you will turn to stone and will struggle to return to human form.'

But, much as the two beseeched him, Agar paid them no heed. The heron called out: 'O huma of the land of love. I am a heron made of tilism. What is it that you are about to do! I pity you. Do not think of me as your enemy. Follow my advice. It is true that:

VERSE

Your arrow has emptied the world of prey
Even the weather vane's bird lies pierced

But in the matter of tilism all your prowess will come to naught. It is a pity that a beautiful beloved like yourself will fall prey to a wretch like me.'

King Agar said:

VERSE

'I know not if the stone fallen from Fate's sky
Would first destroy you or make me its mark'

Thus speaking, he shot the arrow. But the arrow did not hit its mark. He shot a second arrow which also missed. And so did the third one, and all three of them were presently turned to stone.

VERSES

That lovely body was turned to stone
That beloved became all adamantine
Hameed's head lay at his feet, turned to rock
And like its rider the steed too was stone

OF AGAR'S DISAPPEARANCE BECOMING MANIFEST AND EVERYONE AGONIZING IN DISTRESS

It is said that when King Agar turned to stone, he was caught in a terrible fate. Even strangers bitterly lamented his lot, and the flint-hearted Roshan Rai Pari too felt a mountain of sorrow crushing her.

VERSE

Leaving the accidents that happened here
Let us hear what transpired on the other side

For some time, King Mansoor believed that Agar was visiting with the jogi, and the jogi thought he was at King Mansoor's court. Others also made similar assumptions. But when his disappearance was finally known, every inch was searched to find any trace of him. His disappearance was mourned and threw everything into upheaval.

Like a stone engraving, grief and sorrow were imprinted on every heart. Everyone put ashes on their heads to mourn the disappearance of that mercurial personage. Awaiting his return, their eyes became dry and turned into sores, and their hearts' glass was crushed by the stone of separation. King Gul, Prince Laal, Mahmood, Quraish, and Lal Dev set out in one direction, and the jogi, his wives, and Buqalamun in the other. King Mansoor, Khush-haal and other viziers, and the forty kings took one path, and Manuchehr, Jawahar, Basant, and Shahryar along with their wives took another. Friends, acquaintances, relatives, non-relations, nobles, subjects, servants, attendants, whoever heard of his disappearance set out crying and lamenting and throwing dust in mourning to search for Agar, and many turned themselves into the form of animals for the purpose. They searched in thousands of places and in all directions, and left no stone unturned, but could find no sign or trace of Agar. All they could learn from their many searches was that Yusuf of the Times had heard Zulaikha sing the praises of Roshan Rai Pari in reference to the proverb, *What a pity that the hawk is at hand but there is no bait*, and perhaps he had set out in search of the pari. Upon learning this, the avis of their senses took flight. They became convinced that the huma of excellence had become the prey of the heron from the tilism, and that moonlike beauty was now turned to stone. Everyone reproached and blamed Zulaikha, and cursed and abused her. They lost all hope of ever seeing Agar, and became despondent. Everyone dressed themselves in black and some garbed themselves in clothes dyed in red ochre.

King Gul struck his head against the walls and fell on the ground in grief, and lost all consciousness of himself. The jogi was inebriated on the wine of separation, and King Mansoor and Vizier Khush-haal fainted from ecstasies of grief at their loss. The forty kings would not touch food or drink, in mourning. All four of King Gul's viziers were equally frenzied. One beat his head; another cried; one acted insane. One wrung his hands in grief; one roared with agony; another made plaints. The places Agar frequented were thronged every day, and a great lamentation rose at his absence. There was rioting in the cities, and great excesses were committed. No one lit a lamp in a mosque or gave the call to prayer, and the temples were in ruin and deserted. The populace suffered and there was no protector or succor to come to their aid.

Reports of thefts and dacoities were received from every neighbourhood. Thugs and insurrectionists were encountered at every nook and corner. Money lenders stopped providing credit and hundreds of traders lost all their possessions. Whole markets closed down, the land became a desolation, and the subjects were in uproar. Lakhs of buildings, thousands of houses, and scores of palatial palaces became desolate ruins. Wolves and jackals made their dens in the summerhouses. Vultures and owls made their perches in the courtyards. Dust gathered in the rooms, and sticks and straws in the cellars. Owls flew in the mansions and bats hung from the ceiling. In the courtyard, female snakes, serpents, black koriala[77] and patthar-chata[78] lay claim, and on the platforms many coloured scorpions and bis-khupras[79] reigned. Here one saw wild cats fighting; there one saw donkeys rolling on the ground. Badgers lay sleeping in one spot while dogs howled in another. The swallows flew about and the kites hovered. The ceiling curtains were in tatters and the floor was covered with dust. Every place was desolate and a howling wilderness met the eye wherever one looked.

For a long time, things remained thus. When someone recovered his senses, he retired into a forty-day meditation. Some wrote out amulets, others burnt papers written with spells, made offerings at prayer houses, and sought help from the pirs. Some recited spells, some prayed, some humbly touched their foreheads to the ground.

77. Koriala: A kind of braided or spotted snake.
78. Patthar-chata: A kind of serpent.
79. Bis-khupra: A species of venomous lizard.

With the offerings of dona,[80] puriya,[81] hazri,[82] koonday,[83] sehnak,[84] and tabaq,[85] everyone made offerings and pledges according to their custom.

King Gul lay oblivious to the world. When he opened his eyes he did naught except make sighs.

PERSIAN

There is power in the sighs of those whose hearts are burdened with pain

In the end, the jogi sent Mah-e Taaban in search of Agar.

OF THE ROYAL FALCON SETTING OUT AND BRINGING BACK AGAR THE COQUETTISH PEACOCK

At the time of Agar's departure, upon Hameed's advice and from the consideration that the falcon was native to Mah-Parwar Pari's land, and perhaps oppressed by captivity he may refuse to return, Mah-e Taaban did not release him.

Agar's disappearance had shocked everyone and made them self-absorbed. Nobody remembered to feed and water the falcon, and he starved for a number of days. Finally, he said to the jogi: 'O cherisher of servants, that huma of the pinnacle of felicity has disappeared, whose bond of love has bound me. The avis of my soul flutters inside my body's cage. My life is a burden. Now release me as his sacrifice so that I too can spread my wings to go in search of him, and test the strength of my wings against the challenge. Perchance,

PERSIAN

'The huma of felicity may fall into my power'

80. Dona: Offering of sweetmeat wrapped in leaves.
81. Puriya: An offering of sugar wrapped in paper.
82. Hazri: Food sent as offering to prayer houses.
83. Koonday: An offering made in a person's name.
84. Sehnak: An offering made in the name of Prophet Muhammad's daughter Fatima, in which pious women participate.
85. Tabaq: An offering made in the name of paris.

The jogi broke his cage and released the falcon. As it flew away, the falcon cried and said:

VERSE

'O King of Beauty! The bird released as your sacrifice
Becomes the huma, once freed

'O my captor, may God bring me to you, and you capture me once again.'

The falcon first went to his land. All the falcons presented themselves in his service. He said to them: 'My master had gone in search of Roshan Rai Pari, and was turned to stone. Help me find him.' Upon hearing this, thousands of falcons accompanied their king and arrived at a mountain. They saw pellets of deadly poison strewn everywhere. The falcon said: 'Everyone must pick a pellet in his claws.' When they arrived in the land where dragons lay with their mouths open, the falcon said: 'Drop the poison pellets into their mouths.' The dragons died the moment the poisonous pellets fell into their mouths. The falcon advanced with his army.

They came upon a well. Inside it, an old woman, a procuress and Satan's aunt, was hanging. The falcon ordered his followers to pull her out of the well with their beaks and chop her to pieces. A great commotion broke out upon her death, like the tumult on the Day of Judgment. When it subsided, they found themselves in a bare and uninhabited wasteland. With great difficulty, they traversed the desert, and many of them dropped from exhaustion.

The falcon finally reached the gate of the castle. He saw Hameed Dev lying on the ground with his hand touching Agar's feet and the horse beside him, all three of them motionless and turned to stone.

The falcon flew around Agar several times, and cried bitterly at his sorry state. Then he said to his companions: 'Go into the castle and catch the heron you find there.' Whole flocks of falcons rushed into the castle, and soon captured the heron and brought him out.

The falcon said: 'If I were to rub the heron's blood with my claws on Agar's delicate body, it would scratch him. The heron is captured. Now we must bring some jinn or human to do the needful.'

OF MAH-E TAABAN BEING FOUND AND FLOWN ATOP THE FALCON, AND HER RUBBING THE HERON'S BLOOD ON THAT COQUETTISH PEACOCK AND OF AGAR RETURNING TO HIS ORIGINAL FORM AND HIS MARRIAGE TO ROSHAN RAI PARI

The falcon was flying in search of a jinn or human when he saw an animal sitting in a tree and even though it tried to spread its wings to fly, it was unable to do so. The falcon asked him: 'How do you fare?' The bird answered: 'A little while ago, I had perched here to rest when someone let out such a heart-searing sigh from an anguished heart that it burnt up my wings.' The falcon realized that the jogi must have sent one of his wives to bring him news of Agar. He called out: 'O Woman, burning in the fire of separation! The feathers and wings of the birds of the air are burning from your fiery sighs. God has taken pity on your restiveness and I have found trace of your son. Now descend to earth and rub the heron's blood on Agar's body.'

When Mah-e Taaban heard the falcon's speech, she descended like an eagle and narrated the distress of her heart. The falcon gave her the entire account of his arrival and brought her to Agar. She embraced Agar's stony form, cried copiously and shed a sea of tears. Then she rubbed Agar's body with the heron's blood and by the grace of God's consummate nature, that stony shape returned to its original living form.

Then Agar himself revived Hameed Dev and the horse, and marveled at the falcon finding his way there. The falcon told him how he had found him and brought Mah-e Taaban there. Agar rushed and kissed Mah-e Taaban's feet. She embraced him and gave him the whole account of the jogi's suffering. Agar answered: 'I had reconciled myself to the thought that I would remain in my stony state until Judgment Day, and everyone would grieve at my absence. But God erased my suffering and I am indebted to you.' Then he sent for a palanquin worked with gold thread and himself graced the saddle, and twelve thousand falcons followed him row after row in the sky.

POEM

Whoever even glanced at him, said
This king is a Second Suleiman

He is indeed a worthy guest for this house
She is Bilqis, he is Suleiman
Said one: Have you any idea
What hardships did he undergo?
For months he remained in stony form
This vicissitude of fortune he daily endured
Who would have thought he would come alive
The God of the universe gave him life anew

While the populace made these comments, Roshan Rai Pari awaited his imminent arrival. She beheld him and pledged to take all his calamities upon herself. She would say: 'God be praised! This man of singular prestige has fallen in love with me. Thousands of kings came here but fortune did not favour any one of them.' She would utter these words and recall the account of her maternal cousin Giti Aara.

The story goes that one Masood Shah fell in love and became besotted with Giti Aara. For fourteen years he pined away in the love of that full moon. Finally, that crescent had its conjunction with that full moon and took pleasure from their union. After some time, Masood Shah lost interest in Giti Aara, fell in love with another woman, and was bent upon hurting Giti Aara. In short, Gaiti Aara separated from him, and the report of his infidelity to her became known to one and all. Roshan Rai Pari told herself that she had made this tilism for that reason, so that no human could find his way there and provoke her heart with his beauty.

VERSES

These humans only seek their purpose
Their love and fidelity are not durable
They are faithful only to their own kind
What benefit does a parizad have from their affection?
A pari may ruin herself for them
But they feel desire for their own kind

Then it occurred to her to inquire from the astrologers whether the Creator of the sun and the moon had put her, the one with the fate of Venus, in conjunction with a brilliant star. The astrologers said: 'Indeed, that beauty whose forehead is bright as Venus will find conjunction with a luminous moon; a happy union with a human being.'

Upon hearing this, Roshan Rai Pari made preparations for the nikah ceremony. She received Mah-e Taaban at her house with great honour and the functionaries from both sides busied themselves with the preparations for the ceremony.

At an auspicious hour Agar was made into a bridegroom. The qazi[86] arrived to recite the nikah with the orange end cloth of the turban tied around his neck, and wearing the sehra like a bridegroom himself. Hameed Dev said: 'O Qazi, you are decked out like a bride!' The qazi answered: 'Like the longing for Roshan Rai Pari made the bright world all bleak for your king, I too pine away in love for Roshan Rai Pari's singing girl.

VERSE

'Her love makes me dance with joy
Ever since she has been my companion

'I learned from astrological calculations that King Agar would arrive here, and release me from my suffering in love. I am desirous that when His Honour's betrothal with Roshan Rai Pari is held, I should be betrothed to the singing girl.'

To tease him, Hameed Dev said: 'It appears that your good self is also fond of songs and music.' The qazi said: 'Many of my friends have started calling me a wedding domni[87] since I have fallen in love with her.'

Finally, Agar's sehra was lifted and he was asked his name, Agar answered: 'My name is Manuchehr and I am known as King Agar because, from the luminosity of the sun and the light of tapers, my body becomes redolent with the smell of aloes.' The qazi married Roshan Rai Pari to Manuchehr and later the qazi was married off to the singing girl freely and without ado. Thereafter, King Agar returned triumphant and victorious to his land.

OF KING AGAR RETURNING TO HIS LAND AND FIRST VISITING KING GUL'S HOUSE

When Agar arrived in his city after traversing the stages of the journey, he met a weeping and wailing Shahryar and Basant on the way. Seeing

86. Qazi: An official responsible for administering the Muslim marriage contract.
87. Domni: A woman who sings and dances at public events.

them in that beggarly state King Agar became angry and said: 'O fools! Why did you stop dressing royally and reduce yourselves to this state? Where are my sisters, your wives?' They answered:

VERSE

'You should imagine them in the same state as us
Everyone is in a state of worry and frenzy'

Meanwhile, Manuchehr also arrived there with a similar appearance. Agar embraced him and gave him the gifts given to him as the bridegroom, and conferred Roshan Rai Pari as well upon him.

VERSE

Manuchehr came into possession of the pari
Who was sought by the sun and the moon

Meanwhile, Prince Laal and Mahmood arrived there with their collars rent. King Agar cried copiously and with his tears washed away the dust of the journey. For a long time, he discussed every calamity he had faced. When King Gul was mentioned, Prince Laal said:

VERSES

'How to narrate his wretched existence
He scrapes moments of life from death
One can't bear to see the terrible state he's in
You are kind to enquire about him

'He lies in a faint, at death's door. Whenever he opens his eyes, tears issue from them.' King Agar said: 'To call on the sick is akin to praying. Let us go and visit him.'

Agar sent away Prince Laal and Mahmood, and entered King Gul's garden chamber by himself. There he beheld a strange sight: the pools were dry and the fountains were in disrepair; the garden was in ruins and the waterfalls in need of repair. The promenades were covered with dry leaves and thorns lay in heaps in flower beds, instead of roses. Except for the ringed turtle dove's loud calls, no other birds sang.

VERSE

A few feathers lay in a garden nook
witness to the nightingale's longing for flight

In a few places, disfigured kaunla,[88] rangtara,[89] and meetha[90] trees stood, and in some places bhat-kataiya[91] and arand[92] flowers and fruit lay on the ground. Screens of dried-up vines and creepers lay covered in dust. The lush, pleasure-giving verdure was nowhere to be seen. Everywhere, one saw kakronda,[93] and smelled the stench of hulhul[94] trees. Upon seeing the garden in this state, King Agar wept involuntarily and recited these verses:

VERSES

'You who live under the roof of cruel heavens
For how long will you lament your sons, women, cities and homes
Recite the verse, O people with eyes take heed!'[95]
Should you come upon the desolation that is Faridun's[96] *palace*
Once court used to be held there
And an emperor gave audience there with majesty and grandeur
Night and day the court officials exchanged pleasantries
Everywhere people reveled in comfort and luxury
The rose bough was ever the home of songster birds
The songs of the nightingale resounded there like organ notes
Autumn never found a hold on that garden ever
It was either the spring of the balsam flower, or the bloom of the red poppy
Bravo, O vicissitudes of the heavens! Congratulations! Well done!
What a marvel is your small-heartedness despite your grandeur and majesty
The flowers which reflected the assemblies of parizads
Today they reflect the flight of the inauspicious owl
Countless swallows nest in its roof
And a dove makes a home in every decorated niche
The kites circle above, everywhere whirlwinds blow
In the avenues the feathers of crows and kites lie in heaps

88. Kaunla: A large and sweet species of orange.
89. Rangtara: A kind of orange.
90. Meetha: A green-skinned orange.
91. Bhat-kataiya: A prickly medicinal plant.
92. Arand: The tree from whose fruit castor-oil is made.
93. Kakronda: The plant *Celsia*, and its fruit.
94. Hulhul: The medicinal plant *Cleome viscosa*.
95. The Quran (59:2).
96. Faridun: A renowned Persian king.

Ignore the palace and search for those who lived there
And you will find their graves the haunts of the deer and wild ass
Their breasts full of longing, and the seal of silence on their lips
Neither friend, nor sympathiser, nor consoler remains
Neither that form, nor face, nor hue nor beauty are to be seen
Neither those eyes, nor those features, nor that gait remains
Neither pleasantries, nor whims, nor rituals of adorning
There's only a dark nook and a world of loneliness

Upon beholding this scene, Agar was astonished, and wondered about it as he headed to the summerhouse, where he found King Gul lying unconscious. Finding him in that state, Agar panicked and cried. He pressed his breast against King Gul's, his mouth with Gul's mouth, pressed Gul's legs and shook him by his shoulder. After some time, Gul opened his eyes, and beheld Agar's visage, and thought he was dreaming. He wished to behold his face without blinking but his eyes closed from weakness. Agar pressed his lips, the cup of Water of Life, against King Gul's, and helped raise Gul's head. Gul opened his eyes, and lowered his head at his beloved's feet.

King Agar said: 'I had imagined that you would be wandering in search of me like the zephyr. But no, you found a nice ruse and declared yourself sick.' Gul replied softly: 'I lost myself in search of you, and the handful of dust that is my existence was ravaged.'

Agar gave a detailed account of himself and said: 'I got four paris, who are the finest of their race, for your four viziers, and removed this burden from your shoulders. I ruled in a manner that the names of great kings were wiped away from history. My only desire now is to help you achieve success in your mission, and then withdraw myself into happy seclusion.' Thus speaking, Agar rose, and Gul painfully heaved a sigh and recited these verses:

VERSES

He said: Adieu! Go!
But do keep me in your thoughts
I have indulged all your caprices and whims
You should return the favour by giving shoulder to my corpse

Upon hearing this, Agar returned to his bedside, and departed after offering his condolences and consolations. Agar arrived at the jogi's house and found him, as well, frail and cloven by the sword of separation. Agar raised him from the floor and applied the salve of union on his wound. Then he went into Khashkhaash and prostrated himself at the King's feet and embraced the vizier. An assembly of revelry was organized. Every love-sick person was revived by Agar's Messiah-like breath, and King Gul and all his well-wishers celebrated the festive occasion.

OF AGAR PLAYING CHOGAN AND KING GUL FALLING FROM THE AIRBORNE THRONE

One day King Agar said to his companions: 'I feel like playing chogan.' All of King Gul's four ministers and the nobles assembled together. The news also reached King Gul, who arrived on his flying throne to see his beloved playing chogan. Unmindful of the vicissitudes of fate, the lover was engrossed in his beloved's beauty and grace in the midst of game, when he fell like a ball from the airborne throne. He was gravely injured by the fall, and his body shattered like glass. His four viziers, who were also busy playing chogan, rushed to his aid. Surprised and upset by this incident, King Agar said to King Gul's viziers: 'Make haste to get him treated and bring me news of his welfare.'

That weak and injured soul called out to his viziers: 'Why do you worry! I am well!'

VERSE

'Fallen into the ground, the seed breaks through to sprout
Vanity though reduces human dignity to dust

'God be thanked that I was not demeaned in the eyes of my king. I would attain my heart's desire if my life and soul become his sacrifice.'

As King Gul was carried away, King Agar went to Mah-e Taaban and asked her: 'Do you know of any physic for someone whose bones are fractured and broken from a hard fall?' Mah-e Taaban answered: 'No matter the height, I have a physic that has cured even those fallen from the roof of the heavens.' King Agar said: 'Kindly do me a favour and give me some and also tell me how it should be administered.' Mah-e Taaban handed him a few tablets of the medicine called the Pill of Life, and said: 'Mix it in milk before administering it, and massage his body with sweet oil. This tablet is the physic and he should have a chicken for his diet.'

Agar returned to the palace, and after changing into a healer's guise, arrived in King Gul's city.

OF KING AGAR COMING TO KING GUL'S LAND IN THE GUISE OF A HEALER

VERSES

Fortunate is the love-sick one
Whose healer has the Messiah's breath
For whom the sight of the beloved is the cure,
Union is the physic, separation being fatal

The word soon spread that a consummate healer had arrived in the city. Everyone said: 'Congratulations! The Ultimate Healer has sent a gifted healer from His House of Healing and Mercy.' They sought the healer for Gul but the healer refused to visit him. Employing wisdom and stratagem, and after much ado, Lal Dev finally prevailed upon him to visit King Gul. The healer held the patient's wrist in his hand to take his pulse. After comforting and consoling Gul, he raised his healing hands in prayer, and said: 'O Consummate Healer, pray grant swift recovery to this true lover at my hands.'

Thereafter, making an istakhara[97] on Gul's tears, he administered him the medicine and fed him chicken broth. Restored to his senses, Gul recited these lines impromptu:

VERSES

'Rise, O foolish healer, from my bedside
There is no medicine for the lovesick except the beloved's sight'

The healer said: 'O wounded of the sword of dalliance and vanity! O injured of the stone of coquetry and airs! Tell me truthfully whether you are sick, or laid low by someone's stony heartlessness.' He made reply: 'O healer, in God's name, pray stop with your medications. Think of death as the best of lives for me. Do not ask anything of me.'

VERSE

It is my resolve to take poison and die
There is release only in death

97. Istakhara: Looking into the Quran for an augury or omen.

The healer answered: 'Dear fellow, the season of youth is the treasure trove of pleasures and life. To wish for death in one's prime is folly. Who is it who has destroyed a flower like you, and repudiated and denied you the happiness of union?

VERSES

'Regard the rent collars of ten million roses,
Although a sole nightingale died a lone death
No moth escaped the taper's flame
In tears the taper was carried away at dawn

'It is against wisdom and sagacity to become besotted with a candle, that does not itself melt away at the fate of the moth. And to dote on and become infatuated with a rose, which does not tear its collar at the nightingale's cry, is sheer folly. O King, the saying that the world only exists as long as one has life, is proverbial. You have wagered your life in love for no reason whatsoever.'

The healer softened King Gul with such words, and in the end, King Gul could not hold back and recited this verse:

VERSE

'I am unable to give an account of my suffering
And I cannot remain silent either, alas!

'O healer, you appear to be a consoler of the sick, and I am racked with pain. For this reason, hear my account, that for a long time I have been burning in the fire of separation from King Agar like the oud, and being blown like smoke. For six months, I did not touch food or drink on account of his disappearance, and was called a lunatic. Since I am weak and infirm, yesterday I fell off my airborne throne while watching Agar play chogan, which broke every single bone in my body.'

The healer said: 'There is no power nor strength except from God! Your Honour, that handsome youth is an attractive man. Indulging in such abominable habits is most disgraceful.' King Gul answered: 'What habits? What are you saying? Ah, how may I tell you, dear fellow, that that calamity of the times is not a man but an elegant woman.' The healer replied: 'Even if one were to assume that Agar is a woman, could you not find someone better?' King Gul answered: 'First of all, she is indeed the embodiment of light; she is in fact the flame of the light on Tur. Furthermore, it is proverbial that one must regard Laila with Majnun's eyes. Anyone who questions that is short on wisdom and deficient in experience.'

The healer said: 'I still maintain that forfeiting your life for that jogi's son is against all dictates of wisdom.' Upon hearing this, King Gul heaved such a deep sigh that from its impact even the healer turned pale. The healer said: 'O True Lover, my heart quivered with your sigh, and a belief in your contention was obtained from the touchstone of experience. It seems that you were reminded of the same cruel fellow who has tormented you.' King Gul pressed the healer's hands to his eyes, and said: 'O Healer, truth be told, your hand greatly resembles my beloved Agar's hands.'

VERSE

'For the present this resemblance has cured me
Otherwise no physic could have helped me'

Upon hearing this, the healer frowned, twitched his nose, raised his eyebrows, looked at him intently, then said: 'God be praised! You compare me to a youthful boy?' King Gul cried at his unfeeling comment, and said: 'By God! I am tired of my life, and am willing to give it up. Pray give me some medicine so that my life's link is severed, and the avis of my soul is released from the body's prison. I shall never take the Pill of Life. It is my firm resolve to die in utter agony.' The healer said: 'God be praised! You wish to find release from your grief and anger, and escape disrepute and notoriety, while I receive the blame for your death on Judgment Day!'

Gul answered: 'O Dear healer, first of all, as per this verse:

VERSE

'The lover's blood remains uncompensated in this world, and
unaccounted for in the other

'But to simplify matters, let me forgive you my blood. In God's name, please take the seven treasures[98] from me and give me the medicine that releases me from the hold of grief.' The healer asked: 'Who will give me these goods after your passing?' King Gul said: 'You may take a promissory note attested with my seal.'

98. Seven treasures: An allusion to the seven treasures of the Persian king Khusrow.

Then Gul sent for an attendant and asked him to bring the pen box.

Lal Dev said: 'O Kindly Healer, I am greatly indebted to you that King Gul's senses have been restored. God be thanked, when he has had his recovery bath, I shall present you with half the income from the tributary lands.'

The healer answered: 'Have faith, and do not at all worry. He is on the path to recovery.'

King Gul wrote out a promissory note to the healer. The healer told him that he was giving him poison as requested, and administered a second Pill of Life by that ruse, and instructed the harem attendants to keep a careful watch over him.

Then the healer took his leave and returned to his house. The jogi had also gone to visit King Gul, and he too left. Upon returning home, Agar, feigning ignorance, inquired of the jogi what he saw on his visit. He answered: 'Gul was at death's door but a healer revived and healed him.'

The following day the healer again called on King Gul and he was shown great hospitality. The healer asked King Gul about his condition. Gul answered: 'God be thanked, I feel much relieved of pain and anxiety, but my heartache remains as before.'

VERSE

There is no cure for it, alas, what to do?
My beloved does not heed my dying cry, what to do?

The healer answered: 'There's no remedy for this sickness except abstinence. As you drive away thoughts of the person from your heart, you will start regaining health.' King Gul cried bitterly and said:

VERSES

'Why shouldn't I be a burden on strangers
For my beloved who caused my sickness does not visit my bedside
Ah, how can I forget the mole on her eyebrow
I'd sooner eat poison or run a sword across my neck'

The healer said: 'As per my diagnosis, you must withdraw yourself from that person's love, or reduce it by slow degrees. But if Your Highness is unwilling to countenance the thought, you are your own master.' King Gul said: 'Ah! You neither know the taste of love, nor know the bond between clay and water! Indeed, you know very little! My condition is representative of this verse:

VERSE

'I received sword blows from him at every plaint
And continued my plaints from the mouth of every wound

'Even should the millstones of the heavens crush me a hundred times like a grain; or the executioner of the heavens saw off my head a thousand times with a blunt instrument in recompense for loving her; or the Wine-maker of Nature mould my shape from clay a hundred thousand times and destroy it each time; or my humble self be strung up like Mansoor[99] ten hundred thousand times for the crime of loving her, I shall still not withdraw from my claim of love. If I long to die it is merely because I do not wish the ecstasies of my passion to result in my beloved's disrepute or calumniation.

VERSE

'Whether or not suppressing my sighs kills me
I only desire my beloved not to be defamed'

When the healer discovered that King Gul was indeed true in his love, and besotted with the taper of Agar's visage like the moth, he said: 'O King, I again tested you today. A thousand accolades on your courage! Despite Agar's indifference towards you, you burn like the aloeswood in Agar's love and your suffering heart is revived by mention of Agar's name. There is a strong likelihood that the wilted bud of your humours will soon flower in the spring of union with Agar, and the dust from Agar's robe skirts will give colour to your wan cheeks.'

Gul said: 'O Messiah-breath, indeed, this is a prescription to completely restore me and speedily revive me.'

In a short while, King Gul took his bath of recovery, and the whole royal household felt indebted to the healer.

OF KING AGAR HOLDING A FEAST, ENJOYING THE COMPANY OF FRIENDS AND TURNING KING GUL INTO A WOMAN

It is said that after King Gul had taken his bath of recovery, King Agar sent him an offering as his sacrifice. Agar's emissary felicitated King

99. Mansoor: The mystic al-Hallaj who was killed for making claim to divinity.

Gul and presented the items. Gul said: 'Convey my salutations to the jogi, and communicate to King Agar this: I offer myself as a sacrifice to your kindness and your gift. While you did send me these offerings, you did not find it in your heart to visit my bedside.

VERSE

'Such generosity and such lack thereof'

After Agar's emissary had departed, Agar himself arrived there. King Gul feigned ignorance to his presence, and recited this verse:

VERSE

'Bravo, my friend, a hundred accolades
For visiting me on my sickbed'

After sending away Gul's viziers on various pretexts and creating privacy, Agar said to Gul: 'You hold me in such disdain that let alone answer my greeting, you are loath even to look at my face.' Then King Gul rushed forward and prostrated himself at Agar's feet and wept and sought forgiveness for his conduct from Agar, and received his forgiveness. Agar asked him: 'Tell me, what reward did you give the healer?' Agar answered: 'Besides a reward and robe of honour, I also conferred upon him seven treasures of jewels.' Agar said: 'You are telling a lie, for if it were true, he would not have complained to me. Here is the promissory note with your seal, for you to see!' Gul said: 'O Prince, I am convinced that you were the healer of the one whom you made sick.' Agar replied: 'Why would I bother in the least to cure a low creature like you, who would compare the healer's hands to mine, and dare utter my name before him.'

Meanwhile, the two viziers whom Agar had sent away presented themselves and hesitated in joining them, lest their presence be deemed unwelcome, but for a time they regaled themselves in Agar and Gul's company. Then Aflatun arrived and said to Agar: 'I left no stone unearthed in search of you.'

King Gul was offended by Aflatun's arrival. Agar made ready to depart, and taking along Gul's viziers, pierced Gul's heart with the thorn of separation. He returned to his palace, played chogan for a few hours until it was mealtime, and sat down to eat with his friends. He also sent some food with Hameed Dev for King Gul. Delighted by the favour shown him, Gul offered many sweet words in praise of

Agar and bestowed a robe of honour on Hameed Dev and sent him away.

Agar ordered his officials to arrange an assembly of revelry in honour of Roshan Rai Pari. He sent out summons throughout his kingdom, and invited Lal Dev, along with King Gul. King Mansoor arrived accompanied by his viziers. Prince Laal with Mah-Parwar Pari, and Mahmood with Gulnar bedazzled the onlookers. Vizier Shahryar presented himself with Moti Rani. Jawahar arrived holding Ajooba Pari's hand, and Basant holding Sarv-Aasa's, while Manuchehr brought Roshan-Rai Pari along.

VERSE

Everyone was shown regard according to their station
Everyone was treated with thought and consideration

Someone received offerings, some were given a robe of honour. Great munificence and liberality was shown to everyone. An array of delicacies, and cups of delightful wine were consumed by all in an atmosphere of great cheerfulness and merriment. After the feast for the guests was over, Agar ordered melodious singers to sing. Pari-bodied mellifluent singers of delicate airs began singing, and those present in the assembly became absorbed in their euphonious strains.

King Gul alone disregarded all music and singing and burnt his heart like the ispand seed,[100] as an offering to ward off the evil eye from Agar. Of a sudden, he heaved a sigh and fell unconscious.

Agar handed Hameed Dev a flower to make Gul surreptitiously smell its perfume, without Lal Dev finding out. Hameed Dev made Gul smell it and he immediately revived, but all signs of manhood disappeared from his body. Gul felt himself and was shocked at the transformation, and finding his manhood gone, drowned in the well of shame. He finally stopped, thought he was dreaming, and rubbed his eyes. Then he carefully felt himself again, and once again felt ashamed and came very near to dying from his heart's violent palpitations. Hameed gave him another flower to smell, whereupon his missing manhood was restored to him. He no longer felt shame, but every so often he would touch himself to ensure that the grain of barley had not become the grain of wheat. Seeing him thus mortified, Agar laughed uncontrollably. Meanwhile, Hameed Dev said to Agar: 'Come

100. Ispand seed: Wild rue seeds.

and see this marvel: Manuchehr is playing the zangoola[101] in a musician's guise.' Agar said to him: 'Produce him before me this instant!' When Manuchehr was brought before him, Agar said to Hameed Dev: 'Just like the qazi who was betrothed to the singing girl, Manuchehr should be married to Chanchal Bai.' Hameed Dev produced that female musician. Manuchehr found an opportunity to slip away and then returned and presented himself before Agar in his real form. He was made fun of for many days.

The festivities continued in a befitting manner for several days. Finally, they came to an end, and the guests were bid farewell.

OF AFLATUN FALLING IN LOVE WITH GUL ANDAAM AND GETTING BETROTHED TO THAT BELOVED

It is narrated that, when visiting the land of Roshan Rai Pari, King Agar had appointed his maternal cousin Aflatun as his vice regent. As chance would have it, Aflatun fell in love like a nightingale with Agar's female attendant Gul Andaam, beside whose exquisite beauty the elegant rose looked coarse and crude. Presently, the flame of love lit up on both sides. For a long time Aflatun hid love's sparks in his heart's fire temple, but it could no longer be hidden.

VERSE

One can hide love from the world
But chapped lips and wan looks give one away

One day, upon witnessing his anxiety and uneasiness, King Agar said to him: 'From your state it appears that you have become engrossed in the mirror of some beauty's cheeks, and entangled in someone's long locks.'

VERSE

He did not utter a word but his tears answered for him

Agar said to him with great caring and solicitude: 'For no reason you burnt like a taper and singed yourself like a moth! O silly fellow, I underwent great hardships on behalf of strangers; I even suffered myself to be turned to stone for them for months, and underwent hun-

101. Zangoola: A rattle.

dreds of other hardships. You are, after all, my brother and the strength of my arm. Why wouldn't I help you in your difficulty?' Aflatun said: 'I feel mortified. What is there to say, for I feel embarrassed. My account is not one that can be uttered. Verily there is no power over one's heart.'

Upon hearing this Agar reckoned that perhaps he nursed a love for his female attendant in his heart, and his beloved was Gul Andaam, whose captivating gait robs sleep from one's eyes.

VERSES

It is her mark on the moon's surface
She is the one all eyes regard with engrossment
She is pari-limbed and of delicate airs
She is besotted with him, and he smitten with her

Agar joined those two roses in bonds of matrimony, and Aflatun was beside himself with joy. In the assembly his ecstatic heart sang out in jubilation. He began playing the sitar and made the entire assembly enraptured with his playing. Although there were no guests at the wedding, the strains of his singing were so captivating that people began arriving from far away to listen to him. King Gul and Lal Dev, and the jogi arrived. The beasts and the birds encircled him. Aflatun took a garland from his neck and put it around a deer's neck. Then he put down the sitar and the deer went away.

Then he said to King Agar: 'Pray get my garland back. I imagined that it was your pet deer.' Agar answered: 'It was your singing that attracted him here. Use the same enticement in your voice that attracted him here, and get the deer to bring back the garland.' He answered: 'It is not in my power to summon him, and I have no power over the beasts of the desert. You are a past master in this art, and adept at this device. Do complete what I left unfinished.'

Much though Agar refused, Aflatun did not relent and in the end, seeing no recourse left to him, that envy of Venus began singing, and opened his lips to intone this ghazal:

GHAZAL

Replete like the rain clouds
These eyes made forests verdant
O heart, whom have you crossed, that an army of tears approaches
Carrying before them the pieces of the heart

—MIR DARD

The ghazal had not quite ended when the deer, which had run away, returned, and put its head at Agar's feet. Agar removed Aflatun's garland from its neck and replaced it with one of his own. The deer blossomed like a rose and retired into the desert. King Gul felt madly desirous of the garland, and the assembly rang out with praise and accolades.

OF ASKARI PAHALWAN BEHOLDING KING AGAR'S GARLAND AROUND THE DEER'S NECK, AND BECOMING RESTIVE AND FALLING IN LOVE. OF HIS ARRIVING WITH A HOST TO CARRY AWAY KING AGAR, AND RETREATING IN HUMILITY AND SHAME IN THE END

It is recounted that one Askari Pahalwan lived in the wilderness who was as powerful as Nariman[102] and before whom the warrior Rustam[103] was like an insignificant mote. He was such as would make the doughty Sohrab[104] quail, vanquish the mighty Zal,[105] and rub out Tahamtan's[106] existence in the flash of an eye. He was, in size, like the revolving skies, in his height a pillar of the heavens, and the haft-sar[107] should be considered headless before him. The lion was a bedbug in comparison to him. He was peerless in combat and renowned for his strength. The jungle was in turmoil from fear of him, and the cities empty from his tyranny and excesses. Like a wild creature, he lived in the forest.

The deer was attached to Askari Pahalwan, and returned to him. When the deer returned wearing King Agar's garland, the tyrant reckoned that the garland had come from Agar's neck. He said to himself: 'God be praised! The one whose garland's perfume has made Earth and heavens redolent must be as dainty and delicate as the rose; one must investigate the matter.'

102. Nariman: A Persian champion. Rustam's great grandfather.
103. Rustam: A legendary Persian warrior.
104. Sohrab: A legendary Persian warrior. Rustam's son.
105. Zal: Rustam's father.
106. Tahamtan: Rustam's title.
107. Haft-sar: A lamp holder that has seven "heads" or places for oil lamps.

In short, that rutting dev, driven by lust, started from there with an army. The news spread that a sleeping terror had awoken, to wit Askari Pahalwan had come with an army.

King Gul and Lal Dev arrived with their viziers and companions. They beheld that Askari Pahalwan had besieged Agar, and when he spoke to Agar he addressed Agar as "My life!"

King Gul was consumed by a fire of jealous rage, and wished to kill him with his dagger but Agar made a sign to him to desist, and said to Askari Pahalwan: 'O imbecile made of idle talk, what nonsense you spout! It behooves one not to make tall claims. If you feel pride in your strength, know that despite my youth, I have defeated many a Rustam. Are you worthy enough to take me as your son-in-law?' Askari answered: 'I know that you are a woman. I wish to hear you sing.'

Agar wished to resolve the matter by recourse to the sword, but the jogi said to him: 'He is a guest. Make arrangements to welcome him. Serve him food and play a round of chausar.'

Askari agreed to the proposition. They had food and the chausar cloth was spread. Agar and Gul put their men in the same square. That was the best play at the moment. A wager was made that whoever won would receive the other's kingdom. Agar won three consecutive games.

Askari Pahalwan said: 'Indeed, I have lost my kingdom to you but I have not given up on my desire of union with you.' Agar answered: 'Now you are my subject and I have the power to raise you to honor or destroy you.' While they were engaged in conversation, Askari Pahalwan's eyes fell upon Agar's Testament of Victories in which a brief account of each campaign was given as follows:

First Campaign: The attack of forty kings on the land of Khashkhaash and their humiliation, and the attackers swearing allegiance.

Second Campaign: Turned into a dragon for Raja Basik's daughter, jumped into the cauldron of boiling oil, bathed in the hot hammam, and presented her to Vizier Shahryar after winning her by overcoming all challenges.

Third Campaign: Marched on Shah Lala's kingdom and conquered it and brought Ajooba Pari and conferred her on Vizier Jawahar.

Fourth Campaign: Heard the news about the falcon from the Simurgh, departed all by himself in search of it, and captured it after fording seven oceans.

Fifth Campaign: Left his brother Mahmood's wedding and departed for his maternal Uncle's kingdom and defeated the enemy and restored the kingdom to his uncle.

Sixth Campaign: With great subterfuge brought Sarv-Aasa and married her to Vizier Basant.

Seventh Campaign: Suffered himself to be turned to stone for six months for Roshan Rai Pari and finally acquired her with these labours and presented her to Vizier Manuchehr.

Thus anyone who seeks equality with her must be able to win such laurels.

Askari Pahalwan quailed upon reading Agar's Testament of Victories, and came to his senses. He said to himself: 'The one who has accomplished such signal deeds of manliness would never consent to have someone govern her. It is an idle thought, a hopeless dream.' He felt greatly ashamed and mortified at his contumely. He excused himself on the pretext of attending to the call of nature, and departed for his domicile in the wilderness.

King Gul said to Agar: 'Hear, and try to comprehend the situation. We were somehow able to ward off this calamity from our heads today and the ploy worked. But everyone now knows that you are a woman in disguise. And everyone is infatuated and besotted like the nightingale with your rosy cheeks. Every day thousands will die, vying for you. It would be far preferable to settle down with someone and give up the facade.' Agar answered: 'Praise the Lord!

VERSE

'One hears that the frog has caught cold[108]

'I am not Shirin that I will be affected by some extortionist like Farhad cutting open his head and dying,[109] nor am I Laila that someone like Majnun could feign madness and smear my name with his professions of love. Anyone who raises his recalcitrant head shall receive condign punishment.'

In short, Lal Dev and King Gul departed. Then Agar said to Aflatun: 'Your foolishness and importuning are responsible for this vexatious

108. Literal translation of a proverb that alludes to an unlikely prospect.

109. A sect of mendicants who extort alms by threatening to split (or wound) their heads.

business. If that deer hadn't been attracted here, it would not have carried away my garland.' He answered: 'Indeed, it was my fault and I seek your forgiveness.'

OF LAL DEV BECOMING AWARE OF KING GUL'S ANGUISH AND CAREFULLY SETTLING UPON A STRATEGY TO EFFECT HIS UNION

When King Gul parted from Agar, he was convulsed with tears. He said to himself that there was no possibility of his union with his beloved, as that unkind creature cared for him not a whit.

VERSE

When do I ever see the face of hope
Even despair I am not fully apportioned

He told himself that death would be far preferable a prospect to a life such as his.

VERSE

I would like my passion to reach its culmination
Why not find renown by dying in the beloved's name

He wept and cried throughout the journey. Returning to his home, he locked himself in a secluded chamber. After he had passed many a day crying and wailing,

VERSE

Even his sighs stopped issuing
His strength and vigor ebbed away

Quraish received news of his condition and arrived at the door of his chamber. She called out his name many times but received no answer. She struck her head against the wall and made lamentations and a stream of blood issued from her forehead. When Lal Dev heard this news he lamented Quraish's sorry state, and broke down the door of Gul's chamber and brought out his wilted flower. He put him in his lap, and found him at death's door.

Gul revived after a long while, and Lal Dev said to him with great solicitousness and care: 'O Gul, seeing your grief makes me suffer great anguish, and I have lost all will to live. For God's sake share what ails your heart.' He answered: 'What do you care? In comparison with Prince Laal, you would reckon even a stone worthier than your own son. What did you not do for him? You struggled and underwent great difficulties to effect his union with Mah-Parwar. I have pined for Agar since forever, suffering misery and gloom, with my last breath about to leave me. But no matter how wretched or desolate I felt, you did not inquire after me, or ask about my welfare.'

Lal Dev said: 'Now I have heard the details. Come out of seclusion, cheer up, have food and drink, and I will make a plan and bring it to happy fruition.' Gul said: 'I want you to swear to it in Prophet Suleiman's name.' Lal Dev asked: 'But what if I were to swear in his name and am unable to fulfill it?' Gul replied: 'For the plan to be successful, you must fulfill Agar's parents' wish to have Prince Laal returned to them forever.'

After some reflection, Lal Dev said: 'Although I cannot bear separation from Prince Laal, for your life's sake, I shall even consent to what is unbearable for me.' Lal Dev forthwith sent for his viziers and ordered them to ready the baggage for Prince Laal and Mahmood's journey. They put all other matters on hold, and busied themselves with the preparations.

Hameed Dev heard that in a few days Prince Laal would return to his city and communicated it to Agar, who felt great consternation at the news. Outwardly, he spoke cheerfully, but internally he suffered great distress. Finally, he retired into a chamber and ordered seclusion. Much though Hameed Dev queried him, Agar gave no reply.

Agar travelled through the tunnel to see the jogi, who received him with kindness. Seeing his swollen eyes, the jogi wept and inquired: 'What suffering did the heavens visit on you today that reduced you to this state?' Agar said: 'Have you not heard the news that Prince Laal will enter his city in just a few days? At Mahmood's wedding, it was agreed between Lal Dev and Khush-haal that when Prince Laal is released from captivity, and ascends the throne, they will marry Agar with Gul. Thus, upon his return the agreement will be fulfilled. It is just a matter of time before they send a message: 'We carried out our part of the bargain, and you must now alleviate our suffering.' I am very vexed by the matter. If I defy the wishes of my mother and father, I will be embarrassed before God and his prophet (Peace be upon him); and if I were to obey them, I will feel ashamed at embracing what I am loath to do, and allowing myself to become a subject when I am a ruler.'

The jogi answered: 'My son!

'What is written on the forehead must come to pass[110]

'The only thing your refusal would lead to is bloodshed.' Agar said: 'I feel grieved and inconsolable at the prospect of leaving you, and distressed at the thought of your being left alone.'

Upon hearing this, the jogi shed many tears, and washed away the dust of sorrow from his face. He persuaded Agar to do as he had advised. Agar said: 'Have my house pulled out from its foundation, and installed beside your house.'

In just a few days the building was pulled out from the ground and installed beside the jogi's quarters. So despondent and downcast was Agar that the forest rent its tunic in grief.

OF PRINCE LAAL RETURNING TO KHASHKHAASH WITH VIZIER'S SON MAHMOOD, TO TAKE UP RESIDENCE THERE

Prince Laal with Mah-Parwar Pari, and Mahmood along with Gulnar, set out for their land with great fanfare. Lal Dev and Quraish wrung their hands in grief at their separation. Gul, too, looked dejected, and accompanied them for a distance to see them off. When Prince Laal and Mahmood arrived near the land of Khashkhaash, they dispatched a missive to King Mansoor, which read:

By the grace of God, our fortune proved auspicious and we are desirous of augmenting our honor by kissing your feet.

King Mansoor kept the letter pressed to his eyes for a long time, and wrote a reply in his own hand, which read:

O light of my eyes! I have no strength left to wait. Your seeking permission is an oppression for someone dying to see you.

110. Written on the forehead: A belief that one's fate is written on one's forehead.

VERSE

Come and populate my heart's country
Which grief has despoiled for years

Upon receiving this reply, they set out eagerly for the court. King Agar had made arrangements for a feast suitable for the festive occasion. When they arrived in the city, the king mounted an elephant and set out to welcome them with his entourage with great pomp, and greeted them with love and affection. He seated Prince Laal beside him, while Mahmood sat on Vizier Khush-haal's elephant.

Prince Laal saw that every street in the city was caparisoned like the streets in heaven, and saw mirror-works decorate every wall and every door. The redolence of flowers was akin to the perfume of heaven's flowers. The populace was joyous and well apparelled. At every step along the way, they kept praising King Agar's tasteful organization.

Finally, Prince Laal and Mah-Parwar arrived in the palace. The prince's kindly mother was beside herself with joy at the sight of her son and daughter-in-law. Vizier Khush-haal, too, received a new lease on life from the arrival of Mahmood and Gulnar. Sacrificial offerings were received from all over the land, and many who awaited gifts and bestowals received what they sought.

King Agar provided a sumptuous feast for the guests. Prince Laal sent Agar a message: We long to see you and the guests will find no zest in the celebrations until you arrive to regale us with your company.'

Hameed Dev brought the missive and upon receiving it Agar arrived in the assembly. Prince Laal exclaimed: 'O brother! Come, and let us embrace!' Agar answered: 'I am the disciple of a jogi, and find it against deportment to embrace.'

The food cloth was spread and the meal eaten. As Agar was feeling heavy-hearted and disconsolate, he felt anxious, and left through the tunnel, closing the tunnel door behind him. Prince Laal inquired: 'Has the jogi's disciple left?' The nobles were stunned into silence upon this remark. Some of them took courage, and said: 'Your Honor, do not employ such a term in connection with His Honor, as his prestige has kept alive the name and prestige of the kingdom.'

POEM

The garden is in bloom on account of him
Or else it was nothing but a thorny wilderness

If that brave and courageous king were not there
Neither this kingdom nor this life would have been here

Prince Laal said: 'When did I ever refute that? It was he who described himself as a jogi's disciple.'

They searched for Agar but could not find him. Prince Laal said: 'I wish to be properly introduced to him.' Mahmood answered: 'I did not get a chance to see him either. Now it is well nigh impossible that he will visit of his own volition.'

Prince Laal sent out a letter expressive of his desire to meet Agar. Upon receiving it, Agar sent the reply: 'Disciples of jogi have no business meeting with kings.'

OF LAL DEV GOING BEFORE KING MANSOOR TO REQUEST THE NUPTIALS OF THE LOVER AND THE BELOVED, AND OF THE KING GIVING HIS CONSENT TO THEIR MARRIAGE

After some days, Lal Dev wrote a missive to King Mansoor, which read:

This sinner is most contrite on account of carrying away the prince of noble lineage, whose absence inflicted great suffering on Your Honor. I have not yet offered myself in Your Honor's service, and if engrossment in your son's beauteous vision has cleansed the mirror of your worthy heart of the dust of grief, I would request the honor of presenting myself before you for an audience.

Upon reading the letter, King Mansoor asked Prince Laal to write a reply. Prince Laal said: 'O guide of the world, the torment that you suffered on account of our separation, is akin to the affliction he suffers on account of brother Gul.' The king asked: 'What are you alluding to? What power have I to alleviate Gul's affliction?'

Prince Laal said: 'My release was contingent upon the agreement that Agar shall be married to King Gul, who is madly in love with her. Otherwise, our entire army will find it impossible to hold off even one soldier from their host. It would be preferable to grant him leave to present himself, and during the meeting, you should be cognizant of what he seeks.' The king said: 'Very well!'

Then Prince Laal wrote out a reply from the king, which read:

Dear Brother, may you abide in safety. I am in receipt of your letter and immensely pleased at the prospect of your visit. I am looking forward to our meeting.

VERSE

Show favour and come without delay, for my house is your own

Upon receipt of the letter, Gul sent Lal Dev to King Mansoor's court. He arrived, and after expressing great remorse and asking for King's Mansoor's forgiveness, said: 'By the grace of God you found happiness and joy again. I am desirous that you resolve my anguish through your favour, that is, allow my son, a piece of my heart, to betroth your ward.' The king said: 'King Agar's temperament is manifest and well known. But do have hope, and I will do all in my power to help.'

They stayed together for a long time, and King Mansoor showed him the very best hospitality.

After taking leave of the king, Lal Dev visited Vizier Khush-haal. Khush-haal received him warmly and performed the duties of the host, inviting him to a repast and serving him sherbet and chobha.[111] When Lal Dev's daughter Gulnar presented herself and greeted him, he pressed her head to his chest, and seated Mahmood beside him. He congratulated Khush-haal and his wife on reuniting with their son and daughter-in-law. In the same vein, he narrated the purpose of his visit. Khush-haal answered: 'We do not have the least say in what has been settled between His Honour and yourself. As God is my witness, we have been miserable since the day we heard Mahmood narrate the cause for your anguish. God willing, your heart's desire will come to fruition. Dispel all worries, and nurse hope.'

Lal Dev returned jubilant from the land of Khashkhaash, and shared the happy tidings with Gul, who became exultant at the news.

111. Chobha: Steamed rice decorated with sweetmeats and dried fruit sent as a gift for wedding ceremonies.

OF KING AGAR SLAPPING AFLATUN WHILE PLAYING CHOGAN, AND OF HIS FRENZIED LOVER GRIEVING AT AFLATUN'S TRANSGRESSION

It is related that ever since Agar had his quarters moved to be near the jogi's abode, he remained in the female quarters, and refused to participate in amusements and entertainments.

One day, viziers Shahryar, Basant, Jawahar and Manuchehr presented themselves to him. Agar asked: 'Where were you the last few days?' Jawahar replied: 'Your slave had presented himself yesterday as well, but Your Honor was in the female quarters. I waited for a long time, then turned back. King Gul has said that he will soon have a bridal dress made, and will be wroth if there are any delays in its preparation.' Agar replied: 'Your king is always beset by some trouble or the other; he seems to be in a bad way.'

Basant spoke: 'This slave too is pressed for time these days, for I am given the charge of preparing the jewellery.' Shahryar said: 'I am responsible for organizing the lighting, and making arrangements for the procession.' Manuchehr said: 'This slave is responsible for organizing the assembly and the preparation of food. It seems that King Gul is about to be engaged to someone.' Agar said: 'Take heed, lest the ecstasies of joy carry him away from this world.' The viziers replied: 'Your Honor must not utter these words; rather, pray for the happy culmination of the event.' In short, they conversed on the subject for a long time.

Thereafter, King Agar occupied himself with playing chogan. Perchance, the aigrette from Agar's crown fell off. Aflatun rushed to pick it up, lest someone should step on it, and in his hurry, his cheek touched Agar's cheek, and Agar slapped and castigated him at the violation of his modesty. Aflatun began crying at the harsh treatment he had received.

Agar worried that King Gul may be watching from his flying throne and might feel jealous. As it happened, King Gul was riding his flying throne and had witnessed the incident and become morose, and flown away. Agar, too, no longer felt any joy in playing, and stopped and headed to the river to hunt. He said to Basant: 'Prepare and bring me some fish kebabs from your home.' After Basant had left, Agar said: 'O Jawahar, my heart is uneasy.' He replied: 'Let us visit King Gul and rest there for a while.'

Agar went into the palace but did not find Gul, and lay down to sleep in his bedchamber.

Upon hearing of Agar's arrival, Gul left everything and rushed home. He called out Agar's name several times but Agar was sound asleep. A hot rage had lit up in his heart at Aflatun touching Agar, and he could no longer bear it, and lightly slapped Agar.

Agar started from his sleep. The flower of his cheek had turned blue like an Iris. He said nothing and returned to his house and said to Hameed Dev: 'Do not admit anyone.' Meanwhile, Basant arrived with fish kebabs. Hameed Dev announced him and Basant was conducted before Agar. He offered the kebabs, then said: 'Yesterday, I beheld your moon-like visage, free of all blemish when you slapped Aflatun; it's a marvel that its mark has manifested itself on your immaculate face.'

Agar engaged him in conversation and distracted him. Then Agar affected seclusion for a few days. After many days viziers Jawahar and Shahryar came to visit him, and requested Hameed Dev to announce them. Agar said: 'Do not bring me their messages. Tell them to go and take care of their king and attend to his burial.' After much pleading and entreating, the viziers were allowed to present themselves. They met and a food cloth was spread, and Agar asked them to have a meal. But they made an excuse and said: 'Would Your Honor extend the invitation to our court?' Agar asked: 'Tell me, what qualms do you have about having the meal here?' They replied: 'We only know that King Gul was occupied with the business of the state until the day you visited the palace. Since your visit he has been afflicted with a strange malady, and spurns food and drink. He is unwell and suffers palpitations and in just a few days has been reduced to a corpse by the good fortune of his enemies. There is no knowing the real cause of his illness, and none has been able to diagnose it. We, his slaves, will partake of food and drink when he does.'

Agar said: 'Come brothers, have a few bites. He puts up these acts every few days. Nobody dies with another merely out of sympathy.' The viziers again excused themselves. Then Agar said: 'Seeing you sorrowful, I also do not wish to eat. Remove the food cloth and take this food with you, and feed it to that starving fellow.'

In short, the viziers departed. They took the food from the royal table to King Gul and said to him: 'King Agar has sent this feast for you, and it would be improper to refuse it. You must have a little something.' Gul said: 'But he is angry with me.' The viziers replied: 'Not at all. Indeed, he is inclined to indulgence and favour.'

OF KING AGAR GOING INTO KING GUL'S BEDCHAMBER AND EXACTING RECOMPENSE FOR THE SLAP DURING THEIR MEETING

It is related that one day Agar was enjoying the moonlight when someone suggested: 'O Generous Prince! It is my desire to behold the moonlight spread on water's surface, and avert the eyes from the expanse of the forest, to regard the breadth of the sea.'

King Agar allowed the pearl of appeal into the oyster of his approval and headed towards the sea. The beauty of the seaside, the cold breeze, the play of moonlight on water cannot be described in words. The waves of sleep closed the fountain of Agar's eyes. Agar's senses slid into the whirlpool of sleep from disorder. To ward off sleep, Agar stirred the water with his hand and took some in his cupped hand to wash his face.

VERSE

Because the water became perfumed at his touch
The rising bubbles became flagons of rose water

At that moment, the moon could not compete with his beauty and the mighty sea felt embarrassed before his majesty. All the beasts of the sea came out to see the sight of two moons shining above water. Some of them dove in the sea of wonderment, and most leapt with joy and elation. Agar tried to ward off sleep, but it did not release its hold on him. Vizier Jawahar said: 'King Gul's bedchamber is not far from here; please head there and take your rest.' Agar answered: 'That beastly creature would be disturbed in his sleep.' Jawahar answered: 'For several days he has been staying at his uncle's house.'

Agar went to King Gul's place and slept in his bed. It so happened that King Gul also arrived then, and asked Jawahar: 'Has His Honor come here?' Jawahar answered: 'Indeed, he has, but you arrival now does not augur well for your slave, as I told him that you were staying elsewhere as a guest.'

King Gul entered the bedchamber and removed a pillow from Agar's side and lay down beside him. Mistaking him for a pillow, Agar snuggled into Gul in his sleep.

VERSE

Why must I not thank my auspicious fortune
For my beloved's side is now become my pillow

In short, Gul took great pleasure from that fairy-limbed beloved's embrace and in his ardor he forgot all sense of himself, pressing his breast against Agar's, and putting his cheek against his face. Upon that Agar woke up, and he was furious at Gul's taking liberties with him. He punched Gul's side so powerfully that he clutched his heart in pain and fainted. Agar mounted his horse, took Hameed Dev, and departed from there.

OF KING AGAR BRINGING THE MAGIC SLAVE GIRL AND MAKING PLEASANTRIES WITH KING GUL, AND OF KING GUL BECOMING EMBARRASSED AT THE MAGIC SLAVE GIRL'S DOINGS

One day Agar said to his companions: 'Report who is present today! Let us have an archery competition, and see who is a master marksman.' One after another, everyone offered thanks that Agar was ending his reclusion which was the cause of despondency for all of them, and that Agar felt elated and ecstatic. They all joined him as a group.

When Vizier Jawahar asked for the mark, Agar said: 'Go and place a flower for the mark.' Jawhar said: 'What crime has Gul committed that even his namesake must suffer?[112] You do not show him the least respite, even though the poor fellow has become bent like a bow from grief.' While they were having this conversation, Gul arrived and saw that Agar stood there with a drawn bow. He stood in front of him as the mark and said: 'O Prince,

112. Namesake of Gul: Gul means flower.

VERSE

'You inflicted a wound in my heart without mark
I marvel at the arrow shot without a bow

'Gul is here. Pray make him your mark.' Upon that Agar broke out laughing.

Gul asked: 'Has any wager been made?' Agar answered: 'The one whose arrow shoots through the tree will have power over the other.' Gul said: 'Tell me now, how will you treat me if my arrow did not hit its mark?' Agar answered: 'I will have your nose and ears pierced and dress you in women's clothes.' He replied: 'Have them pierced. I submit to you, as I have already lost my heart, and am your slave.' Gul deliberately missed the mark while shooting an arrow at the tree. Upon his turn, Agar shot the arrow through the tree and triumphed over his rival. Agar turned his face away, smiled, and said: 'I won the wager from you!' Gul answered: 'I sacrifice my life over your claim of victory over me, and offer my life as your sacrifice at the bashful manner you smile. Hurry now, change me into a woman's guise, make me attend upon you, make me press your legs, and then I will show you my marksmanship.'

In short, the two of them prattled together in this manner. At parting, Agar said to Gul. 'Have a bath and dress yourself as a woman. I will come for you.' Then Gul departed and Agar returned home. He asked Mah-e Taaban: 'Do you have such a tilism that would embarrass a man?' She answered: 'I have a magic slave girl. If you put her beside a man she turns into a woman, and speaks in such a brazen manner that even men blush.'

Agar headed for King Gul's bedchamber with that magic slave girl, and took Hameed Dev along. Agar found him asleep and put the doll beside him, and hid himself to watch the spectacle. The magic slave girl suddenly turned into a hundred-year-old woman. Her hair was white, she seemed to be at death's door, her back was bent, her eyes watered, and her hands and feet trembled. She was a thing of mirth for the young, and more hideous and revolting than any monster. Indeed, she was the very aunt of Satan, with a face like a procuress. Whoever saw her lamented the viciousness of life.

VERSES

So ancient was that crone
Her eyelashes, too, had turned white

When the morning breeze struck her
She trembled like a grass leaf
She had not a single tooth in her mouth
That she may cry at her state of eld
Wrinkles covered her body
As if it were the crumpled skirts of a robe

But dressed all in red, lips dyed with lac, eyes lined with lampblack, teeth tinged with missi, and hands painted with henna, she caught hold of Gul like a veritable monster, and started vigorously kissing him. Gul was consternated by her lustfulness and got furious with her. He asked: 'O wretch, who are you?' She answered: 'Of course! Why would you recognise me! You only recognised your lust in that moment. Since the time we have met, I have fallen in love with you and become besotted with you. You long for others, but I long for you. Today I found you alone after a long time and came to you.'

Gul rent his collar in frustration and called his viziers. While she was wrapped around him, Agar presented himself. Gul tried to shake her off him and escape, but the magic slave girl would not let him go. In his panic, Gul caught Agar's hand. Agar said: 'Show this lust to your great-aunt. She has been in love with you for a long time.' Gul felt mortified and lowered his eyes and head. He reached for his sword but Agar made a sign to Hameed Dev who removed it from his side. Then Agar said: 'Shame on such deeds and a curse on your actions. That day, while playing chogan my cousin Aflatun inadvertently did something for which I slapped and insulted him before a thousand people, but that was not enough to allay your suspicions and mistrust, and you acted indelicately towards me. How should I seek recompense for that from you? I should humiliate you in a thousand ways!' Gul said: 'I beg you in the name of Suleiman! Release me from this unforeseen calamity, this catastrophe from the heavens.' Agar said: 'Do not swear falsely and make idle talk. God be praised! You try to hoodwink me, act as if you do not know, and attempt to ward me off.'

Then Gul prostrated himself at Agar's feet. Agar laughed, raised him and went away, leaving Gul marvelling at what had happened.

THE ACCOUNT OF BETROTHAL AND WEDDING OF THE SEEKER AND THE SOUGHT, AND THE UNION OF THE LOVER AND THE BELOVED

The author of this sweet tale writes that Lal Dev and King Mansoor continued their parleys for a long time, but the king could not facilitate the match. In the end, King Gul went to see the jogi, and entreated and pleaded with him. The jogi said to him: 'Although you venerate me on account of my accomplishments, and consider me accomplished, I feel greatly embarrassed as there is no comparison between us: You are a king, I am a beggar.' Gul answered: 'The pious ones and men of faith are the kings of faith and the world, and men of the world like me, are like dogs. It is forever so:

'The kings arrive to kiss the beggar's feet

'Furthermore, you are also my uncle. And isn't an uncle just like a father? I have every right to seek your assistance.' After making these comments, Gul displayed to the jogi a glimpse of his lovesick heart and alluded to the marriage proposal. The jogi forthwith said: 'I do not have a daughter. If I had one, I would not have refused you, or defied the religious law. Everyone knows that after twelve years of austere labour, God Almighty gave me a son. This free cypress[113] has borne no fruit, besides him.' Gul said: 'Forgive my saying so, but your words do not corroborate with her circumstances. Contingent upon your approval, Vizier Khush-haal has engaged her to me. If Agar were his son, why would he have agreed to the proposal?' The jogi answered: 'I shall make inquiries and have an answer for you by tomorrow.' Then jogi went to Mah-e Taaban and said to her: 'Send for Agar and tell him about the visit of King Gul and our conversation, and ask him why he feels abashed in a matter sanctioned by religious law. Tell him that, by the grace of God, he has attained the age of majority and is wise and discerning. If he has no objections to the match, we can facilitate the matter; otherwise he must give a reason for refusing it; even though I

113. Free cypress: The cypress is alluded to as the free cyprus on account of not having any fruit.

fear a refusal would end badly for all parties, and lead to destruction on both sides.'

Agar heard what Mah-e Taaban said to him, then replied: 'Even though I am loath to enter into marriage, but for fear of bloodshed, I shall agree to it upon some conditions: Firstly, that I shall not give up dressing like a man; secondly, that he must give precedence to my wishes over his own; thirdly, that nobody should have a say in matters that relate to me; and fourthly, that he should not stop me from meeting with the jogi.'

Mah-e Taaban related Agar's answer to the jogi, who communicated it in Agar's own words to Gul. Upon hearing it, Gul forthwith wrote out a covenant in acceptance of Agar's terms, and attested it with his seal. The jogi sent for King Mansoor and Vizier Khush-haal, and narrated the details of the arrangement. He greatly lauded Gul's skill and adroitness, and King Mansoor praised him. King Gul returned to his palace triumphant, happy and joyous. Lal Dev and Qurasih got busy making preparations for the wedding, while the bride and the bridegroom observed the manjha[114] ceremony. The next few days passed quickly. The offerings of sachaq[115] were sent from the bridegroom's house with great fanfare in thousands of pitchers of gold-inlaid work. Hundreds of thousands of enchased thrones, such that

Each throne was the envy of the throne of heavens
The sun and the moon looked with covetousness at its every flower

In the crowd of the commanders, decorous arrangement of the viziers, the sound of exploding fireworks, the whinnying of horses and trumpeting of elephants, the flight of the anars[116] and the whirring of charkhis,[117] the offering was sent in great array with lines of troopers and rows of foot soldiers.

The jogi seated the bridegroom on the throne with great honour, served him sherbet and paan, and dressed him in a robe of honour. He conferred on the bridegroom's companions salvers of garlands, and

114. Manjha: A ceremony also called mayoon during which, four days before the wedding day, the bride and bridegroom stop going outdoors and stay in their homes.

115. Sachaq: The bride's dress, sweetmeats, oil and fruit sent from the bridegroom to the bride's house before the wedding day.

116. Anar: A kind of sparkling firework that shoots up like a rocket.

117. Charkhi: A kind of firework resembling a rotating wheel that is also used in battles.

gave rich rewards to the retainers. Once these rituals were performed, the bridegroom was sent off.

The preparations for sending the menhdi[118] were in the offing at the bride's house.

[Narrator's note: This author, who is a font of gaiety, felt exuberant, and wondered whether he should narrate the festive events in bright cinnabar, or in the colour of henna so that the narration affords twice the pleasure. My devoted friends said: 'This subject is in itself colourful. There are thousands of subjects that may be recounted with greater colourfulness. You should capture them in joyous narration like one captures the thief of henna.][119]

The henna alone was carried in thousands of salvers. It is hard to describe the profusion of decorations, glass orbs, lamps, the heaped salvers, and the beautifully made tapers, the platters of chobha, and flower-covered sticks.

Agar's four sisters, Sarv-Aasa, Ajooba Pari, Moti Rani, and Roshan-Rai Pari gathered like the four elements and set out with the menhdi with great pomp and ceremony, and entered the bridegroom's house with great fanfare.

In short, Sarv-Aasa applied the henna on King Gul's palm, and put a band on his finger and said: 'This band is from the one in whose love you have made yourself notorious.' Ajooba Pari said: 'In the end you were able to bring her around, and attain your purpose.' Roshan Rai said: 'God be praised! The bridegroom is handsome but pales in comparison with the soles of the bride's feet.' Moti Rani said: 'Remember well! Once you have beheld even the sight of her shoes, you must not have eyes for another!'

These jests and lively banter greatly pleased King Gul. In this manner, the bride's maids made raillery and flippant allusions to the union. If Mah-Parwar and Gulnar tried to offer a retort they were soon overwhelmed by their repartee. The play with flower-sticks was followed by distribution of salvers of garlands. The bride's companions returned home after the ceremonies for the day.

118. Menhdi: A ceremony before marriage in which, along with henna, cosmetics are sent to the bridegroom's house and the bride's sisters apply henna on the bridegroom's palm and put the wedding ring on him.

119. Capturing the thief of henna: Filling out with dye, spots on the palm that have escaped the application of henna.

Finally, it was the wedding day, and King Gul dressed up as a bridegroom. He sported a sehra[120] strung with pearls, and his steed was also groomed like a pari with dyed hooves, draped with a saddle cloth strung with roses and surmounted by a golden saddle. If Mani and Bihzad were to make a faithful portrait of the groom, they would feel embarrassed before their coequals, and even the prospect of painting the steed would make their senses take flight.

In short, King Gul arrived with great majesty and circumstance at the bride's house. While all these grand preparations were made by the bridegroom, the bride was loath to indulge in the least flamboyance. Agar would object to every little thing, fight over it, and offer a million ruses. Her fair, crystalline hands, her teeth that were like a string of pearls, all that she agreed to adorn she did so after much ado. Mah-e Taaban asked her to change into the bridal dress, and offered a hundred inducements but she would not consent. Whatever rituals she submitted to, she did contrary to the tradition. Knowing Agar's delicate nature, nobody forced her, but all of them were disconsolate, the bridegroom being the only exception. Gul was not called indoors nor allowed to participate in aarsi-mushaf.[121] Agar had it announced that Gul was being married to Agar's sister.

Once the nikah was done, sherbet was served, garlands and paan were distributed and jewels were offered as the sacrifice of the couple. Finally, it was time for the wedding procession to conduct the bride to the bridegroom's house. Then Sarv-Aasa was dressed as a bride, seated in a golden palanquin, and sent away with the procession. She was accompanied by such a large dowry that even the accountant of heavens would be at a loss to enumerate it, the bookkeepers of the universe unable to record it, and the Organizer of Cosmos alone able to reckon its value. Witnessing the rapture and euphoria of the bridegroom, the jogi was racked with anxiety and worry that he may be carried away from the domain of mortals by the good fortune of his enemies. He purposely warned Gul in harsh words, but Gul hardly had ears for any such talk and answered all comments with: *I accept!* and *Very well!*

120. Sehra: A decorative headgear for the bridegroom.

121. Aarsi mushaf: A wedding ceremony in which the bride and the bridegroom are shown their faces in a mirror.

Finally, the wedding procession started in great state and arrived at the bridegroom's door, who himself helped the bride's palanquin into the palace. Then he prostrated himself on the ground for a long time to offer thanks, made a few rounds around the bride's palanquin, and offered himself as the bride's sacrifice.

Then Vizier Basant said to him: 'O King, do not become bereft of your senses! Get a hold of yourself. Today all your desires will be fulfilled. The bride has already been accommodated in a separate house, and you should proceed there speedily. Do not be taken in by the spectacle, for it is Sarv-Aasa inside the palanquin.'

Then King Gul hurried inside and made rounds of Agar's bed and offered himself as her sacrifice. He observed that from keeping awake at night, the bride's sorrowful mind had been overpowered by the host of sleep, and she had cried herself to sleep. The drops on her bedewed visage were like so many diamonds studded on the moon's face, and many a pearly tear had fallen beside her cheek-pillow. Gul could not bear the sorrowful sight, and himself broke into tears. Agar woke up from his sleep, and said: 'You have humiliated me before the whole world! Everyone turns their face and laughs when they look at me. Some whisper, some point fingers, some hurl comments. You did what you had to do! But now I cannot show my face to anyone. Know well that your power ends here, as I shall now destroy my life.' Thus speaking, Agar took out a poison pill from her handkerchief. Gul feigned indifference and asked: 'From where did you get this poison.' He distracted Agar with his questions, then quickly snatched the pill from Agar's hands. Then Gul said to her: 'What you say is true and you are right to grieve. But you gave me hope when I was drowning in sorrow and revived me when I was near death. I shall be obedient to you as long as I live, and will never forget the favour you did me.'

In this manner, he placated and consoled Agar, and kept cajoling and paying tributes to him.

Then he returned home and told everyone to always address Agar as Prince, and to make sure not to ignite his anger.

. . .

Gul had a cantankerous nanny, who was cosseted and overindulged by him. She felt angry at Agar's irascible manner and crotchety behaviour. She interfered in Agar's business and Agar cursed and chastised her and sent her away. The nanny went crying to Gul in hopes of garnering his support. But Gul also reprimanded her and blamed her, saying: 'Why did you have to interfere in her business? I had warned you not to do so. I am glad that you got what you deserved!'

After some days Agar himself said to Gul: 'You were raised by the nanny, and she carried you in her arms. I cursed and abused her and sent her away. What will the people say when they hear that! It will make me infamous.'

Agar sent for the nanny, and showed her much indulgence, and said to her: 'Do not interfere again in matters that concern Gul and me. Here, take this gold armlet!' The nanny took the armlet from him and wore it, and made a careful note of what Agar had told her.

OF THE JOGI'S FOE HANDING HIM A RESOUNDING DEFEAT, AND OF KING AGAR COMING TO HIS AID AND VISITING RETRIBUTION ON THE FOE

It so happened one day that a eunuch from the jogi's attendants, presented himself in Agar's service. Agar asked: 'My good fellow, give me news of the venerable jogi's well-being.' The eunuch replied: 'I do not know where to begin, as he has suffered a calamity: enemies have surrounded him from all sides; his land has been occupied, and his armies dispersed and not heard from.'

VERSE

'You were his star of majesty
Since you left, his fortunes have reversed'

Agar could not rest upon hearing this adverse news, and sent for Hameed Dev and his horse. King Gul tried to reason with Agar that he would send his armies instead, but Agar did not accept, and departed forthwith for the jogi's land.

On the way, Hameed Dev sighted the jogi lying despondent in the forest, pierced by the thorn of grief. Agar picked him up and put him on a war elephant. Upon hearing of Agar's arrival, the jogi's viziers, Humayun and Buqalamun arrived in his triumph-securing presence, and gave a full account.

Agar said: 'Rest your minds as that precious pearl has been recovered by sifting the soil.'

In short, Agar encountered the foe. Before the sun of Agar's beauty, the enemy host scattered like the stars. That Rustam of the Time did not wait for reinforcements or help from others but fell upon the enemy.

VERSES

He encountered and combated them in a manner
That he dispersed them like dust
When he weighed his sword and dealt someone a blow
His opponent put his shield at his feet
Intrepid warriors quailed before him like women
Agar was no woman, a swordsman was he

Agar returned triumphant from the battle but received two wounds to his body. He said: 'I refused to wear any garlands as I desired and waited for these ornaments for my body.'

Gul received news that Agar had routed the enemy but received deep wounds. He said to Vizier Jawahar: 'Regard, he made me a target of the arrows of reproach. Before I could think of a strategy or arrive there, he exposed himself to mortal danger.' Gul complained of this to anyone who would lend him their ears, and was vexed by Agar's courage which had put his life in danger.

Agar said: 'Do not be cross with me. I promise that for as long as I live, I shall not step out of the house, nor will I show myself before familiars or strangers.' Gul, who wished it from his heart, was most pleased to hear it, but for appearances, he said: 'I felt miserable because, had you died from the good fortune of your enemies, I would have sacrificed my life but yet earned the blemish.'

Then Gul said to Sarv-Aasa: 'Make pledgets of Suleiman's liniment, and apply them to the wounds.' From the power of the liniment, the wounds were healed in just a few days. Agar took the bath of recovery, and festivities were held and sacrificial offerings received from all over the land.

OF THE TALE OF UNION AND HOW IT CAME ABOUT

It is said that Gul had an ardent desire to see Agar, who was like Venus in countenance, in women's clothes, but Agar always refused it, and on account of his delicate nature, he would not do it even for show. On days when Gul found Agar indulgent, he embraced him, and when he was loath to see his countenance, he consoled himself by beholding him from afar.

VERSE

A beloved is never obedient
Even should he be a bought slave

One day Gul's nanny praised Agar, offered herself as his sacrifice, and blessed him. Agar said: 'Tell me, what is it you wish to say?' She said: 'I will only speak, if you promise not to refuse my request.' Agar replied: 'I shall not refuse it.' The nanny said: 'I wish to see you dressed in women's clothes.' Agar answered: 'We have never worn women's clothes but shall do so to honour your wish.' Then Agar put on the bridal clothes made for her wedding day.

CAP A PIE

Let me begin the chapter of her beauty
From head to toe she was a treasure house of beauty and airs
If the darkness of her hair were added to the night
Dawn until Doomsday would not be seen
In darkness and length, they were without equal
Like the night of separation, and the age of Khizr
Her locks reached down to her feet
Their shafts were under her feet
That beloved's forehead was like the book's illumined title-page
And each eyebrow like a choice line of poetry
Her eyelashes a pack of poplar arrows
Her glances, lightning strikes of a diamond sword
Doomsday lay hidden in her eyes' corners
Death's house situated in her angry frown
The heart saw virtue in her nose
They were two narcissi on a branch bloomed
In the manner of a book's gilded page did her cheeks shine
So delicate were her endearing ruby-like lips
They could not keep the glory of her teeth hidden
With jewelry her ears were adorned like peacocks
Perched on her shoulders, bedecked like a pari's wings
With such industry the Maker made her hands
The finesse itself paid tribute to the Maker's hands
Her arms were rounded and the shoulders full

The glance that fell found no purchase
Her wrist had no front or back, was perfectly round
Like a candle's sides are indistinguishable
I can say her hand was a reflection of divine essence
And write its beautiful attributes with gold
No part of her body I saw that was hard
Except her breasts, that were firm
Ah, those protruding breasts
At whose sight the discerning would comment:
Because her body was in clarity like a mirror
Her nipples were the reflected image of her eyes
It smelled of roses when she dewed
The moon was envious of the luminosity of her stomach
The shiny navel of that immaculate pearl
Was the like of Venus under earth
Her waist's existence by its delicacy was manifest
For it was invisible to the eye like the line of sight
So perfectly molded were her thighs
The glance would not find a purchase on them
And why should her shin not compete with the light of Tur
The convex of her foot was luminous like a houri's cheek
If someone restively put her delicate feet on his eyes
The eyelashes would pierce her soles like thorns
Her height and stature were a calamity for lovers
Doomsday itself would bow before her
Manifest from those silent eyes were the words:
I am proud that the Maker created me thus!

The moment pari-like Agar was fully decked out, King Gul arrived. Upon seeing him, Agar went into the bedchamber. Gul, too, surreptitiously followed her there. She tried to stop him but he picked her up in his arms and laid her down in bed, and said:

VERSE

'On the night of union, cast aside all reserve and join,
Your tongue with mine entangled, your mouth with mine enjoined'

In short, he teased and tickled her, and annoyed her and brought her to the verge of tears, picked her up and laid her down again.

VERSE

In his desire's embrace, when he pressed Agar
From her dainty lips, many a protest issued

Although she desired union, yet she shook her head, frowned and turned up her nose. But Gul was overpowered by his desire, and drunk on his passion, he would not be stopped.

VERSE

Then Gul took her in his embrace
And sated his desire after their long separation
With his cheeks against hers
He showered her with kisses
He enjoyed her succulent chin
And fondled the pomegranate of her breasts
Then all her glories were laid bare
And nothing was left unexplored
With his diamond he perforated her pearl
And filled up her oyster with the pearl-forming rain
Then they rose from the bed of sleep
And from modesty each felt reserve from the other
She changed the dress that lay in shreds
Lest the night's proceedings should become known from its state

That damsel tore up her dress into shreds and said: 'This wicked thing disgraced me.'

King Gul came out of the room laughing. The curtain of reserve lifted between them, they daily indulged in pleasure-seeking. And at all hours of night and day they took pleasure from each other.

Agar had four palatial houses reserved for her four sisters near her residence, and handed them to her sisters after furnishing them to the last ceiling-cloth.

Just as everyone in this tale saw his desire come to fruition, may every seeker's desire and purpose be met with a happy end.

CULMINATORY VERSE

O Lord, in the name of the king of prophets
Pray forgive all of Nasir's trespasses and sins

End

ABOUT THE AUTHORS AND NARRATORS

RAI BENI NARAYAN (B. CIRCA 1776 CE?–D. CIRCA 1838 CE)

Author of *Char Gulshan* (The Ingenious Farkhanda and the Two Conditions). Rai Beni Narayan was born in Delhi. He belonged to a literary and political family. His literary works include qissas and biographies of poets.

KHUSHDIL KIRATPURI (D. 1788 CE)

Author of *Qissa Sipahizada* (The Adventures of a Soldier). Khushdil's Kiratpuri's real name was Muhammad Ibrahim. He was a teacher. His father's name was Qazi Zia-ul Haq, and the family belonged to a Chishti order from Lahore.

MEHR CHAND KHATRI MEHR (B. 1868–1869 CE?)

Author of *Nau Aaeen-e Hindi* (Azar Shah and Saman Rukh Bano) Mehr Chand Khatri who used Mehr as his nom de plume. He authored two divans of Urdu and Persian poetry.

HAFIZ AMIRUDDIN MAANI (ACTIVE MID-NINETEENTH TO EARLY TWENTIETH CENTURY?)

Author of *Qissa-e Maqtool-e Jafa* (The Victim of Malice). His real name was Muhammad Amiruddin and he used Maani as his nom de plume. He was a little-known poet, and except for the verses attributed to him in *Qissa-e Maqtool-e Jafa* (The Victim of Malice) no other record of his poetic or other literary work has survived.

SAADAT KHAN NASIR (AFTER 1796 CE–BEFORE 1869 CE)

Author of *Qissa Agar o Gul* (A Girl Named King Agar). His real name was Saadat Khan, and he used Nasir as his nom de plume. He was a known poet and biographer. Other than a biography of poets titled *Khush M'arka-e Zeba*, none of his other works has survived, which included five divans of Urdu poetry, two masnavis, and another qissa titled *Gulshan-e Suroor*.

ABOUT THE TRANSLATOR

MUSHARRAF ALI FAROOQI

Farooqi is an author, translator, and storyteller. His most recent work of fiction is *The Merman and the Book of Power: A Qissa*. He is the translator of the critically acclaimed *The Adventures of Amir Hamza* (2007, Modern Library) and Urdu poet Afzal Ahmed Syed's collection *Rococo and Other Worlds* (2010, Wesleyan University Press). He heads the publishing house Kitab and is the founder of the interactive storytelling program Storykit.

Web: micromaf.com | Twitter: @microMAF